The
TWENTY-YEAR
Death

The
TWENTY-YEAR
Death

by Ariel S. Winter

A HARD CASE CRIME NOVEL

A HARD CASE CRIME BOOK

(HCC-108)

First Hard Case Crime edition: August 2012

Published by

Titan Books
A division of Titan Publishing Group Ltd
144 Southwark Street
London
SE1 0UP

in collaboration with Winterfall LLC

Print edition ISBN 978-0-85768-581-0
E-book ISBN 978-0-85768-741-8

Design direction by Max Phillips
www.maxphillips.net

Typeset by Swordsmith Productions

The name "Hard Case Crime" and the Hard Case Crime logo are trademarks of Winterfall LLC. Hard Case Crime books are selected and edited by Charles Ardai.

Printed in the United States of America

Visit us on the web at www.HardCaseCrime.com

The
TWENTY-YEAR
Death

Malníveau
PRISON

A HARD CASE CRIME NOVEL

in memoriam G.S. with apologies

I.
A Man in the Street

The rain started with no warning. It had been dark for an hour by then, and the night had masked the accumulation of clouds. But once it began, the raindrops fell with such violence that everyone in Verargent felt oppressed.

After forty minutes of constant drumming—it was near eight o'clock, Tuesday, April 4, 1931—the rain eased some, settling into the steady spring rainfall that would continue throughout the night.

The rain's new tenor allowed for other sounds. The baker, on his way to bed for the night, heard the lapping of a large body of water from behind his basement door. He shot back the lock, and rushed downstairs to find nearly two feet of water covering the basement floor. A gushing stream ran down the wall that faced the street.

Appalled, the baker rushed up the stairs calling to his wife. She hurried past him, down the stairs, to see for herself, as he went to the coat rack to retrieve his black rain slicker. This had happened before. Something blocked the gutter at the side of the street, and the water was redirected down their drive, flooding the basement. Somebody in Town Hall would hear from him in the morning.

He opened the front door and went out into the rain just as his wife arrived from the basement. The force of the storm pressed the hood of his slicker over his forehead. He hurried down the drive with his head bowed; rivulets of water formed long v's on the packed earth beneath his feet. Now he'd be up much of the night bailing out the basement, and he had to be up at three-thirty to make the bread. The mayor would hear about this in the morning!

He reached the end of the drive, about twenty-five feet, and looked along the curb towards the opening to the sewer. The streetlamps were not lit, but there appeared to be a person lying in the gutter. The baker cursed all drunks.

"Hey!" he called, approaching the man, who was lying face down. The baker's voice was almost covered by the rain. "Hey, you!" He kicked the man's foot. There was no response. The street was dark. No one else was out in the storm. The houses across the way and along the street were shuttered. He kicked the man again, cursing him. Water still coursed along the drive towards his house.

His schedule was shot; tomorrow was going to be a nightmare. Then he noticed that the drunk's face was buried in the water coursing around his body, and the baker felt the first flicker of panic.

He knelt, soaking his pants leg. The rain felt like pins and needles against his shoulders. Choking back his discomfort, he reached for the drunk's shoulder, and rolled him away from the curb so that he was lying on his back in the street. The drunk's head rolled to the side. His eyes were open; his face was bloated. He was undisturbed by the rain.

The baker jerked back. The concrete thought: *He's dead!* coincided with a gathering numbness and the uncomfortable beat of his heart in his throat. The baker turned, and hurried back to the house.

His wife, elbows cupped in opposite hands, held herself at the door. "Did you fix it?"

"Call the police," the baker said.

His wife went to the phone stand at the foot of the stairs. "You're dripping on the floor; take off your coat."

"Call the police," the baker said, not explaining himself. "Call the police, call the police."

His wife raised the phone to her ear. "The line's down. It must be the storm."

The baker turned and grabbed the doorknob.

"Where are you going? The basement…"

"There's a man dead in the street."

The baker lived ten minutes from Town Hall, which was also the police station. Nervous, he avoided looking at the dead man as he turned towards the center of town. The rain was still steady, a static hush over everything that served to both cloud and concentrate the baker's hurried thoughts: A man was dead. The basement was flooded. It was late. A man was dead.

At the police station, he found that it would not have mattered if the phone lines had been operational. Of the three officers on duty, two had been called to assist with an automobile crash before the phone lines had gone down.

"The rain makes the roads treacherous," the remaining officer explained. "People shouldn't be out."

"But the man's dead," the baker insisted, confused that these words had not inspired a flurry of activity.

"We just have to wait for Martin and Arnaud to return."

The baker sat on one of the three wooden chairs that lined the wall between the front door and the counter where the officer sat. Small puddles of water refracted on the tile, tracing the steps the baker had taken since entering the police station. The officer had already taken his name and statement, and now was trying to pass the time, but the baker was unable to focus. He was exhausted.

Martin and Arnaud returned twenty minutes later. They were young men, the fronts of their slickers covered in mud from their recent work at the automobile crash. They glanced at the baker, but ignored him, talking to each other, until the officer on duty interrupted them and explained the baker's situation.

It was decided that Martin would accompany the baker back to his house, while Arnaud would go in the police car to the hospital to retrieve a medic and an ambulance.

Back out in the rain, the men were silent. The streets were still deserted. Even the few late-night cafés and bars at the center of town were closed. Martin and the baker arrived at the baker's house to find the body unmoved. It was still blocking the gutter, still sending water into the baker's home. They stood several feet away in silence, their hands in the pockets of their slickers, their shoulders hunched against the rain.

They only had to wait a minute before a police car followed by an ambulance pulled up in front of the house. The medics jumped out of the ambulance and retrieved a stretcher from the back. Arnaud came to where Martin and the baker were standing.

"We will contact you tomorrow, if we need anything else," Martin said.

The baker watched the medics load the body onto the stretcher and then into the ambulance.

"Somebody needs to fix the drainage," the baker said, his mind clearing some now that the body had been removed.

"You'll have to bring that up with the town in the morning."

"I have to be up early, and my basement is flooded."

The officers were unconcerned.

The baker's heart wasn't really in it.

The ambulance pulled away. One of the officers said, "We'll let you know," but he didn't say what they would let him know. They got back into the police car and pulled away, leaving the street once again empty.

The baker could see that the water was already flowing correctly, draining into the sewer. He turned back up his drive, preparing for a night bailing out the basement.

Inside, his wife came downstairs. "What happened?"

The baker peeled off his dripping coat, and began to roll up the sleeves of his shirt. "Some drunk was taken unexpected."

These were the details as related over breakfast the next morning to Chief Inspector Pelleter by the Verargent chief of police Letreau. Pelleter was in town to hear the testimony of a murderer at the nearby Malniveau Prison. This murderer, Mahossier, was one that Pelleter had arrested several years earlier for a brutal multiple child slaying in which he had kept children in cages in his basement in order to have them fight one another to the death. On two prior occasions, Mahossier had contacted Pelleter, claiming to have information. Pelleter hated to be on call to a convicted criminal, but Mahossier would talk to no one else, and his information had both times proved accurate. Over the course of the previous visits, Pelleter and chief of police Letreau had become friendly.

As they ate, the rain streamed down the café windows, distorting the town square, rendering it invisible.

The café was empty of other customers. The proprietor stood

behind the counter with his arms crossed, watching the water run. Two electric wall sconces had been lit in deference to the continued storm.

An automobile passed around the square, its dark form like some kind of lumbering animal, its engine sawing diligently, audible and then gone.

Nobody was out who didn't have to be, and not many people had to be out in Verargent early on a Wednesday morning. The weather had been worse last night. Why would a drunk choose to be out in the rain instead of sitting it out in some bar?

"Tell me about the dead man," Pelleter said.

"We don't know him. None of my men had seen him before, and in a small town like this, you get to know the faces of all the night owls. He had no documents on him, no billfold, no money. Just a drifter. We've sent his fingerprints in to see if there are any matches."

"You get many drifters here?"

"No."

Pelleter sat back and retrieved a cigar from his inner coat pocket. He lit it, and blew out a steady stream of smoke.

"Would you go with me to see the baker?" Letreau asked.

Pelleter chewed his cigar. Seeing Pelleter smoking, the proprietor came to clear the plates. The two lawmen waited for him to leave.

"I need to get to Malniveau. Madame Pelleter expects me home."

"It won't be a minute. This is exactly what it looks like, a drifter drowning in a puddle. I just need to be careful, and if I arrive with you, an inspector from the city, if there's anything to know, we'll know it. Benoît will be too scared to hide anything."

The rain continued outside.

"Not that I think he has anything to hide. I just need to be careful."

"Tell me about the baker."

"Benoît? He made the bread we just ate. His father was the baker here before him, but the old man died many years ago. He works seven days a week, and does little outside of his house and his shop. In his domain, he can seem very commanding, but when you see him anywhere else, at the market, at the cinema, he is a small man. My men said he sat last night in the station as though he had been called to the headmaster's office at school. And he's fifteen years older than my oldest officer! His wife works in the bakery too."

Pelleter called the proprietor over to pay, but Letreau told him that it was taken care of.

"I have a tab," he explained, standing.

Pelleter made sure that his cigar had gone out, and then placed it back in his pocket. He took his rain slicker from the standing coat rack just inside the door, and his hat.

Letreau called goodbye to the proprietor, who answered as though he had just been awakened. Fixing his own coat, Letreau said, "I hate to go out in this rain." Then he opened the door, and the sound of the weather doubled in strength, like turning up the radio.

There were more people on the street than it had appeared from the café, but each walked separately with the determination of someone who had places to go. Most walked with hunched shoulders and heads down, but there was the occasional umbrella.

The bronze statue atop the ten-foot concrete column in the

center of the square watched the faces of the shops on the north side of the street.

It was cold.

The two men walked in silence. Letreau led, but they walked so close together it would have been impossible to say whether or not Pelleter knew where they were going. They crossed the square, and took the southern of the two roads that entered the square from the west. The buildings here were still a mixture of shops and houses. The baker's shop was on the first floor of a two-story brick building, five storefronts from the square. The words *Benoît and Son Bakery* were emblazoned on the plate glass window in green and gold paint.

There were several women in the store buying bread for the day, but when Benoît saw the policemen enter, he came out from behind the counter. "Monsieur Letreau! I'm glad you came. This terrible business from last night has my wife very upset. She could hardly sleep. And we have to get up very early. Very early to make the bread. We could hardly sleep."

Despite his loud greeting, the baker looked exhausted, the spaces under his eyes dark and puffy. There was a small patch of light stubble on the left side of his chin at the jaw line where he had missed a spot shaving.

"And my basement is ruined. One day my house will collapse. You'll see. The town must do something about this. Every time that gutter gets clogged, I must spend the next two days bailing out my own house. The worms come through the walls."

The customers conducted their business with Madame Benoît, the women apparently used to the baker's little tirades. As each one left, the sound of the bell hanging from the top of the door mixed with the shush of the rain.

"This is Chief Inspector Pelleter," Letreau said. "He's come to see about this business."

Pelleter was annoyed by the introduction. He could see himself becoming more involved in this investigation than he wanted to be. He moved his lips, but it was unclear what the expression meant.

Benoît stepped in towards the two men. "Is it that serious?" Then he got excited. "Or are you here to inspect our sewers, and solve this problem? I can take you to my house right away. My wife can take care of things here. There's still water in my basement. Let me show you."

"I'm with the Central Police," Pelleter said.

Benoît became grave again. "What happened?"

"Nothing as far as we know," Letreau said. "We just wanted to hear it again from you."

The door opened. The bell tinkled, letting the last customer out. Madame Benoît watched the three men, but she remained behind the counter.

"I was going to bed when I thought to check the basement. As I said, these storms often cause floods. When I saw the water, I rushed out to the street, and found the drunk lying there. We tried to call the police, but the lines were down, so I went to the station myself. It probably caused another two feet of water, leaving that body there like that."

"The men said he was face-up when they got there."

"He had been face-down. I rolled him over to see if he was all right. Then I saw he was dead..."

"Did you hear anything? See anything?"

Benoît gripped his left hand in his right, rubbing the knuckles. His voice had grown much quieter, almost timid, and he glanced at his wife before looking back at Pelleter. "What was there to hear? Only the rain… Only the rain…"

Benoît turned to his wife. "Did you hear anything last night?" he called to her.

She pressed her lips together, and shook her head.

Letreau caught Pelleter's eye, and Pelleter nodded once.

"Okay, Benoît," Letreau said. "That's fine."

"Did…" Benoît looked at his wife again. "Was… Did something…happen? The man was drunk, right?"

"Sure. As far as we know."

Benoît's expression eased slightly at that. He had clearly been shaken very badly by the whole incident, and the idea that something more might have taken place was too much for him.

"Ah, the mop!" he said looking down. "We need the mop."

The door opened, letting in another customer, and before it closed a second new customer snuck in as well. They commented on the terrible weather.

Benoît looked for permission to go, and Letreau said, "Thank you. We'll let you know if we need anything."

Benoît stepped back, his expression even more natural now. He reached one hand out behind him for the mop, which was still several feet away in a corner behind the counter. "Come to my house, and I'll show you the flood. The water was up to here." He indicated just below his knees with his hand.

Pelleter opened the door, and Letreau followed him out into the street.

"What do you think?"

"There's nothing to think."

"I just had to be sure."

Pelleter nodded his approval. Water sloshed off of the brim of his hat.

They began to walk back towards the square. "Come back to the station. I'll drive you to the prison."

They waited for an automobile to pass, and then they crossed the street. The rain had eased some again, but it was still steady. Lights could be seen in the windows of various buildings. It was like a perpetual dusk even though it was still before ten in the morning.

They stepped into the police station through the entrance on the side street beside Town Hall. The station was an open space separated into two sections by a counter. In front of the counter was a small entryway with several chairs. Behind the counter were three desks arranged to just fit the space. Doors led to offices along the back and left-hand wall. Letreau needed to get keys to one of the police cars.

"Chief," the young man behind the counter said. "There's a message for you." The officer looked at Pelleter, and then back at his commanding officer. Pelleter had never seen the man before, but it was obvious that the young officer knew who he was.

"This is Officer Martin," Letreau said to Pelleter. "He's the one who went out to the baker's house last night." Then to Martin as he started behind the counter towards his office, "Did we get an ID on our dead drifter?"

"Not yet," the man said. "It was the hospital."

Letreau stopped and looked back.

The young man picked up a piece of paper from the desk on which he had written the message, but he didn't need to look at it. It was more to steady himself. "Cause of death was multiple stab wounds to stomach and chest. No water in the lungs."

Pelleter looked across at Letreau who was looking at him. Letreau's face had gone pale. His drunken drifter had just turned into a homicide. And no water in the lungs meant the man had been dead before he ended up in the gutter.

The young officer looked up. He swallowed when he saw the chief's face.

"Anything else?" Letreau barked.

"There were no holes in his clothes," the officer said. "Someone stabbed him to death, and then changed his outfit."

2.
Malniveau Prison

The sudden silence in the station was stunning. It was made all the more awkward when two other officers appeared from the back, laughing over some shared joke.

They saw the state of the room and fell silent as well.

Letreau stepped heavily across the small space to the counter, and took the message from out of the desk officer's hand. "I have to call the hospital," he said, and disappeared into his office, slamming the door behind him.

Pelleter saw Martin look up at him, but he turned away, uninterested in any paternal conversation. He retrieved the cigar he had started at the café from his pocket, lit it, and took the seat that the baker had occupied the night before.

The two officers who had been joking returned to their respective desks.

Pelleter concentrated on the fine taste of the smoke from his cigar. He opened his coat. Light drops of water continued to fall on the floor around him.

If Letreau was going to be long, he would have to take a taxi. Visiting hours at the prison were short. The warden refused to be accommodating, annoyed by Pelleter's visits. He felt that they were unprofessional, that the prisoners, once under his guard, were dead to the outside world. Pelleter's own displeasure for these visits didn't soften the warden's opinion.

The three officers talked amongst themselves in quiet tones.
A murder in this town was big news.

Pelleter looked at his cigar as he blew out a plume of smoke.
It was more than half gone.

Letreau's office door opened. The officers fell silent, but he
ignored them as he strode across the station to the door. "Come,"
he said to Pelleter. "Let's go."

Pelleter stood. It was obvious that Letreau was distraught,
his easy nature covered by a set jaw and a gruff manner. "I can
take a taxi."

"No. There's nothing to be done right now. Let's go."

They went back out into the rain to one of the police cars
parked just outside the station. The doors had been left unlocked.
Letreau got behind the wheel and Pelleter sat beside him in the
passenger seat.

Letreau started the car, turning on the windshield wiper, and
then he pulled out of the spot, and headed east out of town.

"Any news?" Pelleter said.

"Just what you heard."

The two men remained silent for the remainder of the half-
hour drive.

When the town fell away, it was replaced by fields that extended beyond the wire fences on either side of the road. There
was the occasional outlying farmhouse or barn. Cows milled
in a large enclosure, the hair on their undersides hanging in
muddy clumps matted by the rain. Even in the countryside all
colors were muted and everything seemed pinned down by the
spring gale. The sky was large and gray.

The prison was visible ten minutes before they arrived there.
It was a heavy, awkward structure imposed on the land, a dark
blotch. It appeared a remnant from some earlier age.

They pulled into the drive. A guard, so bundled as to be indiscernible, appeared from the guard house, waved at them, and went to open the twenty-foot iron gate.

"A man could kill himself here," Letreau said, "and no one would blame him."

The guard had the gate open. Letreau pulled the police car through, and the guard waved again, but Pelleter still could not make the man out.

There were several other vehicles—a truck, two police cars, three civilian cars—parked in the small cobblestone courtyard before the front entrance. There was another courtyard in the center of the building where the prisoners took their exercise. The narrow windows in the stone walls were impenetrable black slits, dead eyes watching over them.

"There's something wrong about having this place out here," Letreau said, parking the car. "The men they put here come from far away, from other places. That way the rest of the country can forget about them. And my town is the closest. All the men who work in the prison live in Verargent. Don't you think they bring some of this back to town with them? We're a peace-loving community. Most of our complaints are petty thefts and the occasional late-night drunk."

Pelleter didn't point out that somebody had been murdered in town the night before. After all, Letreau was right.

"It looks this bad on a sunny day too. I hate coming out here."

At the front door, there was a loud clank as the lock was released, and then the door was opened to admit them. It was musty inside, and the only light came from two exposed light bulbs high on the wall.

"I'll take your coats, gentleman," the guard said.

"How are you today, Remy?" Letreau asked the guard.

"I'm still alive, Chief," the guard said, hanging the coats in a small booth just inside the door.

"There's always that."

Pelleter pushed open the door to the administrative offices, while Letreau stayed to talk a moment with the guard. Nothing had changed in the two years since Pelleter had been there last. It was the same large room with two rows of desks down the center. The same filing cabinets lined the walls. The same people sat behind the desks. The same drab paint reflected the electric bulbs hanging from the ceiling.

The warden, a large gray-haired man, must have been informed that Pelleter was there, since he was waiting with a look of impatience just inside the door. He managed to use his irritation to add to his air of importance.

"Inspector Pelleter. I'm so glad. If you had been even five minutes more, we would have missed each other. I have promised my wife a holiday in the city, and she is expecting me an hour ago."

A neat, sharp-angled man stood with his hands crossed in front of him just behind the warden.

"Let me introduce Monsieur Fournier. I don't believe you've met. Fournier is the Assistant Warden here now. He takes care of the jobs I don't want to."

Fournier took Pelleter's hand. "He jests."

None of the men smiled.

"Fournier will be in charge while I am away, and he will be more than capable of assisting you with anything you need. Not that you need much assistance. You are an old hand at this." The warden smiled at that, but it was an expression of pure malice. "You could have probably gone to get the prisoner yourself."

He looked around the office. The people at the desks made an effort to focus on their paperwork, but they were clearly uncomfortable.

"I really must be going." He looked at his watch and then the clock on the wall. "I shouldn't have even stopped to say hello. Fournier, you have everything you need."

"Yes, *Monsieur le Directeur*."

The warden stepped towards his office, but stopped when the outer door opened to reveal Letreau.

"Chief Letreau," the warden said, and he glanced at Fournier, confused and accusatory. "Nothing is wrong, I trust."

Letreau paused in the doorway, surprised at being addressed so suddenly. He looked at Pelleter, but Pelleter was unreadable. "As Remy says, I'm still alive."

"Yes," the warden said, almost sneering as he took possession of himself. "There's always that."

Letreau stepped in and greeted the other people in the office including Fournier.

The warden excused himself, and disappeared into his office.

"If you'll follow me, Chief Inspector," Fournier said. They left the administrative offices, and went down a barren hallway. Fournier conducted himself with an icy precision throughout. "I understand you have been here before."

"This will be my third visit."

"The warden feels you give this man too much credit and that you make him feel important. It is our job to be sure that these men do not feel important. They are criminals."

Pelleter said nothing. He retrieved his partially smoked cigar from his pocket and put it between his lips without lighting it.

"There is no question that there is a certain intelligence in some of them, and that their crimes require guts. Perhaps in another time they would have been something else. But here they are still criminals. They are to be punished, not applauded. And it is dangerous to make any of them feel important."

They were outside one of the visiting rooms, which also served as interrogation rooms if needed. "Is that what the warden says?"

"It's what I say," Fournier said, his expression unchanged. He unlocked the door with a key on a large ring. "Wait here."

Pelleter paused, but resisted asking Fournier if he knew just what Mahossier had done. The assistant warden hadn't seen the way those children had been brutalized. A man who could do that felt important all on his own.

Pelleter went into the room. The door closed behind him, and his jaw clenched around his cigar at the clang. The room was devoid of any distinguishing features, just stone below, above, and all around. No sounds penetrated the walls. If this was not enough punishment for a criminal, than Pelleter didn't know what was.

The door opened only a moment later, and two guards led Mahossier in. He was a small old man, bald, with deep wrinkles across his forehead, and a beaked nose. His hands had been cuffed in front of him, and another set of cuffs chained his legs together. These had been linked by a third chain between the two. The guards sat Mahossier in the seat across from Pelleter.

Fournier had also come in with the three other men. "We will be right outside the door. If he tries—"

"We'll be fine," Pelleter interrupted.

"But if—"

"We'll be fine."

Fournier flared his nostrils, the first time he had allowed his emotions to be seen.

"The Chief Inspector and I go way back," Mahossier said, his eyes locked on Fournier, his voice so quiet it was almost soothing.

Fournier nodded to the guards, and the three men left the room, closing the door behind them and engaging the lock.

"How's Madame Pelleter?" Mahossier said.

Pelleter moved his cigar from one side of his mouth to the other. Facing the man, it was all he could do to keep the images of those children out of his mind.

Mahossier seemed to know it.

"Still no children?" Mahossier smiled. "But, of course... That ship has sailed. It's much too late for you now. Such a shame. Children really make the world worth living in." His eyebrows furrowed and his lips fell in a theatrical frown. "Of course, there are never any children here." His expression went cold. "Plenty of rain though."

Pelleter bit his cigar again. He'd have to light it soon just to help him breathe.

"But of course, even if it's too late for Madame Pelleter, it's not too late for you. A Chief Inspector! Plenty of young girls out there. Someone to take care of you in your old age. Think of it!"

Mahossier's excitement at his own fantasy took him over, and he looked up, almost overjoyed. The chains weighing him down were nothing to him. He looked back at Pelleter.

"So how is Madame Pelleter? Well, I trust."

Pelleter waited patiently. It wouldn't do to rush him. If Mahossier thought that he was getting a reaction from the inspector, then he would go on forever.

"How do you like this room? You must...they keep putting you in it. It's much like mine, although I do have a little window." He held up his right hand, which forced him to draw his left hand with it because of the cuffs, and he indicated a narrow space with his thumb and forefinger. "It's a small window, but at least it's a window. And I have you to thank…Thank you… Thank you…I must have you up some time. You should tell the warden that you are more than welcome…Or Fournier. But then he'll think I like you, he's not as smart as you, he wouldn't know you're not my type."

He looked up again, and it made the wrinkles in his forehead even deeper.

Pelleter chose to light his cigar. He took his time about it, ignoring the chained man across from him, extracting a single match from his pocket, scratching it on the table, and taking several puffs, making sure the cigar was really lit. Mahossier watched in silence.

"Okay, I understand you." His expression had turned serious. "And it's not as though Fournier will leave me in here forever. The rules are the rules are the rules are the rules…But it's safer in here with you than it is out there…You've had more than one chance to kill me, but I'm still here." He tapped his chest, and the chains jingled together.

"There's a first for everything," Pelleter said. The smoke from his cigar hung in the air between them.

"Well said! Right to my point. That's why I can talk to you. Your wife is a very lucky woman…Still no children?" He raised his eyebrows, but then shrugged when the inspector made no response. "Here is the thing—there are fewer of us than there were before…At first it was just one, but now it's two, three, four…I don't really know, it's a big prison and they don't let me out all that often." His theatrical frown again. "Glamieux's gone. He was another one of yours, right? They slit his throat. And there have been others."

"What's that have to do with me? People get killed in prison all the time."

"Not all the time…not all the time…Sometimes. Not that often, actually. Not many people in one month. Not many people and nothing's done about it, said about it…outside. Even here."

"What's the warden say?"

"What does the warden say?"

The two men watched each other, both calm, but each in his own way. Pelleter smoked. Mahossier smiled.

"We need somebody on the outside. Someone we can trust… Someone like you. There should at least be an inquiry."

"You want an inquiry into several dead prisoners?"

"They were people too." Mahossier's theatricality undermined any sense of real feeling in his expression. It was chilling as always.

Pelleter leaned forward. "You want an inquiry?" He stood up. "That's easy. Let's have an inquiry. Fournier's right here. He's Assistant Warden. He'll know." Pelleter was at the door now, his hand raised to knock on the door. "I'll ask him about all these dead prisoners. He doesn't seem to like the lot of you very much, but if someone's killing you…" He motioned to knock. "Let's inquire."

"Please don't do that," Mahossier said. His voice was still quiet and even, and for that reason it was commanding.

Pelleter let his hand drop. "Is there nothing to inquire about then?"

"It's just that there are the right people to inquire it of."

The two men stared at one another. Mahossier's face remained self-assured, Pelleter's steely. The last time Pelleter had come out here, Mahossier had given him the information necessary to capture a murderess in a case that was nearly three years cold.

He waited for Mahossier to say something else, but the prisoner just sat looking up at him, the lines in his forehead drawing deeper as he widened his eyes in mock innocence. It certainly felt as though he was simply making trouble, but it wouldn't hurt to ask a few questions. Pelleter could always turn it over to the central prison commission, if need be.

Pelleter waited a moment longer and then turned and knocked on the door. There was the sound of the key in the lock.

"Send my regards to Madame Pelleter," Mahossier said behind him.

The door opened, and Pelleter stepped out of the tiny room.

Fournier didn't ask what Mahossier had said as he led Pelleter back to the front offices. It was hard to know if this was out of professionalism, a show of contempt, or a genuine lack of interest. The man was so particular in every movement that it was hard to read him at all.

Letreau stood as they came into the front office. "Ready?"

"Yes."

"Please let me know if you need anything else," Fournier said.

"I'm sure I will. Send my regards again to your boss."

"Yes, I'm sure he regrets that he could not stay. His wife can be really insistent sometimes."

They shook hands, and went out to retrieve their coats from Remy.

"So?" Letreau said as he slipped his on.

"We'll see," Pelleter said, and then to Remy, "Have you had many prisoners die recently?"

Remy thought about it, helping the inspector with his coat. "There was one about two months ago."

"Disease?"

"Stabbing, I think." Then he shrugged. "People die anywhere, I guess."

"Any others?"

Remy shook his head. "I don't know. There have been other stabbings, if that's what you mean. But that happens."

Pelleter pressed his lips together. There was no way to know what he was thinking.

Outside, the rain was still coming down strong. The two men hastened to their car, and slammed the doors behind them. It was hot and humid in the car, adding to the general sense of discomfort.

"Have you heard anything about prisoners dying?"

"No," Letreau said, starting the car. "But I might not have. It's not really our business."

"Where would they get buried?"

"Depends on where they're from, I guess."

"But you haven't heard of any bodies getting shipped out on the train?"

Letreau shook his head. "No. But that doesn't mean anything."

"No, it doesn't." Pelleter looked out the window.

"Is that what Mahossier got you out here about?"

"Yes."

"You think it's anything?"

"I don't know."

They remained silent the rest of the trip, but this time Pelleter didn't see the wet landscape before him, didn't see the barns, or the cows, or even notice when the town started up again.

When they pulled in front of the station, the rain had eased up enough so that they could get out of the car without hunching their shoulders.

"Are you going back to the city tonight?" Letreau said.

"I don't know."

"If you stay around, my wife wouldn't hear of you having dinner anywhere else."

"Thank you."

Letreau waited, and then he went into the station. Pelleter followed him.

The same young officer, Martin, was behind the desk. He didn't even wait for the chief to get around the counter before saying, "Another message for you, Chief."

Letreau crossed and took the paper before the officer could say another thing. "This just gets worse."

Pelleter came up behind him, and looked at the paper.

The fingerprints of the dead man had turned up in the system. His name was Marcel Meranger. He had a long record as a safecracker who had worked with a number of the large crime cartels around the country.

This meant that there could be any number of people who would want to kill him.

The only problem was the last note taken down in the young officer's looping hand.

Marcel Meranger had been arrested thirteen years ago and sentenced to forty years in prison.

The prison was Malniveau.

3.
The American Writer

Letreau rushed into his office, leaving Pelleter holding the paper with the message. Once there, he picked up the phone and could be heard barking, "Hello…Get me Fournier…"

Pelleter approached the young officer who had taken the message, still seated at the front counter. He pointed to the phone. "May I?"

The young officer, surprised that he had even been asked for permission, nodded, and managed a "But of course."

Pelleter spoke to the operator and hung up.

Letreau could be heard saying, "This is a problem, and it's your problem…"

"Has anyone ever escaped from Malniveau?"

The young officer was startled again at having been addressed. He had clearly been eavesdropping on the chief's conversation. "Not in my memory and I've lived here my whole life," the young officer said. "But when we were kids they used to talk about the three great escapes since the prison's been open."

"Three?"

The officer nodded. "In the 1820s sometime a man faked consumption. He coughed and coughed for days. Then he cut his fingers on the rocks and used the blood to stain the front of his shirt so that it looked like he'd been coughing up his lungs…

Of course the warden didn't want to infect his whole population enclosed like that, so he ordered that the man be brought into town where he was to be quarantined in an old shed... He escaped as soon as he was in town. There was no train here then so he had to go on foot or get a ride and he didn't want to risk getting a ride, so he didn't get very far before they caught him...He was in solitary for good after that."

Pelleter looked across to Letreau in his office, who was pacing as he spoke, the phone cord making a mess of the papers on his desk.

"And the other two?"

"The second wasn't really an escape. One of the men who worked in the laundry hid himself among the sheets that were to be discarded. Rather typical, I guess. Of course, the sheets were checked before they were taken out the front gate and the man was found, so he didn't even make it beyond the prison walls."

Letreau was shouting now in the other room. "You listen, Fournier. You better find a way to get in touch with your boss, because he's looking at a scandal that may lose him his job!"

The young officer ignored the commotion behind him, flattered at the attention the chief inspector was giving him.

"The last escape was during the war. By then the prisoners were allowed some exercise time outside in the courtyard. Three men got together and planned their escape...They arranged themselves so they would be the last out in the courtyard with a guard just behind them...As the last man stepped out into the fresh air, all three fell back and overpowered the guard, taking his gun and forcing their way back into the prison using the guard as a hostage. They made their way to the front gate, but the warden had a chance to arrange a team of guards outside. They killed two of the prisoners on sight, and the third one surrendered claiming that they had just wanted a chance to serve in the war. He was sent to the trenches and killed there. If he'd just waited that would probably have happened anyway."

"So none actually made it."

"Never."

"Do you think that one could have now?"

"Not without help."

"That's what I think too."

Pelleter touched his hand to his mouth.

"Chief Inspector?"

Pelleter focused on the young officer.

"You went to see Mahossier...I mean, you caught Mahossier. You know the man. What kind of a man could do—?"

Officer Martin broke off, and Pelleter realized that he was glaring at the young man.

Martin swallowed, but to his credit did not look away. "I just wanted to know if you could tell."

Pelleter tried to relax his pose. The Mahossier business had been big news at the time of the killings and was perhaps not as forgotten as Pelleter sometimes hoped. Officer Martin was just the right age that he had no doubt followed the story avidly, perhaps even deciding to become a police officer because of it. And now here was Pelleter, and there was a murder to be solved.

Pelleter shook his head, trying to soften his expression. "You never can tell. Later, afterwards, of course, and then you wonder if you always knew." He considered his words. "Men are capable of anything."

This upset Martin. "But what Mahossier did, I mean—"

Pelleter put a hand on the young man's shoulder wishing he could honestly relieve his anguish.

Martin said, "I just want to be ready."

"If you saw the man now, you would know," Pelleter reassured him, which of course was not quite the same as knowing in advance.

Martin was slightly relieved, and Pelleter forced a close-mouthed smile, thinking of the power Mahossier wielded now because people knew what he had done. He tried to remember the first time he interviewed Mahossier, when he was just a suspect, if he had known then. He really couldn't say.

Letreau slammed the phone down in his office, drawing everyone's attention. He was breathing heavily, trying to get control of himself.

The phone on the counter rang and Pelleter picked up. "Yes…Chief Inspector Pelleter…I need you to pull the file on a Marcel Meranger…All known associates, family, friends, accomplices, enemies, anyone…How long will it take…Good, then I'll wait…"

Letreau came out of his office. His face was red, but he otherwise seemed to be under control. He watched Pelleter on the phone.

Pelleter said, "Wait…Actually I'm going to put another officer on, you give the information to him…He'll wait for it…Thank you." Pelleter handed the phone to Martin. "Write down everything he tells you."

When Pelleter turned to Letreau, the chief of police's face went a deeper shade of red before he even started talking. "Fournier said he'd look into it."

"I see."

"I could—"

Pelleter stepped forward and took Letreau by the arm, leading him towards his office. All eyes were on the two senior men. Once in the office, Pelleter closed the door, and then stood watching Letreau pace once again, working himself up over the situation.

Letreau stopped and looked at his friend. "I'm sorry. We haven't had an unsolved homicide in this town in thirty years."

"You don't have one yet."

"Fournier said that he would look into whether or not they were missing a prisoner, but that he thought he would know by now if the man had been missing over twenty-four hours."

"He should. Did you say we would come down there?"

"He said that wasn't necessary, because he'd be tied up trying to find out what happened and the warden, of course, isn't there, so if we want to, we should come tomorrow. I told him that perhaps the warden would want to know about this. He said there was no way to get in touch with the warden at the moment, but that he would have everything under control, and that if we felt it was necessary, we could come tomorrow."

From the outside, it was impossible to read Pelleter's expression, it appeared to be so calm, but in fact, he felt exactly the same way as Chief Letreau.

"I could kill that man Fournier. He's so cool. It's not natural," Letreau said.

Pelleter had thought the same thing earlier in the day. The man acted as though nothing could surprise him. And the warden rushing out of town like that was a bit convenient too.

Letreau said, "I guess I'm going to go see Benoît again. Take a look at his basement."

"The baker?"

"I need to do something, damn it!" And Letreau went red once again. "We didn't know it was a murder when we saw him this morning. Maybe we missed something."

Letreau went to the hook behind the door to retrieve his overcoat. He pulled open the door. An old woman stood in the public space of the station holding a small soaked dog under her right arm as though it were a handbag. A young man who had not removed his hat was standing next to her, and they were both talking at the same time to the two police officers who normally occupied the desks. The noise of the argument filled the small space of the station, creating an increased sense of tension. Martin was still on the phone, his left hand pressed against his free ear.

Letreau crossed the station, ignoring the scene. Nearly at the door, he said to Pelleter, "Are you coming with me?"

Pelleter said, "Go ahead."

Letreau went out, the sound of the rain momentarily blending in with the noise of the argument before the door slammed shut.

Pelleter sat down in one of the waiting room chairs watching the scene. There was nothing to do but wait.

The officers managed to get the two parties separated, and the story unfolded that the young man had nearly hit the old lady's dog with his car as he parked it on the square. The young man claimed that the dog had been in the street. Nobody was hurt.

Pelleter wondered what it would be like to be a policeman in such a town. The weather had everyone on edge.

"Chief Inspector!"

It was Martin at the counter. He had hung up the phone. Pelleter went up to him. "Got anything?"

The young officer handed over a list in the now familiar handwriting. "Here's the list. It's a long one." He was proud of his work, and watched Pelleter expectantly as the inspector scanned the names.

There were at least ninety names on the paper written in small even lines. It was a lot of names to go through, but it could be done if it had to be. Pelleter scanned the list and recognized a few of them from many years ago, but for the most part they meant nothing to him. Many of them were probably also in prison or dead.

"Chief Inspector," Martin said, and he stood up from his stool to lean over the counter. He pointed to a name on the top of the list. "I thought I recognized that name," he said.

The name was Clotilde-ma-Fleur Meranger, and a note beside the name identified her as the dead man's daughter.

"It's such an unusual first name, I figured how many people could there be? So I had the person on the phone look up whether or not Mademoiselle Meranger had since been married, and it turns out she is. She's married to Shem Rosenkrantz, the American writer. She's now Clotilde-ma-Fleur Rosenkrantz."

The woman with the wet dog had been appeased, and the group was now talking jocularly in more normal tones.

Martin waited for a reaction from Pelleter, and then he said, "They live here in town."

Pelleter registered this new piece of information. Meranger's daughter lived in town. If anyone knew anything about this, it would be the daughter.

"Where?"

*

The Rosenkrantz home was on the western edge of town on the
Rue Principale where the houses were spaced further apart
before giving way wholly to farmland. It was a small two-story
wooden house painted a faint olive green with white shutters.
The low fence surrounding the property was more decorative
than anything.

The rain was holding steady, but Pelleter had refused a ride
to the house, preferring to see the town on foot. The baker's
house where the body had been found was in another quarter
of the town, to the north, but that didn't mean anything. The
town was not very large. Meranger could have been on his way
to see his daughter, or he could have already been there. And
there was still the matter of who had helped him out of the
prison, and who would want to.

Pelleter let himself in through the front gate. The house was
well maintained, and somehow managed to look cheery even in
the rain. At the door, shielded by the overhang, the remaining
water streamed off his hat and coat before settling to a steady
drip. There were no lights at the front of the house, but he could
see that there were some lit towards the rear. He knocked.

A car passed in the street, on its way to town, not yet slowing
its country pace.

There was no response from the house. Pelleter knocked
again, looking up and around him as if he could gauge if the
house was empty.

It was possible that the Rosenkrantzes were out, although in
this rain it seemed unlikely. And Pelleter thought they would
not have left any lights burning if that were the case. He was
thankful for the overhang, but he was growing tired of the

sound of the rain, of the weight of his coat, of the clammy feeling of the weather in general.

He knocked again with great force and the door shuddered a little in its frame.

A figure appeared from the back of the house, a silhouette blocking the light, visible through the window in the door. The man came up to the door with quick strides, and pulled it open violently. "What do you want?"

He was about Pelleter's age. His French was almost unaccented, but something still gave him away as a foreigner. Perhaps it was his manner.

Pelleter showed his papers. "Is Madame Rosenkrantz at home?"

"No. What's it about?"

"I'd like to speak to her directly."

"Well, she's not here. And I'm trying to work. So sorry." He made no motion to close the door, but by his stance it was clear that he was about to.

"It's about her father. I think she would want to speak to me."

The man's stance opened up, and he took a step so that he was standing at the threshold of the door. "If it's about her father, then she definitely doesn't want to speak to you. She's done with him. Finished. She hates his guts."

"That doesn't change that I need to speak to her."

The man repositioned himself, as if readying for a confrontation. He was a broad man, of a similar build to Pelleter. He had not let himself get soft with age or with the comfort of working at a typewriter. "My wife doesn't talk to her father and hasn't for thirteen years. So anything she has to say, I can say right now, which is nothing. You got that?"

Pelleter didn't answer.

Monsieur Rosenkrantz backed up. "Now I'm working." He started to close the door.

Pelleter turned slightly as if to go, and then turned back just as the door was almost shut, Rosenkrantz still visible through the window. "One more thing. If your wife no longer talks to her father, then why did she choose to live in the town closest to his prison?"

Rosenkrantz jerked the door back open, and stood glaring at Pelleter as though he were going to start a fight. Instead he slammed the door without answering, and stormed off into the back of the house, disappearing in the low light.

Pelleter found the stump of his cigar in his pocket and put it in his mouth. He chewed it first in the left corner of his mouth and then shifted it with his tongue to the right corner. It was too wet out to light a new cigar, so the stump would do for the walk back into town.

He stepped down from out of the protection of the overhang, walked the length of the path, and out through the gate.

The storm brought an early evening. As he walked through town, many windows were lit, but their lights didn't extend far beyond the panes of glass. Benoît's bakery was closed; it kept early hours. The café where he and Letreau had eaten breakfast was lit and filled with evening patrons stopping for a drink before heading home, or having an early dinner. At the edges of the streets, the rainwater was above the cobblestones as it gushed towards the sewer entrances.

Pelleter could have returned to the station, but there was little to report and most likely even less to learn. It also would have made it harder to refuse Letreau's offer of dinner. He didn't want the conversation or the comfort. He turned instead to his hotel, the Verargent, at the northeast corner of the square.

He left instructions at the desk that he would be down for his dinner in one hour and he asked to have a toddy sent up to the room.

Upstairs, he peeled off his coat and hat, retrieved a fresh cigar and lit it and then picked up the phone.

"Get me the police station...Yes." He hung up.

He sat at the edge of the bed, smoking. The phone rang. It was Letreau.

"Yes...No, nothing...She wasn't there...I didn't expect as much...No, I'm going to stay in the hotel tonight. My apologies...We'll meet in the café in the morning and go to the prison...Good. Goodnight...Call if you need to."

He hung up. The world outside was invisible from the bed, the window a black mirror, but the sound of the rain trickled in, interrupted occasionally by the sound of a motor.

It bothered him that Mahossier had said somebody was killing prisoners and then the dead man in town turned out to be a prisoner.

And the American writer had seemed awfully argumentative, but perhaps if your father-in-law was in prison it would be the cause of some anger. People reacted differently to the police anyway.

A girl brought him his toddy, and he dressed for dinner while he drank. The warm drink, the smoke from his cigar, and the dry clothes made him feel a new man, and he realized that he was hungry. He pushed aside the questions of the day, and went down to dinner in an optimistic mood.

The girl who had brought him his drink was behind the

counter reading a magazine. The dining room, just off of the lobby, was a small ill-lit room with six round tables fit close together. There was only one other guest there, at a table in the far corner. Pelleter took one of the smaller tables near the window to benefit from the wall sconce. He could feel the outside cold seeping through the glass windowpanes.

The hotel owner appeared through a door in the back. He clapped his hands together and spoke in a loud voice while still across the room. "Inspector! Your dinner's coming right away. It's finished right now. The girl will bring it. Some weather, no?"

The other guest turned from his meal at this performance. He and Pelleter exchanged an embarrassed, apologetic look, and then the man returned to his meal.

The owner was standing over Pelleter now.

"You must tell me all about this business," the owner said. "A man killed in the streets? In Verargent? No, no, no, no, no." He clucked his tongue and shook his head.

Pelleter's good mood soured. It was inevitable in a small town that these things would be discussed, but it was not preferable. "We don't know," he said.

"But Benoît found him in the street, the poor man!"

The girl appeared with the meal, chicken in a wine sauce with sautéed asparagus on the side. She set the plate, which was still steaming, in front of Pelleter and stood behind the owner.

"Ah, here it is. You will love it. A personal specialty. *Bon appotit.*" He turned to the girl, and shooed her away. "Leave the inspector alone. Go, go." He turned back, and opened his mouth just as Pelleter put the first bite of chicken into his own. Then he must have realized that he too was pestering the inspector, because he said *"Bon appetit"* again and turned to leave, stopping at the other guest's table before disappearing into the back.

The food was good, but Pelleter ate mechanically, without tasting it. The owner's inquiries had once again turned his mind back to the matter at hand. Who had gotten Meranger out of prison, and was he dead before or after?

Halfway through his meal, a young woman appeared in the entryway to the dining room. She was very pretty in a delicate way. She wore an expensive dress, which accentuated her slight form, but it was clear that she was not comfortable in it and used her shawl to cover herself. She stood just inside the entrance looking into the dining room, turning her wedding ring on her finger with her right hand.

Pelleter waited to let her make up her own mind, and then he waved her in.

She fell forward as though she had been released from someone's grip, and rushed across the dining room to his table. "Chief Inspector, I am so sorry to disturb you."

The other guest turned again at the sound of her voice. In such a small town, there was never any privacy, always somebody close at hand. And yet no one had seen or heard a thing the night before when Meranger had been murdered.

Pelleter indicated the chair across from him, and she pulled it out far enough that she could sit at the edge of the seat, not quite committing herself to staying.

"I am Madame Rosenkrantz," she said, and then looked down at her hands in her lap as though this were something shameful.

"Yes," Pelleter said. She was younger than he had expected— this girl was no more than nineteen. He could see why Rosenkrantz had married her. She was charming to look at.

She looked up at him. "My husband said that you came to see me."

"And he let you come out to find me at this time of night in this weather?"

"He was not happy. But in the end he does what I tell him to do." She looked down again at this confession.

Pelleter tried to imagine the American writer taking orders from a woman, and he saw that it might be possible. "I'm surprised he even told you I had come. He wasn't happy to see me."

"That's just because you caught him when he was working. He's a different person when he writes. That's why I often go out."

"Where?"

"Just out," she said, and left it at that, her gaze fixed on him, some of her shyness gone. "He said you came about my father."

"Yes."

She waited for him to say more, but when he didn't, she said, "He's dead, isn't he?"

"Yes."

She looked down again, and he could tell she was twirling her ring by the movement of her arms. He watched for any change in her expression, but there was nothing, no tears, no surprise. "Murdered?" she said, her voice soft but firm.

"How did you know?" Pelleter said, eager.

"This man the baker found, and then you arriving..." She looked up. "What else could it be?" And with that a nervous smile sought to hide any other feelings.

"Your husband said that you hated your father. That you hadn't spoken to him since he'd gone to prison. He was very emphatic."

"Please, please eat," she said, indicating his food. "I've interrupted your meal."

"Why did you hate your father?"

"I didn't."

"You don't seem very upset over his death."

"He was dead to me already. But I didn't hate him. He was still my father." She shrugged. "He killed my mother."

Pelleter was surprised. "That's not in his record."

"Well he did." She pursed her lips. "He didn't kill her directly. He put her in danger, and she was killed. He owed money. He ran away." She shrugged again. "That's how these things work."

Pelleter looked at her again. He saw now that her initial shyness was a product of her current luck, the unexpected wealth of her husband, and her newfound domestic happiness. She was not a stranger to a rougher life. It had probably served her well to remain unnoticed in that life as well, and that would not have been easy as pretty as she was.

"I should think your husband is now a father to you."

"Because of my age? No, not at all. We're—"

"Why would someone have wanted to kill your father?"

"He was a bad man," she said.

"But you can think of no specific reason? There was no one in particular who would have wanted him dead?"

She shook her head, flustered again by his insistence. "No…I don't know…I had nothing to do with my father."

He pressed on. "But you went to see him."

She looked down once more. "Yes," she said.

"Your husband didn't know that."

"No…I don't think so."

"Why not tell him?"

She didn't answer.

"If it needed to be kept a secret, why go see your father at all?"

She looked at him, and her expression was strong. "Because he was my father," she said.

"When did you see him last?"

"I don't know. A month ago. Maybe more. I didn't go regularly. Sometimes a whole year or more…"

"Did he say anything? Was he afraid? Did he talk of being together again soon, of getting out of prison?"

"No. Nothing. We didn't talk long. Somebody had been killed that week in the prison, but that happens. It was nothing…I never stayed long…Once I was there, I could never figure out why."

Pelleter watched her. She looked at her hands fidgeting in her lap, then up at him defiantly, then back at her hands, in a cycle. He thought of the American writer, of his bluster. "Tell me," he said suddenly.

She looked at him in panic. "There's nothing! That's it!"

He slammed his hands on the table in fists, rattling the china. "Tell me!"

"There's nothing! My father's dead, I just wanted to be sure. That's all!"

They stared at each other, neither looking away, neither backing down.

At last Pelleter said, "Well, he's dead." He picked up his silverware and resumed eating. The food was cold now. It made no difference.

Madame Rosenkrantz gathered herself, taking a deep breath, and then got up. She stood over him for a moment, watching him eat. Then she said, "Are you going to do something about this?"

He looked up at her, watching her carefully for a reaction. "Do you care?"

There was no reaction. "Yes," she said.

He looked back at his plate. "I am."

She left, taking strong steps across the dining room, but pausing in the lobby, once again appearing like a lost young girl.

The dining room was quiet. The rain had stopped.

Upstairs, the other diner was just stepping out of the door to the room across the hall from Pelleter's. He stopped short at the sight of the inspector, and then tried on an ingratiating smile, extending his hand as he stepped up to meet Pelleter halfway down the hall.

"Inspector Pelleter!"

The man took Pelleter's hand almost against his will and pumped it, blocking the inspector's path.

"I don't mean any familiarity. I couldn't help but hear some of the conversation downstairs. It's very exciting to meet a celebrity."

Pelleter freed his hand and tried to step around the man. "A pleasure," he said.

"Could I ask you a few questions? I hate to be an imposition, but you read things in the papers and you're never able to tell if they've gotten it quite right. Like our own local celebrity, Mahossier."

The man had placed himself in such a way that Pelleter could not pass him without force.

"Is it true that he kept the children in cages?"

Pelleter felt tired. Was there not enough sadness in the world that people had to revel in the worst of it?

"I remember reading that you found a child in a cage, and

that there were other small cages next to it…And that he had dug a pit in his basement where he would force the children to fight each other if they wanted to be fed…An image like that stays with you. I still have nightmares about it, and that's just from reading the stories. Is it true?"

"Excuse me," Pelleter said, but he made no attempt to get by.

"I just don't understand how somebody could do that, how it works. He would kidnap the children, and then starve them…"

The man paused, observing Pelleter with a keen eye, as though he were testing him, to see the effect of this story.

"Meanwhile, he would have two of the already starving children fight each other to set an example. Am I getting this right?"

All these years later and people were still talking about this monster. He should be forgotten, not famous.

The man went on. "Yes. Then the children would fight to the death, and the winner was allowed to eat the other children's carcasses, locked away until the next battle. Amazing."

"Why are you so interested?" Pelleter said, determined to give no signs one way or the other.

"Oh, just curiosity, curiosity. I have an amateur interest in the mystery of crime, let's say."

Pelleter felt his anger rising. "Excuse me," he said again.

"Oh, of course, it's getting late. But just tell me, is that really true? Surely the newspapers must have exaggerated. No one would do that to children just for his own entertainment."

"I have nothing more to say on this. It was a long time ago."

"Then maybe you could tell me about our local murder. Have you any suspects there?"

Pelleter took a step forward as though to walk through the man.

The man held his ground so that he was too close, directly in Pelleter's face. "I don't believe that anyone could get away with what Mahossier did even if he would do it. You have to tell me that. It can't be that that is how it was."

It was as though the man needed some reaction out of Pelleter, as though he were deliberately pushing him to see what kind of a man he was.

"There were really bones with children's teeth marks on them? That detail always seemed too extreme."

Pelleter grabbed the man's shoulder then and pushed him out of the way. The man fell against the wall, and hopped to regain his balance as Pelleter stepped around him. "There's nothing more to be said."

The man called at Pelleter's back, "So it really is true, and you saw all of that. Why didn't you kill him on sight?"

Pelleter turned back and rushed the man, stopping inches away from his face. "Because that's not how the law works."

"When there are murdered men in the streets of Verargent, maybe the law doesn't work."

Pelleter glared at the man. He could have told the man of the years of scars on the surviving boy, the evidence of many battles fought and won. That the bite marks on the bones suggested that this last boy had killed no less than six other children in his short life, and that he was still in an institution in the city unable to talk, often in restraints. They had managed to keep that out of the papers, for the boy's sake.

Instead he said, "Good night," and turned away.

Behind him the man said, "I didn't mean anything by it. I just wanted to know."

Pelleter unlocked his door.

"You—"

But the man stopped himself before Pelleter had even closed the door.

In the room, the inspector felt too wound up for such a small place. Mahossier was one case. He could have told the man of so many other cases over the years that the papers were too busy to notice. Was one horror really more terrible than another when somebody was dead?

And somebody was dead again, and Mahossier was close at hand again. Even if Mahossier had nothing to do with this, it just made Pelleter uncomfortable.

He took a deep breath and let it out slowly. It had just been a tactless man. As he had told Officer Martin that afternoon, people can do anything. Right now, only the questions were important:

Who moved the body?

Why hide that Meranger was a prisoner by changing his clothes?

He shrugged off his jacket and stepped over to the bed. He tried to review his interview with Madame Rosenkrantz as he sank onto the mattress.

Instead, the image of that lone boy in a cage in Mahossier's basement crowded everything else out. His anger flared up again at the guest from across the hall, and he clenched his fists and ground his teeth.

Of course the papers had left out the smell. Mahossier's basement had smelled like a latrine outside a slaughterhouse. Pelleter had had to discard the suit he wore that day, because the smell had woven its way into the cloth.

These were the memories that he had to fight against when he saw that clownish glee on Mahossier's face in the interrogation room at Malniveau. There he had succeeded in being all business. And now some curious civilian threw him off his guard.

He looked at the phone sitting in the pool of light from the bedside lamp. He checked his watch.

It was too late. If he called Madame Pelleter now it would only make her worry.

4.
Another One

The next day was clear as Pelleter and Letreau set out for Malniveau Prison. The fields were muddy and there were occasional twin stripes of tire tracks on the pavement from where trucks and automobiles had turned onto the main road from unpaved country roads.

Fournier met them himself at the front entrance. He wore a tailored gray suit that looked as though it had been pressed that morning. He had a clipboard in hand, and began to speak before Remy had managed to relock the front door.

"Meranger was present at roll call two nights ago, April 4... The guard who took roll call yesterday morning counted him as present...There was no exercise yesterday because of the rain, so the next roll call would have been last night, and you contacted me before then."

"Where's the guard who made the mistake?" Pelleter said.

"He's already been reprimanded."

"I still want to talk with him."

"It will not happen again...I have long suggested to the warden that certain reformations must be made to our roll call procedures." His manner was sharp and authoritative. He was not going to be pushed around in his own domain.

Pelleter and Letreau locked eyes. Fournier was impossible.

Letreau said, "We're all in this mess together."

Fournier opened the door to the administrative offices. "The Meranger file—"

"I'd like to see Meranger's cell," Pelleter said.

Fournier looked back at him, still holding the office door. "We have been through the cell," he said flatly. "There's nothing to see."

Suddenly Inspector Pelleter stepped so close to Fournier that the two men's coats were almost touching. "I am trying to do my job. Your job is to assist me in doing my job. So I don't care if you've reprimanded your guard or if you've searched the cell or if you think you've got everything under control. I want you to help me when I say help me and otherwise I want you to stay out of my way."

Fournier's face remained impassive during this speech, but when it was clear that Pelleter was done, he looked away first. "Right. He was on cell block DD, which is on the second floor."

Pelleter stepped back. Fournier pushed past him and led the way through a door at the end of the hall, only several doors down from the room in which Pelleter had met with Mahossier the day before. It opened onto a set of stone stairs. There was a cloying smell of mildew, and the temperature was noticeably cooler than it had been in the hall.

Fournier seemed to have recovered from his dressing down, and was using the opportunity to proudly show off the prison. "The doors lock behind us as we go, so that anyone caught without a key at any juncture would be trapped until somebody else came through…We've of course never had a successful escape here, and there hasn't even been an attempt since the war."

"Until now," Pelleter said.

"Well, we'll see."

"What do you mean?"

"The man was dead, after all."

They reached the second floor landing, and Fournier sorted through his keys. "You'll notice the two doors. The one to the left here leads to the inside hallway between the cells, and the one further to the right," he said stepping over to it, "leads to the outside gallery that overlooks the inner courtyard." He fit his key into the outer door. "You'll want to look at this…The prisoners weren't able to go out yesterday because of the rain, so they were eager to go out today."

He opened the door, and a breeze rushed in, blowing cold air. They stepped out onto the gallery, a narrow iron walkway only wide enough for one man. A guard stood ten paces away, carrying a shotgun.

The prisoners were in the courtyard below. Many held their arms across their chests against the cold. They were like the random crowd on a market day, jostling against one another, walking with little regard as to where they were going.

"The guards down there carry no firearms." Fournier pointed out the other guards along the gallery. "The men up here have shotguns…The prisoners that are allowed outside get one hour in the morning and one hour in the afternoon."

"Did Meranger have outdoor privileges?"

"Yes. He was a model prisoner. He'd been here a long time."

Pelleter watched the prisoners milling about in the relative freedom of the yard.

Suddenly a cry came from the far corner. Everyone's attention was drawn to the sound, and immediately the prisoners were shouting and rushing into the area.

The guards on the ground began to run as well, joining the general melee.

Fournier turned back to the door, shuffling through his keys. His movements hurried but precise. He went through the door, leaving Pelleter and Letreau locked out on the gallery with the armed guards.

As they watched, the guards on the ground got to the center of the crowd, and forced the prisoners back. A prisoner was lying on the ground, his hands clutching at something on his chest.

"They've knifed him," Letreau said.

The man's mouth was wide open in agony.

Fournier appeared below them. He cut across the yard, directly into the crowd, yelling at the prisoners as he went.

The guards on the gallery had their rifles in hand, and watched with care.

Two men appeared with a stretcher through one of the doors. The prisoners parted to let them through. The noise had diminished enough that the injured man's cries could be made out as he rolled on the ground.

Fournier was at the center of the crowd, yelling at the prisoners. He grabbed one man and pushed him back.

The injured man was moved onto the stretcher, and rushed inside.

Fournier, still yelling at the prisoners, followed.

By the time the prison yard was emptied and one of the guards could readmit them into the building, Pelleter and Letreau were thoroughly chilled. The guard who escorted them to the infirmary talked continuously, still energized from the excitement of the stabbing.

"You sure saw something…It can be so dull out here, just standing for hours and hours at a time. You forget that these are dangerous criminals. You almost let your guard down…Then, pow! It's a powder keg…You don't know if you should shoot or not."

Every door they came to required two sets of keys. There were locked guard boxes at all major intersections. The guard had to return his shotgun to the armory, a locked room in which the guns were locked in cages and overseen by the arms keeper.

"How often does something like this happen?"

"It could be months. When I first started here, there was a whole year before anything happened. I didn't believe the older guys who said different. But this month! Wow! There must be some kind of gang war going on. Here we are."

Pelleter stopped him outside of the infirmary. "How many?"

The guard rocked on his feet, he was so excited. "I don't know, four, five. The guards don't always find out about everything, you know?"

"Any dead?"

"Not that I know of."

Pelleter nodded at that, as if all of the answers had been expected. He pushed his way into the infirmary.

It was a small white room with six beds, three on each side of the room. The knifed man was in the furthest bed on the right. His shirt had been cut off, and two guards and a nurse were holding him down as the doctor stitched the wound on his chest and stomach. The man did not seem to be struggling.

"He's been given morphine," Fournier said from just inside the door. He was taking notes on his clipboard. "He'll live. It's only a gash."

"Can we talk to him?"

"He doesn't know who did it. He was walking and then he was on the ground in pain. It could be any number of people who were in his vicinity, but he's not even sure who was nearby."

"Any enemies? Did he have a fight with someone?"

Fournier held his pencil against his clipboard with a snap. "No. Nothing. I asked him."

"Would he tell you?"

Fournier's nostrils flared, and his movements were sharper than usual, the only indication that he was under a great deal of stress. "Listen, Inspector. If we're all in this together, then you're just going to have to trust me. He didn't see anything. He doesn't know who did it. That's it."

A moan came from the prisoner. The doctor could be heard placating him. They were almost finished.

"Now if you still need to see Meranger's cell, let's go and be fast about it. I have a lot of work to do. We've got to search all of the prisoners and all of the cells. Not that we'll find anything, but it has to be done."

Pelleter would have liked to question the prisoner himself, but he had seen the incident and it was quite possible that the man knew nothing. It could wait.

"Yes, let's," Pelleter said, and he stepped back as if to let Fournier pass. Then he stopped him. "And what does the warden say of all of these stabbings?"

"All of them?"

"The guard said that there have been at least four this month."

Fournier's brow furrowed, his eyes narrowing "If you count Meranger then this is three that I know of, and for all we know Meranger was stabbed on the outside."

Letreau started to speak, but Pelleter held up a hand to hold him off. "Surely, you will be calling the warden about this?" Pelleter said.

"The warden has left me in charge because I am fully capable of being in charge. He will be informed when he returns on Monday. No need to ruin his vacation."

"Of course."

Fournier nodded his head once for emphasis, then led out the door.

Letreau stepped in close to Pelleter. "What's going on?"

"There's been a stabbing."

"I know there's been a stabbing, but…"

"Then you know what I know."

Fournier had gotten ahead of them, and he waited at the next door for the two of them to catch up. In the hallways, away from the courtyard, with no one in sight but the occasional guard, it was impossible to know that a man had almost been killed within these walls less than an hour before. The stones were gray and impassive.

Meranger's jail cell was on the outer wall, with a narrow window that looked out onto the neighboring fields. The space was large enough for the iron cot and steel toilet with barely enough room left over to stand. Fournier stood impatiently in the hallway, reviewing the papers on his clipboard, and Letreau stood outside the cell door watching Pelleter survey the room.

Meranger's few possessions had been dumped into a box on the bed from when Fournier had made his own investigation. There were three books—a bible and two mystery novels—a travel chess set, odd-shaped stones most likely found in the yard below, a dried flower, and a small bundle of letters tied with a string.

The letters were all in the same feminine hand, although it had grown more assured over the years. There were four letters in total. The most recent letter was from only two months prior:

Father,

It's unfair of you to be so demanding. You don't know what it costs me to make those visits or to even write these letters. Every time I tell myself that this will be the last, that I can not take it anymore. I remind myself of what you have done and all the reasons I have to hate you, and I make new resolutions. But I still fear you, and I still wish to please you, and all I end up doing is reprimanding myself.

You must believe though that my husband would be enraged if you were to contact me or even if he knew that I contacted you. He treats me like a dream, but he can still be a rash man.

I will not promise to visit you again or even to write, but you must know that you are in my thoughts. And I will be here in Verargent when you are on the outside. You shall see. As you said, your little girl is all grown up now already.

Clotilde-ma-Fleur

The other letters were much the same. A photograph had been inserted in one of them, of a couple standing with a young girl. The woman looked much like Madame Rosenkrantz, and Pelleter figured that it was Clotilde-ma-Fleur's mother.

He refolded the letters along their much-folded creases, and put them back into the box. He bent down and checked beneath the bed, beneath the toilet, and ran his hands along the walls. Then he stepped out of the cell. "Right," he said. "It was as you said."

Fournier looked up from his clipboard. "Of course," he said.

Letreau tried to catch Pelleter's eye, but Pelleter put on an air of one who was wasting his time and was ready to leave.

Fournier started to lead them back the way they had come, but they hadn't gone two steps when a voice said, "Hello, Pelleter."

The three men stopped, and Pelleter looked at the door to the cell beside the one they had just been in. A smiling face was visible in the small window in the door.

"How is Madame Pelleter?"

It was Meranger's neighbor: Mahossier.

In the police car in front of the prison, Letreau turned to Pelleter before starting the engine. "Can you tell me what's going on?"

Pelleter stared straight ahead at the prison walls. The sun had come up fully, and now, with the last traces of the rain burned away, even the prison appeared gayer in the light. "Was Meranger slashed or stabbed?" Pelleter said.

"Stabbed. More than once."

Letreau waited, but the inspector remained silent.

"Pelleter, talk to me. I appreciate that you've chosen to help, but this is still my responsibility."

"Start the car. We should get back to town. It's time to eat."

Letreau sighed and started the car. The pavement on the road had dried to a slate gray. Puddles of rainwater in the fields reflected the sun, little patches of light dotting the fields.

Pelleter pulled a cheap oilcloth-covered notebook from his pocket and flipped it open. "This is what we know…*Tuesday, April 4, just after eight PM: A man is found dead in the gutter by Monsieur Benoît outside of his house. At first it is believed that he drowned in rainwater while drunk, but it is later discovered that he had been stabbed several times and then had his clothing changed to hide the wounds.*"

"Or to hide that he was a prisoner. He would have been wearing his grays."

Pelleter went on: "*Wednesday morning the murderer Mahossier claims that the prisoners at Malniveau are being systematically murdered, and that he doesn't feel safe."*

"Wait a second."

"The dead man turns out to be Marcel Meranger, a prisoner at Malniveau Prison."

"Wait one second. Is that what Mahossier told you? Then do you think that this Meranger murder is tied up in something larger?"

"I don't think anything. This is just what we know. *Wednesday night Meranger's daughter Madame Rosenkrantz says that she knows nothing about her father's murder. She claims at first to have nothing to do with him, then to have visited him on occasion. Her letters are found in Meranger's cell.*

"Thursday morning another prisoner is knifed at the prison… Nobody can agree on the number of prisoners stabbed or killed in the last month." Pelleter closed his notebook and put it away. "And that's it, which is nothing." He said it with the bitterness of a man who has failed at a simple task.

"Somebody had to have gotten Meranger out of prison whether it was before or after he was killed. If we could figure that out, then we might know a lot more."

Pelleter didn't answer. Instead he reached into his pocket, retrieved his cigar, and smoked in a restless silence without enjoying it.

Suddenly, he said, "What do you think of Fournier?"

Letreau shifted in his seat. "You know what I think of Fournier. I could wring his neck. Although really until today, I didn't know anything about him. He's only been here a few months. He came from another prison, and the word was that he is extremely good at what he does…But I don't know. The prison really is its own entity."

"You said the men who work there live in town," Pelleter said.

"It's as if there's a wall of silence somewhere along this road. Sometimes things get said, and others…" He shrugged. "If only the warden were here. This Fournier seems intent on blocking us out at every step. That's what I think."

"And the warden?"

"He's brutish and controlling. He started at the bottom, so administration might not be his forte, but he's been there forever, and the prison gets run."

Pelleter nodded, considering this.

"What are you thinking? That the staff has something to do with all of this? These are prison stabbings. They happen. This wouldn't even be our problem if it wasn't for this body in town."

"I'm not thinking anything. I'm just trying to understand. What can you tell me about the American author? Do you think he would have killed his father-in-law?"

"Rosenkrantz? He keeps to himself mostly. That's why he chose to move out here, as far as I understand. He was part of the American scene in the city for many years, getting his photograph taken at bars, drinking until sunrise. He produces a book every year or two, and they're apparently big sellers back in the States. He can seem loud, but I always figured that's because he's American. Clotilde caused him to settle down. She means everything to him."

"Enough to kill for."

"I don't know. Somehow I doubt it."

"Why?"

"He's all bark and no bite."

"So we still know nothing."

"We know that one man's dead," Letreau said. "There's that."

"There's that," Pelleter said like it was a curse.

The mud-drenched fields made the whole countryside appear dirty.

Letreau looked over at the inspector, but Pelleter was lost deep in thought again, a scowl on his face.

The town had come alive in the sunshine. There seemed to be an impossible number of people on the streets, hurrying from shop to shop, sitting out in the center of the square along the base of the war monument. The café where Pelleter took lunch had every seat filled, and the inspector had to sit on one of three stools at the counter.

Letreau had returned to the station in order to see about his other duties.

Pelleter ate with his back to the crowd. Occasionally he would hear the name Benoît, and he knew that the town was discussing the murder, but the tone was of idle gossip, with little regard for the reality of the crime.

The man beside him pushed his plate back, and stood up, and another man took the seat immediately.

"Inspector Pelleter?" the man said. He sat sideways on the seat and had a notebook and pencil in hand. "Philippe Servières, reporter with the *Verargent Vérité*. Could I ask you a few questions about the Meranger murder?"

"No," Pelleter said without looking at the man.

"What about what you're doing in town? You arrived before the body was discovered. Was there another matter you were investigating?"

Pelleter drank from his glass and then pushed back his plate.

"I know that you and Chief Letreau have made two trips to the prison already, and that the warden has left town. This sounds like something that's bigger than just Verargent. Malniveau is a national prison after all. The people have a right to know."

Pelleter stood up, turned to the reporter, and stopped short. It was the man from the hallway last night.

"You…"

The man flinched as though the inspector had made a move to hit him. "I had to try," he said.

"Try what?" Pelleter growled.

"If you would talk about an old case, even out of anger, maybe you would talk about the new case too."

The man was a small-town reporter, practically an amateur. He mistook Pelleter for an amateur too. "I know you're doing your job, but you better let me do mine."

Pelleter called the proprietor over and settled his bill.

The reporter stood too. "I'm going to write this story for a special evening edition either way. You might as well get your say in it."

Pelleter gave him one last look, which silenced him, and then the inspector went out into the street.

He crossed the square. People went about their daily business. It was as Letreau had said: the town seemed unaware that twenty miles away there was another community where somebody had just been attacked that morning. The newspaperman hadn't even mentioned the knifing.

He turned the corner at Town Hall to go to the police station, and as he did a figure jumped out from between two of the police cars parked at the curb and rushed Pelleter.

Pelleter turned to face his attacker, and was able to register the face just in time to not draw his weapon.

"I warned you, damn it!" Monsieur Rosenkrantz said, forcing

Pelleter back against the wall without touching him. His face was red, and he leaned forward, crowding Pelleter, his chest and shoulders pushed out.

Pelleter watched the American writer for any signs that he would actually turn violent. He remembered that Letreau had said all bark and no bite.

"I told you to stay away from her. That she had nothing to say."

"She came to me," Pelleter said.

"I told you!" Rosenkrantz leaned even further forward, and then he pulled himself away, spinning in place and punching the air. "Damn it!" he said in English. Then he turned back to Pelleter, and said in French, "She didn't come home last night. Clotilde is missing."

5.
Five Wooden Boxes

Pelleter watched the American writer pace the sidewalk in front of him, full of nervous energy. The inspector stayed on his guard, but it soon became clear that Rosenkrantz's violence, like at the house the day before, was entirely auditory. There was no danger.

"Come, let's go inside," Pelleter said.

Rosenkrantz shook his head. "I've been looking for you. They won't let me make a report anyway, it's too soon."

"Has she ever run away before?"

Rosenkrantz jerked towards him. "She hasn't run away." Then his manner eased again. "When she got home yesterday from her shopping, I told her that you had come around...She insisted on going to see you. She was in a panic. She was convinced that her father must be dead."

Pelleter nodded.

"I know now that he is, but then...Well, good, I hated the man for all that he put Clotilde through as a girl, for what he did to her mother. He deserved to die. I hope he suffered...But last night, I told Clotilde to not get involved...That it only ever upset her, and that she should stay home...It was raining still... But she went out anyway."

"I saw her."

"Was she upset?"

"I wouldn't say that."

Rosenkrantz shook his head. "That's Clotilde. You can't always know."

"Does she have friends she would stay with? The hotel?"

"I checked. Both. No one has seen her."

The two men looked at each other. Neither said what they were both thinking, that it would be easy for her to have gotten on the train and to be almost anywhere by now.

"Do you think that she hated her father?" Pelleter asked.

"If you're suggesting that Clotilde might have killed the old man, you can forget it. She can't kill a fly."

"But if she thought she were in danger, or if she were angry..."

"No," Rosenkrantz said, shaking his head and frowning. "You met her. She's so small, and gentle, and quiet. Like I said, you hardly ever even know what she's feeling, she just keeps to herself..." The American writer's eyes got soft. "She's practically a kid. She's never run away before..."

Pelleter nodded. "I'll let you know if I find anything."

Rosenkrantz's eyes flashed and his fists closed, his rage returning. "Listen you..." But then he swallowed it back, taking a deep breath. "Thank you," he said.

Pelleter turned to go into the police station, and Rosenkrantz grabbed him by the arm. Pelleter looked back, and this time the American writer just looked sad and scared. He let go of Pelleter's sleeve, and Pelleter went into the station.

A country woman in the waiting area looked up at Pelleter with an imploring, forlorn expression that did not see him.

This was a police station face. It was the same everywhere.

The inspector went behind the counter and into Letreau's office.

"Rosenkrantz was just here," Letreau said, running his hand through his hair, which only caused him to look more harried.

"I saw him outside."

"Now the girl's missing."

Pelleter took a seat.

"I don't like this. Things are happening too fast. There was apparently a reporter around here earlier. One of our local men. The *Vérité* is usually a weekly paper, but they're putting out a special edition about this business. I think my boys know not to talk, but who knows…Do you think we should worry about it?"

"The newspapers don't mean anything."

"The missing girl."

"You can worry if you think it'll make a difference."

"I guess it never does."

"Where's your man from the front desk?"

"Martin? I sent him to Malniveau. Your questions about how much we knew about the prison got me thinking. We need to have somebody on site if this whole thing started there…I told him to demand to see the files, any files, to dig up what he could."

Pelleter nodded his approval, some of his own concern fading from his face. "Good. Very good."

"He left this for you," Letreau said, handing across a paper. "It's not much help, unfortunately."

It was the paper that listed Meranger's known associates. Martin had systematically gone through the entire list, and marked it "up to show the present location of all of the people on the list. He had even included a key at the bottom: a cross-out meant the person was dead, a circle meant prison, otherwise he had

penciled in their address. Nobody was near Verargent. None of
the prisoners were at Malniveau.

"Good," Pelleter said, reading over it. "This is good work."

"It leaves us just where we were before. Knowing nothing."

"Maybe."

"What?"

"Nothing."

There was a knock on the opened door and an officer stood
at attention just inside the office.

"What is it?" Letreau said, his frustration spilling over onto
the man.

"Sir. Marion is still waiting for you…"

"Oh, I know Marion is waiting for me. Doesn't she know I'm
busy here!" He stood, banging his thighs on the underside of
his desk. "God damn it!"

He leaned his hands against his thighs, turning his head to
the side, a sour expression on his face, biting back the pain.

Pelleter watched his friend. This murder was too much for
him.

"And…" the officer started.

"What!"

The young man lowered his voice almost by half, cowed. "We
just received a call from a farmer outside of town. It seems that
he has found a box in his field."

"So," Letreau said sharply, standing to his full height with a
deep intake of breath.

"Well, he said that it seems to him like it may be a coffin. He
wants us to come have a look."

Letreau turned to Pelleter, shaking his head. "See, it just
keeps getting worse." He turned back to the officer. "Well, go
ahead."

"Right, sir," the officer said.

Letreau continued, "I've got to see what Marion wants. She's been waiting all morning."

"Wait." Pelleter stood up, stopping the officer as he turned in the doorway. "Where is this box?"

"On the eastern highway, about ten miles out of town."

Pelleter looked at Letreau. "And about ten miles from the prison." He turned back to the officer. "I think I'll go with you."

By the time Pelleter and the officers arrived at the farm, the farmer and his son had uncovered the whole length of the so-called coffin.

The excavation site was no more than ten feet from the road, halfway between the town and the prison. The officers parked just off of the pavement behind a rusty truck and another automobile already there.

A group of four men and a boy stood around the open grave watching the inspector and the officers approach. The pile of dark brown dirt beside them was like a sixth waiting figure. The mid-afternoon sun had burned away the morning cool, and it was hot in the unshaded field.

"It's a coffin, all right," one of the officers said when they reached the spot. The box was unfinished pine, imperfectly crafted.

"The rain did the first part of the digging for us," the farmer said. He was a mustachioed man of about forty. "My son saw the wood sticking up while he was plowing, and then he came back and got me."

"So you don't know anything about this?" Pelleter said.

"The family plot's back up near the house…This is good soil here. Why would I bury a body where I wanted to plant?"

"And so shallow," one of the other men said.

Pelleter looked at him.

"I'm a neighbor. I was just passing by with my truck. I'll help take it back into town if you need."

Pelleter didn't respond. Instead he looked at the two officers and said, "Open it up."

They looked at him without comprehension, their expressions lost. They had let Pelleter take charge, and did not expect to be called upon.

"Open it," Pelleter said again, throwing up his hands. "We need to know if there's even a body inside, and what it's wearing."

"What it's wearing?" somebody said.

The officers stepped forward, but it was the farmer and his neighbor who each picked up a shovel, and fitted the ends of the blades into the space between the lid of the coffin and its body.

Pelleter stepped away, pacing the ground to the side of the coffin, looking at the dirt as he went.

The sound of wood creaking cut the air, somebody said, "Easy," and then there was a snap.

A car passed on the road heading towards town, slowing as it approached the site where the men's vehicles were parked, and then resuming speed.

"Oh, my god."

Pelleter turned back, and the men parted so he could see.

There was a body in the coffin. It must have been there for several weeks, because the face had softened, distorting the features into a ghost mask, and the body appeared caved in. A large patch of blood stained the man's shirt over his stomach. But the important thing was what the body was wearing: Malniveau Prison grays.

A sweet moldy smell caused more than one man to gag.

Pelleter squatted beside the grave, and pulled the man's shirt taut to reveal the number above the breast. He pulled out his oilcloth notebook and jotted the number down, then he stood and waved a hand towards the body. "Close it back up and get it out of there. This gentleman will take it back to town." And he nodded at the man who had offered his truck.

The officers, embarrassed now over their delay in moving to open the coffin, stepped forward, taking the lid from the farmer. "We've got that. Let the police handle this."

Pelleter began to walk along to the side again, watching the ground. It was clear that he was looking for something by the careful way he stepped, examining each inch of dirt before moving forward.

He called to the boy, who came over at a jog.

"What did you see when you found the box?" he said.

"Just a bit of white, sir. It was the corner sticking up from the ground."

"Look again now. See if you can find anything. You do that side."

The boy ran off to the other side of the grave, and then he also began to pace the ground step by step. The farmer and his neighbors saw what was happening, and they too began to spread out, looking down.

The officers were awkwardly extracting the coffin from its shallow grave.

"Here! Here!"

Everyone looked up. It was one of the men who must have come from the car. He was only a few feet to the west of the grave and several paces closer to the road, looking at Pelleter, waving him over. He knelt.

The whole crowd approached, and the man indicated what

he had seen. There was an impossibly straight line in the dirt as though the ground had sunk into a crack. The man was digging with his hand, and he quickly revealed what appeared to be the edge of another coffin.

The group went into action without Pelleter saying anything. The two shovels were brought over, and the farmer and the man who had made the discovery began to dig. Meanwhile, the truck owner helped the officers load the coffin into the bed of his truck, while Pelleter had the boy and the fourth man continue to scan the ground.

The seven-man team fell into a rhythm as will any group of men who have a large physical task before them, and they worked silently and efficiently, as the sun traversed the sky overhead. Pelleter took his turn with the shovel when it came, but he soon appeared overtaxed, and the men relieved him of the task. He smoked a full cigar, and walked far afield, determined to not leave any of the coffins undiscovered. One was revealed almost twenty feet away.

Cars and trucks passed in both directions on the road, but no one else stopped.

When the fifth box was found, the owner of the truck said, "I hope this is the last of them. My truck can take only one more."

Pelleter had the officers begin to fill in the holes that had been made, while he and the boy went around thrusting the shovel in at random points on the off chance that they would strike wood.

The sun was nearing the horizon, and the weather had once again turned cool. The two men who had come in the car said their goodbyes and left. The officers loaded the last coffin on top of the others in the truck bed.

Pelleter had five numbers written one under the other in

his notebook, but one of them he didn't need. He recognized Glamieux at once. As Mahossier had said, his throat had been cut.

"Come on, that's enough," he called.

The boy turned a few feet ahead of him, his spade sticking upright from the earth. The men near where the holes were being filled in looked up as well.

"Fill in the holes, and we're going home. There's no point in working in the dark."

The farmer came up to him nervously. "But what if there are more down there, and we go over them with the plow? You see? I wouldn't want to desecrate the dead."

"You won't."

"But if we uncover one…"

"You let the police know, just like last time. But I think we got them all. We'll know soon enough anyway."

"How?"

"Because we'll be able to ask somebody who knows."

Pelleter walked off before the farmer could ask anything else.

The man with the truck was already on his way back to town.

The graves had been mostly filled in, at least enough to satisfy the farmer whose son would be plowing over them the next day anyway.

"You let us know," Pelleter said again, as he got into the police car. The officer who was driving started the automobile and turned on the lights, which lit the few feet of road just ahead of the car.

Verargent's town square was almost unrecognizable. It was as though it had been an empty stage waiting for its players. A subdued crowd of serious men had gathered around the base of the war monument, spilling into the roadway and blocking traffic.

Flickering lights from kerosene lamps and open torches dotted the crowd, casting moving shadows that made the mass of people seem like one large anonymous organism. This was Verargent. With its population spread out over the houses and outlying farms the town could feel abandoned. But brought together, the group was large enough to raise alarm.

The officer driving Pelleter inched the car forward through the throng, forced to let out the clutch again and again. He repeatedly sounded the horn to no effect. The men in the square were unconcerned with allowing the police car through.

The truck carrying the coffins was only just ahead even though it had left the farm a good deal before Pelleter and the young gendarme.

"What is this?" the officer said.

Pelleter caught sight of Letreau huddled with Martin and the mustachioed officer beside the war monument. Letreau had his hands in his overcoat pockets and his shoulders hunched against the brisk April evening.

The car jerked again, the gears groaning.

"Let me out here," Pelleter said, and he released the door. The cool night air rushed into the closed space of the car.

The crackle of the open flames sounded over the murmur of people. Some of the men carried electric torches as well. Pelleter began to push his way towards Letreau.

"Some week to visit Verargent," a man said close at Pelleter's side.

It was Servières. His expression was overjoyed.

"If things keep up like this, we'll have to make the *Vérité* a daily."

"You would like that."

They were almost to Letreau now, but Letreau and his men were breaking apart.

Pelleter would not ask the reporter what had happened. He would know soon enough.

"Have you seen this evening's edition?" Servières said, and then a copy was floating in front of Pelleter. The headline, which took up almost all of the space above the fold read:

ESCAPED CONVICT MURDERED
IN THE STREET

Pelleter did not reach for the paper, but Servières forced it on him. "Please. Please take it."

Pelleter folded the paper and stuffed it into his coat pocket. They were through the crowd to where Letreau had been standing, but Letreau was now atop the bottom step of the monument's base calling over the crowd.

"Gentlemen! Gentlemen!"

The mass of noise dropped, but it was tentative, the crowd unsure if they had been called to order.

"Gentlemen!"

The silence spread then in a ripple from the spot where Letreau was standing, out to the back of the group where the square started once again. All eyes turned to the chief of police.

"I want to thank all of you for coming out like this."

There was a renewed murmur, and Letreau held up his hand.

"I know we would each want the same if it was our children."

Children? So this did not have to do with Meranger?

"As you have all heard, Marion Perreaux's two little boys Georges and Albert have gone missing. They were last seen Tuesday afternoon at Monsieur Marque's sweet shop here in town, and they were to walk back to the Perreaux farm in time for supper."

Letreau spoke with calm and command, so different than in his office earlier. Organizing a search party was in his purview, a murder investigation was beyond him.

"Everyone should split into three-man teams and search from here outward. If you locate the boys and can bring them back here, do so at once. If they are injured, two men stay with the boys and the third man should come here to get help. Everyone should return to report at sunrise regardless of what they have found. Are there any questions?"

There was a moment's pause in which a murmur began.

"Okay, let's get to it."

The crowd began to split, talking and shouting in an indecipherable cacophony.

Pelleter pushed his way to where Letreau was stepping down from the monument by leaning on the shoulder of one of his men. Servières stayed close to Pelleter's side, but Pelleter paid him no attention.

When he finally reached Letreau, Pelleter said, "Our case just got a lot more complicated." He did not want to mention the details of the five bodies in front of Servières, although it was unlikely that the man had not seen the loaded-down truck make its way through the square towards the hospital.

"I can't be concerned with that now," Letreau said. "Meranger is dead. Those boys might still be alive. You can search or meet up with me in the morning."

Pelleter nodded once. Letreau was right that if the boys were alive, that was the priority.

"I'll search."

Letreau nodded, but he had already turned back to his junior officers.

The square had emptied out and taken on its normal sleepy quiet. The only thing out of place was the occasional raised voice a block or two away that indicated that the town was not at rest.

"I'll search with you," Servières said.

Pelleter looked at him, and then started away. "Fine."

"What about our third?"

Pelleter turned back. "You," he called to Officer Martin.

Martin looked around him to see if Pelleter had meant someone else. Then he jogged over to Pelleter. "Sir?"

"Have you been assigned a duty?"

"No, sir."

"You're with us. Lead the way to Benoît's house. I want to see where you found Meranger's body."

6.
Hansel and Gretel

The three men walked in silence down the center of the street. Martin led the way, a half a pace out in front, and Pelleter and Servières hurried side by side. The chief inspector walked with his head down, an unlit half-smoked cigar clenched in his teeth, his jaw moving in contemplation. Servières watched him.

The air was heavy with moisture, and a slight breeze was enough for a chill to cut through the men's clothes.

The occasional call, "Georges! Albert!", echoed in the streets.

"Should we be looking?" Servières said.

They had passed two other search parties on their route, each deliberately examining the alleys towards the center of town.

Pelleter said, "If those boys are to be found, they're not going to be found in plain sight a few blocks from the square."

Servières did not reply.

They were in a completely residential area now, a quiet street at the edge of town lined with two-story homes built much closer together than necessary. There were no streetlamps. The few lit windows in the surrounding homes did little to light the street.

Martin stopped, looking at the ground. He then looked at the house which they were standing in front of. "This is the spot," he said.

It was exactly as it had been described to Pelleter, complete with the details he had filled in himself, such as the broken trellis beside the baker's front door. If there had been anything to see, it would have long since been washed away by the rain. He could just see the tracks of mud on the baker's driveway, where the water had streamed from the street into the house.

"Spread out. Look around," Pelleter said.

Martin started for the opposite side of the street.

"What are we looking for?" Servières said.

"The children."

Even in this residential district, it was as Pelleter had said. There were no places where the children could be hidden for long. The spaces between the homes were little more than alleys, and the houses on the neighboring streets backed up almost to the rear stoop of the houses in Benoît's street.

Pelleter took special care to examine any external basement entrances, but most were locked.

Servières began to call "Georges! Albert!" and soon Martin took up the call as well. No one would get much sleep in Verargent tonight.

Pelleter was three houses down from the baker's now, using the back alley for passage. He found an unlocked basement, and looked up at the house. There were no lights on. He knocked on the back door, and then, satisfied, he pulled open the basement, folding the hatch back onto the ground.

"Hello!" he called. The basement was pitch black. The dank smell of wet earth and mildew rose to meet him. There were no children's voices.

He took a few steps down, and ducked his head to enter the small space, the earthen floor soft beneath his shoes.

As his eyes adjusted, he could see why the door had been left unlocked. There seemed to be nothing in the shadows. He lit a match to be sure, and used it to light his cigar. Nothing. Not even a coal box or a modest wine rack.

He shook out the match, and stood for a moment in the dark, enjoying the warmth of the cigar. If nothing else, it was as if he had seen Benoît's basement. But there was nothing to be learned here. He needed to get a medical examiner to come and work on those bodies. He needed to talk with the prisoner who had been stabbed that morning. He needed to find out how Meranger got out of Malniveau. Only if he went back to his hotel to get the sleep he needed for the next day, then Servières would be all too happy to report in the *Vérité*, Inspector Pelleter uninterested in saving lost boys.

He forced his mind to pass over his instinct to link the missing children to the dead bodies.

There were too many people missing—the warden, Madame Rosenkrantz… Who else?

Pelleter made his way back to the gutter where Meranger had been found. Away from Servières, he squatted to see if he could find anything that had been missed, even in this low light. He paced the edge of the street, still squatting, but there was nothing out of the ordinary grit and grime.

Martin returned. "No sign of them, sir."

Pelleter did not answer.

"Did you find something?"

Pelleter stood to his full height, stretching his back. "I didn't expect to. But I still wanted to see."

"It was raining really hard," Martin said. "The water pooled around him, about here." He pointed. The young officer wanted to know that he had not missed something crucial, that he had not made a mistake.

"It's okay," Pelleter said. "There's nothing here."

Servières called from halfway down the block, hurrying towards them, "What are we doing now?" He did not want to miss anything.

"We keep moving," and this time Pelleter led the way, away from the town center, passing Servières before he had a chance to turn around.

The Benoîts were really at the edge of town. Only a few houses away from the baker's, the paved road gave way to a dirt road cut through fields. There was enough light from the stars to see by.

"Were we even looking for the Perreaux children or are you still continuing your murder investigation?" Servières said.

"You take that side of the road," Pelleter said to Martin, ignoring Servières. "Keep your eye on the ground and ahead, but don't leave the road."

"Because it seemed to me like you were awfully interested in that patch of ground, and it was clear that there weren't any children there."

Pelleter turned to Servières, "You take that side."

Distracted by the command, Servières dropped to the side of the road, scanning the darkened field beside him.

"What are we doing?" Servières said in a loud voice. To have any kind of conversation spread out along the road as they were required them to raise their voices.

"Searching."

The fields here were of wild grass as high as a man in places. Off in the distance, black blotches were islands of trees rooted in the otherwise open expanse. Leaving the road at night would be foolish, but if the boys had not been located by the morning, those small patches of woods would have to be searched. If Georges and Albert had gotten that far away from town, they would have likely stopped at the edge of the woods for shelter.

"Georges!" Martin cried. "Albert!" The sudden noise left the night silent.

"When those boys are found, they're going to have a lot of people angry at them," Servières said.

"If..." Pelleter started.

"If what," Servières said, looking at the chief inspector.

Pelleter said nothing. The end of his cigar burned a bright orange and then faded.

"Oh." Servières had put it together. "Georges and Albert went missing on Tuesday night—" Servières took out his notebook and held it close to his face to take notes.

"That's the same night Meranger was found," Martin said, excited now that he had caught on too.

"So we *were* looking for the children," Servières said as he wrote. "Because if they had seen something, like who dumped Meranger's body..."

"Keep your eyes on the side of the road," Pelleter ordered.

Servières brought down the pad in surprise, then put it away without comment. He really was not a bad sort. He was just a man who loved his job.

There was a tense silence for a moment, and then it passed into the silence of a shared task. A cry of "Albert!" came from the distance behind them. The moon was high in the sky. It must have been near to midnight.

"It poured that night," Martin said, almost to himself. Then he called, "Georges! Albert! Georges! Albert! Your mother is worried for you! Call if you hear me! It's Officer Martin!"

There was nothing.

The damp had gotten into their clothing, and Pelleter hunched his shoulders against the cold.

"You probably think this is a bit below you," Servières said.

"In the city, you have a whole team of men to do this kind of thing for you. Didn't I just read you solved a case because your wife had found the suspects?"

Pelleter said nothing.

"A double homicide solved by your wife."

"It's still the chief inspector who organizes the investigation and must take the responsibility," Martin said, rising to Pelleter's defense.

"I asked the chief inspector about responsibility last night, and he got very angry with me."

"Reporters!" Martin said, as though he had been troubled by reporters his whole career.

"What were you doing in Verargent before Meranger had even been murdered?" Servières asked Pelleter suddenly in the hard tone he had used in the café before. "There's something happening here, and you knew something before anyone else."

"Perhaps it was a coincidence," Pelleter said.

"It was not a coincidence. You went out to the prison to see Mahossier. I know that. I also know about the other two times you came to see him, and the two cases that were solved, the bank robbery and the woman murderer. You see I'm not as provincial as you thought. I know some things."

Martin was watching the two men as they walked. No one was searching the side of the road anymore.

"What did Mahossier tell you?"

Pelleter did not like to be questioned, least of all by a reporter. It was his job to interrogate people, not to be interrogated.

"Tell me. I'll find out anyway."

Pelleter stopped and pivoted towards Servières. "Watch the side of the road!" He then raised his chin and cried, "Georges! Albert!" and continued on.

The two other men fell into place to either side of him, once again scanning the flowing gray grass.

"Did…" Martin started, but then shook his head.

Servières was still smarting. "You have no call to yell at me," he said. "I apologized about last night."

"What happened last night?" Martin said, forgetting himself.

"I posed as a hotel guest and I asked the inspector some questions about Mahossier. About what it was like."

Martin did not respond, perhaps embarrassed that he had also asked Pelleter about the case the day before, but his own curiosity was apparent in his silence.

"This was big news here," Servières said. "I know it was big news everywhere, we followed the case like all the other papers, but when it became clear that Mahossier might end up in Malniveau…We followed it long after everyone else had dropped it…People were angry. They know it's a federal prison over there. They know that there are bad men who have done bad things. But they don't stop to think about it. It's vague. What this man had done could not be ignored."

"But they ignore it now."

"Except when you show up."

"And why would anybody know when and why I showed up?"

"The people have a right to know."

"Are you going to hide behind that again?"

Servières did not respond. His face was turned away, scanning the side of the road for any sign of the missing children.

Pelleter softened his voice, and tried a different tack. "Do you pay attention to what's going on out at the prison then? My understanding was that there wasn't much intercourse between the town and prison."

"We don't report on every little incident out there if that's what you mean. Half of the *Vérité* is devoted to the school's football scores and the church's bake sale."

"And the train station," Martin said.

"There's never going to be a train station."

"The town officials love it when you point that out."

Pelleter blew a plume of smoke, thick in the night air. "So Fournier…"

"The assistant warden?" Servières said, trying to read Pelleter's expression. "What about him?"

Pelleter made a theatrical shrug. "What about him?"

"He keeps to himself. He practically lives at the prison. We did a profile on him when he first moved here, but it was a dry c.v. He took his degree here. He worked at this shipping firm. He worked at this prison. There was nothing interesting about the man, and he has not made any attempt to get to know any of the people here since. He seems like a particular administrator and nothing more."

Pelleter nodded, but only because Servières' description fit his own idea of the man. If anything, it was more banal, not taking into account how violent Fournier's particularity was. But a violent passion was different than a violent man, and sometimes the reverse, as Pelleter knew all too well. Still, he did not like that the assistant warden had kept him from interviewing the stabbed prisoner or that he was in control of what information was at hand. He turned to Martin. "What do you think?"

Martin stood up straighter, wanting to please and forgetting to scan his section of the road. "The Assistant Warden? He seems very good at his job. He knows everything that's supposed to be done, and what's actually getting done."

Except he did not know that five of his prisoners were dead

and buried in a field. Or maybe he had known and had not felt that it was necessary to mention.

"He always acts angry about it, but he lets me see everything I ask for."

The tip of Pelleter's cigar glowed orange again. It was close enough to his face now to cast an eerie light on his features. They were tense in contemplation.

"This is pointless," Servières said, throwing up his hands.

An engine sounded in the distance behind them. Martin and Servières both looked back to see headlights as a single distant speck, and the dots of light that marked the town floating in the silhouette against the blue night sky.

Pelleter inhaled deeply on his cigar, pulling the flame into the last of the tobacco. He then dropped the butt in a puddle standing in one of the ruts of the uneven road.

"What about Rosenkrantz? Is he big news, one of the other local celebrities along with Mahossier?"

Servières turned back. The sound of the engine grew steadily, but it was still a good distance off.

"People don't care much about an American, or a writer. His books aren't translated into French either. His wife is something to look at, though. And there was some scandal there. They married when she was barely eighteen, a girl. He left his wife for her too. But she's learned to carry herself like a much older woman."

"So you wouldn't think that he would kill his father-in-law?"

"No, I wouldn't think it. But what does that mean?"

"Nothing."

"Exactly."

Pelleter was beginning to like Servières a little. His stunt the night before was just the kind of thing Pelleter would have tried if it served his purpose.

"I understand why you have to look at Rosenkrantz, but I wouldn't expect too much of him. He makes Fournier look like a society man, except when he's on his rare drinking sprees, but then they usually go to the city for that."

"When was the last time that happened?"

"Four, maybe five months ago."

The engine was loud enough now that Pelleter looked back to see how close it was. He started to get over to the side by Martin.

"Won't you give me one quote," Servières begged, "about Mahossier? People out here were indignant, but they really can't imagine what it must have been like to find those cages and the pit."

"And the boy still alive," Pelleter said.

"Yes. And that." But Servières seemed unable to actually say boy or child.

"When Mahossier was brought here, my mother wouldn't let me out of the house for a week," Martin said beside Pelleter. "And I was thirteen!"

The headlights resolved and it was a truck that was almost on them.

"Wait a second," Martin said.

Servières at the last moment decided to jump and join them on their side of the road, a shadow dancing across the head-lights.

"Do you think Mahossier..." Martin said, upset.

"There *are* two boys missing," Servières said.

"We should go back," Martin said. "Perhaps Chief Letreau didn't think to check the prison."

The truck pulled to a stop beside them, and the man in the driver's seat rolled down his window. There were two other men beside him, although their faces could not be seen.

"You find anything out this way?"

"No, Jean," Martin started, "but—"

Pelleter gripped Martin's shoulder, cutting the young man off. He glanced at Servières, but there was no need to worry there. Servières understood how information could be used to stir up the public and the value of releasing that information at just the right moment.

"They haven't found anything back in town either. I offered to drive out a good ways to extend the search, and some other people were going to drive out on the highway too."

"We'll cover the next few hundred yards," Pelleter said. "You go on."

"We're not going to find anything at night anyway," one of the other men said from the darkness of the truck.

"Madame Perreaux is hysterical," Jean said. "I heard they gave her something to calm her down, but Letreau promised that we would search all night if we had to."

Martin said, "Thanks, Jean," as though he had the power to thank the men on behalf of the Verargent gendarmes.

Jean nodded, and began to roll up his window, bobbing in his seat with the activity even as he released the clutch and let the truck begin to roll forward.

When the taillights were a good deal ahead of them, Pelleter said, "I saw Mahossier at the prison myself this morning. He's not involved in this."

"But two boys missing and just when we found that a prisoner had gotten out of Malniveau—"

"That's not what this is," Pelleter barked.

Martin closed his mouth, and looked away.

It was hard to tell in the light from the moon, but Servières looked pale.

"That's not what this is," Pelleter said again. But he had been thinking the same thing from the moment he heard the boys were missing. For two young boys to go missing with Mahossier close by…

Pelleter took control again. "Let's finish this. I'll take that side this time, Monsieur Servières. You join young Martin here. We don't have far to go."

He pointed. The red taillights of the truck were small, but still visible in the distance. They had only to cover the ground that would not be covered by the men in the truck.

They spread out and began to pace along slowly without speaking. The distant sound of voices would sometimes reach them when the wind blew, but the words were indecipherable. The movement of the grass was like the sound of a poorly tuned wireless.

The more they looked, the more Pelleter felt like the man in the truck, that they would find nothing at night.

Across the road, Martin and Servières began to talk in quiet tones that did not reach the chief inspector. He may have heard the name Mahossier, or it might have still been weighing on his mind.

Georges and Albert Perreaux. They had never determined the name of the boy they had found in the cage in Mahossier's basement.

A sudden gust of wind cut them hard, the grass yelling in anger. The tension in Pelleter's neck and shoulders from the cold pained him. It was time to turn back.

They continued forward.

Servières laughed, and Martin then joined him.

Pelleter shivered. If Mahossier was involved, the boys wouldn't be out here somewhere, they would be in town in a basement. He had searched the one basement, but all of the others had been locked. They would have to be opened.

Pelleter thought of the cages…small prisons…

"Servières," Pelleter called.

It silenced the two men's laughter, and they stopped to face the chief inspector.

"You want a quote about Mahossier?"

Servières' face turned somber then. He slapped his chest to feel for his pad.

The chief inspector spoke before he had found it.

"It was a horror."

7.

Visiting Hours

The morning found Verargent soaked in sunlight, but Pelleter could tell even from his hotel room that there was a nip still in the air by the way the people in the square walked with their hands in their pockets and their elbows pulled tight to their bodies.

Pelleter left the hotel still pulling on his overcoat, a troubled expression across his brow. He shoved his hands in his pockets against the chill, and found a wad of folded paper there. He pulled it out. It was the newspaper Servières had pushed on him the night before.

ESCAPED CONVICT MURDERED
IN THE STREET

After last night's unsuccessful manhunt, this seemed like old news. But it was big news for a town like Verargent, and the *Vérité* had treated it accordingly, devoting the entire front page and most of page two and three to the article. The byline was Philippe Servières.

It was all speculation, although none of the facts were incorrect. They had interviewed the baker. They had Meranger's name and history. They mentioned the Rosenkrantzes by name, although they didn't yet have Clotilde's disappearance. Pelleter figured the paper could expect to hear from an irate Monsieur Rosenkrantz today anyway. Otherwise there was nothing new.

There were also public opinions, and a brief history that re-counted the three previous escape attempts from Malniveau much as they had been described to Pelleter the first day of the investigation.

Pelleter refolded the paper and stuffed it back into his pocket. He didn't see how it would affect his investigation one way or the other, but he still didn't like it. Newspapermen were just sensationalist leeches.

There was a tired group of men standing outside of police headquarters, smoking cigarettes in silence. This was what was left of the volunteer search party, men who could put off their day's work or had no work to go to.

Pelleter went inside. The entire Verargent police department was there behind the desk that divided the public space from the department offices. Officer Martin tried to catch Pelleter's eye, but Pelleter ignored him, intent on Letreau's office.

Letreau was squatting before a tearful woman who Pelleter recognized as the woman that had been waiting the day before as he left to investigate the coffins in the field. Madame Perreaux, no doubt. Had that been just yesterday? There was too much happening too fast without enough answers.

Pelleter lit a cigar, and leaned in a corner beside a filing cab-inet without a word.

"We will find them no matter what," Letreau was saying, as the woman shook her head back and forth, back and forth. "We will find them, but you need to let me give my men orders."

Madame Perreaux shook her head again. She was hysterical.

Letreau came to the same conclusion, and stood with the woman still shaking her head, tears pouring down her face. He looked over at Pelleter with grave eyes, and then took a step towards the door.

Pelleter met him in the doorway, and put a hand on his friend's shoulder.

"You must search the basements."

"What basements?"

"All of the basements."

"I was going to do another concentric circle search based from the Perreaux farm. If that was where they were heading from the sweet shop and they got lost, it's most likely they're out there."

Pelleter nodded. He could not argue with that. As he had told Martin and Servières the night before, Mahossier was in prison; he most likely had nothing to do with this. Still, the basements needed to be checked.

"Then assign only two or three officers to check the basements. Whatever you can spare."

"What are you thinking?"

Pelleter looked back at Madame Perreaux, who was still bawling, twisting a handkerchief in her lap. He pulled Letreau out of the office.

"If they got lost, you're right, they're probably somewhere close to home. But if they got taken…"

"You think this is a kidnapping?"

"I think we need to search everywhere."

"Fine. You can have four men. I'm going to organize the rest."

Pelleter shook his head. "I'm going to Malniveau."

Letreau lost his cool then, puffing out his cheeks. "Pelleter, I have six dead prisoners in my jurisdiction and two missing children! I've said it before, I appreciate your help, but I'm not sure I see how you're helping."

Pelleter ignored this outburst. "I'll take a taxi to the prison. Search the basements."

Letreau's cheeks puffed out again, and his eyes blazed.

Pelleter said nothing. Letreau had a tendency to get overwhelmed, but in the end he was a good policeman. He would do what Pelleter had suggested, because he knew that Pelleter might be right.

The chief inspector pushed his way back through the officers towards the front door. As he did, he heard Letreau begin to give orders behind him.

Verargent's sole taxi sat parked outside the café across the square. As Pelleter reached for the rear door handle, the driver came out of the café straightening his paperboy hat.

"Malniveau Prison."

Pelleter settled in to the backseat relieved that the driver was one of the astute drivers rarely found in provincial towns, who knew when his fare preferred silence to small talk.

He pulled out his oilskin notebook, and added the details he had been too tired to add the night before.

His notes ended:

Thursday morning another prisoner is knifed at the prison... Nobody can agree on the number of prisoners stabbed or killed in the last month.

He corrected himself so that the entry read, *Thursday, April 6, approx. 10 AM.* It wouldn't do to be imprecise. With so many happenings, it would be important to know exactly when everything took place. He continued:

Approx. 1 PM—Coffin uncovered in field halfway between Malniveau Prison and Verargent. Further investigation reveals a total of five coffins containing murdered prisoners.

The chief inspector looked out the window at the passing landscape. It was so uniform that it was incredible to him that whoever had buried the bodies had been able to locate the same burial ground each time, since he was convinced that the bodies had been buried on five separate occasions. He would know for sure when the medical examiner had examined the corpses.

Tuesday, April 4, Approx 5 PM—Georges Perreaux (six years old) and Albert Perreaux (five years old) go missing. Last seen at Monsieur Marque's sweet shop.

Letreau had interviewed Monsieur Marque himself. He assured Pelleter that Monsieur Marque was in no way involved with the children's disappearance. And why would he be? In a small town like Verargent the owner of the candy store could not afford to have a bad reputation with regards to children.

Pelleter turned back to his earlier entries, and tried to fit in the margin beside the entry on Madame Rosenkrantz's visit to the hotel,

Last time Madame Rosenkrantz is seen.

He did the same for the warden beside the entry on Mahossier's claim that prisoners were being systematically murdered.

He looked at what he had written, and he felt the anger well up in him again. It was time to take the offensive. There was too much going on, and up until now they had been reacting. Events happened and they tried to keep up. Even the manhunt the night before was a reaction. But today, at least, he would find out what Mahossier knew.

To calm himself he started at the beginning and reviewed everything so far, but it didn't help. He knew what had happened

in many instances, but he did not know why or how, and there-
fore he did not know who. He knew nothing.

The prison loomed before them. The taxi drove up to the
gate, and Pelleter got out, instructing the driver to return in
two hours and to wait if he was not yet ready. The chief inspector
showed his documents to the guard at the outer gate, crossed
the space where several cars were parked, moss and wild grass
growing in places from between the cobbles, and then he showed
his documents again at the inner door, where he was admitted
to the prison.

"I hear there was more excitement in town last night," Remy
said.

"Any excitement out here?"

"Oh, it's always exciting here."

"That's what I thought."

Pelleter passed in to the administrative offices. The young
woman at the first desk took one look at him and reached for
the phone. She was a plain girl who would have been prettier if
she had had the conviction to either cut her hair shorter or to
grow it longer. Instead she had settled on an awkward style that
paid homage to a bob without being one.

She whispered into the receiver with her head bowed, blocking
her mouth with the closed fist of her free hand.

There was a kind of lethargy in the rest of the office that
came perhaps from some of the men having been involved in
the search the night before, but Pelleter had spent enough time
in police stations, courts, and prisons to know that the usual situation in those places was of utter boredom.

He saw a desk towards the back of the room stacked with
files. This, no doubt, was Officer Martin's workspace. The prison

workers had been unsure if they were allowed to clean it up yet. Pelleter made a mental note to get Officer Martin back out here as soon as possible. Even if he found nothing, it was better to have someone on hand.

The young woman replaced the receiver of the phone, and sat up rod straight as though the phone cradle were a switch attached to her spine. She looked up at the chief inspector with pursed lips, took a breath, and said, "Monsieur Fournier is otherwise engaged at the moment, and does not know when he will be available to assist you. He suggests that you come back another time."

She waited then, as if to see if she had passed some recitation exam.

Pelleter could not help but smile, and the girl slumped a little sensing that she had failed.

"That's fine," the chief inspector said. "I wasn't here to see Monsieur Fournier anyway. I can just show myself around," and he began to turn back to the door.

"But…"

"No need to bother," Pelleter continued in his light tone. He pointed at the door. "I'm on my way to the infirmary. I know the way."

The young woman looked around at her colleagues, imploring for help. They were paying attention now, but only with surreptitious glances that relieved them of any responsibility.

As Pelleter pushed open the office door, the young woman stood up behind her desk but did not move. He turned back. "You could do me one favor," he said as though it were an afterthought. "I'll need to see Mahossier again. Please have him brought down."

The woman's shoulders sank, but Pelleter did not wait for an answer. As he stepped back into the entry hall, he could only just see one of the other men stand behind her.

"Open this door for me, Remy. I'm going to the infirmary." Pelleter tried to remember if there was another locked door between this one and the infirmary, but he thought it best to keep moving and worry about it when the time came. If the young woman had recovered herself, she no doubt was on the phone to Fournier once again, and it was only a matter of a few minutes before the assistant warden made an appearance.

As Remy unlocked the inner door, Pelleter said, "Could you be sure that they're bringing Mahossier down to the interrogation room for me as well. There seemed to be some confusion about that in the office."

"I'm sure there was," Remy said, smiling. "There needs to be a paper for everything, and god forbid if you miss one little paper." Remy pulled open the door, stepping aside to allow the chief inspector to pass.

Just as he was about to step into the hall, the office door jerked open and one of the clerks appeared. He pulled himself up short in an attempt to regain some composure, and then he said, "Right this way, Monsieur Pelleter."

They must have decided that it was safest to have somebody accompany the chief inspector if he was going to force his way into the prison. Or perhaps Fournier had given the order that Pelleter was to be watched. In either case, the young man stepped ahead of Pelleter, and then led the way to the left towards the infirmary.

"Any more incidents since yesterday?" Pelleter asked the nervous young man from one step behind him.

The man did not turn. "Incidents, sir?"

"What's your name?"

"Monsieur Vittier."

"Okay, Vittier. Fights, stabbings, murders. Incidents."

"I'm sure I can't say, sir."

"I'm sure you can't."

They came to a steel partition with a door in it that divided the hall into equal intervals. Vittier fumbled with a ring of keys he produced from his pocket. So there *had* been another locked doorway before coming to the infirmary. Then Pelleter was glad for the chaperone.

Vittier managed to get the door open, and this time Pelleter stepped through first. The air in this stretch of the hallway had a bottled-up mustiness to it, cut with the ammoniac smell coming from the infirmary.

Pelleter strode along the hall, unconcerned as to whether Vittier was with him. The door to the infirmary stood open. Apparently it was assumed injured prisoners were in too much pain to try to escape.

In the infirmary, there was none of the hurried excitement from the day before. A guard sat in a straight-backed chair just inside the doorway. The stabbing victim was the only prisoner taking up one of the four cots. He was small, pale, and gaunt, as though he had been in hospital for weeks instead of twenty-four hours.

Pelleter crossed the room and set himself on the edge of the cot beside the prisoner. He saw that the prisoner was hand-cuffed to the bed.

Vittier came up beside him, standing at the foot of the bed.

Pelleter held out his papers, but the prisoner, whose eyes darted between Pelleter and Vittier, showed no inclination towards reading what was held before him.

"I am Chief Inspector Pelleter with the Central Bureau. I've come from the city to look into things here. I was hoping you could tell me something of what happened yesterday."

The prisoner's eyes again darted between Pelleter and Vittier. No other part of him moved. His face remained blank. He seemed unimpressed with Pelleter's credentials.

"Do you know who it was who stabbed you?"

The man turned his head away from the chief inspector, wincing as he did.

Pelleter shifted his weight on the cot. The metal rod of the frame cut into the back of his thighs.

"Vittier!"

The young man jerked towards Pelleter. He had been lost in contemplation of the prisoner's wasted form. Now he looked as though he were awaiting a sentence of his own. Was it the prison itself that made everyone here somber, or did Fournier have his men—both his staff and his prisoners—on edge at all times?

"Give us a moment," Pelleter said, and he nodded his head in the direction of the door.

The young clerk went to the entrance and stood beside the guard. They did not speak to one another.

Pelleter leaned forward then, his elbows on his knees, and lowered his voice. "Can you tell me who stabbed you?"

For a moment it seemed as though the prisoner was going to act as though he had not heard the repeated question. But at last, without turning his head, he said just above a whisper, "I don't know."

"Do you know why you were stabbed?"

The prisoner closed his eyes and shook his head. He had been thinking about it, and he didn't know. Prison gave a man lots of time to think, but almost getting killed must make him think in new ways.

"What about the other men that were killed? Are people saying anything about them?"

There was another long pause, and Pelleter was worried that he would have to start from the beginning again. But at last the wounded man said, "No one's saying anything."

"If you say something," Pelleter said, leaning even further forward until he felt the cot begin to tip beneath him, "then maybe I can help."

Still there was no reaction.

"No one will know it was you. I'm going to talk to other prisoners as well."

The man turned his head quickly towards Pelleter now, his eyes wide. "I don't know anything. It was crowded in the yard. It could have been anyone who went for me. I had no beef. I don't know nothing else."

"Okay," Pelleter said.

The whites of the man's eyes showed around large pupils, his nostrils flared, the look of a man afraid and in pain and backed into a corner.

"Okay." The chief inspector stood. He watched the man carefully. "But this will probably be the last chance I have to talk to you without Assistant Warden Fournier."

There was no reaction. The man's face remained the same, full of pain and indignation. Fournier's name had changed nothing.

The chief inspector considered the man for another moment, frustrated that he had not learned anything more from him. With each new incident, Pelleter seemed to know less, and even the victims were ignorant. Sometimes there was nothing that could be done on a case—it was just a matter of waiting—

but Pelleter was unwilling to believe that was true here. Too many things were happening, and somebody knew why. It was just a matter of asking the right person the questions in the right way.

Pelleter turned away from the man on the cot.

"Vittier," he called. "Take me to Mahossier."

Mahossier was already in the examination room, his hands and legs once again chained. To Pelleter's surprise, Monsieur le Directeur Adjoint Fournier had still not made an appearance. Pelleter left Vittier with the guard outside the door, and took up a position behind Mahossier and just to the side.

"Why did you stab the man in the yard?" Pelleter said.

Mahossier made no attempt to turn around. "Why, Inspector! I'm surprised at you. Surely you know that I didn't have yard privileges yesterday. Some days I do, some days I don't. Monsieur Fournier sees to that. It's for my own protection, you see. Some of the boys here don't like me very much. I couldn't say why."

Pelleter could hear the hilarity in Mahossier's voice. The criminal did not seem put out to have Pelleter behind him. Pelleter was in no mood to be toyed with. He tried to keep his voice calm. "What do you do those days for meals? Are you allowed in the mess?"

"One of the good boys brings it to me in my cell, but assistant warden's careful for it to be a different one as often as possible. What's the matter? He didn't tell you any of this? Is he not being helpful?"

Pelleter would not be drawn in.

Mahossier put on a tone of absolute concern. "Have they found those two little boys yet? I've been so worried about them."

"And how do you know about the missing children?"

"How is Madame Pelleter by the way? Well, I trust. But why wouldn't she be?"

Pelleter grabbed Mahossier by the shoulders then, and threw him to the side, causing the prisoner to fall heavily to the floor, his head knocking the stone with a dull thump, followed a second after by the clatter of the chair falling to the ground. With his hands chained to his legs, Mahossier was forced to remain in a fetal position in the shadow of the table, a small old man, unable to even raise himself.

Pelleter kicked the chair, which had settled partially on Mahossier, into the corner.

The old man was shaking, laughing soundlessly.

Pelleter circled the table to prevent himself from kicking the downed man. He thought of Servières asking him that first night how he could be in the same room with this monster and not kill him. The thought cooled his anger. The play had been made, and it was not a bad one. He would see what effect it had.

He came around so that he was standing in front of Mahossier's face. The murderer, still laughing, was straining to see the floor beneath his head.

"Very good," he said. "I think I'm bleeding." He licked the cold stone, and his grin spread even wider. "I am bleeding! Very good." And he laughed some more.

Pelleter squatted before Mahossier and said the one thing he thought might force a straight answer out of the man. "I will leave on tonight's train. I don't have to be a part of any of this."

"I suppose you could," Mahossier said from his place on the floor. "Whether you have to be a part of it…that depends on what the press thinks and what the Central Bureau thinks about what the press thinks when Le Maire and Letreau and Le Directeur decide that it would be nice if it was the fault of that detective from the city that several dead bodies turned up and several people went missing. It's true you have no obligation to me."

Mahossier thought he had Pelleter in his control and the chief inspector bristled at the notion.

"But you know these small towns…It never seems to be the people in charge, just people drifting through."

"Now you're a political activist? Or is it a social reformer?"

"I prefer concerned citizen." The shadows on his cheek deepened as a grin spread. "I love the word concerned. It's so… useful."

Pelleter stood to relieve the ache that had begun to burn in his thighs from squatting. He pulled out the still-standing chair, the one that he had sat in two days prior, and sat down. From there he could not see Mahossier, but instead, looked across the table at the sweating stone wall across from him. The rough-hewn faces of the stones were a miniature topography in which an ant could be lost forever. From his point of view, able to take in the whole wall's surface, Pelleter did not think it made any more sense to him than it would to the ant.

Mahossier filled the silence. His one weakness when he felt as though he had a worthy conversationalist. "I don't know anything about those missing boys. They have nothing to do with this."

"Then if you know about everything else, wouldn't it be easier to tell me?"

"I don't know about everything else."

"Then what do you know about?"

"Dead prisoners."

"I know about them too."

"See, you're not a total loss, Chief Inspector. And I was trying to come to terms with the disappointment."

It was easier to talk to the man without being able to see him, his voice floating up from below.

"Who moved the bodies?" Mahossier said.

That was the question. But he responded, "Who killed the men?"

"Perhaps…" Delight returned to Mahossier's voice again, as though ice cream had been suggested and the question was now which flavor. "Perhaps you answer my question and I'll answer yours!"

"You're not worried about being a snitch?"

Mahossier's delight turned to anger. "Listen, detective! I am already reviled. I told you that to start. But being reviled isn't always a bad thing."

Pelleter wondered how that could be. Still, Mahossier had highlighted once again the question that seemed most pressing. How had those prisoners' bodies gotten out of Malniveau? Who had moved them?

Pelleter contemplated the wall. After a few moments, Mahossier began to hum, and the tune eventually penetrated the chief inspector's thoughts. It was a children's tune. If Pelleter remembered correctly it was about going to grandmother's house.

Pelleter stood, his chair scraping the floor, cutting off Mahossier's song.

He had learned nothing here. The initial summons, the oblique aspersions regarding the assistant warden…it all seemed to be for Mahossier's own amusement, and Pelleter was jumping through his hoops like an amateur.

The chief inspector went to the door. He raised his hand to knock, but held it there, suspended in the air. A noise came from the other side of the table, a shuffle, and the clank of chain on stone, but Pelleter could not see what Mahossier was doing.

"Mahossier," Pelleter barked.

The movement stopped.

"If those boys don't turn up soon, and alive, you may find that you have yard privileges every day again."

There was no response from the floor.

"Or perhaps the next time I send guards in here to pick you up off the floor, I'll only have to follow your body to find out how they get dead prisoners out of Malniveau."

With that, Pelleter allowed his fist to drop against the metal door, a hollow echoing clang, signaling that he was ready to go.

8.
Lost and Found

The temperature had climbed so that the brow of Pelleter's hat was clammy and a faint sheen of sweat coated his body beneath his overcoat as he stepped out of the taxi in front of the café. It was the humidity that was particularly oppressive. Most of the sky was clear, but to the east there was a dirty-sheep-colored expanse of clouds that may or may not have threatened rain.

Verargent Square was quiet, the town about its post-lunch business. Only the old men who lined the base of the monument were to be seen, and they were as still as the statue above them.

The café was equally silent. Pelleter ordered some beer and a ham and cheese sandwich for carry away. He wanted to get back to the police station to find out any news about the missing children. He also needed to send Martin back to the prison files and to call Lambert at the Central Bureau.

The waitress appeared from the back and the proprietor bullied her to fetch the inspector's meal.

Pelleter pulled out his watch. One o'clock, three days after the first body was found. This was the difficult time in a complicated investigation that so few people understood…the waiting.

The proprietor turned to Pelleter with an ingratiating smile.

"So they found those boys." The proprietor shook his head. "They're too old to have gotten lost in a field," he said, and he snorted. "When I was their age, I had to walk miles just to milk the cows."

Pelleter did not reply, but there was a subtle relaxation of his shoulders. It was the first he had heard that the boys had been found, but he was not surprised. It accounted for the town's quiet. He reached for a cigar, then remembered he was about to have lunch, and dropped his hand.

"To cause so much trouble," the proprietor continued, "I hope they get a sound thrashing."

The waitress returned with Pelleter's sandwich, wrapped, he noticed with some satisfaction, in yesterday's *Vérité*.

"But how are they? Is everything okay? And this other thing with the dead prisoners and the missing girl?"

Pelleter ignored the proprietor's questions, making a point to say thank you to the waitress as he took his lunch.

Outside he took a long refreshing swallow of beer. The sandwich was good. Benoît, even in his crisis, made good bread, crisp and firm. He ate as he crossed the square, the sweat beginning again to pour down his back. It was good that the boys were safe, but he felt lost in this other thing. He could not help but feel as though he kept forgetting to do the simplest things that would lead him to the answer. There were too many distractions. He contemplated for a moment how a small town could seem to have more distractions than the city.

He saw the man standing in the shadow of the police station steps before he recognized him. "A happy ending, Monsieur Pelleter!"

"Servières."

"We're doing another special edition tonight. The headline…" He traced his open hand across the air. "*FOUND*."

Pelleter continued to eat. "You really are becoming a daily."

"This may be my chance for a larger market."

"Then who would write the *Vérité*?"

"Inspector! It's good to see you in high spirits as well. I'm not the only reporter at the *Vérité*."

Pelleter finished his sandwich and made a point of balling up its wrapping, but Servières did not notice.

"What happened?"

Servières took out his notebook. Pelleter could not fight the feeling again that Servières was very much like him, and he felt a burst of warmth for the young reporter.

"Tuesday, April 4th at approximately five in the evening, Georges and Albert Perreaux left Monsieur Marque's sweet shop, and headed west on the Rue Principale on their way home to the Perreaux Farm.

"Georges decided it would be faster to cut across a field, but the boys quickly became lost, circling in the high grass in an ever-increasing panic."

"That's how you're going to write it?"

"I haven't settled on it yet. Dark fell, the rain started, and the boys were pinned down, lost in the field. In the morning, Albert was ill and unable to move. Georges was frightened to leave his brother.

"Madame Perreaux assumed that the boys had stayed with an aunt in town because of the weather and so she did not inform the police until Thursday, April 6th. Chief of Police Letreau organized an all-night search that continued into the morning until the boys were located in the field west of town, now both with fevers.

"They were removed to the hospital, and there will be more here with quotes from the police and the men who found them and maybe the boys themselves if I get lucky."

"Then why are you waiting out here?"

"Monsieur Rosenkrantz is inside, and I thought it best to stay out of his way, since it seems he's unhappy I mentioned his wife in yesterday's paper."

Pelleter smiled at that. He turned up the steps.

"Inspector, wait!"

Pelleter stopped, now looking down at Servières.

"Do you have anything new to report in the Meranger murder?"

Pelleter's smile softened.

"Or would you care to comment on the five prisoners' bodies that were found yesterday? Or Madame Rosenkrantz's disappearance?"

Pelleter's expression had turned dark, and he growled, "I thought you were running good news tonight, Servières."

"Good news is news that sells papers."

"Stick to the boys," Pelleter said and began to turn away. He stopped again.

"What is it?" Servières said.

Pelleter didn't reply. He thought again about how he felt as though he were forgetting something or some things and how he was at a loss as to what to do next, as he had thought that morning, that he was only reacting. Maybe the trick was to get something else to react to. He turned to Servières.

"Take this down. Inspector Pelleter is very encouraged about his investigation into the prisoners murdered at Malniveau Prison. He has some promising leads and hopes to have the case tied up by the time this paper goes to press tomorrow."

Servières was writing feverishly. When he finished he looked up at Pelleter, his eyes gleaming with excitement. "Is it true?"

"We'll know tomorrow, I guess." The chief inspector thought of the young, attractive woman standing in the entryway of the

Verargent Hotel's dining room like a lost little girl. She did not need to be dragged through the papers. "And leave out Madame Rosenkrantz's disappearance."

"But everyone already knows—"

"Leave it out," Pelleter said, climbing the last step. "I gave you plenty." He pulled open the door to the police station at the back of Town Hall.

The police station was as deserted as the rest of the town, only it was as noisy as ever.

"You bastards search night and day when its two little boys missing, but you don't give a damn about a young woman!"

Monsieur Rosenkrantz was standing against the desk that separated the public space from the department offices. There were two police officers Pelleter did not recognize sitting at the desk furthest from Monsieur Rosenkrantz watching the angered man with silent determination. There was no one else in the office. Letreau had probably given everyone else leave for the rest of the day after last night's search.

Rosenkrantz was shouting in English now, and Pelleter was able to pick out more than one of the words he had learned in the war from an American soldier in return for teaching him the equivalents in French.

Pelleter came up behind the tall American, and slipped a hand under his elbow.

Rosenkrantz jerked away in surprise, but Pelleter had a tight grip.

"What are the police doing?" Rosenkrantz said, switching back to French. "Nobody's doing anything here. They searched night and day for those little boys. My wife's been missing for a day and a half now. Because of these two little miscreants, I haven't even been able to file a report."

"Come on," Pelleter said, nodding his head towards the chairs in the waiting area and tightening his grip on the American's elbow. "I'll see to you in a moment."

"Are you going to help me look for my wife?"

"Why don't we talk about it?"

Rosenkrantz regarded Pelleter for a moment. The two men were almost the same height, but Rosenkrantz managed to look down at Pelleter nevertheless. He pulled his arm away and Pelleter released it. "Okay. We'll talk."

The American straightened his overcoat, but did not sit down. Pelleter went behind the desk and approached the two officers, whose expressions had not changed since Pelleter had come in, even now that the shouting had stopped. "Where's Chief Letreau?" Pelleter said, glancing into the chief of police's office.

"At the hospital with Madame Perreaux."

"Inspector!" Rosenkrantz called from the waiting area.

Pelleter held up his hand, and said to the officer, "And everyone else?"

"Skeleton crew until tomorrow. Don't want to pay us too much overtime."

The other officer tapped his companion on the shoulder, and the first officer realized what he had said.

"I mean, sir…"

"I know what you mean," Pelleter said. He turned.

"Any message, sir?" the second officer said.

"No."

"Inspector!"

As Pelleter approached Monsieur Rosenkrantz, he said, "Let's go."

The American writer said, "Where?"

"To talk about it," Pelleter said, taking out a cigar and busying himself with lighting it.

Rosenkrantz watched this performance, and then said curtly, "Okay. Fine." He turned and led the way out of the police station, and Pelleter followed.

Outside, the chief inspector was glad to see that Servières had had the sense to disappear. He was probably on his way to the hospital to try to get some quotes. Or perhaps he needed to go type up the chief inspector's comments immediately.

Rosenkrantz led them away from the square, into an area of town that appeared residential. He walked with long angry strides, his outrage far from gone, but for the moment invested in walking. At a small alley, no larger than one man across, he turned. The windows at ground level were all shuttered. Empty laundry lines crisscrossed between the buildings above their heads, each line just long enough for a single shirt or several socks.

Halfway down the alley there was a steep set of stairs, almost vertical. Rosenkrantz went down, holding the side of the building for support, guiding his head beneath the low passage and through a door.

Pelleter followed and found himself in a private pub, just a board across the width of the room held by evenly spaced posts acting as a bar. There were no tables. The place smelled of stale cigarette smoke and sour beer. Pelleter's shoes stuck to the floor, each step giving way with a resisting crack as he stepped up to the bar.

They were the only people there. The ancient barman had been sleeping on his stool with his head leaned against the wall, but he stood, rubbing his eyes when Rosenkrantz knocked on the board. He set two pints on the bar without either patron ordering.

Rosenkrantz stared ahead as he drank, still standing. The ceiling was only inches from the tops of their heads.

The barkeep went back to sleep in his corner.

Down in this basement, it was already night.

Pelleter took a seat and left his beer untouched. He watched Rosenkrantz drink, smoking his cigar and waiting for the man to speak. He remembered what Servières had said about Rosenkrantz's drinking bouts.

Half a pint gone, Rosenkrantz, still facing forward said, "Why would she have gone away?"

"You tell me."

Rosenkrantz turned. There was real hurt in his face. He shook his head. "She wouldn't have." He downed the rest of his beer, and turned to wake the barkeep, but Pelleter said, "Have mine."

Rosenkrantz took it, but he only held it. "I didn't know her father was in Malniveau until you showed up at our door. I knew he was in prison, of course, but it had never occurred to me that he was in our prison."

"She visited him there."

"How do you know?"

"She told me."

Rosenkrantz drank then.

"I know I'm an old man to her," Rosenkrantz said, setting the empty glass down. "That sometimes it must seem like I'm a father to her more than a husband. But I love her more than anything, more than my country, more than my writing."

He knocked on the bar, and the barkeep startled, then shuffled to refill their glasses.

"I can understand that people might keep secrets from each other, that's how I make my living, making up all of these little lies that people tell each other, but why keep this about her father? And why disappear without a word? She knows it would kill me."

He drank the newly poured beer.

"So you were never in communication with Meranger?"

"Never. I hated the man without having met him."

"And anyone else at the prison?"

Rosenkrantz motioned with his glass. "Here. In town. Maybe. But not to talk to. I don't really know anyone here, except Clotilde. That's why those bastards at the police department won't help me." His eyes opened wide. "That's why you have to help me. You have to find her. And prove…"

"Prove what?"

"Whatever it is that they say about her in the papers is wrong."

"The papers just said the murdered man was her father."

"That's already too much."

"You'll have to take that up with Philippe Servières."

Rosenkrantz finished his pint and began the second one without asking Pelleter if he wanted it. The writer was unsteady on his feet. He probably hadn't eaten since Madame Rosenkrantz disappeared, and he was drinking very fast.

The barkeep saw the mood that the American writer was in, and decided that he would not get any more sleep.

Rosenkrantz began to ramble, to tell of how he had met Clotilde and left his first wife, an American who still received half of his earnings in the States, and their son.

Five pints…six. Pelleter was not yet finished with his cigar.

He talked of how they had chosen to move to Verargent despite Hollywood's clamoring for him to come out there and work on a salary, and how he loved the solitude, the way that his whole world could be wrapped up in his writing and his wife.

The barkeep went to refill Rosenkrantz's glass, but Pelleter shook his head, and the barkeep pulled back.

Rosenkrantz turned to the chief inspector, almost falling. "Do you think she's all right? You don't think that whoever went for her father would also go for her?"

"I think she's fine," Pelleter said. "Come sit down."

"Is it true what they're saying about these other murdered prisoners?"

"What are they saying?"

"That there were other murdered prisoners."

"It's true."

Rosenkrantz went to lift his glass and noticed that it was empty. "More beer," he bellowed. "What are you thinking!"

The old man refilled the writer's glass, too timid to even cast an angry look at Pelleter.

The chief inspector said again, "Why don't you sit down?"

Seven pints…eight. Rosenkrantz at last sat down and put his head on the bar at once. His voice muffled, he said, "I just don't know what to do. They searched everywhere for those boys and no one found my wife. What do I do?"

The chief inspector called to the barkeep about a taxi.

"There's no phone in the house," the old man said.

Pelleter went out to get the taxi himself. The threatening clouds had broken up and were now thin white wisps against the darkening sky. Night was falling and with it, how many missed opportunities? How long before he could go back home to his own wife?

The taxi was in its usual place before the café, and when

Pelleter explained what he needed, the driver knew the place at once. He had been called there many times.

It took all three men, even the old barkeep, to get Rosenkrantz up the steep stairs and down the alley. Once the American was in the back seat, Pelleter took his place beside the driver, and the barkeep went back to his pub.

Rosenkrantz had a tab. The barkeep would be paid in time.

When they reached the Rosenkrantz home, night had fallen. The other evening, huddled down as it had been against the storm, the house's charm had still come across, but now empty in the night, it just appeared lifeless and forlorn.

Pelleter stepped out of the car and thought he saw a shadow move at the end of the drive, just a darker patch of dark. He stepped towards the street without closing his car door, fixing his eyes on the spot. It could have just been a shrub moving in the breeze, or was somebody out there…following him? He continued along the drive, ignoring the sounds of the cabman behind him. The shape moved again, and then joined a hedge.

"Hey," the cabman shouted behind him. "A little help."

Pelleter continued towards the shadow, still peering into the darkness. He saw no more movement. Had it been Madame Rosenkrantz? No, she would have let herself into the house.

"Inspector!"

Pelleter held still, listening for sounds. "Come out now," he called. The bushes swayed in a faint breeze. Nothing. Was he overtired from the night before?

"Inspector!" the cabbie shouted again.

Pelleter turned back. If someone was following him, he would find out who and why soon enough.

The cabman was leaning into the back seat of the car, his

silhouette lit by the dash as he struggled with Rosenkrantz's inert form.

The chief inspector came up alongside the taxi driver, and leaned in beside him, the two men shoulder-to-shoulder as they hoisted the unconscious American writer up off the seat and into the cool of the night. The rank smell of alcohol caused Pelleter to wince even more than the dead weight of the large man.

They shuffled up to the house, the taxi driver muttering the whole time, "Come on, you bastard, come on, you bastard, come on..."

At the door, Pelleter began to look for the writer's keys, but the driver tried the handle and found it open. Perhaps Rosenkrantz had been afraid that his wife would come home and not be able to get in. Perhaps, even with all of the excitement, it would not have occurred to the American to lock his door. After all, wasn't that one of the reasons they had moved to Verargent?

The two sober men turned sideways to manage the doorway, and Pelleter darted his eyes back to the street to the spot where he had seen the shadow. Sure enough it seemed again as though someone was out there. But Pelleter couldn't give chase until he'd set down the American, so he just staggered forward. What had the chief inspector discovered that was reason for being followed?

Inside, the door swung slowly closed behind them. They labored in the darkness of the small hallway, dragging the writer between them.

"This way," the driver said at the first opening. Enough light came through the window to make out the shadow of an armchair. They deposited the drunken man, and Pelleter stretched, his hands at the small of his back, his heart racing from exertion.

"I should get paid extra for this," the driver said. His brusque voice seemed too loud in the darkness.

Pelleter reached into his pocket and pulled out some francs, handing them over without making out the denominations.

"He should pay."

Pelleter looked for a lamp. There was a gasoline sconce beside the door, which Pelleter lit with one of his matches, revealing a standard sitting room. "You go back. I'll be fine."

The driver shrugged. He had been driving the inspector all day, but he was not a curious man and it was getting near dinner. He left the room.

Pelleter stepped to the window. He knew it would make him visible to anyone who might be watching—the light behind him and the darkness outside—but that was fine. It might lure his tail into a false sense of security, that he could see but couldn't be seen. However, the only movement outside was the cabman reversing his car down the drive. As his headlights swept the hedge and the street, they revealed no one. The man who had been out there was probably long gone.

Pelleter turned around. He regarded the slumped form of Monsieur Rosenkrantz. Clotilde was loved if nothing else. And that was something. That was a lot.

The chief inspector took another look around the room. It was hardly used, much of the furniture brand new and the rug on the floor unmarked by footprints. The only thing that gave the room a feeling of habitation were the two built-in bookcases to either side of the fireplace jammed with books in French, English, and Spanish, two-deep in places. The liquor cart in the corner was devoid of liquor, the glasses in need of a dusting.

Out in the hall, the day's mail was still in a scattered pile on the floor. Pelleter picked it up, and flipped through. It was actually the last several days' mail: bills, airmail from the States, a printed envelope from a well-known magazine in the city. He set it on a sidetable in the entryway.

Across the way was a dining room that he could make out well enough in the light from the sitting room. It was a small room, the table filling the whole space. He went through, pushing into the kitchen, which was so dark that he lit another match, looking for a lamp. He found one hanging from the ceiling in the center of the room over a butcher block table. Clotilde kept her kitchen clean. The surfaces were all spotless, as was the floor. The drawers and cabinets were kept neatly, the silver-ware stacked, the pots and pans inside one another. There was a porcelain double sink with running water. It made sense that the American writer would be sure to provide his young bride with the luxuries that she would most appreciate.

There was a rear door to the kitchen that opened further along the main hallway. One door in the hall led to the back yard while another across the way revealed Rosenkrantz's study. He'd left a lamp burning on his desk, and it cast a glow on the room, revealing the disarray of papers and books in stacks on every surface including the floor. There were framed photographs of Clotilde on the desk, along with several older photographs of an elderly couple that must have been the writer's American parents.

Rosenkrantz and Clotilde did appear to be the content pair they seemed. They lived in isolated marital bliss. Clotilde had been troubled over her father's death, confused really, when Pelleter saw her. But she hadn't seemed frightened. There would have been no reason for her to run.

He forced his way to the small window between two of the bookcases, and looked between the blinds out into the back yard. There was nothing there to see. So his supposed tail, if there was one, was probably alone, which meant that he was effectively useless, two men required to follow someone successfully. There were too many players and it seemed that all of the important ones he couldn't see. He blew out the lamp on Rosenkrantz's desk before going back into the hall.

He went upstairs to be thorough, not expecting to find anything. The upstairs was a large single room with the staircase opening in the center of the floor, a railing around the other three sides of the opening. There was more light from the windows here than downstairs. The bed was unmade, and the armoire left opened, but these were the signs of an absent wife, not of a hurried departure. There was nothing to find here.

Pelleter went back downstairs without further investigation.

Rosenkrantz had not moved during Pelleter's search. His chest rose and fell with labored breaths. With luck he would be out for the rest of the night.

Pelleter left, feeling the front door latch behind him. The evening was clear and pleasant, an evening meant for enjoyment. As he reached the street, he listened for footsteps behind him, but heard nothing. At the first closed storefront with a display window, the chief inspector stopped as though to look inside, and glanced behind him, but there was no one there. If he had been followed earlier, he wasn't being followed now.

In the lobby of the hotel, Pelleter asked the girl at the desk to ring up headquarters for him. The missing children had distracted him. He should have gotten in touch with Lambert before this. Hopefully the lost time would not prove too costly.

The girl left for a moment and when she returned she said the call would be put through directly.

He asked for a newspaper and told her that he was ready to take his dinner.

She pulled a fresh copy of the *Vérité* from under the counter, and then came around and disappeared into the dining room.

Pelleter didn't watch her go. His eyes were fixed on the headline:

FOUND!

Of course Servières could not leave it as a simple story. He placed emphasis on the fact that the boys had been found by two civilians, not gendarmes, and he cast aspersions on the effectiveness of Chief Letreau and the local police department given the recent rash of crime. Yes, he was making his bid for a larger market. Stirring up trouble was a good way to do it.

Pelleter flipped through the rest of the two-sheet paper and stopped at the article on the Meranger murders. As of right now, the *Vérité* was not committing to the idea that Meranger's murder was connected to the five murdered prisoners from the field. They had been found in different places after all, and in different circumstances. The *Vérité*, however, was encouraged to find that visiting Chief Inspector Pelleter of the Central Bureau was very optimistic about the case, having uncovered a promising new lead that he would follow up immediately.

There was no mention of Madame Rosenkrantz's disappearance. Pelleter hoped that Monsieur Rosenkrantz would appreciate that he had done that much for him. He was pleased that Servières had gone along with his ploy. Now the inspector would have to think of something to back it up with in the morning.

He turned to go into the dining room, and he saw out of the corner of his eye that there was a man sitting in an armchair in the corner, a second before the man said, "Chief Inspector."

The inspector turned fully then.

The man sat with his right ankle on his left knee. The same newspaper was spread out in his lap. His suit, as always, was impeccable.

"I think we need to have a talk," Fournier said.

9.

The Assistant Warden

Pelleter realized that Fournier must have been waiting for him since before he arrived, which meant that the assistant warden had been able to watch the inspector turn through the paper unobserved. Pelleter had done nothing inappropriate, but he was still rankled at being caught unawares. There was nothing to be done about it now.

"Yes," he said, and with a false bow, he invited Fournier into the dining room. "Let's talk."

Fournier refolded the paper, taking care to pull at the end of each crease so that when he was finished the paper appeared brand new. He stood, left the paper on the seat, and led the way into the dining room.

Once inside, Pelleter took his seat so that he faced the door, and spread his napkin in his lap as though he were simply sitting down to dinner. He looked uninterested, a man at the end of an exhausting workday, when in reality he was watching Fournier's every movement.

The assistant warden took the seat opposite, where Clotilde-ma-Fleur Rosenkrantz had sat two nights before. His face was set, as though he were determined to say what he had come to say without being waylaid.

As he prepared himself, the girl from the counter approached behind him.

Fournier began, "You can not come and go as you please at the prison. It's unacceptable!"

"Monsieur Inspector?"

Fournier jumped, and turned in his seat to see the girl who was leaning in towards them with her hands clasped.

"The phone…"

"Ah, yes," Pelleter said, bunching up his napkin. "You'll excuse me, Monsieur Fournier, of course. It'll only be a moment." Pelleter stood, pushing back his seat, and extracting himself from the table. "And you should let the chef know that it will be two of us for dinner."

Fournier looked frightened by this sudden turn of events, looking at the girl and then Pelleter and then the girl again. "No, I'm not staying for dinner."

"Of course you are. You've had a very trying few days, after all. I won't be a minute."

Fournier's fear had converted to frustrated anger, but Pelleter passed out of the dining room, and went to the phone that had been left on the front desk for him.

He picked up the receiver:

"Lambert? It's me…Yes, I need you to locate somebody for me…" He gave the name. "Check the hotels…He's with his wife, so he shouldn't be hiding too carefully…Call me when you've found him, either at the hotel or through Letreau. But don't lose sight of him…Very good…Yes."

He hung up, and went back into the dining room.

Fournier was sitting facing forward, his back to the door. He sat up straight, his shoulders squared. Pelleter spoke before Fournier could see him, but the assistant warden did not act startled. He'd regained his composure.

"Sorry about that. The telephone must not be ignored. Never

know when it's going to be something important. Or when you'll be able to get in touch with the other person again, the chances of you both being at the phone at the same time…" He resumed his seat, and replaced his napkin. He continued to ramble, setting a nonchalant, jovial tone, knowing that it would further anger Fournier and make the man more likely to make a mistake. "Perhaps it's best to communicate through telegraph, but a telegraph can be too easy to ignore, so…here we are. You were saying?"

Fournier pressed his lips together, and exhaled through his nose. In a tight voice, he said, "You can not come—"

"Oh, yes, I can not come and go as I please at the prison. Well I had an escort, and I was told you were busy."

"That's beside the point. The prison must remain secure, and to do that, certain rules must be followed."

"Ah, of course." Pelleter said, remaining offhand. "Where were you today, by the way?"

"The results of our search turned up many things that had to be dealt with even if it didn't turn up the knife used to cut our prisoner. Running a prison is complicated enough without outside forces meddling. For instance, you can not have your man at the prison. That too is unacceptable."

"My man?"

"Going through our files."

"Well, it's not my man. It's Letreau's. You must take it up with him."

Fournier scoffed. "Letreau? The chief of police is adequate at his job, but this is a small town, and his job does not ask much of him. Everybody knows that you are running this investigation."

"But it was Letreau who sent the officer to Malniveau."

Fournier clenched his teeth. His eyes lit with anger. "I will not—"

The proprietor appeared then with two steaming plates of ratatouille. "Ah, here you are, Chief Inspector, and Monsieur Fournier, what a pleasure to have you. You will love this, I am sure. *Bon appetit! Bon appetit!*"

He set a plate down before each man, and clapped his hands together. There was a pause, and then he edged away from the table.

Pelleter took up his silverware. "What's the problem with *my* man?"

"He's distracting my staff, and interfering with my systems. I can't have an outsider requesting to see every piece of paper we have produced in the last two months."

Good boy, Martin, Pelleter thought. He was the right choice for the job. He has shown more big-city pluck than any of the others. I have to be sure he gets back out there first thing in the morning.

"I told you earlier, if you insist that we're all in this together then you must trust that I will come forward with anything I find."

"Then can you tell me what you know of the five prisoners who were buried in a farm field ten miles from the prison?" Pelleter said. He took a bite of his meal after this quiet question, but his eyes didn't leave Fournier's face.

"What! I will not be mocked. Surely you're not serious."

With the same calm, Pelleter said, "I am serious." He reached into his pocket, took out his notebook and flipped it open to the page with the five prisoner numbers on it, and slid it across the table. "You haven't heard about this yet?"

Fournier glanced at the numbers without touching the notebook. "I don't know anything about it."

Pelleter took another bite of his food, but still watched Fournier. The assistant warden's anger had shifted away from Pelleter and broadened, as he looked off to the side, thinking. It seemed as though he were genuinely surprised at this discovery. He *was* isolated out at the prison. And it seemed he did not know everything that went on there either.

The assistant warden turned back to the inspector. "When was this done? Perhaps this was from years ago…"

What he meant was, before his time. "In the last few weeks."

Fournier looked to the side again. When he turned back to the inspector, his anger had dissipated, and he was now conspiratorial. "You must understand…the warden…" He paused, and Pelleter could see him struggle with his political self, trying to decide if it was yet time to speak out against his superior. "The warden started his career as a guard at Malniveau. He did his time, his years pacing those corridors, standing watch with a shotgun, sitting in a cold guard box alone for hours. He didn't go to school. He's never been out of Verargent for more than the occasional trip to the city or the seashore. For him, the prisoners are the enemy to be controlled, and that's it.

"And they are! I don't disagree, but there's more to that then violence and a show of force…I studied administration. I worked in the private sector for an importer, overseeing shipments, arranging transport. Everything had to be planned in advance, calculated on paper—the paperwork! And the reality of it all had to be addressed, of the people out there on the boats or on the docks, real people, you understand. Real people.

"All of these things are the same in a prison. The prisoners are people. But they are also the things that must be transported, stored, maintained. That means paperwork. And diligence. And understanding."

He was really opening up now. Pelleter had fallen silent, not wishing to interfere with the assistant warden's confession. And Fournier took that silence as a sympathetic invitation. They were both in law enforcement, after all. Pelleter understood.

"The warden is all violence and might," Fournier said. "He has no finesse."

"Are you saying the warden killed these men?" Pelleter said suddenly, leaning forward.

Fournier looked confused. "No," he said, shaking his head. "The warden? No, he's not a murderer…"

Pelleter sat back, and took another bite of his ratatouille. He was almost finished with it.

"I'm simply saying the warden is incompetent. That you have no idea what work I have had to do to get things in order, and I have had to fight at every step. We need a form for this. We need a form for that. And the warden always resists. But then things slip between the cracks." He raised his hand and let it fall on the table in frustration.

Pelleter pushed back his dish. "Like people getting counted present, when they are missing."

"For example," Fournier said, and sneered.

Pelleter waited in silence to see if the assistant warden would say more.

Fournier renewed his vigor. "You can not push me around. I've worked in the city, and I worked my way up at two other national prisons." He stopped, sitting up in his seat. He had not touched the food in front of him. He felt empowered by recounting his story. "Call off your man."

Pelleter took a cigar from his pocket, and took the time to light it. He blew out the smoke, which hung over the table between them. Then, in a quiet, deliberate voice, he said, "How did Meranger get out of the prison?"

Fournier, surprised by the question, exploded, "I don't know! I'm doing everything—"

"Not enough!" Pelleter barked, and the benevolent confessor was gone, as was the babbling fool from the beginning of the meal.

Fournier for all of his bluster, blanched at Pelleter's quiet indignation. "Are you accusing me of being involved?"

"It had crossed my mind," Pelleter said.

Fournier looked down at his untouched meal, and then out through the thin curtain, and then into the empty dining room, unable to settle his gaze. At last, he looked back at Pelleter, and he was seething, his anger from earlier nothing compared to the white anger that was paralyzing his body. "How dare you," he managed, choking on the words.

Pelleter blew a plume of smoke, calm and dismissive.

Fournier pushed back from the table, almost knocking over his chair, which was only saved from falling by the chair behind. He righted it, and then stormed across the room, and out the door. A moment later, a car could be heard as it started and screeched around the square, the man still controlled by his outrage.

Pelleter sat, enjoying his cigar, the air above him filling with smoke. Verargent was quiet, a small town after dark.

In his room with the lights off, Pelleter could not sleep, despite the physical activity of the afternoon and evening.

Fournier had been genuinely surprised when Pelleter had

told him of the five murdered prisoners found in the field. If Meranger constituted a sixth murder, and the man stabbed the day before was meant to be a seventh... Well, it stood to reason that somebody was committing the murders inside the prison. The real question was the one that Mahossier had put to Pelleter and Pelleter had put to Fournier and was now putting to himself over and over:

How were the dead men removed from the prison without anybody knowing?

Or the other way to ask that was, Who was removing the dead prisoners from the prison without anybody else knowing?

Because Pelleter was certain that Meranger had been killed within the prison walls as well. And if Fournier truly knew nothing...

He tried to remember everyone who he had seen in his three trips to the prison, but there were too many to recall, and he had not seen everybody. That was definitely the case: he had not seen everybody.

His mind turned the facts round and round, and then at some point, as he asked himself again who had moved Meranger, he fell asleep.

10.
A Lineup

Pelleter had not taken two steps out of the Hotel Verargent the next morning when he was accosted on the street.

"Inspector Pelleter! Were you happy with my article? Another special edition, no less."

It was Philippe Servières.

Pelleter turned towards the police station without even casting a glance towards the reporter. The town was busy with early morning activity. People who worked in the businesses in town hurried to their jobs, while housewives who liked to do their shopping early already carried parcels. Two senior citizens had taken up their place on the shaded side of the war monument.

It all seemed quite normal. Pelleter had seen small towns like this in a panic once an article like Servières' came out, but it had had no serious effect. Perhaps they viewed it as a prison problem, something outside of town.

Servières hurried two steps to fall in beside Pelleter. "We're doing another special today. This is big news. Do you want anything else to go into the paper? Do you think we can help flush out the murderer?"

Pelleter walked with quick assurance, ignoring the reporter. He had awoken with an idea that he was eager to put into effect, something to support his claims in the paper, and it felt good to be on the move, acting instead of reacting.

"I need to keep the story alive. I can't keep the Rosenkrantz girl's disappearance out of it forever. Inspector, a comment?"

They were outside Town Hall now, a police car parked out front. Pelleter turned the corner towards the police station.

"It seems to me," Servières went on, "that the only reason Madame Rosenkrantz had to run off was because she killed her father. And that your lack of interest in finding her is a gross failure."

Pelleter turned back then, already on the steps to the station so that he towered over Servières. Servières fell back, surprised and off-guard.

"Is that what you're going to say in the paper?" Pelleter said.

Servières' assurance had vanished. "Well, yes."

"You may want to think twice about that. Monsieur Rosenkrantz will be very unhappy."

"I don't print things to make people happy. I print the news."

"But this is just your opinion," Pelleter said, and turned away, going into the police station, and leaving Servières cowed on the steps.

The station was in direct opposition to the sunny calm outside. Martin was back at the front desk. The woman with the yappy dog had returned, dog in hand, another poor driver accused of attempted canine slaughter, the yelling parties handled by two officers. Pelleter was surprised to see that Monsieur Rosenkrantz stood in front of one of the other desks, shouting over the noise at one of the officers who had assisted Pelleter with the coffins.

When Rosenkrantz saw Pelleter, he walked over, leaving the officer who was taking his statement behind. "She still hasn't turned up," Rosenkrantz said.

"Sir?" the officer said. "I'll help you."

"You seem steadier on your feet this morning."

"I'm beside myself with panic."

"This officer will take your statement," Pelleter said, inviting Rosenkrantz to turn back around.

"These officers should have taken my statement days ago! She's disappeared. She could be dead somewhere, but what are they doing? Looking after dogs and children! Someone killed her father, why not kill her too? Wipe out the whole family. This is what you should be working on."

"Sir?"

Pelleter readjusted his stance. "That's the second theory I've heard already today. The first was that your wife killed her father and then ran off."

"Who said that?"

"Have you checked with the conductor? Has she taken a train?"

"I checked. She hasn't. Who said she killed her father?"

"And the car?"

"I have it. But she could have hitchhiked out of town. That doesn't mean anything. I think she's been murdered. Now who's saying this other nonsense?"

The officer who had been taking Rosenkrantz's statement gave up, and sat back down at his desk.

"Servières. He's going to put it in the *Vérité*. He's right outside."

Rosenkrantz scowled. "I'll…" he started, and then hurried through the front door.

"Good work," Pelleter said, smiling at the officer at the desk.

The yappy dog barked, the sound cutting through the small station.

Letreau appeared at the door to his office. He looked haggard, as though he had not slept the night before, his hair out of place and his clothes wrinkled. "What is going on out here?"

Pelleter went over to Martin, taking his oilcloth notebook from his pocket.

Letreau saw the inspector, and joined him at the front desk, but when the dog barked again, he turned and yelled, "Get that animal out of here!"

The woman holding the dog immediately turned her tirade on Letreau who found himself pulled into the argument.

Pelleter had Martin copy the prisoner numbers from his notebook. It was obvious from the care that Martin took making the notes that he was proud to have been singled out by the inspector for this task. When he finished writing the numbers, he looked up at Pelleter expectantly, like a disciple given precious time with the master.

"I want you to go back to the prison," Pelleter said. "Look up everything there is on these five prisoners. Check Meranger too. See if there's anything unusual in the files."

Letreau rejoined them. "It's been like this all morning. Rosenkrantz left?"

"I sent him after Servières."

Letreau tilted his head in a confused question.

Pelleter patted him on the shoulder. "It's going to be all right. We're on the path now."

This made Letreau only shake his head in disbelief. "I don't know what you're talking about."

Martin was still looking up at Pelleter, waiting for more orders.

Pelleter nodded his head towards the door. "Go on."

Martin clambered to his feet.

Pelleter stopped him. "And tell Fournier I'll be out there

shortly, and that he should have all of his men available to me, even those who are not on duty. I want them all out there."

Martin waited a beat to see if there was going to be anything else, and then he rushed out the door.

"Now, I'm really confused," Letreau said. "You're ordering my men?"

"I hope you don't mind. I've got an idea, and I'm ready to put it to the test. We'll head out to the prison shortly."

"Back to the prison?"

"Come, let's walk by the baker's house first."

Letreau shook his head. "You really are ahead of me. Between this and the children, I haven't been able to get a moment's rest, and you look happier than a kid on Christmas."

"Well, we still have to see. We still have to see. How are the children?"

"Marion…Madame Perreaux…is in a worse state than they are. The boys just have a fever. Nothing a few days in bed won't cure."

"Good," Pelleter said, his expression serious. "Good."

Outside, the weather was the kind of inviting spring weather that fell into the background just because it was so perfect. Verargent continued to look like a picturesque town, a completely different place than the rain-drenched community that Pelleter had found when he first arrived.

Before they had even left the square, Monsieur Benoît appeared.

"Inspector. Chief. Something must be done about this… Everyone wants to hear how I found the body. There is a crowd in my store."

"That's good," Letreau said.

"Yes. Good." The baker hunched his shoulders, and his eyes wandered to the side. "But I know how this is. If you don't find the murderer, then soon my name will be the only one attached to this thing, and people will think of my store and they'll think of a dead body, and then business will be bad, very bad."

Pelleter said, "We are on our way to your house now, for another look at where you found the body. We're taking care of this. It will all get resolved."

Benoît looked at Letreau. "Yes?"

Letreau said, "Enjoy the extra business. Doesn't your wife need your help?"

Benoît looked behind him, back towards his store. "Yes," he said, nodding. "Yes." He paused. "And you will find this murderer. My name…" He didn't wait for an answer, but turned and rushed back towards his store.

Letreau shook his head when he left. "The whole town is crazy."

Pelleter didn't respond, but started north.

"I thought you already examined the baker's street when you searched for the Perreaux children."

"I did."

"Then what do you expect to find?"

Pelleter smiled, lighting a cigar. "Fresh air and pleasant company."

Pelleter walked on. His principal purpose was to give Martin time to get to the prison so that Fournier could round up his men. The assistant warden had made an effort the night before. It was only fair to give him warning this time.

They came to Benoît's house. In the intervening days, the street had returned to what it had always been, simply a quiet residential street. A stranger to the town walking by this spot would never know that only days before a man's body had been found here in the gutter. There was nothing to see.

Pelleter smoked his cigar as he paced the street, observing the ground, and the houses around just in case there was something he had missed. If his plan didn't work, he could always interrogate all of the neighbors to see if they had seen anything that night. But it had to work. He had gone to sleep wondering how Meranger had gotten out of the prison, and he woke up even more convinced that if he could answer that, then he'd have the whole thing.

He continued to pace and smoke until he had smoked his entire cigar. Then he looked up and said, "Okay."

"Did you find anything?" Letreau said.

He nodded as though the trip had been very fruitful. Then he looked at Letreau. "Let's go to the prison."

The now familiar sight of Malniveau rose up before them. The sunny weather might light the walls, but it did little to make the prison appear other than what it was, a dreary place for the confinement of souls.

They waited for the outer guard to open the main gate.

"I don't understand why we're here," Letreau said. "Martin can handle going through paperwork well enough on his own."

"We're not here to go through paperwork," Pelleter said, staring straight ahead as the inner courtyard was revealed through the opening gate. "We're here to have a lineup."

Letreau inched the car forward, and the walls of the prison closed around them. There were more vehicles parked in the small courtyard than there had been on their previous visits, and Letreau had to maneuver the car along one of the walls and onto a small patch of crabgrass.

"You can't really expect to interrogate all of the prisoners," Letreau said, getting out of the car.

"Not the prisoners."

A look of understanding softened the features of Letreau's face. Then he frowned. "Fournier's not going to like that."

"That's why I gave him some time to get used to the idea."

Inside, Fournier was not happy to see them at all. He could not bring himself to look at Pelleter, forgetting himself one moment, and then hurriedly averting his eyes the next, using his ever-present clipboard as a shield.

Pelleter outlined his plan. "I want to interrogate each and every one of the prison workers—the guards, the infirmary staff, the office workers, the cafeteria people, everyone. We'll take them one at a time. The room where I saw Mahossier on Wednesday should be fine. Just line them up outside."

"This is an insult to my people," Fournier said, looking at his clipboard. "And a disruption to the entire prison."

"At least one of your people has something to do with this. It's the only way the dead prisoners could get transported out of the building."

"I still don't understand how there could be dead prisoners I don't know about."

"But there are, so let's get started."

"When the warden…"

Pelleter raised his eyebrows at this, and Fournier didn't finish. The assistant warden waited another moment to show that he wasn't being bullied, and then he set off to make the arrangements.

A guard let Pelleter and Letreau into the interrogation room. An extra chair was brought from another room, and the inspector and the chief of police sat side by side on one side of the table, leaving the chair across from them blank. Pelleter put his note-book and pencil on the table in front of him, opened to a new page, but he didn't reach for it once the interrogations began.

"Please, sit down," Pelleter said, to the guard who had led them in.

The guard looked confused, and he checked behind him to see if somebody else was standing there.

Pelleter indicated the chair, and nodded his head. "Might as well start with you."

The guard rubbed his palms on his pants legs, and then sat down heavily in the chair across the way, slouching in the seat with his legs spread under the table. He looked at a point just to the right of the inspector's head.

Once the inspector began, his questions came quickly, his expression serious.

"What's your name?" Pelleter asked.

"Jean-Claude Demarchelier."

"How long have you worked at Malniveau prison?"

"Since I got out of school."

Pelleter raised his eyebrows.

"Three years."

"Do you like it here?"

The guard shrugged. "It's a job."

"But they don't pay you enough."

The guard shrugged again.

"Perhaps you look to make a little extra money on the side. Help get things for the prisoners. Maybe help hide things that need to be hidden."

The guard looked directly at Pelleter then, shaking his head in wide sweeps, "No. Never. Nothing like that. I just do my job, and go home. That's it."

"But when you're asked to do something you know is against the rules, you help out. Maybe it's an important person asking you. Fournier. The warden. You don't want to lose your job."

"Never," the guard said, and he looked at Letreau for help, to confirm what he was saying, but the chief of police sat impassive, watching. The guard looked to the door. It had been left open. Then he looked back at his interrogators. "I just do my job." His expression was pleading. It looked as though it would not take much to make him cry.

"Okay, you can go."

The guard sat for a moment, unsure if he had heard correctly. Then he sighed, and got up. He started for the door, but Pelleter stopped him.

"Before you go, just write your name down in this notebook."

The guard turned back, and he bent over the table in order to write. His handwriting was large, like a schoolboy in elementary school. He finished hurriedly, and left.

Letreau turned to Pelleter. "Do you really think that you're going to find anything this way? He could have been lying."

"He wasn't lying."

"How do you know?"

"I know."

"This could be a big waste of time. Maybe we should be looking for Madame Rosenkrantz. Benoît is right. It'll only be a matter of time before the town grows nervous with the thing."

"Call in the next person."

Letreau stood up, and went to the door. He came back with another guard. When he sat down, he leaned over to Pelleter and whispered in his ear, "They're lined up all the way down the hall."

That interrogation went much the same way as the first, as

did the next one, and the one after that. Pelleter found a rhythm, and he asked the same questions again and again, even if he adjusted his tone and manner to fit each of the people he was interrogating. Soon the list on his notepad extended to a second column.

Fournier came by once, and he stood in watching some of the interrogations from behind the inspector. But soon after, he left, and Pelleter continued to have prison employee after prison employee brought in. He thought once that he might have found something, and he pushed, but it was only that the man brought in cigarettes for some of the prisoners. One of the cafeteria workers admitted to bringing home some of the food to feed her family and cut back on grocery costs.

None of them responded to the question of whether or not a superior had asked them to do something against the rules. Everyone had a different opinion about the number of prisoners who had been stabbed and how many had actually been killed.

After four hours, Pelleter held up his hand for a break.

"I told you this would get us nowhere."

"On the contrary."

"You think that you've learned something from this?"

"How many more are out there?"

"A lot? At least thirty."

"Then we're not done."

Pelleter lit a cigar, and took several puffs in contemplative silence. He glanced at the notebook on the table with the varied handwriting covering the page. Another list of names. So many names, but none of them were the right one.

The smoke from his cigar floated to the ceiling and formed a cloud with the smoke from his previous cigars. The interrogations were exhausting, but he was convinced that he would find something. One of these people had to know something about removing the bodies. He just had to find which one.

He waved to Letreau to let the next one in. Letreau brought in a young guard, and they each took their respective seats. The guard was no more than twenty-two, and the scruff that he must have considered a beard was still patchy in parts, the space under his lower lip completely bald.

"What's your name?" Pelleter began.

"Jean Empermont."

Pelleter frowned. "You're the guard who marked Meranger as present the morning after he was killed."

The man looked down at his hands, which were in his lap. "Yes," he said, almost so quietly as to not be heard.

II.

Getting Somewhere

Fournier had said that the man had been reprimanded, and Pelleter would not have been surprised to find that Fournier knew all too well how to dress a man down. He softened his tone.

"How long have you worked here?"

The man was slow to answer, and at first it seemed as though he might not. At last, still looking at his hands, he said, "It will be a year next month."

"And before this?"

"Nothing…I tried university, but I was no good at it…I helped my father with his painting business…then this."

All the time the man had not looked up. Here was a man who was familiar with failure. Who, in his short years, had tried his hand at several things, but always seemed plagued by ill-luck. He no doubt felt as though this new failure would soon lead to his termination, an action for which Fournier was no doubt simply awaiting the warden's return, and that he would once again be forced to make a fresh start of things.

Pelleter sat forward, eager but also gentle. "Can you tell me what happened Wednesday morning?"

"Nothing!" the man burst out. Then he looked up to see what effect this ejaculation had had, panicked that he had damaged his case by showing his exasperation. "Nothing," he repeated quietly, his eyes pleading. He took a deep breath. "Each guard is responsible for roll call on his cell block. But it's almost a formality in the mornings because where would the prisoners have gone? I guess they could have died."

He stopped short, realizing what he had said.

Letreau shifted in his seat beside Pelleter, but the inspector stayed still, watching the guard intently.

He started again, holding his hands palm up. "We don't even let them out of their cells at that point. Each guard has a list, and he walks along the block, calling the names, and the prisoners respond. Then you mark them as here. I guess we're supposed to look through the windows, but nobody does. I went along the block. I called Meranger. Somebody said, 'Here,' and I marked him as present."

"They said it from inside the cell?"

"I thought so." He dropped his hands to his sides, and shook his head. "I don't know."

"Who told you to mark him as here?"

"No one."

"Fournier?"

The guard shook his head, confused. "No. No one. Somebody said here. It was just like every day."

"The warden?"

Letreau coughed suddenly, and turned in his seat.

"No." The guard's eyes were wide. "No. He said, here. I marked him here."

"Okay," Pelleter said, and sat back. He put his cigar in his mouth, but found that it was no longer burning. He tapped the gray bud of ash from the end of the cigar onto the floor.

"Okay?"

"Oh. Write your name on the notebook, and let in the next person." Pelleter was relighting his cigar.

The guard reached for the notebook as though he were waiting for some kind of trap. But as he wrote, Pelleter looked off into the distance, as though he had already forgotten that the man was there. The guard left on silent feet.

"Pelleter—" Letreau started, but the next guard had already come in.

He was a large man—over six foot—and older than most of the other men they had seen so far, at least as old as the inspector, with hair graying at the temples. He sat up straight in the chair, pushing out his broad chest over his rounded belly, and met Pelleter's eyes. "I've got nothing to say," he said.

Letreau noticed that Pelleter's manner changed. The inspector's movements, already slow, grew slower, and his eyelids dropped halfway. "How about your name? Will you say that?"

The guard sucked in his lower lip, and resettled his bulk on his chair. "Passemier."

"How long have you worked here?"

"Thirty-two years."

Pelleter raised his eyebrows and nodded. "Impressive."

"I've been here longer than most."

"But not the warden," Pelleter said. "He got his start here as well."

"We started together. We've been here the same amount of time."

"How come you're not warden?"

Passemier shifted, pressing his lips together. He paused before answering, weighing what he had already said versus what he was going to say. "We can't all be the warden. The warden's a good man. A great friend."

Pelleter turned the notebook towards himself. There was apparently something very interesting there all of a sudden that was more pressing than the interview.

Passemier waited him out, not saying anything.

"So you don't know anything about any of this?" Pelleter said, still looking at the notebook, although he wasn't reading a single line there. All of his energy was focused on the guard.

"Any of what?"

"Any of this?" Pelleter pushed back the notebook, and looked at the old guard.

"Meranger?" the man said, squinting. He brought a hand to his chin.

Pelleter made a gesture with his hand, but it was impossible to tell what it meant.

Passemier resumed his self-assured military pose. "Nothing."

"Okay," Pelleter said. He picked up the notebook and turned to a fresh page. "If you could just write your name here..."

"Okay?" The guard looked surprised. He had been prepared to get grilled. He glanced at Letreau and then back at Pelleter. "That's it?"

"You have nothing to say. You don't know anything about this. You're a long-standing guard here. What more can I ask?"

The guard shrugged, and his whole figure loosened up, the weight of his stomach pulling his shoulders forward. He reached for the outstretched notebook and pencil, and held the notebook in hand while he wrote instead of setting it down on the table. When he finished he set it down, sighed, looked at both men again, and then stood by pushing his hands against his thighs.

When he was at the door, Pelleter said, "One last thing...

How many stabbings would you say there have been in the prison this month."

"Seven," Passemier said, his hand on the doorknob.

"Is that a lot?"

Passemier shrugged. "It's happened before. But it's not usual."

"Thank you. No one else was sure."

Passemier nodded, and stepped out into the hall.

"You think he knows something," Letreau said as soon as they were alone.

"I know he knows something," Pelleter said, smoking again. "He knows that there were seven stabbings. No one else guessed more than four."

"So what now?"

"We continue."

But as the remainder of the employees filtered in one by one, Pelleter seemed disinterested, eager to get through them so that he could move on. He allowed Letreau to question some of them. Letreau followed the same method that he had seen Pelleter use all morning, and Pelleter would step in if he thought that something was missing. But no one else excited the same interest.

In the administrative office, Pelleter went directly to Martin, who had indeed been given the desk in the corner that Pelleter had spotted the day before. He had stacks of files spread out before him.

"So?" Pelleter said.

Martin handed him a small stack of six folders without saying anything. The top one was Meranger. At the end of the file it said that Meranger had been transferred to the National Prison at Segré.

He went through the other five folders. They were the men who had been found in the field. They too had each been transferred to the National Prison at Segré.

"Good," Pelleter said, and handed the files to Letreau, so he could see.

"There is no national prison at Segré," Martin said, still seated and looking up at the inspector.

"I know."

"My god," Letreau said.

Pelleter stepped over to one of the nearest desks and picked up the telephone. He waited while he was connected.

Fournier arrived then. "Are you satisfied, now that you've terrorized my staff?"

Pelleter turned his back on the assistant warden, and spoke into the phone.

"Who is he calling?" Fournier said to Letreau, annoyed that the inspector was ignoring him.

"I don't know," Letreau said.

Pelleter hung up then. "Good. How's our stabbing victim from yesterday?"

Fournier seemed put off by this question. He had been expecting something else. "He's fine."

"Good. We'll see you later, I hope."

"Wait one second. What's going on?"

Pelleter turned to Martin. He showed him his notebook. "Pull these two files. Then go through all of the employee records. I want to know anyone else who started at the same time and is still on staff." Pelleter paused for a moment. Then he added, "Or was on staff until recently."

Martin stepped off.

Fournier sputtered. "I demand that you tell me what is going on."

Pelleter smiled, and it seemed to only make Fournier angrier. "Soon," Pelleter said. "When the first train arrives in the morning. We're almost done now."

Pelleter turned to Letreau, and then headed for the front door. Letreau fell in behind him.

Fournier called behind him, "Wait!"

Pelleter said, "We'll let you know."

Then he and Letreau went out to the car, which was just then in a bright ray of sunshine.

12.
Madame Rosenkrantz is Found

It was dusk when they reached the police station in Verargent. As always, the town in evening was a shadow of its daytime self. The square was deserted. The lights in the café, the hotel, and a few other buildings were the only indication that the town was more than a stage set.

"You must join us for dinner tonight," Letreau said, slamming the police car's door. "My wife's appalled that I've let you take dinner by yourself through all this."

Pelleter met Letreau at the front of the car. "I haven't eaten alone yet. If people know where I am, they can reach me."

Letreau shook his head. He looked worn out, the lines in his forehead deeper than usual, his cheeks lax, pulling his eyes down. "Do you really have this thing nearly wrapped up? Because I don't see it."

"Some of it. We'll see what I actually know in the morning."

Letreau studied the inspector's face to see if he could read the solution there. He sighed, and dropped his hand on Pelleter's shoulder. "You're sure about dinner?"

"I want to go for a little walk now," Pelleter said. "But thank your wife."

Letreau shook his head. "You're not making things easy for me." He laughed, but it was strained, his face muscles tight. He dropped his hand, nodded, seemed as though he was going to say something else, nodded again, and then went up the station steps. At the top of the steps, he turned, hand on the door, and called, "First thing in the morning." Then he disappeared into the station.

Pelleter wanted to check on something before he returned to his hotel. He walked away from the square.

The streetlamps had been lit, and the light from the houses cast a pale glow into the night. The evening had a safe coziness to it proper to the town, and it was hard to imagine that Verargent could ever feel unsafe. When he came to the hospital, the extra light from the building seemed harsh and unnecessary.

The hospital was a single-story structure that had been built at what was once the outskirts of town, but was now embedded in the town proper. The building was simple and functional, which made it appear institutional even from the outside.

Pelleter went inside. A nurse sat at a desk just inside the door, reading the new special edition of the *Verargent Vérité*. Its headline simply read, "Murder!", which meant that Rosenkrantz had been very convincing when he spoke to Servières about not mentioning his wife in the paper.

"May I help you?" the nurse said, looking up.

"I'm Inspector Pelleter. I've come to look in the morgue."

"We don't have a morgue. More of an all-purpose storage room in the back. But they've sure filled it up with bodies this week…Take that door there. That's the men's ward…There are double doors straight back, which lead into a hall…The first door in front of you will be the storage room."

The ward had twelve beds along each of the longer walls. There were windows lining the outer wall, but the inner wall was a solid partition separating the men's ward from the women's. It didn't extend to the ceiling.

Only eight of the beds were occupied, two of them by children, both asleep. Pelleter stopped and looked at the boys. They must have been the Perreaux brothers. It was amazing that such little forms could stir up so much trouble. The chief inspector's mind turned involuntarily to the fate he had imagined for these two boys when it seemed as though Mahossier could have them. He looked away. A nurse was distributing dinners from a cart in the center aisle. Pelleter went on.

No one paid attention to the chief inspector as he went through to the doors at the back of the room. The hallway there lined the rear of the building with evenly spaced doors down the length of the hall. One door was open at the center of the hall, and a radio could be heard playing a slow jazz song.

Pelleter opened the door to the makeshift morgue and was met with a hurried, fearful face that stared out over the draped form of a body on a gurney.

"I hope you've had something to eat since I saw you last," Pelleter said to Madame Rosenkrantz.

She hung her head, resuming the position she no doubt had held for the last three days, her knees together, her shoulders hunched forward, her hands held in her lap, the pose of a praying supplicant. In other words, a daughter in mourning.

"Yes. The nurses feed me."

Pelleter found another chair and turned it around just inside the door. He straddled it, resting his elbows on its back. The five coffins had been piled in two stacks to the side, and there was a sour smell of decay in the enclosed room.

"Your husband has been quite distraught over your absence."

"But you knew where I was." She spoke to her hands.

"Yes."

"And you didn't tell him."

Pelleter remained silent.

"When I was a girl, I would tell people that both my parents were dead...It was easier than admitting that my father was in prison...I never saw him and I had nothing to do with him, so it was almost like he was dead, and I would forget that it wasn't true. Every now and then the thought would startle me that my father was still alive. I'd stop whatever I was doing, and think, my father is alive, but it wasn't real. In truth, I believed my own lie."

She spoke mechanically. There was none of the self-assurance, or meekness, or emotion, or any of the conflicting tempers she had shown at dinner three nights before. Her face was white, and her tone was flat.

"I didn't even tell my husband the truth until after we had moved to Verargent, and at that point I had known him for over a year. Verargent was his idea. It was small, quiet, had the train but nothing else to attract people, and so he thought it would be the ideal place to live so that he could write undisturbed. I went along with it, only half-realizing the proximity to my father. It seemed to me, what difference could it make if I was twenty miles or one hundred from him, so I didn't say anything until after we had bought our house. Even then I only explained that my father was in prison, not that he was in Malniveau."

She spoke as though the body before her wasn't the man she was speaking of.

"I told you that I believed my father had murdered my mother, and that's true, and I told you that I didn't hate him, and that's true too...

"When I was little, he taught me how to take apart his watch and put it back together. My mother told him that was for little boys, but he said he didn't care. His daughter could do anything. He set the watch on the table, and took out his tools, and he showed me piece by piece, pulling each little gear and spring out of the bronze case and spreading them out on a cloth. There were all these pieces of metal, and I couldn't understand how they could keep track of all of the seconds in the day. I thought that somehow the time must be contained in them, but when they were apart, everything went on, and when they were together, it wasn't really different. Except, I remember when the last pieces went into the watch, and he would wind it, and the second hand would start turning, it felt as though we had started the world again.

"He was so patient with me those times. And he was not always a patient man. My mother got plenty of smacks and beatings when he felt things weren't being done right..."

Pelleter reached into his inside pocket for a cigar, but he found that there were none there. He had smoked them all during the day.

"Other than that, I don't have any good memories of my father. He wasn't around a lot, and when he was, he frightened me. He could be laughing and he'd have my mother laughing, and then he'd suddenly start hitting her, or he'd storm out. I tried to stay out of his way.

"Do other people feel as though they are a part of their parents? Do they feel that the pieces of each of these grown strangers are really the parts that make them up? Can they say, this part is my mother and this part is my father? And if so, does it matter if their mother or father is still alive? If your parents die, are you the only part still living, or has a part of you died as well?"

She looked up as though she expected Pelleter to answer, and he could see just how young she was.

"I don't know," he said.

She looked at the shrouded form on the table in front of her. "I don't know either. But I don't want to be what's left of my father. He was a bad man. I know that, even if I don't feel it.

"When my mother was killed, they took me away to live with my aunt and cousins. My father was missing at that point… They found him later and then he went to prison, but I had already started telling people that both of my parents were dead…For me it was as though I was an accident created out of nothing. Maybe I was a bad person, and that was why I was all alone."

"I don't think you're a bad person," Pelleter said. "What your parents do is not your fault."

"Then why did I lie all those years?"

"That doesn't make you a bad person. And in a way, it was true."

"No," she said, shaking her head. She reached out as though she were going to touch the sheet, and then drew back, gripping the hand that she had extended in her other hand. "It wasn't true. I can tell you that now. There's absent, and there's dead, and there's a difference. Because when he was just absent, then he was still out there in the world, affecting people, causing things, even if it was only to cause the prison cook to cook one extra meal and for a guard to check his name on a piece of paper. And even if I couldn't imagine his life, and I didn't know who he was really, my idea of him seemed as though it were outside of me.

"But now that he's dead, he's nowhere but in my head. What was he to the people in the prison? Nothing. One more prisoner. He's just gone. But here…" She paused, and her eyes narrowed, the great strain of her thoughts and emotions somehow making her more precious, more delicate. She shook her head. "Now it's only building that watch, and…" She shook her head again as though shaking the thoughts away.

Pelleter could see how hurt she was, and he wanted to step around the gurney and to put a fatherly arm around her, to reassure her. But he knew it wasn't his place. He stayed seated in his chair.

"I haven't pulled back the sheet," she said. "I haven't looked at him directly…But I don't need to."

"Why don't you go home? Your husband's worried about you."

She nodded her head, but without taking her eyes off of her father's corpse. She had not cried once during her whole confession, but she looked wan and emptied.

"He loves you. He thinks you are not just a good person, but the best person. He'd do anything for you."

"I know," she said, almost a whisper.

"I'm just about finished with the case."

She looked at him then, but it didn't look as though she saw him. "It doesn't matter."

"It might not. But for the living, it's all we can ever do."

"It's still nothing. I am nineteen years old and I am finally an orphan for real. Knowing that it's going to happen, and having it happen…Not the same."

Pelleter stood at that. The smell of the dead was going to his head. He felt as though it was surrounding them, and pulling them away from the world outside. He went to her then, and helped her to her feet with a firm hand on her elbow.

As he did, there was the squeak of a rubber soled shoe on the floor in the hallway. Pelleter listened without showing that he was listening, not wanting to alarm Madame Rosenkrantz. Had he been followed again? There was no other sound and he began to guide her towards the door.

Madame Rosenkrantz didn't resist his guidance, and he led her out into the hall, where the door to the men's ward was still easing shut on its hinges, no doubt the footsteps from a moment before. But when they went into the ward, there was no one there other than the same nurse who was now removing the dinner trays from each of the patients' tables.

The nurse looked up at them with a matronly frown.

Pelleter stopped. "Did someone just come through here?"

"All you folks running through, and it's not even visiting hours. I'm going to give that girl at the front desk a talking to."

Pelleter looked ahead, and then he steered Madame Rosenkrantz back the way they had come.

The back hallway was empty still. The radio was off.

"What is it?" Madame Rosenkrantz said, awakening somewhat from her mourning stupor.

"Nothing yet."

Pelleter stood in the center of the hall, holding tight to Madame Rosenkrantz's arm and thinking. He pushed her up against the wall shared with the ward, and he went back to the morgue doorway.

He opened the door, but the room was as they had left it, storing the dead.

He returned to Madame Rosenkrantz and took her arm again, steering her down the hall as though she were luggage. She had to take small hurried steps to match his long strides, but she didn't complain and didn't ask questions.

They passed through a windowless door at the end of the hall, and found themselves in an alley beside the building.

There was a man at the end of the alley, a large silhouette peering around the side of the building watching the front entrance. He turned at the sound of them, startled to find them behind him, and then he ran out into the street, disappearing from view.

Pelleter pushed Madame Rosenkrantz back into the hospital, saying sharply, "Wait here," and he ran down the alley after the man.

The chief inspector reached the street just in time to see his quarry turn down one of the side streets that would lead him back into a series of uneven small passageways where houses had been built with no regard for keeping a thoroughfare.

The chief inspector darted after him. The blood was rushing up his arms and into his chest, constricting his airway. His heart beat dangerously in his head. He had not seen the man's face, but he had seen the man's size. He was a hulk.

The side street the man had taken was little more than an alley itself, and unlit. The crisp spring Verargent night was bright, but little of the light from the sky found its way down to these twisted cobble passages.

Pelleter plunged forward, almost twisting his ankle on one of the cobblestones, running after nothing, since there was nothing visible ahead of him.

He passed other openings, any one of which his man could have taken, and so he slowed his pace, trying to hear the other man's footsteps over his own labored breathing. Running through back alleys was a young man's work. Pelleter was no longer young.

He stopped, but heard nothing but his own body's protest.

An oval ceramic tile screwed into the side of one of the buildings read "Rue Victor Hugo." The provincialism of this almost made him laugh. To have a Rue Victor Hugo had apparently been deemed necessary, but that Verargent had settled on this back alley for the designation was small town politics in its most essential form.

He waited another moment, straining for some sign, and then he turned back.

As he did a large form materialized out of one of the doorways and brought both hands down on the back of the chief inspector's neck, dropping Pelleter to his knees. A sharp jolt of pain shot from his kneecaps into his stomach, which threatened to empty itself.

The man swung again, still a two-fisted blow, this one landing across the chief inspector's cheek, unbalancing the downed man, who fell to the ground.

Dazed, the chief inspector tried to look up at his attacker, but there was not enough light. The man pulled back, preparing to kick Pelleter in the ribs, and the chief inspector instinctively put his arms around his head, pulling his body into a ball.

The blow did not come.

Footsteps echoed and were soon beyond hearing.

The chief inspector rolled onto his back, looking up at the lighter patch of sky between the buildings. He took deep breaths, trying to control his breathing, to steady his heart rate.

He looked at his surroundings to distract himself from the pain. All of the windows were shuttered for the night. No one had seen the attack. The ceramic street marker caught a glint of light from somewhere, winking at Pelleter on the ground. Wink, wink. Wink, wink.

It was not the first time he had been beaten, but it had been a long time, many years, and he had forgotten what kinds of little details got imprinted on the mind in such moments. The winking Rue Victor Hugo! There was one in every town!

When his body had recovered enough to let him feel the throbbing ache stemming from the top of his spine, and the sharp pain radiating from his cheekbone, Pelleter pulled himself up to a standing position, leaning one hand against the wall beside him.

His body had to accommodate the pain to his upright position, sending a shiver over Pelleter's frame. He was thankful that his attacker held off that final kick. The man could have gotten away without any confrontation. But a panicked man too often made bad decisions. Once he struck he must have come to his senses.

Who had Pelleter angered? Or maybe the right question was, who had he scared? The lineup at the prison had clearly worried someone, if he was being followed and attacked. But too many of the guards could be described as large men for Pelleter's shadowy impression of his assailant to be any help at identification. Pelleter had thought he was close, at least to identifying the people who knew most of the answers, but there must be some piece that he was missing.

He took his hand away from the wall, testing his weight on his feet, and rolled his head to one side, wincing with the movement. He started back the way he had come, towards the hospital.

The nurse behind the front desk stood as he came in. Half of the lights in the building had been doused, creating the cavernous feel of a public institution at night.

"I'll get the resident physician," she said, her weight already shifting, ready.

"No," the chief inspector said. "I'm fine."

Madame Rosenkrantz was sitting in one of the chairs along the wall of the main entry hall, her lost blank expression back on her face. She looked up at Pelleter as he came in, but she made no comment about the bruise he could already feel welling up on his face. When he held out his hand, she stood up, and walked past him out the front entrance.

The nurse, still standing, watched them go, shaking her head, but whether in disapproval or disbelief, it could not be said.

Outside, Madame Rosenkrantz did not speak, nor did she ask where they were going. He took her by the arm and led her back to the center of town where a single car was crossing the square, and then out to the Rosenkrantz home.

In front of the gate to her house, she stopped, resisting, and he at last let go of her elbow.

She looked at him, and there was some color in her cheeks from the walk. Her eyes seemed more focused, but the pain was still written across her face. "Will this ever stop?" she said.

"You should be safe now," he said.

She shook her head. That was not what she had meant.

He nodded. "It'll stop." But his neck ached, and he did not know.

"I guess I thought he'd always be there for me if I really needed him."

"Have you needed him?" Pelleter said.

"No."

"Go home to your husband."

She put her hand on the gate, and Pelleter turned away, heading back into town without watching whether or not she really went home. When he was a few steps away, he heard the gate close behind him.

He ate dinner alone at the hotel, and he called his wife before going to bed just to say good night.

✻

In the morning, Pelleter was in high spirits, even with the soreness from the previous night's adventure. When he had come to Verargent, it had been to receive the testimony of an already incarcerated prisoner, no more than a day trip. Five days later, there were six dead bodies—seven, if he was not mistaken—at least one other murder attempt, and a building full of suspects. But today, Sunday, he was certain that he would have the answers to his questions, and that he could go home.

In the hotel lobby, he found Officer Martin sleeping in the lion's-footed armchair Fournier had waited in Friday night. Martin was dressed in the same uniform he had worn yesterday, now thoroughly wrinkled, and a day's growth of beard covered his face. He had a number of files clutched to his chest, his arms crossed over them.

Pelleter called to the boy behind the counter, somebody he had never seen before, "How long has he been here?"

"I come on at seven and he was here then."

It was only a little before eight now. The first train from the city came into Verargent at nine-forty, and Pelleter wanted to be there when Lambert arrived with his prisoner.

He hated to wake Martin if the man had been working most of the night, but there was nothing to be done about it. Besides, Letreau wouldn't want one of his men to be seen with his mouth hanging open in the hotel lobby. He reached out and touched the young man's shoulder.

Martin started, grimaced, and looked around without moving his head, a quizzical expression on his face. "Inspector," he said, stretching in the seat, and then sitting upright, letting his burden of files down into his lap. He rubbed a hand across his face, and then became aware of the fact that he was being observed by a superior officer. His eyes went wide, and he prepared to stand.

"Inspector, I'm sorry, I must have fallen asleep. I wanted to be sure to get you these."

He started to sort through the files on his lap.

"It's okay," Pelleter said, amused at the young man's enthusiasm. It seemed to contribute to the upbeat temper at the end of a case. "Take your time. No need to stand. What time did you get in?"

"Maybe five. What time is it now?"

"Eight."

Martin had the files in order now, and he looked up at the chief inspector. His eyes went wide for a second time at the sight of Pelleter's battered face. "What happened?"

"Apparently somebody thinks we're too close to finished. Once you show me those files, I have a feeling we might know who."

Martin handed three of them up to Pelleter. They were thick files with years of paperwork on uneven paper of various colors, the oldest sheets an almost amber-brown.

Pelleter opened the first one. It was Passemier's, the guard who had had nothing to say. He had been a large man. It was possible that he had been Pelleter's attacker, but he had seemed too certain of his invincibility. "Fournier let you take these out of the prison?"

Martin went slightly red. "Fournier wasn't there, and I thought nobody would mind…"

Pelleter opened the second file, which was the warden's. It showed that his service had begun in 1899, the same as Passemier, on cell block D. While Pelleter looked, Martin talked:

"You were right, as you can see. Those three men all started as guards at Malniveau within a few years of one another."

The third file was for a man named Soldaux. He had started in 1896, also on cell block D. The top of his file had been stamped, "Retired."

"And if you look at their detail…"

"All three worked the same cell block when they started. Does Soldaux still live in town?"

"Yes."

Pelleter smiled and nodded, looking off into the distance. It looked as though he might burst out singing. He would not be surprised at all to find that Soldaux was also a very large man.

Martin was startled to see the inspector so pleased. He stood then, and handed the inspector the file in his hand, coming around so that he could look at it at the same time as Pelleter.

"If you look here…Since the files of the murdered prisoners were marked transferred, I got the idea that we should see what a file looked like if a prisoner was murdered and it was marked properly…"

This was another old file, as full as the others. It was for a prisoner named Renaud Leclerc. He had been sent to Malniveau in 1894 on a conspiracy charge, an anarchist believed responsible for a series of bombings in which several people were injured although no one was killed.

Martin, excited over his discovery, talked faster than Pelleter could read. "Leclerc was killed two months ago, at least a month before any of the men found in the field. He had no family any longer, so he was buried here in Verargent, which is why we didn't know about it. The police are only informed if the body has to go out by train."

"Good work, my boy," Pelleter said, still reading through Leclerc's history. "Good work."

Martin beamed, and his broad smile juxtaposed with his shabby appearance was comic. He had the makings of a fine detective.

Pelleter closed the file, and looked closely into Martin's face. "Listen to me, we're nearly finished. This is what I need you to do…Go to Soldaux's house, and bring him to Town Hall. Stop by the station and get a partner first. He may not want to come with you, and I don't want him getting away…I have a feeling he'll be a big man…yes, I'm certain of it…Then the same with Passemier. Again, two men…I have to meet the nine-forty train with Chief Letreau…Do you think you can handle this?"

"Yes."

"Don't take any unnecessary risks."

Martin waited expectantly for the inspector to say something else, but Pelleter continued to look off into the distance with a smile on his lips.

"Yes…" the inspector said to himself. His smile broadened. He saw that Martin was still standing next to him. "Go. Go. I want everybody there by ten-thirty at the latest."

Martin turned and practically ran out the door. Pelleter wasn't far behind.

The weather fit the inspector's mood, not a trace of the storm from earlier in the week. It looked as though it never rained in Verargent.

"Inspector," somebody called as Pelleter turned towards the police station. Officer Martin was already out of sight. "Inspector!"

It was Servières.

Pelleter didn't stop, but instead called behind him, "Come to the station around ten o'clock. You'll get your story then."

Servières surprised at this jovial command, stopped short, and Pelleter hurried on to the police station.

✿

The Verargent train station was little more than a wide patch of beaten dirt at the side of the track just outside of town. A small wooden enclosure open on two sides had been built at some time to offer protection from the elements, but it had clearly long been a target of vandalism for the Verargent youth. There was a hole through the roof, and every square inch had been carved into more than once.

Pelleter and Letreau stood under the post that read *Verargent* outside of the enclosure. The weather was warm, and Pelleter had removed his jacket and held it draped over his arm. He whistled as he looked down the length of railroad track that cut through the countryside.

Letreau paced, impatient. He appeared less ragged than the day before, but still on edge.

"I hope you know what you're doing," he said, not for the first time. He had already asked Pelleter about his injuries and had not been happy that the chief inspector had not given him much of an answer.

"We'll know soon enough," Pelleter said, and resumed whistling.

"It's all well and good for you, but I have to live here. We don't want any problems with the prison. We want to forget that it's there. I haven't spent so much time out there in one week in my life."

The distant steam of the locomotive could be seen on the horizon.

"I hope you know what you're doing."

Now that the train was visible, Letreau stopped, and stood beside Pelleter. Pelleter put his jacket back on, and put his hands in his pockets. He would have liked to smoke a cigar, but he had not had a chance to replenish his supply.

"You hope to leave tonight?" Letreau said.

"That's the plan."

"It'll really be tied up?"

"You might not have all the answers you want, but I think you'll have the ones you need."

"My wife'll never forgive you for skipping all those dinners."

The tracks began to sing their metallic whine.

The two policemen stood side by side like immovable objects. The train whistle sounded, and the air brakes hissed while the train was still two hundred yards away. The chuff chuff of the wheels slowed, the expanse of metal slowing impossibly, and then the engine stopped just past them, and the escaping hiss of gas marked the train's arrival in Verargent.

A round-hatted conductor appeared on the platform of the first car before them, and called, "Verargent," and then Lambert appeared.

Pelleter smiled at the sight of his old friend and colleague, but he didn't take his hands out of his pockets.

"You are some trouble, aren't you?" Lambert called, as he stepped down.

Behind him, a tight, pale face appeared, an older man carrying two large leather cases in front of him.

"I hope you know what you're doing," Letreau said again, a refrain that had long since lost its meaning.

The older man stepped down as well. The warden of Malniveau Prison was home.

13.
Thirty-two Years

Being escorted home by a national police inspector had made the warden quiet. He looked as though he were in danger of throwing up at any moment.

His wife, however, had no qualms about laying into Inspector Pelleter.

"Who do you think you are that you have us taken on a train against our will, and on our vacation, too! My husband is a very important man. You think you can push him around!"

The warden ignored his wife's outburst, and headed directly for the police car that was parked just off the side of the road near the train stop.

Letreau tried to catch Pelleter's eye, but unable to, he turned to follow the warden.

"The reason we have an assistant warden is just so that this kind of thing does not happen," the warden's wife continued, her cloying perfume sweetening the air. "It's not a one-man job, certainly not anymore, now that my husband's not a young man. You take this up with Fournier. We would have been back tomorrow."

"I'm sorry to have cut your vacation short, madame," Pelleter said, and he smiled at Lambert behind her back.

The warden's wife went to the police car and got in back with her husband.

"Did you have any trouble?" Pelleter asked Lambert.

"We were getting that speech from both of them at first, but when I insisted, he got really quiet. He's been like that since."

"Sorry to bring you out here like this. We'll go back together tonight."

"That's no problem. After a day with those two, I'm curious to see where this is all going."

Pelleter opened the passenger door of the police car. The warden's wife was still complaining. "So am I," he said, and got into the car.

The scene at the Verargent police station was amusing to Pelleter's practiced eye for its studied busyness. Every desk was occupied by an officer diligent about his paperwork, and an additional officer stood near one of the walls with a case file open much as a man reads a newspaper while waiting for the bus. Word must have spread that Inspector Pelleter was bringing in the chief suspects. All eyes darted up at their entrance.

"Monsieur Letreau, you tell me what's going on. No one is talking to me. And I keep telling them, if they would just get in touch with Monsieur Fournier, he will take care of any problem at the prison. These city people treat us like we can be pushed around…"

It was the warden's wife, still voicing her complaints with no regard for who was around her.

"Marie!" the warden snapped, the first he had spoken since arriving on the train. He grabbed his wife by the arm and pulled her to him, whispering fiercely into her ear.

She screwed up her face, tightening the muscles of her arm and pulling away from him, but without any serious attempt to break free.

Philippe Servières was in a corner writing excitedly in his open notebook. He caught Pelleter's eye, nodded, and smiled, holding up the notebook in thanks. Pelleter did not acknowledge the reporter.

"Has Martin returned with his prisoners?" Pelleter asked the man at the front desk.

The officer stammered and looked away as though to hide the fact that he had been paying attention to the new arrivals, "I, um, no, Martin? Martin's out with Arnaud, sir."

"Let me know when he arrives." Pelleter turned to Letreau. "Your office?"

"That's fine."

Pelleter nodded, flicking his eyes to Lambert, and then the warden. *"Monsieur le Directeur."*

Lambert stepped in to separate the warden and his wife, and the warden's wife began to complain again at once, her voice carrying despite her attempt at restraint. "No, this will not do." Lambert tried to take her arm, put she pulled it away, and stood her ground. "This is not acceptable."

Ignoring the woman's protestations, Letreau, Pelleter, and the warden went into Letreau's office where Pelleter offered the warden a chair as Letreau closed the door on the now buzzing squad room.

Pelleter had arranged the files that Officer Martin had borrowed from Malniveau Prison into a pile on the corner of the desk closest to the warden. They formed an uneven sheaf of papers as thick as a phone book.

Pelleter leaned back against the desk, reaching into his pocket for a cigar, but he still had not replenished his supply. He was eager for a smoke.

The warden's eyes darted to the files and then to Pelleter.

Pelleter crossed his arms. "Do you know what these are?" he said, indicating the stack with a nod of his head.

Letreau made a noise as he positioned himself against the closed door, and the warden looked behind him, having to raise himself against the arms of the chair in order to do so. He turned back with an exhalation, and shook his head.

Pelleter smirked despite himself. "Do you have a guess?"

"Should I have my lawyer present?" The warden spoke with the restraint of a powerful man uncertain if his power was a handicap in the situation.

"I think we're all interested in keeping this simple," Pelleter said, glancing over the top of the warden's head at Letreau as though they were all coming to an agreement. "We'll just try to keep to the truth, and be quick about it, and it shouldn't be a problem."

The warden sat with his lips pressed together.

"These files," Pelleter said, tenting his fingers on top of them, "are your records and the records of guards Passemier and Soldaux and of a prisoner named Renaud Leclerc."

The warden's shoulders slumped, his whole body adopting the aspect of a man too tired even to sit.

"Could you tell us about the prisoner Renaud Leclerc?"

"Oh—" The warden's voice broke, and he cleared his throat, coughed, and adjusted himself in the seat with the assistance of the armrests again. "Well, I'd have to look in his file and..."

"I would have thought that you would have been familiar with the case of the last prisoner to be murdered under your watch. Perhaps we should contact Monsieur Fournier as your wife said..."

The warden sighed, and looked back at Letreau who was

impassive. He faced forward, adjusting himself in the chair again. "Leclerc was an anarchist back when the anarchists were dropping bombs everywhere...He was involved in a bombing and was caught, and he was sent here. This must have been in the early '90s. But then some years later he killed a fellow prisoner here, and his sentence was extended. After that, he was a model prisoner until he was killed himself two months ago."

"Why would anyone want to kill Leclerc?"

"I don't know."

"But he was the first of this series of killings?"

The warden didn't answer.

"In your opinion, *Monsieur le Directeur*, did Leclerc kill that other prisoner? Think before you answer!" Pelleter added.

The warden opened his mouth. He looked again at Letreau and then back at the stack of files on the edge of the chief of police's desk.

Pelleter jumped on this. "Are you wondering how much the files say? Are you worried you might tell us more than we know? What could we possibly know other than that Soldaux and Passemier were also guards on Cell Block D in 1899? Leclerc's file must certainly show that he really killed the prisoner he was accused of killing."

"Did you say there had been other stabbings?" the warden said, trying on his authority again to see if he still had it. "What does this have to do with that, such an old business?"

He appealed to the silent Letreau again, for there was no one else to appeal to, and this time the chief of police's face did seem to carry the same question.

Pelleter ignored this, leaning in until his face was only inches from the warden's, "What you should really be asking yourself is, how much have Soldaux and Passemier already told us?"

Pelleter sat back and recrossed his arms.

The warden looked around the room, and then back at Pelleter.

"I should have a lawyer here," the warden said, his eyes pleading.

Pelleter didn't soften. Neither of the lawmen spoke.

The warden brought his right palm to his hairline, kneading his temples, and then slid his hand to the back of his head. He looked away from either of the other two men. "It was thirty-two years ago…" he began. "I had just started at Malniveau. I was young and a bit of a brute. There are only so many ways to get into trouble in Verargent without going too far…I had finished school, and I knew I was too old to keep getting into little fights, but I didn't know what else to do. So I started working in the prison. I liked the idea of being in charge…Passemier started with me at the same time. We hadn't been friends in school, but we ran in the same circles…Soldaux was the senior guard on the duty, although he was only a few years older…He was like a big brother to us."

The warden shrugged and shook his head, smiling ironically at the memory.

"Back then, you could do more to the prisoners and get away with it. Sometimes on night duty, if we were really bored, we'd give one of the prisoners…a hard time."

He checked to see if Pelleter had understood. The chief inspector's expression was easy, but his eyes were locked on the warden, and it made the warden look away again. The hand went again to the back of his head.

"One night we went too far and the prisoner died…I wasn't in the room when it happened, naturally…I don't know which of Soldaux or Passemier struck the fatal blow…"

"Naturally," Pelleter said, straining to keep his voice level.

"We were kids really, and we were just fooling around, but this guy was weak, and he didn't make it…"

"Jesus," Letreau said, behind the warden.

"We panicked. We didn't want to end up as prisoners ourselves. The man had clearly been beaten, so we couldn't claim that he had died of natural causes…So we fell on the man's cellmate, Leclerc…We gave him a light beating, just enough to land him in the infirmary, in order to make it appear as though the two men had fought. When Leclerc came around the next day, he learned that he'd already taken the fall for the murder. We let him know we would look out for him, and make sure that nobody bothered him."

"Which was better for him than him having an 'accident' if he ever claimed a different story."

The warden said nothing.

"Well, somebody got to him in the end."

The warden shrugged and looked down. "In the end. I'm warden now, so I'm rarely on the cell block myself. Soldaux had retired. Passemier was on a different duty. We couldn't protect him always."

"And he couldn't go anywhere."

Letreau cleared his throat. "Inspector, this is revelatory, but what does it have to do with anything?" The chief of police needed *his* murder solved, not just any murder.

Pelleter held up a staying hand to quiet Letreau. He prompted the warden. "So when Leclerc was murdered…"

"It was a shock."

"But at the same time a relief, no? You were off the hook. Finally."

The warden didn't respond, and Letreau shifted, impatient.

The buzz from the squad room had grown enough to penetrate the office door, a quiet roar from the room outside.

Pelleter said, "But then another prisoner was killed…"

"It's one thing for one prisoner to die in a stabbing," the warden said, almost annoyed. "That happens. But a second one…it would have raised questions. Maybe even reopened the first case. I couldn't risk my position as warden."

"Especially when you and Passemier are only three years away from retirement yourselves." Pelleter looked up at Letreau and he saw that the chief of police got it, or at least this part of it. Pelleter didn't want the warden to stop talking now that he was so unrestrained. The chief inspector pushed him again: "They had already sent Fournier to look after you. You hoped that he would just be your successor when you retired, but you couldn't know for sure he wasn't there to replace you…"

"It wasn't just me. Passemier was even more worried—and Soldaux, for his pension. I told them, it's been three decades, there's no way the old incident would come to light now, and yet…Unnecessary questions might just uncover unnecessary answers about Leclerc's past…Soldaux built the coffin, and we used his truck. We're not young men anymore, but we were able to rise to the challenge."

"So when the third prisoner was killed, and the fourth…"

"That's right. We just kept on."

"How many in all?"

"After Leclerc? Five, plus Meranger. Six, then."

"What if the prisoners' families came looking for them?"

"Some had no family, or none who cared to stay in contact. For those that did…We'd record the prisoners as having been transferred…The ensuing investigation would either give us time to get out of the country, or come up with an alternate explanation."

"And the prison is large enough that you were able to keep the number of stabbings, and how many of them had ended in deaths, a secret…"

"People might know some things, but no one would know everything."

"But what about Meranger," burst out Letreau, not happy with how long Pelleter was taking to get there.

Pelleter reached for a cigar again, and then remembered that he didn't have any before his hand even went inside his jacket. "The night Meranger was killed it was raining. It was raining much too heavily to bury a body in a field. So they had to get rid of it another way. Am I right?"

"Yes," the warden said.

"They changed Meranger into civilian clothes and dumped him in town, figuring that it would be assumed he had escaped, and then been killed by his accomplices after the fact."

Letreau shook his head, and said, "The things people do."

"Of course, the same downpour that prevented them from burying Meranger uncovered the hastily buried coffins of the other prisoners."

The warden just shook his head in disbelief. "Thirty-two years…" he said.

The pitch of the noise from the squad room changed, and Letreau stepped away from the door, a puzzled expression on his face.

Pelleter stood. When Letreau looked back, the inspector nodded that the chief of police should open the door.

Everyone was on their feet in the station. Martin, Arnaud,

and Lambert were wrestling a large man in his sixties around the booking desk. His arms were pulled back, his hands cuffed behind his back. In the background, a stunned Rosenkrantz, his arm protectively enveloping his wife, floated near the front door.

The warden stood, and Pelleter put a hand on his upper arm, although he was not concerned that the warden was about to run.

Letreau stepped up to where the struggle was going on as the prisoner kicked one of the desks several inches, and then Lambert tripped the man so that he came down onto the desk face first, dragging Martin and Arnaud with him, who held on.

Pelleter was pleased to see that he had been right. The man was six-four, easily two hundred fifty pounds, and looked like a powerhouse despite his gray hair.

Pelleter led the warden out of Letreau's office, and as soon as the downed man saw the warden, he shouted, "You bastard!" Lambert knew to step forward and relieve Pelleter of the warden. "You ran out on us!" Soldaux shouted at the warden.

"Monsieur Soldaux, thank you for joining us," the chief inspector said. "It's so nice to see you again, and really get a good look at you."

The large man struggled on the desk, wriggling his shoulders. "I've never seen you before in my life, and I wish I never did."

Pelleter brought his hand up to his bruised cheek, reassuring himself with the tender throb that was there under pressure. He looked over the prisoner, thinking. The warden's wife stood, so stunned that she was speechless. Servières was writing it all down.

"Where's Passemier?" Pelleter said suddenly.

"He wasn't home."

Pelleter turned to the warden. "Does he have a car?"

"No."

Letreau stepped forward, reasserting his command. "Put these men in the holding cell. Everyone else must have something to do. So start doing it."

The stunned atmosphere began to retake its normal shape. Letreau trailed his prisoners further into Town Hall.

Lambert joined Pelleter, who had not moved since asking about Passemier.

"We need to find the other guard. He attacked me last night."

"I'd wondered what happened to your face. I figured you'd fallen while shaving."

Pelleter gave that as much of a smile as it deserved. There was yelling from the back corridor now, and the warden's wife was arguing with two of the other officers, asking where her husband had been taken.

"Inspector." It was Rosenkrantz.

Pelleter raised an index finger to hold him off and continued talking to Lambert. "See if you can get Letreau. Tell him we need to start a stakeout. The train station, all of the major roads out of town. If Passemier's still here, we don't want him to get away."

Lambert began to go, but stopped when the chief inspector spoke again.

"And we'll need a warrant. I want to search the man's house."

"Inspector, I wanted to thank…"

Pelleter let his raised hand drop. Rosenkrantz had stepped up to the booking desk. He held Clotilde so close that she had to stand at an angle to walk. Her hand lay flat on her husband's chest.

"Inspector…you were as good as your word, and I want you to know I'm grateful. For everything you did."

The words seemed to carry an extra weight, as though he meant to thank Pelleter for more than just his wife's return. Had he told Clotilde of his binge the other night? Probably not.

"No need to thank me," Pelleter said. "Anyway, it's not over yet."

14.
Roadblock

In Verargent, searching for missing children could be done on anyone's authority. Arranging the complicated machinations involved in tracking down a fugitive—the necessary roadblocks, the search warrant for his home, informing the railroad—required the approval of the town magistrate.

The portion of Town Hall used for the administrative operations of the town distinguished itself from the police station with high ceilings. The light fixtures hung on long cords overhead, casting self-important shadows.

Pelleter paced in the hall outside the magistrate's office. Letreau was inside. Pelleter imagined he was taking great care to show that all actions had been taken under his authority, embarrassed now at how flustered he had been in the preceding few days. In the meantime, he had had the sense to set up the roadblocks first and to get the paperwork done afterwards.

Pelleter cast an impatient glance at the closed office door with each pass. The bruise on his face seemed alive with worry, three pinpricks of red in the center of the wound. He had sent Lambert to the train station in anticipation of the midday train to the city. Servières had gone with Lambert, certain that the story was with him.

Pelleter stopped in front of the magistrate's door, willing it to open. Letreau's officers were in the process of cutting off the main routes of escape, but something worried him. It was not that they might be too late. If Passemier had been planning to run the night before, then following and attacking Pelleter would have been counter to his plans. It was the attack itself that bothered him. People made rash decisions when they felt cornered. Passemier was violent and a murderer and he had already shown what something as simple as an informal interrogation would drive him to. If they cut off his escape routes, what would be his next move?

Pelleter touched the bruise on his cheek and rolled his shoulders, satisfying himself that the pain was unchanged. Madame Pelleter would have scolded him for playing with his wounds.

The door to the magistrate's office opened and Letreau emerged holding up a sheaf of papers. "Let's go," he said.

Pelleter caught a glimpse through the door behind the chief of police, but it opened only onto an outer office where a secretary sat at a desk. The town magistrate was hidden away in some interior office, doubly protected from the town he administered.

The two men headed towards the connecting hall that led back to the police station.

"Where are we going?" Pelleter said.

The chief inspector was not surprised when Letreau answered, "Rue Victor Hugo."

In daylight, the Rue Victor Hugo showed itself to be little more than an alley, similar to the one where Rosenkrantz had gotten drunk in the basement pub. At some time after the alley had formed between the surrounding buildings, an attempt had been made for drainage by lining the center of the cobblestone path with a concave well of brick. The project had been ill conceived, however, since puddles lined the edges of the alley even five days after the rain. Pelleter saw that he had been lucky not to break an ankle on his chase the night before.

The concierge for Passemier's building lived two buildings away on the corner of Rue Victor Hugo and another alley that had not been deemed worthy of a name. She was a worn, middle-aged woman doing the washing outside her door in a large tin tub with a washboard.

"Have you been up there yet?" she asked, not stopping her washing.

"An officer was there earlier, and no one answered," Letreau explained. "You see we have the warrant. We just need you to let us in."

She was unconvinced. "I don't know anything about a warrant. I've been concierge of this building, that one, and that other one," she pointed with her chin, "for seven years now, and I've never seen anything about a warrant. Monsieur Passemier works out at the prison as a guard."

Letreau blew out his cheeks, and then opened his mouth to speak, but Pelleter stepped forward. "Madame, I appreciate your caution. If all concierges were as cautious as you, then perhaps the police wouldn't have as much work as we do."

The woman narrowed her eyes, unsure if he was truly complimenting her or mocking her.

Pelleter wondered how close this spot was to where he had been beaten the night before. The concierge might have been one of the many nonexistent witnesses. "We don't think that Monsieur Passemier is home or that there is any trouble in your building. But we need to ask Monsieur Passemier a few questions, and we were hoping that something in his apartment would tell us where he had gone."

The concierge regarded Pelleter for another moment, pausing

in her scrubbing and blowing a stray strand of hair out of her eyes. She looked at Letreau. "That paper means I don't have a choice, does it?"

Pelleter tried a kind smile and nodded an apology.

She began scrubbing again and nodded with her head towards the open door behind her. "All the keys are on the ring just inside the door. It's got the number on it."

Letreau went forward to find the keys, and Pelleter said, "Thank you."

They waited awkwardly a moment while the woman continued washing, before Letreau came back with a key ring.

The two lawmen went partway down the alley, further from the main street that led to the hospital. The concierge watched them.

When they got to the door, which was a few steps below street level, they found it partially ajar.

"Guess we didn't need the key after all," Pelleter said.

"Damn it," Letreau said. He looked at Pelleter. "What do we do?"

Martin had not said that the door had been opened, so either Passemier had been home when the officer had knocked and had since left, had come and gone in the meantime and forgotten to close the door, or the prison guard was home now and didn't expect to be there long.

Pelleter pulled out his revolver, and, taking a deep breath, Letreau did the same. Then Pelleter pushed his way in.

"Hello!" Letreau called.

The apartment had the mustiness of a below-ground room. Pelleter wondered if it flooded when it rained, like the baker's basement.

"I guess you don't make much as a prison guard," Letreau said, looking around.

"Or he didn't have much reason to spend money on anything," Pelleter said.

The flat was furnished with the barest of necessities, a few chairs, a table, a single shelf with assorted books. Everything was neat, because there was nothing to make it cluttered.

A hall opened off to the right at the back of the room, and there was an opening to the left. Pelleter nodded to the left at Letreau. Letreau turned for the opening, and Pelleter went towards the right.

The hall led to two small rooms, one that opened immediately to the right off of the hall and the other that opened straight ahead. The room to the right was a storage area. The man had accumulated some things over his lifetime, but whatever they were he had boxed away and stacked in this small space. Pelleter opened one of the boxes nearest to him and found that it was filled with newspapers. Another one had dime novels.

The room straight ahead was the bedroom. It was as spare as the others, but a chest of drawers had been emptied, the drawers left open. The bed cover had been thrown back from the bottom as though Passemier had retrieved something from below the bed. That would have been his suitcase. The night before he had planned to fight, but something had changed, and he was now clearly on the run. Had Soldaux been able to tip him off? Maybe it had just been his intuition.

Pelleter went back out into the living room and found Letreau holding a gray cat with a white speck off-center above its nose. "Look who I found enjoying a saucer of milk in the kitchen."

Pelleter stepped over to the kitchen and glanced in. It was only large enough for a stove and an icebox. A layer of grime coated everything. A single skillet hung from a nail on the wall, and the saucer of milk was on the floor. It was still mostly full. Passemier must have left only moments before. That was why the door was open. If he wasn't coming back, then the cat needed a way to get out.

"The warden said that Passemier didn't have a car," Pelleter said, back in the living room. "How would he have gotten to work?"

"Many of the guards share a ride."

"So we need to get a list of which guards have cars, and start checking them. He's definitely running for it." They had to keep moving. He took out his notebook, wrote something there, and tore off the sheet. Then he went for the door. "Come on."

Once outside, he put the note between the door and the jamb, closing the door and locking it. In the distance, the faint sound of the midday train's whistle sounded. The two men shared a look, but said nothing.

They stopped back at the concierge's where the woman was still at her washing. There were a few more articles of clothing on a line overhead, but otherwise no time might have passed.

"Here are the keys and a friend," Letreau said, taking both into her apartment.

"What are you doing with that? I can't have a cat in there!"

"Did you see Passemier in the past half-hour?" Pelleter asked.

"No. I thought you said he wasn't home."

"Let the police know if he comes back. He'll know you have his cat, we left a note."

"Is he dangerous?" the concierge said, for the first time showing real concern now that she had been given a responsibility.

The two men turned without answering.

"What am I supposed to do with the cat if he doesn't come back?"

Letreau had given his men orders to report in every hour. When he and Pelleter returned to the police station they found that nothing had changed. Lambert had also reported. The midday train had passed without incident. Letreau went to find out from the warden which of the guards had cars, and who Passemier was most likely to trust.

Pelleter sat in one of the waiting room chairs, pulling on his lips, and occasionally putting his fingertips to the bruise on his cheek. All eyes in the police station were on him, but he ignored the attention. He was bothered by a sense that they were on the wrong track, that Passemier, while brutal, was not stupid, and that he would know not to trust any of the other prison guards. After all, while the lines were perhaps hard to see at times, in the end, the prison guards were on the side of the law, not crime.

The chief inspector bowed his head. He thought of the saucer of milk laid out for the cat. Passemier was not a sentimental man—the meager furnishings in his apartment indicated that—but he was a responsible man. Perhaps that was why he had stayed to the last minute, out of an obligation to see the whole thing through.

And that saucer of milk had still been full. The man was still close. They could not afford to search a list of people. They needed to know where he was going, and be certain of it.

Pelleter rolled his shoulders, the bruise on the top of his spine turning white hot for a moment, and he winced. The Verargent gendarmes continued to watch. He imagined them thinking, This is a real policeman. Injured in the line of duty and still going on. But what was the alternative?

Pelleter looked back towards the hall leading to the holding cell. Where was Letreau?

Pelleter reviewed the precautions they had taken, roadblocks and the train station. The Perreaux boys had been found in the middle of a field. Why wouldn't Passemier just walk around the roadblocks that way and try to catch a ride further on down the road?

Letreau arrived with the list. "There are only ten of them, and two are at the prison now. I just called."

"Good," Pelleter said. "Put some men on it. Then get the word out. We need to organize a search, like you did for the children, and we need to do it now."

Letreau puffed out his cheeks, "Right."

"He was still in town within the hour."

Letreau looked disconsolately at the list of names in his hand. Then he turned and shouted, "Arnaud!" and headed back to his men.

Phone calls were made. Pairs of police officers left the station. Soon there were men filing in from outside. These would be the search party. Having seen the search party from the other night, Pelleter noted that this was a different sort altogether, only young men, some who were still almost boys, all with mean faces. Several of them carried rifles. At least one of them had a pistol in a shoulder holster. They laughed and smoked, filling the public space of the station. There was none of the worried urgency of the other night. This was the excited antici-pation before a football match between rivals.

Pelleter thought of the warden's description of his youth as a Verargent troublemaker.

Reports came back negative. They were losing time.

Letreau interrogated the warden and Soldaux again to see if there were any places that Passemier visited regularly, but the man led a simple life of work and then home, work and then home…and of course disposing of murdered corpses.

At last Letreau appeared with a large map of Verargent and spread it out over the front desk. "Quiet now," he yelled over the noise of the crowd.

Pelleter worked his way beside the chief of police.

"Quiet, please."

The remainder of the police force that was not currently on a roadblock or checking on other prison guards stood in silence behind their chief.

"Gentlemen!"

"Right, now!" Pelleter said, at a stern but normal level.

The men closest to him fell silent, elbowing those behind them. There was a last stray laugh, somebody said, "And she will," and then, "Shut up, blockhead," and there was quiet. The smoke from their cigarettes clouded above them.

Letreau cleared his throat.

"Thank you all for coming." The chief of police glanced at Pelleter for support, but the chief inspector remained impassive. "Right. We are looking for a man by the name of Passemier. He is six foot one, two hundred twenty-five pounds, fifty-one years of age, with dark hair graying at the temples. You are to assume he is armed and dangerous. We know that he was in the Rue Victor Hugo within the last two hours and that he is most likely trying to leave town."

Letreau held up the map and pointed.

"This is Passemier's home. We're going to conduct a house-by-house, block-by-block search from there to the edge of town, and we'll search through the night if we have to. If he's still in town, that will force him to show himself at some point."

"What, we can just go in people's houses?" one of the men said near the front.

"There will be officers with you. You have to explain the situation. If somebody refuses, get an officer, and he'll take care of it."

There was an uneasy pause. The men shifted on their feet.

"Any other questions?"

No one spoke.

Letreau turned to his officers. "Men, divide up the search party, and get started. I want constant updates here."

The noise started then, as the door opened, letting in a breeze and a shaft of bright light over the heads of the search party. The crowd filed through the door.

Letreau turned to Pelleter. "Do you think we'll get him?"

"Maybe not today. But we'll get him eventually."

Letreau rolled the map in front of him with both hands. "That's what I think," he said, the hint of a pleased smile on his face. "But the warden…and the other one…" He nodded to himself. "Surely you won't refuse dinner tonight!"

The crowd at the door had shrunk to just police, and then the last of those were out the door.

"Madame Pelleter will expect me back," the chief inspector said, but even as he said it, he was thinking that there was something that he was missing about Passemier's whereabouts that was important. He wanted to at least see the search through. He wouldn't feel settled if he didn't.

"And what of Madame Letreau?" Letreau said, clapping the chief inspector on the shoulder.

The Verargent chief of police was clearly feeling pleased. He had had perhaps the worst week of his career with six murdered persons showing up and two lost children. But he had suspects in custody for the bodies—even if they were not the murderers, they were responsible—and the children had been found unharmed.

"Let's see how this afternoon goes," Pelleter said.

"Right," Letreau said. "I'll tell her you're coming." And he walked back towards his office.

The police station appeared emptier for the disarray in which it had been left. The desks were scattered with papers, files left opened, fountain pens across their pages. Chairs were pushed back, and a file cabinet drawer had not been shut. The cloud of smoke from the search party's cigarettes drifted, a diffuse haze over the empty scene.

A lone officer had been left to man the phones. He was busy taking notes, the receiver of a phone cradled between his shoulder and his ear.

Here it was again. The waiting. That was perhaps all that was left with this one. It was best to be moving.

Pelleter turned to go outside. He badly needed a cigar. There was a tobacco shop in a little out-of-the-way street just off of the square. He left the station.

The weather was almost too perfect, but the chief inspector did not notice that as he crossed the square. He pictured Passemier sitting across from him in the interrogation room in the prison, first bluster, then confusion, then arrogance. Was he going through those stages again now? He had followed Pelleter two nights in a row. He had attacked him the second night. Now he was on the run. Was he confused or was he arrogant?

The chief inspector nodded to the old men around the war memorial, touching the brim of his hat. He shook his head as though he had been asked a question, and then passed on.

The warm comforting smell of tobacco enveloped him in the tobacconist's shop. Distracted, he bought three cheap cigars, just enough to get him through the rest of the day.

"Beautiful day," the tobacconist said.

"Oh? Yes." The chief inspector snipped the end of one of the cigars. "If a large man with a suitcase comes in, you let the police know."

The tobacconist's brow crumpled into a question, leaving the smile alone on his mouth.

The chief inspector turned to leave the store without answering the unspoken question.

Outside, Pelleter scanned the square almost without thinking, the old habit of a longtime policeman. But nothing registered out of the ordinary. He lit his cigar, and his muscles relaxed with the first inhalation of smoke. He rolled his neck, feeling the now reassuring pain in his shoulders. He wondered if Fournier had heard yet of the warden's arrest. What about Mahossier, who seemed to know everything?

The chief inspector's nostrils flared, and he bit down on his cigar. Yes, perhaps it wasn't quite finished. Maybe Letreau was near satisfied, but what had Mahossier said, that Pelleter was to find who had taken the bodies out of the prison and the madman would supply the names of who had made them bodies in the first place?

Pelleter shook away the thought of having anything more to do with the man. He headed back across the square, forced to nod to the old men at the war monument again as though he had not just seen them minutes before.

✻

Over the course of the afternoon, Pelleter regretted having bought cheap cigars. He regretted having bought only three cigars.

The reports came in from the search party, from the roadblocks, from Lambert at the train station.

Nothing.

15.
Dinner with Friends

"Come then, shall we?" Chief Letreau called across the station, emerging from his office, already arranging his overcoat on his shoulders.

Pelleter looked up without seeing his friend. His gaze shifted to the floor; he shook his head and pulled himself to his feet.

The long uneventful afternoon had unsettled the chief inspector, eradicating any sense of progress from the morning. Pelleter now felt certain that Passemier was within his grasp if only he could remember the correct detail, but he had been through his notebook no less than ten times without stumbling upon the answer.

Letreau gave orders to be followed in his absence. "The warden's wife will be bringing Soldaux and the warden dinner. She can stay with them while they eat. But then she must go. Don't let her give you any trouble."

Letreau clapped his hands on Pelleter's shoulders and kneaded them like a coach with a prizefighter. Pelleter shrugged away, wincing from the pain of his injury.

But the chief of police didn't see, already at the door, turning to check whether Pelleter was following him.

Pelleter said to the desk officer, "When my man calls, tell him to hold his position. I'll be there soon."

Outside the sun had already fallen out of sight but the sky had not yet started to darken. There was an easiness about Letreau as he guided them towards his home. It was the relaxed confidence of a man of authority in control of his domain, something that had been missing in the chief of police since their initial trip to the baker's days before. For Pelleter, on his walk home after work, he always felt the crush of responsibility, the city and its inhabitants too large to fathom, his job to keep out the barbarians by building a gate out of toothpicks. But here, the normal order of business was petty theft and vandalism, and Letreau currently had most of the regular perpetrators conducting a search for a suspect on his behalf.

A girl—or was she a young woman—collided with Letreau in the doorway of his house.

"Whoa there," Letreau said, wrapping his arms around her. "Where do you think you're going?"

The girl ducked her head, crossed her wrists over her chest, and leaned shoulder-first into Letreau, allowing herself to be embraced. "I've just come to borrow some salt, Uncle."

Letreau waddled in place, rotating them in the doorway so that his back was to the open house and the girl was on the street side. He looked at Pelleter over the girl's head, his eyes gleaming, and asked her, "You don't want to stay for dinner? We've got an important guest from the city."

The girl realized that she was being watched by a stranger, and she pulled herself away, straightening her frock with one hand, a teacup held in the other. She slid her hair behind first one ear and then the other with an unconscious turn of her fingers. "We've already started cooking at home," the young woman said, for Pelleter saw that she was a young woman. "But thank you, Uncle."

Letreau pressed his smile between closed lips, and nodded once. "Yes, of course."

The young woman smiled at Pelleter, then her uncle, and darted off, grabbing at her skirt with her free hand.

"My wife's sister's daughter," Letreau said, stepping into his house.

Pelleter watched the young woman hurry along the street for a moment. She went to a house several doors down and pushed her way inside. The sight of her made him think of Clotilde Rosenkrantz, and then in turn of Passemier. Why was he so preoccupied? Why couldn't he feel some of the closure that Letreau clearly felt? If the man was to be found, he would be found.

The chief inspector followed Letreau into the house. The smell of cooking filled the space, chicken and rosemary.

Letreau had gone back to the kitchen, and Pelleter followed.

"Oh, good you're home," his wife said, lifting a roasting pan out of a coal stove with two leather potholders. "Everything is ready. You can sit down."

A gnarled old woman with no teeth blinked and smiled at Pelleter, tasting her lips.

"My mother-in-law," Letreau said by way of an introduction. "She's deaf."

"Would you get her seated?" Madame Letreau said. "She insists on helping, but she's always just in the way. Alice was just here."

"I saw her on the way out."

The name came back to him, and Pelleter realized that he had met the girl on one of his previous visits, only she had been a child then, and Letreau had doted on her. Nothing else had appeared to change.

"Inspector Pelleter, you've decided to have a real meal finally."

"Madame Letreau. Through no fault of your husband, I assure you."

The table was a small round butcher block in an ill-lit corner of the kitchen. There were four wicker chairs, the wicker in two of them broken through in places—Madame Letreau made sure to arrange them so that she and her husband took those chairs. There was just space for the four of them to have the roast chicken, boiled beets and potatoes that reminded Pelleter once again of how many days this business had kept him from home.

"So you've arrested the warden and one of the guards," Madame Letreau said, still on her feet, making sure her mother was settled with her precut meal.

Letreau looked put out that his wife had already heard his news, but he regathered himself, chewing heartily a purplish mass of beets and potatoes. "Yes. It seems thanks to Inspector Pelleter that things aren't a complete mess."

Madame Letreau's mother stared across the table at the chief inspector with a blank smile.

"That's certainly good news," Madame Letreau said without looking up, and then, "Eat!", gesturing to her mother, who frowned, shifted back and forth on her seat, and shrugged her shoulders. "Eat!" Madame Letreau took her own seat, and in a moment, the old woman leaned forward to take her fork in her hand.

"We still have no idea who murdered all of those men," Inspector Pelleter said, troubled by Letreau's good spirits.

"Unimportant," Letreau said, sticking a hunk of chicken in his mouth. "The only crime committed as far as I'm concerned was improper disposal of human remains, and we have people in custody for that and will soon have the last man as well. And with a cold murder solved as a bonus. If Fournier or whoever's in charge out at the prison now feels they have murders to solve, those are on their hands."

Pelleter saw how it was going to be. He heard Madame Rosenkrantz saying it didn't matter if they ever found out who had killed her father. That it wouldn't change anything.

"Didn't Mahossier tell you that he knew who had killed the prisoners?" Madame Letreau said.

"It's never clear what Mahossier has told you," Pelleter said, curt.

"I must not understand," Madame Letreau said.

The four of them fell to eating. Much of the old woman's meal fell back on her plate. Letreau's good mood had been tempered, and Pelleter's troubled mood had grown.

"You're going to return home tonight?" Madame Letreau said after the silence became awkward.

"Or tomorrow."

"Oh?" Letreau said, setting his hand down on the table and looking at Pelleter in surprise.

Pelleter didn't elaborate, but took another bite of the chicken. The food was excellent and he told Madame Letreau.

"Who is he?" Madame Letreau's mother leaned over and asked her daughter in a loud voice.

"A policeman from the city," Madame Letreau shouted.

Letreau smiled, but it was clear he was uncomfortable and embarrassed by his mother-in-law. "So you may stay until tomorrow. I'm glad to have you. I can't thank you enough for this."

Pelleter drank his wine. "There's something I'm missing."

"I always feel like that," Letreau said.

Pelleter tried to hide a scowl with another bite of food.

They were quiet again. The old woman was still fixed on the chief inspector, who suddenly remembered the bruise on his face. His hand went up to it self-consciously.

The old woman nodded, and her smile deepened, her lips falling further into her mouth.

"Do you think we'll find this man?" Letreau asked, as he had before at the station, but it was only to say something, to fill the silence.

"He'll be found. It's only a question of when."

"I don't really believe he's in town anymore," Letreau said.

"Is he dangerous?" Madame Letreau said.

"Well…" Letreau started, and then looked at Pelleter, seeing his face.

"Yes," the chief inspector said. He was ready to go, but dinner was not yet over. They were each only halfway through their meal, each on their first glass of wine. But this was beginning to feel like a poor use of time. Letreau thought Passemier was gone. He was probably right, but somehow Pelleter was not entirely convinced.

There were noises out on the street, distant shouts, and the sound of a dog barking.

The two policemen shifted in their seats, and the silence at the table changed in tone, from awkwardness to expectancy. The old woman was unaware of the sounds coming from the street, and she sat with the same complacent smile.

Letreau pushed back from the table as the shouting grew louder. "Damn it," he said, throwing his napkin onto the table.

The old woman looked up at him, still smiling. Madame

Letreau continued to eat as though nothing was happening.

Pelleter knew that he was not leaving that night.

The sound grew louder. Letreau had opened the front door. His voice joined the shouting.

Pelleter stood up, and left the kitchen without saying anything to either of the women.

There was a young police officer standing outside the front door talking with Letreau. Behind him were several of the rough-looking youths who had answered the call for the search party earlier that afternoon.

A dog was barking, but wasn't visible. The dusk was heavy.

"I'm sorry, sir," the young officer said.

"No, it's absolutely right."

"It's really not necessary."

"No, no, I insist," Letreau said, stepping back. He saw Pelleter there. "They're searching this block now, house by house, and they want to search mine as per my orders to skip nobody. It's only right."

The officer stood in the doorway looking at the two senior officers, unsure of how to proceed.

"Come on," Letreau said.

The officer stepped in, and two of the young men with rifles hurried in from the street behind him. They fanned out in what had clearly become a practiced maneuver over the course of the day, one man heading directly for the stairs, another heading for the kitchen and the back of the house, while the police officer stood at the front door.

The officer wiped his hands along his pants legs. "I'm really sorry, sir."

"No, it's quite right." But now that the men were in his house, his jaw was set, his teeth clenched, his shoulders tensed. "I haven't been upstairs myself yet. What better place to hide than here."

There was laughing in the street. Banging on a door. The dog was still barking. Someone yelled, "Shut up."

The sound of the man upstairs could be heard through the ceiling. Doors banged.

"Sorry, *mesdames*," the man in the kitchen could be heard to say.

Letrcau was stick-straight.

Pelleter felt the invasion too. Their awkward dinner had been their space, and now these strangers had come in and taken it away from them. He saw the house as a police officer now, not as a guest. The living room was small with three men standing in it. The arms of the chairs and loveseat were worn thin, showing the wood beneath the fabric. The framed photographs on the walls were askew, both in relation to each other and to the floor. A water stain browned and bulged the paint in one corner.

The man came from the back of the house. There was still banging upstairs.

"You've had no luck?" Letreau said, although this was apparent.

"No, sir."

"Okay, then."

The man came down from upstairs, taking the stairs so fast as to be almost falling down them.

"Nice place you got, Chief," the man said, cigarette bobbing between his lips.

Letreau said nothing as the man passed by him and outside. Something was said, and there was a fresh burst of laughter as though the group were out drinking instead of searching for a fugitive.

The officer, embarrassed at the lack of control he had over

his men, many of whom were his age or older, tried to smile and said, "Good night, sir," and then turned and left.

The group moved off down the block in the direction of Alice's house. Letreau stood by the open door, his body still rigid, probably also thinking that his niece would soon be visited by the same invasion, but he held his ground, no doubt reminding himself of equity, and how he would rather this intrusion than the fugitive on the run.

Letreau closed the door, and when he spoke his voice was pinched. "They're certainly being thorough," he said. He started for the kitchen, stopped at the bottom of the steps as though he were considering going upstairs to check for any damage or missing belongings, but instead he continued on to the kitchen where his wife and mother-in-law were still eating the dinner they had prepared.

At the table, Letreau sat upright, staring straight ahead, attacking his food. His breathing was shallow. Any jocularity from before was gone. The two women did not react. When Madame Letreau was finished eating, she stood with her plate and her mother's and began to clean up. Pelleter wondered how typical a dinner this was for the household, as he chewed his food on the side of his face opposite the bruise.

It was a chill April night that made any hope for spring seem rash and ill founded. The cold was made more oppressive by the memory of the beautiful day.

Pelleter found Lambert beside the railroad tracks with his arms crossed, his hands shoved into his armpits, the collar of his overcoat bunched up around the bottom of his hairline. Another officer, whom Pelleter recognized as Arnaud, stood unfazed by the weather beside the city policeman.

The chief inspector knew that his friend was exaggerating his discomfort for effect.

"You misplaced your bag, I see," Lambert said.

"I'm not going home tonight."

"Why does that not surprise me?"

"I've got to go out to the prison one more time to see Mahossier. Mahossier…" Pelleter trailed off and looked at Arnaud, who was gazing down the tracks, vague white lines of reflected moonlight. He was either not paying attention to the chief inspector's conversation or trying to show that he wasn't. "The official investigation is over here. They're going to finish their search for Passemier, put his name and description out on the wire, and ignore the murders. The warden was right about one thing. Nobody cares about a bunch of prisoners getting killed."

"So why do you have to see Mahossier?"

"Something he said…And he started this whole thing." Pelleter looked down the track for the train. "I hate that man."

Lambert let out a long breath. "God, it's cold."

"It's not too bad," Arnaud said.

"Are you going to be all right out here for the night?" Pelleter said.

"A night standing out in the country in the cold was exactly what I was hoping for," Lambert said.

"How have you been working it?"

"When the train's coming, Arnaud goes to the other side of the track, we watch the length of the train, walk along it, and then watch it until the train pulls out. Not that we're going to be able to see anything in the dark."

"I'll help."

"You don't expect there's anything to be seen?"

"No."

"He's already gone?"

Pelleter took a moment before he answered. "No, I don't think he's gone yet."

Lambert knew the chief inspector well enough to remain silent after that comment, to allow his boss to think. The three men stood in the cold, not as though they were waiting for something, but as though standing itself was their purpose, and that they could stand forever.

At last the rails bean to sing, the high-pitched hum of the approaching train, and the pinprick star beyond where the tracks were visible appeared. Arnaud moved up the slight rise to the tracks, crossed over the metal rails, and then fell away up to mid-thigh on the other side.

The train sounded its whistle.

The light grew brighter, and more of the engine began to take form in the moonlight, the black plume of smoke rising from the smokestack blotting out the night sky above. The train wheels could be heard themselves now, clacking.

Pelleter pointed, and Lambert went ahead without any other command, jogging down the track so that he would be where the train would stop, near the freight cars.

Pelleter looked around at the darkness surrounding the nearest brush and buildings, but nothing moved.

The train slowed, the clack of the wheels changing rhythm to a labored chug.

Pelleter realized that he had awaited the train with the warden on it only that morning, and he had to consciously remind himself that he had not yet been in Verargent a week.

The train came to a stop.

Pelleter stepped right up alongside the engine, the sooty smoke making the air hot. Lambert jogged the length of the train towards him, and Pelleter watched behind his officer to see if anything moved in the shadows.

Several men got off of the train, talking loudly to one another.

Lambert was shaking his head before he even reached Pelleter.

Pelleter saw nothing either. He looked at the men arriving, and recognized two of them as reporters from the city. So they had finally decided that the incidents at Verargent were something they should get some first-hand information on. He was surprised it had taken them this long, but perhaps the arrest of the warden of a national prison was the first real news. He was glad that they were not yet on the job, that they were idly joking with one another rather than looking around, and so he avoided having to refuse any interviews right now. It would not be as easy tomorrow.

"Nothing, Chief," Lambert said. "This guy's gone. You sure we need to stick around until tomorrow?"

Pelleter nodded.

Arnaud appeared from around the other side of the train.

"Anything?" Pelleter said.

"Nothing, sir."

The train conductor was looking out the window down at the policemen. Pelleter waved him on. His head disappeared, and the train started up its slow steady chuffing, shuddering once, and then pulling slowly away from the station.

"We're done here for the night," Pelleter said. "Go get some rest, and be sure to be back for the morning train."

The three men turned in the direction of town. The reporters were already gone.

The policemen walked in silence. The sound of the retreating train ushered them to their respective beds, a quiet shush after awhile and then gone.

Pelleter promised himself he'd be on that train tomorrow.

The chief inspector lay in bed for a moment after waking but before getting up. This was uncharacteristic of him, who usually was half-dressed before he realized that he was awake. He had had quite a lot of difficulty falling asleep the night before, waiting for the phone to ring with news of the search, certain that it wouldn't, and still plagued with the idea that there was something he was missing, that Passemier was in town and he should know exactly where. Now the sun bled through the curtains, lighting the too familiar room, and the prospect of another trip to Malniveau Prison made Pelleter feel old.

He ran through it in his head again. Friday night Passemier followed him to the Rosenkrantz house but left off once Pelleter spotted him. Saturday the chief inspector had his lineup at the prison where Passemier tried to act tough and impressive. That same night Passemier followed the detective and attacked him when he thought he was cornered. Sunday Passemier packed his suitcase and went on the run.

The facts told him nothing.

Downstairs, the Verargent Hotel's lobby had become a journalists' salon. The four men from the train last night had been joined by three others who must have come by car, and right in the center of the group talking louder than all the others was Philippe Servières.

"Inspector Pelleter!" It was one of the city boys. "You feel like answering some questions?"

The group had fallen silent and turned expectantly to the chief inspector, retrieving notebooks and pencils from coat pockets.

"It sure took you all long enough to get down here," the chief inspector said, without breaking his stride.

"What do you expect with this Richard-Lenoir business?"

Pelleter stopped, and turned to the man who had spoken. "What are you talking about?

"You haven't heard?"

"You really have been out in the middle of nowhere," one of the reporters from the train said.

"Countess Richard-Lenoir murdered her three children, the count, and then shot herself on their yacht down in Nice. You can't hardly expect a few rotting corpses to compete with that."

"I was keeping all the papers informed of the situation here," Servières said.

Some of the reporters seemed to smirk at that.

"Now with the warden in it…"

Pelleter looked at the group of them with disgust, and then turned to go.

"Inspector Pelleter…"

"What does Mahossier have to do with this?"

"Did the warden commit the murders?"

Pelleter turned around, and the group of reporters that had surged towards the door after him tripped over each other as they came to a stop. "If you want a story, go out and find the missing prison guard," Pelleter said, and with that he left the hotel.

The weather was clear, but with some of the night's chill still in the air. Verargent Square was busy with Monday morning activity, the doors to the shops open to the good weather, women out with their shopping baskets on their arms. A few of the men from the search party were smoking near the war monument, their rifles leaning against the base of the statue. Their eyes stared straight ahead. Gone was the joking and laughing of the day before.

Pelleter cut through the traffic to the tobacconist's, knowing he would not make it through the day without a supply of cigars.

The tobacconist said nothing about the previous night's search. He sold Pelleter his cigars in silence—still machine-rolled, but a better brand—and Pelleter lit one before leaving the shop.

In the square by the monument the small group of ragged men with guns had grown. Some of the other pedestrians glanced at them as they went by. Had Letreau called for a resumption of the search this morning?

Pelleter returned to the thought that the Perreaux children had been lost in a field. If they hadn't found Passemier yet and didn't know where he was going to be, there were too many places for him to hide. They wouldn't find him.

Pelleter smoked and watched the square, not yet ready to join the day.

He saw Rosenkrantz in the little café, standing at the counter with a coffee cup in his hand. The chief inspector was surprised that the American would be away from his wife after spending so many days concerned for her safety. He thought again how hard it was to know people as he watched the American gesture with his cup, the broad open movement of a satisfied man.

Letreau was crossing from the police station to where the small group of men was still growing.

Several more men walked towards the group, although it appeared as though it was out of curiosity rather than any interest in joining in the search. Pelleter recognized the nervous form of Benoît, the baker, who still wore his white apron, his hair grayed by flour. He must be coming to hear if there was any news.

The chief inspector's nose flared. Passemier had followed him and he had let him get away! Such overconfidence!

He shook his head, blowing out smoke, and watched Letreau give new orders.

But why had the man followed him, Pelleter asked himself yet again. To what end? Not only would there have been no reason for Passemier to follow him, in fact it would only have been a risk.

Pelleter's head snapped back to Rosenkrantz. There was a man standing in the café doorway now, one of the reporters, and the few people inside were turned to listen to him, soon ready to give any information he would want to hear.

Pelleter began to walk.

When the chief inspector had arrived at the Rosenkrantz home the night Rosenkrantz was drunk, he had come by taxi. If Passemier had been on foot, how could he have followed him?

Pelleter began to hurry.

He had assumed at the time that he'd been followed. But the prison guard must have already been waiting at the Rosenkrantz home.

The reporter was inside the café now, standing at the counter beside Rosenkrantz.

And at the hospital—

Madame Rosenkrantz had been with him when he spotted Passemier following, before the guard fled and then attacked.

Rosenkrantz was yelling at the reporter now, his gesticulations clear even from a distance and through the window.

If Passemier had been at the Rosenkrantz home one night and then at the hospital where Madame Rosenkrantz had been for the past several days the next…

Pelleter was running now, past the café, in the direction of the American writer's house.

The warden and his two cohorts had gambled that the dead prisoners' families wouldn't make inquiries. But when Passemier found out that Meranger's daughter lived right here in town, he must have wanted to make sure that no questions would be asked. Which meant Clotilde...

Someone in the square noticed him, and there were shouts behind him, but the chief inspector didn't look back.

No, Pelleter told himself, even as he ran. He had to be wrong. But it made too much sense. He had thought that for the last few days the prison guard had been following him. But what if the fugitive had been after Clotilde, and the chief inspector had just happened to be there?

Pelleter's cigar had gone out, clenched as it was, forgotten, in his hand.

No, he had not just been overconfident. He had been blind. Now he hoped he wasn't too late. Because now Clotilde was home. And she had a car, which Passemier badly needed, and she was on the edge of town.

And as her husband was here at the café, arguing with the reporter—

She was all alone.

16.
Clotilde-ma-Fleur

Clotilde-ma-Fleur was troubled by the sun. It had come up that morning already bright and clean. It was the kind of spring day in which everything existed in equal calm, the sun intense but not hot, the air cool but still. The house was suffused with light.

It was hard in the face of such perfection to not feel uplifted. Her husband had fallen to his knees before her when she came into the house two nights ago. He wrapped his arms around her waist and pressed his face against her stomach. It was only by a single intake of breath that she knew he was crying. He had then stood, picking her up in the same movement and carried her up the stairs to their bedroom. She had been afraid that he would hurt himself.

The next morning, he grinned at her in the sunlit dining room throughout breakfast, and doted on her all through the day. The attention made it difficult for her to look at him. This morning, after enduring a full day of such attentions, she sent him out under the pretext that she needed to do a proper housecleaning after her negligence of the past few days, but in fact she wanted a chance to check herself.

She did clean. The kitchen first, washing the dishes from breakfast, and then the counter, the sink, the floor, working up a fine sweat and a warm feeling in her chest. Her mind was clear with the task, but then it would come—my father is dead—and she would stop. Her sorrow was a wave of exhaustion. In the pauses between the peaks, she could raise herself before being knocked down again.

She was upstairs in their room now, changing the linens on the bed, humming in her task, no particular tune, just a wispy tone as she exhaled. She tightened the corner of the sheet at the head of the bed, pulling the excess material up in a right triangle before tucking it under the mattress and running her hand across the sheet to flatten it.

There was a noise downstairs, perhaps the door. She thought of calling to say that she was upstairs, but she was not quite ready to give up her solitude. She felt guilty about her inner calm, and felt unsure about herself if it were to break.

She walked around the bed, to tighten the sheet on the other side.

There was a loud crash downstairs as of a drawer being roughly closed and something tottering from a height. She stopped and stood up, looking at the stairs.

"Shem!" she called.

There was no reply.

She went to the window cut into the slanted ceiling, and looked out at the street. Their car was in the driveway—Shem hadn't taken it—but no one else was there, no car parked at the curb.

She thought she heard another drawer being closed.

She went to the top of the stairs, reaching her hand out for the banister. She took a tentative step down. "Shem!"

There was a movement, someone walking. Why didn't he answer?

She went down. When her head fell below the height of the upper floor, she stopped, her free hand going to her chest.

There was a strange suitcase standing just inside the door, which was ajar.

She tried to remember if she had left the door open, listening so carefully that she could hear her own breathing. She hadn't. And that suitcase. The light from the door cast a severe shadow from the suitcase on the floor. She stepped down again.

"Shem, where are you!"

It was nothing, she told herself, an unexpected friend, even as she remembered that policeman's face from two nights before. She started to hurry down the stairs, watching her feet so she didn't trip.

"Lover!"

She stepped onto the first floor, and turned herself around the banister to head back towards her husband's study. There were quick steps behind her then, and she began to turn, "You scared—"

Strong arms went around her shoulders, and a blade flashed in her peripheral vision. Her throat closed and her head went light.

"Hello, Madame Rosenkrantz." The breath of the voice was hot on her ear. "Now, where do you keep the keys to your car?"

The car was still in the drive. That was the first thing Pelleter noticed. He wished he could have Lambert with him, or even Martin, but he was afraid there wasn't time.

He stopped just short of the property, at the edge of the fence, breathing hard but still in control. The front door was open, but he couldn't see anything inside. There were no sounds either. The natural thing would be to go right up to the front door as though he were just there for a visit and to see how it played out. But he didn't like the idea of giving the man any advantage if he was here, and now Pelleter was certain he was. How had he thought that Passemier would go for the circuitous route, bypassing the roadblocks by going through the fields? He should have known that a man like Passemier—a man who would attack a police officer—would opt for a hostage and try to force his way through. Now the most important thing was to get Madame Rosenkrantz out unhurt.

The chief inspector sped along the side of the fence, retrieving his revolver and holding it ahead of him. He couldn't make anything out in the windows as he passed. He let himself through the back gate.

There was no one in the backyard.

The search party had seen the chief inspector running, so there should be men on the way. The trick was to assess the situation if possible, and to prevent Passemier from getting away if necessary.

He hurried to the back door, standing off to the side with his back to the wall of the house. There was a small semi-circular window made of three panes in the upper portion of the back door. The chief inspector allowed himself a quick look.

The hall was shadowed, all of the light coming from the open door at the other end. All the chief inspector could be certain of was that it was empty.

Pelleter reached across the door and tried the handle. It was unlocked. The hinges were mercifully silent.

He entered the house with his gun ahead of him. It took a moment for his eyes to adjust to the lower light. It was bright in the house, but not quite as bright as outside.

There was a suitcase at the end of the hall near the open door. Passemier's, surely. Where would the Rosenkrantzes be going? Monsieur Rosenkrantz had seemed in no hurry back in the square. The chief inspector listened for sounds, but the only sounds were the normal noises of an old country home talking to itself as it aged.

The door to the study on his right was closed. He reached down across his body with his left hand, still holding the revolver pointed towards the front door, and turned the door-knob. The study was as he had seen it two days before, messy and empty.

He left the door open, turned, and brought his head close to the kitchen door, listening.

There was nothing.

He pushed his way into the kitchen. It smelled of strong soap, which stung his nostrils and made his eyes water. This room was empty as well.

He stopped beside the center counter.

Had there been steps upstairs?

He looked up. The creak of a board.

He crossed the kitchen in two silent steps, but before he could push open the swinging door that led into the dining room, he heard the erratic drumming of feet stumbling down the steps. There was a soft cry and a man's voice.

Pelleter brought up his gun and gripped it with both hands.

Somebody yelled, "Clotilde!"

The front door slammed.

Pelleter rushed into the dining room, his gun extended, and hurried past the table towards the front door, but stopped before he got there. The scene was framed in the dining room window as though it were a photograph.

Passemier had his back to the house with Clotilde part of the way in front of him, the suitcase now in his free hand, and the other one wrapped around her neck. Rosenkrantz was there, saying something and inching forward, almost at the front door of the automobile. From the slowness of the action, Pelleter knew that Passemier must have some kind of weapon in his hand.

Passemier began to move away from the house and toward the car, shoving Clotilde before him.

If the chief inspector came through the front door, Passemier would hear him at once, and then they would just be in a standoff, and either Clotilde was more likely to get hurt or they would be forced to let Passemier get away.

Pelleter ducked back into the kitchen and ran out the back door. His only chance was to come up behind Passemier unseen. He hurried around the other side of the house, which led down the drive, bringing the others into view. As he did, the car horn sounded. Once. Twice. Three times. Good man, Rosenkrantz.

Pelleter moved deliberately now, not wanting his footsteps to give him away even with the car horn blaring.

Passemier was yelling, "You cut that out. Cut that out right now or I'll kill her!"

Pelleter was close enough that he could see the strain in the muscles in the back of Passemier's neck. He could also see the knife clasped in Passemier's closed fist.

Rosenkrantz stopped pressing the horn, holding up his hands, saying, "Okay," in that American accent of his.

"I'll kill her," Passemier said again.

Pelleter kicked at the back of Passemier's knee while grabbing at his knife hand, causing the man to lose his balance, and allowing Clotilde to duck away.

Passemier immediately began to pull his knife hand, and the chief inspector felt himself dragged forward, but instead of resisting, he allowed himself to be pulled, raising his knee so that it landed in Passemier's stomach, doubling the man over and causing him to loosen his grip on the knife.

The chief inspector chopped at the prison guard's wrist with the butt of his gun, and the knife clattered to the ground, but Passemier, still doubled over, swung both hands over his head, throwing Pelleter's balance off just enough that the chief inspector had to fall back on the hood of the car with one elbow to keep from tumbling to the ground.

Passemier was around the edge of the car in an instant.

Inspector Pelleter came up with his gun raised, but the Rosenkrantzes were between him and the fugitive. Rosenkrantz pulled Clotilde out of the way. Pelleter ran around them.

Passemier had turned left, away from town. By the time Pelleter reached the street, the prison guard had realized his mistake, zigzagging down the center of the street as the buildings grew further apart from one another, providing no place to hide.

Pelleter called, "Stop!"

The big man was staggering, still winded from the blow to his stomach, his bulk awkward in the first place. He didn't look back. He must have seen the roadblock one hundred yards ahead, where the last of the town's outlying buildings gave way to pure farmland. Pelleter didn't want him to cut into the fields. The inspector raised his revolver, and shot into the air.

Passemier looked back at the noise, tripping, but regaining his balance before going down.

The men at the roadblock had heard the shot and recognized

it for what it was, and they had begun to run towards them.

Passemier saw that he was about to be surrounded, and he chose to turn around and charge Pelleter.

Pelleter paused, and took aim with his revolver. But the men from the roadblock were too close now. He couldn't risk hitting one of Letreau's men. He reholstered his gun, and bent his knees as the large man came.

The young men from the roadblock were almost on him now, too. They had begun to yell, "Stop! Police! Stop!"

Passemier dropped a shoulder.

Pelleter watched the other man's eyes, but they were pinioned straight ahead.

"Stop! Police!"

Passemier was on him. Pelleter tried to step aside and trip the guard, but Passemier anticipated the move, traveling with Pelleter, barreling full-tilt into the chief inspector's chest, knocking the wind out of Pelleter, whose vision went white. He barely managed to keep his feet.

Passemier pushed past the chief inspector, and on towards town.

The younger officers were there now, passing Pelleter.

Pelleter pulled out his revolver again, still gasping for breath. The air felt cold and dry along the back of his throat. "Move!"

He shot in the air.

The young men looked back, and Pelleter had already taken aim. One of the officers called to his companions, dropping to the ground.

Pelleter shot.

Passemier stumbled. Then began to run again. But now it was more of a loping hop.

One of the younger officers jumped to his feet, and was on Passemier in no time. He yelled at Passemier, but Passemier just turned and swiped at him.

Pelleter was there. He saw that his shot had been good. There was blood on Passemier's pantleg at his left calf. Pelleter kicked for the spot, and Passemier went down.

Pelleter was on top of the large man, a knee in the prison guard's back, and his revolver to Passemier's head.

"Your friends are waiting for you," Pelleter said.

He used his free hand to retrieve his handcuffs, roughly pulling Passemier's hands back, first left, then right.

Passemier had too often been on the other side of the equation to struggle at that point. He knew it would go badly for him, and so he let his body go limp.

Pelleter looked up. The young police officer had been Martin. "Good job."

Martin tried to keep a straight face, but he couldn't hold back his smile. "Thank you, sir."

Further along the street, in front of their house, the Rosenkrantzes were holding each other, Monsieur Rosenkrantz watching Pelleter, Passemier, and the police over Clotilde's head. His expression was of a man defeated instead of triumphant. Verargent was supposed to be their safe haven. It had not been that.

Letreau was beaming. "Well, we wrapped this whole thing up thanks to you! You really saved me."

Pelleter laughed. "You'll just have to return the favor next time you visit me."

Lambert rolled his eyes at Pelleter, and the chief inspector gave his man a stern expression.

The chief of police opened the top drawer of his desk and came out with three cigars. He handed them across the desk to the two other men. Pelleter's heart leapt at the sight of it. He had a headache he needed to smoke so badly.

"Now if someone found out who killed all of those prisoners…" Letreau said, but he was still smiling. "But that, my friends is a prison problem. Illegally disposing of remains—that one we solved. And an old murder on top of that."

Pelleter filled his lungs with the tobacco smoke. The cigar was not quite as good as the ones he was used to, the flavor a bit ashy, but it felt good anyway.

Letreau blew a series of broken smoke rings and then adjusted himself in his chair, looking down at his desk. "I really can't thank you enough."

Pelleter nodded.

"This whole business…" Letreau shook his head.

"I still should go out to the prison one last time, although I hate to do it," Pelleter said.

Letreau waved it away. "It's Fournier's problem. His problem."

Pelleter frowned, and tried to convince himself that was true. Really, how had any of this been his problem? "Don't be surprised if Fournier manages to solve at least some of those stabbings."

There was a knock at the open office door. All three men looked up.

An officer said, "Warden Fournier is on the phone, sir."

"Warden!" Letreau said. "He does move fast."

"Assistant Warden, sir, I'm sorry."

Letreau grabbed up the phone from his desk. "You heard our good news?" Letreau's brow furled. "What! When?"

Lambert looked at Pelleter who just shrugged, enjoying his cigar.

"We'll be out." Letreau hung up the phone. "There's been another stabbing. It's Mahossier."

17.
Mahossier in the Infirmary

The infirmary had emptied now. It had been a flurry of activity for the last hour as the doctor and nurse saw to their new patient's wounds, and various law officials were in and out, overwhelmed by the continued excitement of the day. Pelleter had asked Fournier for his chance to speak with the prisoner before he left, and Fournier had agreed, standing guard with Lambert outside of the infirmary door.

The man who had been stabbed four days before was still in a bed across the room. His color had returned, and he was sitting up in the bed without a problem. He would be returned to his cell later that day. He would have been returned already if it had not been for this new stabbing.

Pelleter sat beside Mahossier's bed.

"How's Madame Pelleter?" Mahossier said.

His voice was weak, but Pelleter knew from the doctor that Mahossier's wounds were superficial. His weakness was a calculated act, like so much with Mahossier.

Pelleter ignored the familiar question.

"I hear that our warden is no longer our warden."

"Are you happy about that?"

Mahossier shrugged. "We can't plan what life gives us. We have to take it as it comes."

Pelleter narrowed his eyes, trying to discover the best way to approach his topic. With Mahossier, it was never an easy matter of discovering the truth unless Mahossier decided to give it to you. "Fournier will no doubt be warden now."

"A pity." Mahossier seemed uninterested in that.

"That one's going to live," Pelleter said, indicating the man across the room.

"Oh, he's going to die, inspector. We're all going to die. We're dying right now, as we speak."

Pelleter's face grew dark. He had uncovered too much already. He didn't have the energy or the patience to philosophize with a multiple murderer. "You killed those men."

"What men?" Mahossier said, his eyebrows raised in surprise.

"Those prisoners."

Mahossier's face changed to a sly smile. "Not my type."

"Or you had them killed. You wanted to get at Fournier, and you figured that a lot of dead bodies soon after he showed up was going to make things difficult for him. You didn't expect that the murders would be covered up by other people for other reasons, and so when nothing happened, you had me brought in to stir things up."

"You do like telling stories," Mahossier said. "I hear you've been telling them a lot the last few days."

Pelleter didn't rise to the bait, or ask how Mahossier always was so well informed. He went on.

"You're the one who called 'here' when Meranger was already dead. Your cell was next to his. You just wanted to throw further confusion into the mix."

Mahossier winced, as though suddenly struck with pain, but the gleam in his eyes made it clear that it was just an act.

"You've missed your mark. You've deposed the warden, and put the man you hated in charge."

Mahossier shrugged. "It is what it is."

Pelleter reached out, ready to push on the cuts across Mahossier's stomach. The prisoner didn't move, and Pelleter stopped short of actually hurting the man. "You cut yourself up to put suspicion somewhere else. But what happens when the killings stop now? Fournier won't let up, even if I'm gone."

"Who said the killings were going to stop?"

"Oh, I think they will. You've done enough."

"Perhaps."

Pelleter's eyes narrowed. Was that an admission? No, he could merely have meant that the killings would perhaps stop. Pelleter spoke through closed teeth. "Why?"

Mahossier smiled. "Why not?"

"Seven people!"

Pelleter could feel his face grow red with anger, and he forced himself to take a deep breath. It was wrong to let the man get to him. He was behind bars for life already. What more could be done to him?

Instead of responding to Pelleter's outrage, Mahossier said, "How *is* Madame Pelleter? It really is a shame you've never had any children."

Pelleter stood up at that. "Don't expect me to come next time you call for me." The inspector crossed the room for the door. Just as he reached it, Mahossier said behind him:

"We could all be dead by then, Inspector."

There was joy in the murderer's voice.

Pelleter went out into the hall, and walked past Lambert and Fournier without a word, heading for the front of the building. Seven people killed. And why? Because why not? And who actually held the knives might never be known.

Fournier overtook the chief inspector, and unlocked the doors in front of them as they walked, relocking them behind as they went.

Pelleter wondered if the American writer would use any of these events in his next book. It all seemed so unbelievable.

He reached for a cigar. They were at the front entrance to the prison.

"Thank you," Fournier called from behind him.

Pelleter didn't even wait to answer. He wanted to be out of Malniveau, free, away from locked doors.

The
FALLING
Star

A HARD CASE CRIME NOVEL

in memoriam R.C. *with apologies*

ONE

Merton Stein Productions was twelve square blocks enclosed by a ten-foot brick wall with pointed granite capstones every three yards. There was a lineup of cars at the main gate that backed out into the westbound passing lane of Cabarello Boulevard. Every five minutes or so the line advanced one car length. If you had urgent business you were no doubt instructed to take one of the other entrances. Since I had been directed to this one, I figured my business wasn't urgent.

It was just about noon on a clear day in the middle of July that wasn't too hot if you didn't mind the roof of your mouth feeling like an emery board. I smoked a cigarette and considered taking down the ragtop on my Packard to let in the mid-day sun. It was a question of whether it would be hotter with it closed or with it open. When it was my turn at the guard stand, I still hadn't decided.

A skinny young man in a blue security uniform stepped up to my open window without taking his eyes off of the clipboard in his hands. His face had the narrow lean look of a boy who hadn't yet grown into his manhood. His authority came from playing dress-up, but the costume wasn't fooling anyone, including himself. "Name," he said.

"Dennis Foster," I said. "You need to see proof?"

He looked at me for the first time. "You're not on the list."

"I'm here to see Al Knox."

He looked behind him, then out to the street, and finally set-tled back on his clipboard. "You're not on the list," he said again.

Before he could decide what to make of me, a voice said, "Get out of there." The kid was pushed aside and suddenly Al Knox was leaning on my door, wearing the same blue uniform, only many sizes larger. There was a metal star pinned to his chest and a patch below it that stated his name and the title Chief of Security. He stuck his hand in my face and I took it as he said, "Dennis. How the hell are you?"

"Covering the rent. How's the private security business?"

"Better than the public one. Give me a second, I'll ride in with you." He backed out of the window, told the skinny kid, "Open the gate, Jerry, this charmer's with me," and then crossed in front of my car in the awkward lope his weight forced on him. He opened the passenger door, grunted as he settled him-self, and pulled the door shut. The sour smell of perspiration filled the car. He nodded his head and pointed at the wind-shield. "Just drive up Main Street here."

Jerry lifted the gate arm and I drove forward onto a two-way drive lined with two-story pink buildings that had open walk-ways on the second floors. There was a lot of activity on either side of the street, people in suits and people in painters' smocks and people in cavalry uniforms and women in tight, shiny skirts with lipstick that matched their eyes. Three men in coveralls with perfectly sculpted hair worked bucket-brigade-style un-loading costumes from a truck. Workers walked in both directions across a circular drive to the commissary. Knox directed me to the third intersection, which had a street sign that said Madison Avenue. Messrs. Young and Rubicam wouldn't have recognized the place. We turned left, drove one block over, past a building the size of an airplane hangar, and made another left onto a boulevard with palm trees in planters down the middle of the street. Here there was a four-story building large enough to be a regional high school. It had an oval drive and two flagpoles out front, one flying Old Glory and the other flying a banner with the Merton Stein crest on it. We drove past the oval and pulled into a spot at the corner of the building beside a row of black-and-white golf carts.

In front of us was a door with wired glass in the top half that had the word "Security" painted on it in fancy black-and-gold letters. I suppose the men who lettered all those title cards in the old days needed something to keep them busy now. To make doubly sure we knew where we were, a sign on a metal arm above the door read "Security Office." Knox started around the car to lead the way when a woman's voice said something that wasn't strictly ladylike. We looked, and three cars over a blonde head bobbed into sight and then vanished again.

Knox pulled up his pants at the waistband as though they might finally decide to go over his belly, and went around to where we had seen the woman's head. I followed. Bent over, arms outstretched, the blonde made a perfect question mark, an effect accentuated by the black sundress she wore, which covered her from a spot just above her breasts to one just above her knees in a single fluid curve. She had on black high-heeled shoes with rhinestone decorative buckles, simple diamond stud earrings and a necklace with five diamonds set in gold across her white chest. In light of the earrings and the necklace, I allowed that the decorative buckles on the shoes might be real diamonds too. What she was bending over was the back seat of a new '41 Cadillac sedan. A pair of legs in wrinkled trousers was hanging out of the car, the man's heels touching the asphalt. She said the surprising word again, followed by, "Tommy."

Knox said, "Do you need any help, Miss Merton?"

She straightened up. There was no sign of embarrassment on the sharp face that came into view, just annoyance and frustration. She brushed her hair back out of her face with one hand, and it stayed exactly where she wanted it, in an alluring sheet that just touched her shoulders. "Oh, Al. Can you help me get Tommy into the car again? He's passed out and he's too heavy for me."

Knox started forward and Miss Merton stepped back out of his way. She looked at me, and a smile formed on her face that suggested we shared a private secret. "Hello," she said. I didn't say anything. Her smile deepened. I didn't like that.

Knox wrestled Tommy's legs into the back seat, a process that involved some heavy breathing and maybe a few choice words under his breath too. At last he had the feet stowed in the well behind the driver's seat, and he slammed the door with satisfaction. "There you go, Miss Merton."

She turned to him, and said in a hard voice, "Tommy can't expect that I'll always go around cleaning up after him."

"No, ma'am," Knox said.

Miss Merton looked at me, gifted me with another smile, and then pulled open the door and poured herself into the driver's seat. Knox faced me, shaking his head but not saying anything as the Cadillac's engine caught and started. Only once the car was out of view did he say, under his breath, "Vera Merton. Daniel Merton's daughter. She's always around here getting into some trouble or other. The son doesn't usually even make it this far. He must have found himself caught out last night." He rolled his eyes and shook his head again. "The bosses, yeah?"

"The bosses," I said.

He gave a hearty laugh and slapped me on the back. "I'm telling you. This place is filled with crazies. Come on into my office, I'll fill you in."

TWO

The front room of the security office was a small, air-conditioned, wood-paneled room with a metal office desk on which there were two telephones, a green-shaded lamp, a desk clock, a pen-and-ink set, a calendar blotter, and a message pad. There was a wooden rolling chair behind it, and three orange armchairs along the wall in front of it that had probably served time on one of the movie sets before their upholstery wore thin and they were reassigned here. A middle-aged dark-haired man with a well-managed mustache looked up as we came in and then away as he saw it was Knox, who continued on through a door behind the desk marked "Private." This led to a narrow hallway off of which there were three more rooms. The first was an empty squad room with four desks, two couches, and a blackboard across one whole wall. The second was a kitchenette with a large table in the center and no less than three automatic coffee machines. Knox went into the third room, which was much like the first, only it had Knox's photographs on the wall. There were pictures taken with various movie stars, and pictures taken when he and I had been police, with Knox looking trim in his city uniform, and pictures taken when he was with the DA's office, looking less trim, but much thinner than he was now. "Close the door," he said, sitting down behind the desk.

I did and took the chair across from him.

"Sorry about the kid at the gate. We have a high turnover and it's either old retired cops like me or kids the academy turned away. The old guys can't take the heat in the box, so it goes to the kids. More than half of this job is managing my own staff."

I said I hadn't been bothered.

He nodded and puffed out his upper lip by forcing air into it. Then he moved his lips as though tasting something, and said, "This is a crap job I have for you, I just want to say that up front. It's a crap job, but the money's good and easy and I need someone I can trust."

"I'll just take my regular fee."

He shook his head. "No. I put in for fifty a day. And expenses, of course. This is the picture business, you take as much money as they'll give you."

"Let's leave that," I said. "What's the job?"

He puffed his lips again and rocked in his seat while rubbing one hand back and forth on his blotter as though checking for splinters. He didn't want to tell. Telling me would make it real. At last he slapped his desk and said, "Oh, hell, you've already seen the kind of thing I have to deal with. These movie people live in a different world than guys like you and me."

"That's not what *Life* magazine says. Haven't you seen? Bogie built his own porch and Garbo sews all her clothes." Knox snorted at that. "Well, they love and hate and die like anyone else, don't they?"

"Sure, but they do it to the sound of violins, with their faces ten feet tall." He slapped his desk again. "If you have any sense of propriety left after being on the force, they sure knock it right out of you here. What do you know about Chloë Rose?"

"I've seen her pictures," I said.

"Well she manages that tortured beauty act from her pictures all the time in real life, too. And now we think maybe she's going crazy."

"What's she done?"

"Nothing much. Nothing besides the usual crying jags and mad demands and refusal to work that we get from any number of these women stars, including some who make the studio a lot less money than Chloë Rose. But now she thinks she's being followed. She's nervous all the time about it, and it's making it hard for Sturgeon to shoot the picture she's making. The studio has her on a five-year contract and there are three years to go, so there are people who are worried."

"Worried that she's actually being followed or worried that she thinks she's being followed?"

"Thinks." He drummed his fingers on the desk. "Maybe she is being followed, I don't know. But I tend to doubt it. These people are all paranoid. It's their sense of self-importance. Either way, I've managed to convince her well enough that I've got things under control here, that the only people on the lot are people who belong there. In truth, there's any number of ways to get onto the lot without us knowing. We have to throw people off the lot all the time, people who think they belong in pictures and are ready to prove it."

"So what do you want me to do?"

"Just follow her around when she's not on the set. Stakeout in front of her house at night."

"You want a bodyguard. I'm not a bodyguard."

"It's not a bodyguard job. I told you, she only thinks she's being followed. You just need to make her feel safe. For show."

"So I'm supposed to follow her around to make her feel better about somebody following her around?"

Knox held his hands wide and leaned back. "That's show business."

"Go back to Miss Rose's mystery man. It is a man, isn't it?"

"That's what she says."

"You said that you convinced her that the only people on the lot are people who belong on the lot. Why couldn't her tail be someone who belongs on the lot?"

"He could be. But don't point that out to her. She must not have thought of it."

"What's he supposed to look like?"

"Like every other man you've ever met, if you go by her description. Medium height, dark hair, medium build. You'll talk to her about it. She'll fill you in."

"And she's seen him on the lot?"

"On the lot and off." He leaned forward. "That's if you believe her. I told you already. There's nobody following her. She's going dotty. There've been a batch of tantrums on the set. And her private life is worse than a paperback novel."

I raised an eyebrow.

He took a breath and let it out slowly. I waited.

"Her husband's Shem Rosenkrantz," he said. "He had a few books they liked in New York ten, fifteen years ago, but the last few years he's been hanging around here doing treatments that never get made. They never get made because he's too busy fooling around with the starlets and he doesn't keep it a secret from his wife. This picture they're filming now is one he wrote and it's getting made because she's in it. And he's *still* having an affair with her co-star, this new girl called Mandy Ehrhardt. Meanwhile, Sturgeon, the director, has a thing for Rose, Missus Rosenkrantz if you're keeping score. Which might be fine if she wanted it too, but…"

"You sure he's not involved with this business?"

"Sturgeon? No. Sturgeon's on good behavior. And he's got reason to be. He had his last three productions fall apart in the middle of filming, and if he doesn't prove he can finish something, he's washed up here."

I mulled it over. "That all?"

"It's not enough?"

"Any old boyfriends that might be tailing her around?"

Knox said through his teeth, "Nobody's tailing her."

"Just for argument's sake."

Knox burst out laughing. "You haven't changed a bit. Still treat every job like it's a real case."

"What am I supposed to do when someone's paying me?"

"This is the picture business, boy. We all get paid for make-believe."

"Silly me," I said. "Always trying to do the right thing."

"You didn't learn anything when they threw you out of the department?"

"Sure, I learned that the law's something they print in books."

He held up his hands, palms out. "All right, all right. I'm not asking you to do anything that'll compromise your precious sense of ethics. All I want is for you to sit down with our star, get her to tell you her story, make lots of notes, and then tell her she doesn't need to worry. And then you can go get drunk in your car or sleep for all I care. It's just for a few days until the picture is done."

"I don't like it. I don't like that what you need's a bodyguard, but what you went and got is me. I don't like a job that's not really a job, looking for a man that may or may not exist just to make some actress feel better. Send her to a doctor."

His face turned stormy. "I've already laid out our dirty laundry," he said, and opened his hands over his desk as though it were actually laid out there before us. "More than I ought to have said."

"You didn't tell me anything I couldn't have learned in a movie magazine."

"Come on, Foster. What's wrong with you? This is easy money. I was scratching your back. You got so much work you can turn down fifty dollars a day? Since when?"

"I didn't say I wouldn't do it, I just said I didn't like it."

I could see the muscles of his face relax. He smiled and nodded. He had to be careful, Knox. The littlest thing would give him a coronary someday.

He stood up, his chair rolling backwards as it was freed from his weight. "I did tell you a few things they don't have in the glossies. And I'm sure you'll find out others. If I didn't know how discreet you are…"

And Knox did know. Back on the force, he would have lost his job more than once if it hadn't been for how discreet I was.

"Come on," he said, "let's go meet your client."

I stood too, but waited for Knox to come around the desk. "You're my client, Al."

He opened the door. "At least pretend that you're excited to meet a movie star."

THREE

The first time I saw her in person, it was at a distance and she was on a horse. From what I could make out, she had a small frame; like she weighed less than the saddle they had under her. They had her dressed in a tan leather jerkin with tassels over a blue gingham dress that made no effort to hide a pair of black maryjanes, which I assumed they would keep safely out of the shot. Much of the thick dark hair she was known for was hidden under a ten-gallon cowboy hat. She sat sidesaddle but held the reins like someone who was used to riding the conventional way. Her famous face could have been any pretty girl's at that distance, just a canvas the makeup artist had painted on. Up close I knew she'd look the way I'd seen her dozens of times on posters and billboards and at the pictures. She wasn't a woman, she was a star. Chloë Rose.

We parked the golf cart on the suburban side of the backlot street and walked over to the Old West. The standing set had been built on a stretch of dirt road not quite as long as a football field. There was a ragtag of wooden building fronts lining the street. Some had gotten paint and some hadn't. Each building had a sign, to indicate which one was the saloon, which one was the chemist's, and which one was the jail. It wasn't a bad façade if you closed your eyes and used your imagination.

There were at least fifteen other people on the set—a horse handler, the director, the assistant director, makeup, electric, and some I couldn't identify. As we approached, another woman in a cowgirl costume and a man in a rumpled suit shouted at each other in the shade of the dry goods store. A child of eleven or twelve stood nearby, uninterested.

"You'd better not forget yourself," the man said, "or who got you where you are."

"A washed-up drunk who lives off his wife?"

"You're living off my wife too, aren't you?" That made him Shem Rosenkrantz. "We're all living off of Clotilde on this damn set. I'm just asking for a little favor, that you watch him for a few hours. I've got to work."

She shot her fists out behind her. "Mandy, do this. Mandy, do that. I've paid you back plenty already. Or are you dissatisfied with the service?"

At that, Chloë Rose jerked her horse away from the handler, almost knocking the director over, and cantered to where the couple was fighting. They stopped and looked up at her. The young boy took a step back. "Can't you at least pretend here?" she said in that famous French accent.

Rosenkrantz said something in reply, but Chloë Rose had already turned her horse and brought it almost to a gallop, not slowing until she reached the far end of the Old West set. Rosenkrantz chased after her, running through the cloud of dust her horse had kicked up. As he passed Sturgeon, the director gave him an angry look that was a step away from tears. Rosenkrantz made a placating motion with his hands, still hurrying through his wife's wake.

Knox turned to me. "Wait here. This might not be a good time."

"What makes you think that?" I said.

He started over to the assistant director, who had turned to say something to the director of photography, shaking his head.

I stood with the woman and the kid. She had auburn hair in waves that were too regular to be natural. Her face was angular, so that it was pretty from the front but not as much from the side. When it was angry, which it was just then, all the lines in her face turned sinewy, like she was stretched too tight and might snap at any moment. Knox had warned me off of asking questions, but it was an old habit with me. I said, "Miss Ehrhardt? I'm Dennis Foster. I'm looking into some reports of unusual activity on the set. You see any strange men about? Anyone who doesn't belong? Or maybe he belongs, but not quite as much as he's around."

She didn't turn to look at me while I said all this. She kept her hip cocked with one fist planted on it to show that she was angry. "With all these people around, who knows who any of them are?"

"So you didn't notice anything?"

"Look around. Notice anything you'd like. I'm working."

"I can see that."

She looked at me then. "Was that a crack? You forgot to tell me when to laugh."

"Now would do fine."

She sneered. "Watch it, mister, or I might have to call security."

I pointed to Al Knox, who was making large gestures as he talked, but seemed unable to distract the assistant director from his clipboard. "That's the head of security there. I came with him. Or didn't you notice?"

"I didn't care."

"You don't notice anyone, do you?"

"Sure, today there's been the mailman, the milkman, the iceman, the priest, a guy from the paper, and a talking cow."

The boy beside her gave one short pant of amusement.

I looked at him, then back at her. "I get it," I said. "You didn't notice anything you feel like talking about. Or at least talking about with me."

"You get paid for being so smart?"

"Not enough."

"What's this all about anyway? Is it because of Chloë?"

I said nothing.

"Chloë's scared of her own shadow. Look at all the time we're wasting now because something upset her fragile disposition."

"I wonder what it could have been."

"You know what? —— Chloë, and —— you too."

"There are children present," I said.

She crossed her arms over her breasts and turned her back to me. I noticed the kid staring at me. I smiled at him, but his face remained impassive. "You see any strange men around?" I said to him.

"I see you," he said.

I nodded. I'd asked for that. I looked around for Knox.

He was on his way back towards me. When he saw me looking he shook his head, his lips pressed together, and waved me over with a swat of his hand. "No dice. They're going to keep shooting now. Sturgeon's only got the horse for another two hours."

I fell in beside him. "I'll meet her later."

"I just would have liked to introduce you," he said. "Smooth your way in."

"I'll manage," I said. We were at the golf cart now.

He stepped up on the driver's side. "Just remember, be discreet," he said, and grunted as he pulled himself under the wheel. "We're keeping this whole thing on the Q.T."

"Mandy seemed to know about it. Says Chloë's paranoid."

"What were you talking to Mandy for? Didn't I tell you not to ask questions?"

I ignored that. "The kid goes with Rosenkrantz?" I said.

"Yeah. By his first wife, I guess. Visiting from back east."

"And how does Chloë feel about that?"

He began to answer but someone cried, "Quiet!" and he fell silent. He gestured for me to do the same. On the set, everyone had resumed their positions. The director was behind the camera and Chloë Rose was on her horse looking off into the distance. There was stillness as everyone waited, trying not to shuffle their feet or cough. Chloë's lips moved, a beat went by, and then everyone else moved again.

"It's still amazing to me how small these sets are when they look so big in the cinema," Knox said.

Mandy Ehrhardt was coming our way with the boy trailing behind her. She was moving as though a bee had stung her.

"Maybe they're done after all," Knox said, and leaned out of the cart, "Mandy, hey, Mandy, are they finishing?"

"No," Mandy said without stopping. "But I'm supposed to get the kid a candy bar in the commissary, because co-star apparently means gofer."

"You could get one for me too," Knox called after her.

She held up her hand with only one finger raised. The boy skipped a few steps to keep up with her.

"Too bad she didn't wait," Knox said, letting out the clutch on the cart. "We could have given her a ride."

The cart's engine made a buzzing sound as Knox made a U-turn. We were suddenly in Springfield or Livingston or any of a thousand other towns in the U.S. The street sign even said Main Street. That lasted about fifty yards before we were coursing down a Chicago city street, and after that a dirt road outside a medieval castle.

"So, what's really going on here, Knox? How about coming clean?"

The folds in his face deepened to show insult. "Why wouldn't I be honest with you?"

"I don't know. Why would the studio need to hire a private dick when it has its own security force?"

"Force? That's a laugh. It's me, two retirees, and a couple of kids that don't shave yet. And we're here for the lot, not to be round-the-clock protection for one actress."

"Is it protection I'm supposed to be offering or comfort? I forget which."

"Ah, nuts to you. Just cash the checks and be glad."

"That's fine if you're right and Rose has gotten spooked for no reason. But if she *is* being followed and something happens to her on my watch…"

Knox waved his right hand at me in dismissal. Nothing was going to happen. Didn't I know that?

I wondered why I was being so hard on him. There was no shame in working for the studios. It's not like my other clients never lied to me.

But there was something about an old friend handing out the lies that I just didn't like.

We were nearing the front of the studio lot, driving along with regular traffic now, limousines, delivery trucks, bicycles The traffic noise out on the Boulevard wasn't kept off the lot by the gatehouse or the high wall.

After a time, Knox said, staring straight ahead, "Just go to the Rosenkrantz house this evening. I'll show you where on the map. She knows to expect you."

I nodded, and we rode along for a while more.

"That Mandy was really angry, wasn't she?" Knox said, shooting me a tentative grin. He wanted to show we were friends again, no hard feelings. "And that lover's spat with Rosenkrantz? His wife right there, too."

"You know these creative types. They're creative in everything they do."

"Of course Sturgeon seemed a little liberal with where his hands were too. Positioning her on the horse."

We pulled up to the security office, and I got out of the cart. "Now you're just being a gossip," I said.

The cart bounced on its shocks as Knox got out. He reached into his pocket and pulled out five twenty-dollar bills. My retainer.

I took the money. "Who's the male lead in the picture?" I said. "I didn't see an actor on the set."

"John Stark. They didn't need him today. He's probably out on his boat. Why?"

"Thought it might be worth getting his perspective on what's going on."

Knox's brow turned stormy again. "You're not asking anyone any questions. This isn't an investigation, it's a show. You understand what I'm saying to you? Look pretty for the camera."

"Okey."

That didn't seem to ease his concern. "I can trust you on this, Foster, right?"

I nodded and smiled and handed his lie right back to him. "Yeah," I said. "You can trust me."

FOUR

I had a few free hours on my hands, so I retrieved my car, and drove west on Sommerset. I left the windows open and the wind buffeted me, causing my shirt to flutter and my tie to dance. When the houses started to have enough acreage to farm on, I turned south on Montgomery, following it down the hill to the area San Angelinos called Soso, what the real estate men called Harper's Promise. Despite the ambivalent name this was a fine neighborhood with good-sized Victorian-style houses that a previous generation of movie stars had bought as starter homes before moving up in size and elevation. The only surprising thing was that Chloë Rose and her writer husband hadn't moved up themselves in the years since she'd displaced champagne as America's favorite French import.

I turned onto Highlawn Drive. They lived at the corner of Montgomery and Highlawn in a medium-sized house. The Montgomery side of the property was lined with a protective hedge two stories high, meant to afford some privacy, but the front lawn was open to view from the street. I drove past the house to the end of the block, made a K-turn, and parked on the street three houses down. Then I walked back along the sidewalk with my hands in my pockets.

Their Victorian was gaudy and ornate, and did not belong on the West Coast. The main color was purple, offset by white trim and trellises at every edge that could be decorated. The wide white pillars at the main entrance looked thick enough to give Samson a challenge. They supported a flat second-story porch with a screened entrance. There were wicker lawn furnishings on the porch with rain-stained canvas cushions that looked unused. Anyone who wanted to get some sun at this house would use the backyard, out of view.

The flowerbeds were as gaudy as the house, a choice the landscape designer probably thought was complimentary. There were crocuses and lilies and daffodils and a few others that I couldn't name. They were arranged in a concentric kidney bean pattern to either side of the walk. There was a detached garage that appeared to be a late addition. While it was also painted purple and white, its design was too utilitarian for the Victorians, practically a shed. The doors were open to reveal a maroon LaSalle coupe and an empty spot for a second car.

The backyard was much the same as the front, only the flowerbeds here were butterfly wings. An automatic sprinkler ratcheted around in a ticking pattern, keeping time with long arcs of water. Since I'd left my raincoat home, I decided to skip the backyard for now and check the garage first. It was built on a slab of poured concrete that looked practically scrubbed clean. There wasn't even a spot of oil where the missing car should have been. The walls were covered in pegboards with hooks to hold every tool a servant might need around the property. A wooden bench against the back wall was lined with mason jars holding screws, nails, bolts, hinges, and other hardware. I went to the coupe and opened the door. The registration was in the name of "Clotilde-ma-Fleur Rosenkrantz." I could see why she had chosen a stage name.

"That's about enough," a man said behind me.

I pulled out of the car, but didn't close the door. A short, squat Mexican stood backlit in the entrance of the garage. He wore a red velvet dinner jacket that was too big for him and matching pants that were cuffed at the bottom. His hair was combed straight back from his forehead and plastered in place. He was a young man, old enough to show a little class but not so old that he couldn't best you in a fight. Just your average Mexican. The Luger in his right hand didn't hurt his chances either.

I brought my hands around to where he could see them. "You know, if you point those things at people, somebody's liable to get hurt."

"Who are you?" He had almost no accent.

"My name's Dennis Foster. It's all right. I'm working for Miss Rose."

"Nobody works for the Rosenkrantzes but me, and I don't know you."

"I just got hired today, at the studio," I said.

His gun held steady. "Try another one."

"I don't have another one. That one's the truth. You mind pointing that gun somewhere other than at me? This suit doesn't need any more holes in it."

"Move away from the car. Close the door. And then get off the property before I call the police."

"I get it. You've got the gun, I have to do what you tell me. But if you were really to shoot me, whose side do you think the police would be on?"

His dark face grew darker.

"Look, we work for the same people. No need to act tough."

"I've got my instructions," he said. "Miss Rose was very clear: I am to watch for people that don't belong here. Now I find you in her car. What does that sound like to you?"

"It sounds like the same thing the studio hired me for. To look for people that don't belong around here. I'm a private detective."

He was still unconvinced. "Nobody said anything to me about a dick."

"Well, maybe you're not privy to every last thing that goes on. Hell, maybe I should ask who you are. How do I know you work for the Rosenkrantzes?"

He didn't like that. "Get going. Scram." When I didn't, his voice rose. "I said get out of here."

"Sure. If they have you, what would they need to hire a dick for? You're tough no matter which side of the bed you got up on."

"Enough talking." He moved the gun to call attention to it in case I had forgotten it was there.

"Look, I'll show you my license. I'm going for my wallet here." He held the gun out further as I reached for my pocket. I got out the Photostat of my license and held it towards him.

He took a few steps forward, turning his body so that the gun stayed out of my reach as he took my license. He resumed his position and then looked at it. "This doesn't prove anything. You could have gotten that anywhere, and even if it's yours, it doesn't tell me who you're working for."

I held my hands up in defeat. "You're right. I didn't know they made Mexicans as smart as you. I thought you were just good for a little music and handing out drinks."

"You think that's funny?" His accent showed more when he got angry.

"Not especially," I said. "Listen, if you'll aim that peashooter somewhere else and give the license back, I'll be on my way. We can sort this out later when your boss is at home."

He twitched the gun in the direction of the open garage door but didn't lower it.

"My license?"

He tossed it at my chest. I caught it on the rebound and pocketed it.

"Out," he said.

I edged along with my back to the LaSalle and my hands held high. I'd left the car door open. He followed me with his gun. He was intent on his job.

When I stepped out into the sun, the Mexican seemed to disappear in the shadows of the garage. I assumed the gun was still trained on me. I wondered what his duties actually were. He wasn't driving the car that was gone and he wasn't dressed for yard work. He made a good watchdog, though. It kind of made me wonder why they needed me.

The sprinkler had finished its artificial rainfall, and now it was just a quiet neighborhood without a sound except for the occasional car going by or airplane overhead or delivery being made. It was a nice part of town to live in, safe but not too presumptuous. I strolled along the drive, taking my time about it, just to give the Mexican something else to be angry about. I heard the LaSalle's door slam and then the sound of the garage doors closing. Out on the street, there wasn't a single person in evidence. The whole neighborhood looked like a set. I walked along to my car, got in, and started the motor.

FIVE

North of Sommerset were the Hills. The more money you had, the higher up you got to dig your foundation. Here there were landscaping teams in canvas slacks and bandanas at work on every third yard, and that was just counting the yards that could be seen from the street. There were probably gardeners working on half of the homes that were hedged or walled or gated too. These were the winter palaces of Hollywood's royalty, large Spanish-style mansions dating back to the silent era, southern plantation-style homes from the rise of the talkies, angular mesa homes clinging to precipices for the newly rich. There might have been competition between the residents, but to an outsider, the whole enclave represented those who had the money. To the moneyed, it was probably a much too thin line of defense against the masses.

Several blocks into the development, I stopped along the side of the road, idling in the shadow of a hedge. I only had to wait a few minutes before an open-topped tourist bus drove by, the amplified voice of the tour leader pointing out the homes of the stars. I pulled in close enough so I could hear the tour guide's patter, a cheerful droning of names sprinkled with months-old gossip that had been de-clawed for the out-of-towners. The bus wove its way along the narrow curving street, intent on covering every inch of pavement that had been blessed with the magic of the movies. When the tour guide eventually said John

Stark's name, I tapped the brake and let the bus pull on ahead of me. I was glad to be rid of it. I had swallowed enough exhaust for one day.

Stark's home was open to view. There was a lush expanse of emerald grass venturing up a hill to the house. A circular drive was hidden from the street, which gave the impression that the grass went right up to the mansion's front door. The architect had placed two white columns on either side of the door, and had probably thought it added a touch of antiquity, but mostly it made him look like he was angling to see his work memorialized the next time they re-did the back of the five-dollar bill. The house behind the columns was little more than a sprawling box. It was painted white with decorative black shutters pinioned to the left and right of every window. It was the kind of home that would have a candle lit in each window at Christmastime and a big imported wreath on the front door. It was a modest abode. No more than thirty rooms at the outside.

I pulled up the steep drive until I was even with the front door. There was a short step up to a platform made from a single slate slab. I rang the bell and heard the distant sound of chimes within. The light hanging from the top of the portico looked as heavy as a car, and I made sure to be out from under it as I waited for someone to answer the door.

I was just reaching for the bell again when the door opened. A pretty young man with fair hair and a perfectly even bronze tan stood in the entry. His jaw and his eyes showed that he was fully grown, but there was something about him that remained boyish. Maybe it was the unmarked skin and the hint of down on his cheeks or maybe it was his slender body. He was dressed in pale blue suit pants but with no jacket or tie. It was hard to tell if he was a member of the house staff or a guest. His expression was of minor annoyance. "Yes?"

"Dennis Foster." I held out one of my cards. He didn't reach for it. "I was hired by the studio over a matter of security. I wanted to ask Mr. Stark some questions."

His expression changed to boredom, and he closed the door without a word.

I stood still for a moment, the door too close to my face. I considered ringing the bell again. The man hadn't said that Stark wasn't at home. Then I turned to look down the hill to the street. Everything was green. No one was in sight.

I was considering my options when the door opened behind me. It was the same young man, his expression of boredom now extending over his whole body. I decided he must not be a member of the staff with such an unprofessional disposition. He moved to a position alongside of the door and waved his hand towards himself. "Come on. Come in."

I stepped inside and he closed the door behind me. The entry hall's ceiling went to the roof. The floor was gray marble, and it kept the room cool. It was just large enough to walk your dog without having to go outside. There were two large archways on either side of the hall, and a massive marble staircase directly across from the front door that went up to a landing and then divided, continuing up to the right and the left. He walked around me and started diagonally towards one of the farther archways. His footsteps gave a dull echo.

"You don't go in for much security here," I said.

"People know better than to come."

"Much trouble with the staff?"

He ignored that question. He led me through a sitting room decorated in white and yellow, through a music room with floor-to-ceiling wood slat shades along two walls, and then through a small doorway onto a verandah that looked out on what would have made a good eighteenth hole.

"Presenting this guy, Johnny," the pretty man said with a dismissive flick of his wrist. He went to the edge of the verandah and leaned against one of the white pillars, facing me, with his arms crossed. Definitely not a member of the staff.

Johnny Stark, the face loved by millions, sat in Bermuda shorts and a lemon-colored golf shirt on a large white wicker chair, his bare feet on a matching wicker ottoman. Leather sandals lay neatly on the floor beside him. His dark hair, his cleft chin, his white teeth were all perfect, just like in the pictures. He didn't even seem smaller. He had an open manuscript on his lap, the already-read pages bent back behind the pages remaining to be read. A glass on a table beside him could have been iced tea with a twist of lemon or iced tea with a fifth of vodka. I wasn't close enough to tell. He looked at me with a wide smile and raised eyebrows.

"Your man tell you why I'm here?" I said.

That got a rise out of the fellow holding up the pillar. His hands went to his hips and his mouth opened wide. "Now what is that supposed to mean?"

"Greg," Stark said, making a calming gesture with his hand, and then I knew how it was.

"So are you on the payroll?" I said with a smile.

Greg's hands went up in exasperation. "Johnny—"

"Shhhh," Stark said. Greg crossed his arms again and made a show out of his sulk. Stark turned that gorgeous smile on me. How many women had it made fawn over him? How many men?

"Mr. Foster, Greg *is* on the payroll. He works in the kitchen. But the staff is off this afternoon. Can I get you a drink? We don't usually get unexpected visitors—"

"Even with no gates on the drive?"

"Mr. Foster, the gates are invisible and they're much further away than just my drive."

"I'll make do without the drink, thank you."

He shrugged with indifference.

"The studio hired me to look after Chloë Rose, Mr. Stark. Apparently she's being followed and she's worried for her safety. I'm trying to find out if anyone else has seen this man she says is following her. You notice anyone hanging around the set that doesn't belong?"

"Well it takes a lot of people to make a movie…"

"It could even be someone who works for the studio, but doesn't work on your picture, or someone on your picture that would make Miss Rose nervous for some reason."

He smiled at that and shot his eyes across at Greg who had let his indignation go, but still held his arms across his chest.

"Did I say something funny?"

"Have you met Chloë yet?"

"Al Knox tried to introduce us this afternoon. It didn't work out."

He laughed then, an open laugh that showed all of his teeth. "I'm sorry, Mr. Foster, it's just that it doesn't take a lot to make Chloë Rose nervous."

"Does she have reason to be?"

"Do any of us have reason to be? Certainly. We all do. You do too. Everyone. But that doesn't mean I am nervous. Are you?"

"I'd appreciate an answer to my question still."

Greg tsked and uncrossed and recrossed his arms.

Stark's eyes went up, and he said, "No, I haven't noticed any-one around the set that I would say didn't belong there. I know that Chloë thinks there is someone, but she's never pointed him out to me."

"So you think she's making it up?"

"She might be mistaken," he said diplomatically. He took a deep breath and then said, "I have been threatened and I have been followed. The price of fame. But it doesn't happen nearly as often as you'd think it might and it's never as sinister as you fear. Chloë's just skittish."

"You mean crazy."

"Actresses are their own animal," he said. "May I ask why the studio has hired a private detective to protect Chloë instead of making use of someone already on staff?"

"You'll have to ask someone at the studio that, and if you get an answer, feel free to tell me."

"See, Greg," Stark said, shooting out his hand toward the other man, "we're all good friends."

Greg tried to bolster his gloomy disposition, but it didn't look genuine.

"Was there anything else, Mr. Foster? You just wanted to know if I had seen any shady characters? I feel like we're in a movie."

"That's it," I said. "No one's given me any more to go on."

"Why don't you go ahead and meet Chloë, and then do what everyone in S A with brains does, take the studio's money."

"Thanks for the advice." I leaned forward and floated my card onto the table beside his drink. "I'm sure we'll be seeing each other again. I can show myself out." I didn't wait for either of them to move, just headed back into the house. Be-hind me, I could hear Greg's higher-pitched voice begin to whine. Part of me wanted to frisk the house just on principle, but in a place that size no more than two or three of the rooms are personal, and it would take too long to find them. I went out to the car, and rolled down the drive without having to touch the gas.

SIX

At seven o'clock I was back at the Rosenkrantz place. The house at night looked much like the house during the day, only with enough lamps blazing to light the Queen Elizabeth. There were lights upstairs and lights downstairs. There were mushroom-shaped guide lights along the front walk and two high-powered spots for the front lawn. There was another spotlight shining from the roof onto the drive. If you intended to sneak up on the Rosenkrantzes, you didn't want to do it dressed in burglar black.

I took the front stairs this time. I had on my good suit, a navy blue so deep it looked black, with a pressed white shirt, a red-and-blue-striped tie, a red handkerchief, and freshly polished loafers. I'd had a shower and a shave. It was five minutes after seven. The front door opened before I rang. It was my friend from the afternoon, without the gun this time.

"They let you in here too?" I said. "I didn't know it was that kind of place."

He stepped back to let me pass. "Mr. Foster."

I went in and took off my hat. "I guess they only allow artillery at the servant's entrance. It's certainly more welcoming this way."

He closed the door. "This time Miss Rose let me know you were expected." He hesitated a moment. "I'm sorry about…"

"That's okay," I said. "I like to have people point guns at me every once in a while. Reminds me I'm still alive."

He gave a slight nod, and vanished through the archway on the left without a word.

The front hall was open to the second floor ceiling, where a tarnished bronze chandelier cast just enough light to make the space gloomy. The front door was set between twin staircases that led up to a catwalk hallway. There were three doors on the catwalk along with the French doors directly overhead that opened to the upstairs patio. The floor was largely covered with overlapping Persian rugs that bore the marks of foot traffic from each of the stairwells to the squared arches off to the left and right. Here and there rich maroon tiles could be seen where the floor was exposed. Two large breakfronts at the back of the hall were stuffed with books and porcelain dolls.

The sound of men laughing burst forth from one of the upstairs rooms. It was a frantic sound that suggested alcohol.

The Mexican came back. "Miss Rose, she's not feeling very well tonight."

"I'm sorry to hear that."

"She won't see you tonight." He smiled. "Maybe tomorrow."

"Of course," I said. "We all serve at her pleasure." I started to fit my hat back on my head when a telephone rang with extensions in several of the rooms. The Mexican and I stared at each other in the silence only a ringing telephone can create. Then he said, "Excuse me," and went back through the archway from which he had come.

The noise stopped, and then Shem Rosenkrantz stumbled out of one of the upstairs rooms calling "Clotilde...." He was in his shirtsleeves with black suspenders holding up pants that sagged in the middle. His face was red from drinking too much and his nose was covered with broken blood vessels from drinking too often. His straw hair was parted down the center. He looked like a stereotype of the great American author, which is what he was. "Clotilde...It's that man again about your damn horse!" He saw me then and stopped. "Who the hell are you?"

I tipped my hat. "Just one of the hired help."

"Well tell my wife to answer the damn phone," and he headed back into the room.

I thought about that for a moment and decided Rosenkrantz's order overrode the Mexican's plea of Chloë Rose's frailty. I followed where the servant had gone and was in the dining room when I heard him say in some further-off room, "The telephone, miss." I stopped, and her voice said something I couldn't make out. I looked around the room. There was a phone extension on the sideboard. I went to the phone and picked it up, covering the mouthpiece with my hand.

"I've told you before," Chloë Rose said, "Constant Comfort is not for sale."

I grabbed a pencil by the phone and scrawled "Constant Comfort" on the top sheet of the notepad lying beneath it.

"He'll give you *three* horses in trade, good horses, and he said that you can renegotiate your contract."

"I don't care what he said, he should have the decency to call me himself. And the answer is no, you little," she hesitated to think and then spat, "pissant."

"Hold on, Miss Rose, we're all working for the same guy."

"That's right, working for him, not owned by him. Good evening."

The phone rang off, although I could still hear the man breathing. He could probably hear me. I gently replaced the receiver on the base, tore the top sheet off the pad and pocketed it, and then walked casually out of the room into the front hall. A minute later, the Mexican emerged as well from where he had no doubt had to hold the phone for the ailing Chloë Rose so the weight wouldn't strain her. "Nice place," I said, looking up with my hands in my pockets as though I were admiring the moldings. "Some real nice pieces in there," indicating the other archway with my head, cool and convincing as a long-nosed dummy. "Well, I'll be in my car down the street if I'm needed," and I took the main entrance before he could respond.

I walked the mushroom-lighted path to the street, and then down the middle of the street to my car. It was almost as hot outside as it had been at noon. A perfect night for car sitting, if you were cold-blooded. I got in behind the steering wheel and rolled down the windows on both sides. I thought about breaking the first rule of a nighttime stakeout and lighting a cigarette and decided that it didn't matter if I got spotted. The whole job was cockeyed already. A stakeout and follow job required two people for it to be done properly. And I hadn't even been granted access to my client, Knox's assurances notwithstanding. The only way those two facts added up to something that made sense was if I really was just here for show, a piece of set decoration, and not a very necessary one either. This case already had a mystery man on the set, a mystery man on the phone, the mystery man that the man on the phone was bargaining for, the mystery man who was drinking and laughing with Shem Rosenkrantz upstairs. I was one too many. I felt like I had come to the party late and got seated at the wrong table.

I took out a match and lit it on my thumbnail the first time. I took a drag of my cigarette and watched the tip glow orange. I thought about the phone call. I didn't know what to make of it or even if there was anything to make of it. It was your regular strong-arm phone call. All of the up-to-date movie stars got them. They found it invigorating.

I smoked and watched as one by one the inside lights went out in each of the houses on the block. The outdoor lighting gave the neighborhood an ominous look. At nine, the Mexican came out and walked towards Montgomery. He would catch the Number 3 bus on Sommerset to go home. At 11:30, a police cruiser came around, right on time. It pulled up alongside me and I had to get out my license and laugh at a few corny jokes before they went away. I must have lit at least three more cigarettes, but I wasn't counting. My mouth felt like cotton. I wouldn't have turned down a drink.

Eventually the lights downstairs went out. The front hallway chandelier went next. I waited for the upstairs rooms. If there had been two people laughing when I first came in, and I thought there had been, then someone should be ready to come out just about now, or they had a houseguest that I should have known about. That was if there had been two voices. It could have been the radio.

A car started at the back of the house. I could make out the taillights through the next-door neighbors' hedge as it backed out down the drive. It wasn't the LaSalle I had seen earlier; this was a tan Buick sedan. It pulled out into the street facing me, which gave me a clear view of the driver: Shem Rosenkrantz, his face bloated and sour with drink. Someone was sitting in the passenger seat next to him and when the car passed under a streetlight, I caught the passenger full in the face: Hub Gilplaine. That was Hub Gilplaine the nightclub owner, casino operator, and publisher of pornographic books—the sort with more words than pictures, if that made any difference. I knew him by sight on account of how often he got his picture in the paper for donating to one charity or another. He sat tense and upright, his face pinched, clearly worried for his safety with Rosenkrantz at the wheel, and with good reason.

The glare of the Buick's headlights brightened my windows as the sound of their motor went by and then darkness and the engine draining away. I looked behind me in time to see them turn left at the next block. It would take them out of the development to one of the major arteries, Woodsheer or Sommerset. I looked at the house, and saw each of the upstairs windows go dark. Chloë Rose was in for the night. But Shem Rosenkrantz was out with a known pornographer. And he was in no condition to drive. Some concerned citizen had to make sure they were safe. I started my car and swung around in a wide U-turn.

SEVEN

I caught up with them just as they turned east on Woodsheer. The boulevard was busy enough, even at that hour, for me to keep a car between us at all times. They took Woodsheer out of the quiet prestige of the Hills and into the glut of traffic that was the Mile. As the traffic lights coyly winked, Rosenkrantz drove in fits and jerks, enough to make the most stoic traffic cop swallow his whistle. The retail stores were closed, but people weren't out in the middle of the night to do any shopping. At least not the sort of shopping done in a store. Women in sheer satin blouses and once sensible skirts now covered with spangles strolled alongside men with loud patterned suits and wide-brimmed hats on their way from the fights or to the club or just on their way. These pedestrians had no regard for the traffic, which provided Rosenkrantz several opportunities to turn my knuckles white on the steering wheel.

We managed to reach the comparative safety of Los Bolcanes without incident, and from there we drove all the way out to Aceveda-Route 6. Route 6 took us north, out of San Angelo, into the San Gabriel Mountains. I knew then we were on our way to Arcucia, but I let them lead the way. Hub Gilplaine had a club in Hollywood for all of the movie people to be seen in called The Tip. There were waiters in tuxedoes and a fountain in the middle of the dance floor, and five-course meals, and a mixed jazz band to add a little spice. It made a nice background for when you had your picture taken. But if you wanted a real good time you went to his other operation, The Carrot-Top Club, a casino out in Arcucia, not far from the Santa Theresa racetrack. Players could lose some money at one and then go lose some more at the other.

Rosenkrantz drove on and so did I. It was cooler in the mountains. The road was cut through or dangled over the peaks and rises of the landscape. As the suburbs petered out, larger houses appeared, perched on large parcels of land to either side of the road. We passed a field of cows huddling together in a tight group that shifted in trips of unsteady hooves. There was an orchard that must have been apple trees since this wasn't good land for oranges, and then some more animals roaming free behind a wooden fence. It was impossible to hide in country like that. I tried to leave half a mile between us, but that was just for show, I knew they knew I was there. But it was a public road. I had a right to ride on it. I was just another customer.

After several empty miles, the road curved around an outgrowth of rock and suddenly a smattering of lights could be seen in the valley below. These were the homes of the respectable citizens of Arcucia who had lobbied against the legalization of horse racing but who rolled over for Gilplaine once the track was built. Once you've let a little sin into your life, what's the problem with a little more? The signs warned us to slow down and a moment later, evenly spaced bungalows with pebbled drives and postage stamp lawns lined the road. We sped through the ghost town that was the downtown district, then on to more residential spreads. These homes were a bit larger and set back from the road with woodland around them. There was an uninterrupted spate of trees, and then the Buick turned onto an unmarked back road whose entrance was no more than a gap in the forest, a black cavern out of Grimm.

I followed. There was nothing but dark all around. The headlights of my car lit the road just far enough for me to see something before I hit it. I kept my eyes on the other car's red taillights. Pockets of fog sat in the road's depressions giving the feeling that the woods were closing in. There was a flash, and then a car coming the other direction squeaked by without slowing down. There might have been lights in the distance behind me. Why not? The Carrot-Top did good business.

The Buick slowed and turned off at an angle onto another uneven dirt road. The impression of seclusion was damaged somewhat by the lights from the town now just visible through the woods. As remote as it felt, we were still in civilization. Of course, it had the trappings of exclusivity necessary to make the paying customers feel special. There was probably a secret password at the door. And men in funny hats. And every other word spoken would mean something other than what the word really meant—words like 'tea' and 'horse.' The cops would want it that way too. I had a feeling they weren't going to like me.

A clearing opened up where gravel had been put down and about thirty cars were parked in neat lines. I pulled into the first empty spot I saw, while the Buick drove up to the front door and Rosenkrantz and Gilplaine turned the car over to the valet. I waited for them to disappear through the front door before I got out of my car.

The Carrot-Top Club had originally been built as the guest house of a mountain retreat for some new-money oil millionaire who lost the property when his money ran out. Gilplaine had gotten it cheap at auction. It was a two-story frontier home with unpainted cedar shingles and a slate roof. A canopied porch of wooden planks ran the entire length of the front of the house with two rocking chairs still off to the side waiting for ma and pa. There were two windows to either side of the door and three more upstairs, all blocked by blackout curtains, which left the parking lot shrouded in night, except where the open front door cast a yellow carpet of light leading into the club.

I arrived at the door just as the valet returned from parking the Buick. A dark-haired sharp in a tuxedo stopped me in the doorway and tapped my shoulder clip. "No guns."

"This? I just wear it out of habit. It's like my wallet."

The tuxedo gave me a smile and held out his hand. "I'll take good care of it for you."

"Like hell you will," I said and walked away from the door. I peeled off my coat, unbuckled my shoulder holster, and tucked the whole thing under the passenger seat of my car. When I got back to the front door, neither the tuxedo nor the valet so much as looked at me as I entered.

Inside, the whole first floor was one large open room about the size of a small ballroom, with exposed support beams and a stairway in the middle going up to the second floor. A mahogany bar lined one wall, its mirror doubling the four rows of liquor bottles. That part was all strictly legal now, although the bar was scuffed enough to suggest that it had been dependable through Prohibition too. The bar's brass edges could have used a shine. That didn't prevent half of the barstools from being filled with dark-suited men and women in cocktail dresses shouting over one another to be heard.

The other side of the room was where the real action was. There were three blackjack stations, two craps tables, and a roulette wheel. The dealers wore red vests with brass buttons and black bowties. Small crowds of boisterous onlookers partially hid the gaming tables. The sound of the ball skittering around the roulette wheel could be heard over the noise of excited conversaton. There was no band. No one would have listened to them if there had been one, so Gilplaine probably figured he might just as well save the cost.

I went to the bar first. As I did, a heavyweight champion in an ill-fitting suit followed after me. I leaned against the bar and he leaned against it right next to me. It was an empty space. No reason he shouldn't lean against it.

I caught the bartender's eye and ordered a Scotch. I scanned the room while he poured my drink. There was no sign of Rosenkrantz or Gilplaine. I tasted my Scotch. It was too good for me, but the studio was picking up my expenses. I paid and started for the nearest blackjack table. My oversized shadow followed with all of the subtlety of a white suit at a funeral. I watched several hands and for all I know so did he. The house went over once, hit blackjack twice, and paid out to a dealt blackjack once. I thought I'd check on the other tables just to make sure that my new friend got his exercise. At the craps table, he stood so close I could feel his breath on the back of my neck. I turned and looked at him, but he just smiled a closed-mouth smile. I showed him all of my teeth, then turned back to the game.

When I had had enough of that, I went around to the other side of the table, crossed behind the croupier at the roulette wheel, squeezed past a couple leaning against the wall, and hurried over to the stairs. I was only halfway up when the heavy-weight's tread sounded behind me. I turned and was able to look him in the eye from two steps up. "Did somebody stick a candy on my back?"

He grinned again. "I'd've thought your mother'd have taught you the golden rule."

"I know a few golden rules. Which one do you mean?"

"Treat others the way you'd want 'em to treat you back."

"Yeah, I've heard that one," I said. "I don't remember following you though."

This time he showed me that he was missing a few of his teeth.

"Yeah, well," I said, "then it's time to switch places. You take the lead and I'll follow you to Gilplaine's office."

The heavyweight raised his chin. "You'll find it. It's the second door on the left. I'll be right behind you in case you get scared."

I thought of something smart to say to that, but then I remembered I wasn't smart, so I just turned up the stairs.

EIGHT

Gilplaine's office looked like a storage room with a desk stranded in the center. Three of the walls were lined with brown cardboard boxes that had been labeled in a scrawl with the titles of erotic pulp novels: *Leslie's Love*, *I Married a Man's Man*, *Never Enough*, that kind of thing. The musty smell of old cheap paper filled the room, somewhere between a library and a locker room. There was a couch along the fourth wall, itself half covered in boxes, and three tall green filing cabinets taking up valuable real estate. Rosenkrantz, still dressed as informally as he had been at the house, occupied the free spot on the couch.

Gilplaine sat at his desk, leaning back in a swivel chair, its spring audibly protesting his weight. He was a sharp-faced man, with a head twice as high as it was wide. This had the effect of making his nose seem longer than it was, which didn't inspire any confidence in his honesty. He had piercing dark eyes that he focused with all of his attention on only one thing at a time. He wore an army-green three-piece suit with a gold chain coming out of the watch pocket and running to the gold watch in his hand. He looked at it, making note of the time, before placing it open on the desk blotter in front of him where he could consult it with a minimum sacrifice of attention. "What do you want?" he said.

"Hold on, I know him," Rosenkrantz said. The drive must have sobered him, since his speech no longer showed any sign of alcohol.

"You do?" Gilplaine said without taking his eyes off of mine.

"He was at the house before."

"Yes, he followed us when we left."

"No, inside the house. He's the detective they hired for Clotilde."

"Well, Mister...?"

I handed over a card, and he glanced at it.

"Well, Mr. Foster, you don't seem to be doing a very good job of protecting Miss Rose."

"How do you figure that?" I said.

"Right now, for instance, you're here with us."

"Maybe you're the ones she needs protecting from."

His eyes darted to the watch and then back to me.

"Just throw him out, Hub," Rosenkrantz said.

Gilplaine moved his mouth like he had just tasted something sour. "My men tell me you tried to bring a gun into my club."

I shrugged. "I thought I might need it."

"And what do you think now?"

"I was right."

"Are you certain you want to make an enemy of me, Mr. Foster?"

"No. But I am certain there isn't much that's honest about you. I'm certain you're a dirty little man who makes his money in dirty things for dirty people. I'm certain that a man like you anywhere near Miss Rose is something to protect her from."

Gilplaine's eyes narrowed. The champ shifted behind me and the floor creaked.

"Hah," Rosenkrantz said. "I should be writing this stuff down." He patted his pockets for something to write on.

Gilplaine continued to consider me with the scrutiny a mother gives her child before the first day of school. Then his face loosened and he spoke quickly. "Mr. Rosenkrantz and I are business acquaintances. Mr. Rosenkrantz is a writer, I am a publisher. We are discussing a forthcoming book. None of it has anything to do with his wife. Is that satisfactory?"

I shrugged.

"Not that it's any of your business. But if we get this straight now, I hope you won't go on annoying me in the future." Gilplaine looked once more at his watch and then clicked it shut. "Listen, Mr. Foster. I don't like cops who think they're smart when they're not. I don't like cops who think they're clean when they're not. I don't like cops who talk out of turn, and I don't like cops who talk in turn."

"Since we're all being so honest here," I said, "you have any ideas about who's been following Miss Rose?"

Rosenkrantz had found a notepad and was jotting notes with a golf pencil.

"Why would I have any idea about that?" Gilplaine said. "I'm not involved with the movies, even if my business sometimes involves people who are. I don't know who'd be following her around."

"No one's following her, Hub. Clotilde is imagining it," Rosenkrantz said. And to me he said, "You're busting yourself up for nothing. Just sit in your car and watch her and collect your money."

"That's what people keep telling me," I said.

"I have no information about this," Gilplaine said. He picked up his watch and tucked it away in his pocket. "And you've taken up all the time I care to give you."

The chair squealed as he turned to face Rosenkrantz. "Where were we, Shem?"

The creaking floor warned me to step out of the way before

Hub's man could get a grip on my shoulder. "I'll walk myself out," I told him. "That's one thing my mother did teach me."

He grinned that same closed-mouth grin that could have meant that he found me amusing or might just have meant that he had gotten hit in the head one too many times. He opened the door, and I stepped past him and hurried down the hall. I'd been wasting time, like the man said. Gilplaine was a publisher and Rosenkrantz a writer. It made sense that they would be working together, even though the critics would be surprised to find out that Rosenkrantz, the great golden boy, not only had sunk to writing for the pictures but even a step lower, writing for the under-the-counter trade.

Outside I went back to my car and sat behind the wheel without turning the ignition. I had been hired to sit in my car, as Rosenkrantz had reminded me, and Hub Gilplaine's parking lot was as good a place as any to sit. At the end of the night, Rosenkrantz and I were going back to the same place after all. The Carrot-Top Club wasn't too particular about what time it closed, but it was late and it couldn't stay open forever. I lit a cigarette and listened to the crickets buzz in waves, the sound rising and receding. There was a light breeze, offering some relief from the heat in the valley. The smell of the trees was cloying. It made me miss the city.

Laughing groups and couples came out the front door and I watched the valet flitting around the lot. Headlights cut across the trees two by two as people made their way out. After an hour, about half of the cars were left. I could see the Buick several cars over. A breeze swept through the clearing and I shivered. I began to wonder if there was something back at the house that I shouldn't be missing. Just as I was about to start my engine, Rosenkrantz appeared in the doorway and handed the valet his ticket. He was alone. The valet ran off, and Rosenkrantz talked to the doorman while he waited. It was ten minutes to three.

I started my engine and backed out of the spot, pointing the nose of my car away from the club. I pulled onto the private back road just ahead of the Buick. Maybe if I was in front of him, he wouldn't notice he was being tailed. We retraced our route through the endless wall of trees, past the town, up into the mountains and Route 6, and then eventually into the city and Woodsheer. I thought it would be better for me not to go directly to the house, so I drove past Montgomery and turned in the next block. But as I did, I saw the Buick continue west on Woodsheer in my rearview mirror. I hurried around the block, but had to wait for passing traffic before I could follow.

I caught up with the Buick at a traffic signal. If Rosenkrantz was worried about being followed, he showed no sign, and took no measures to shake me. He pulled off the highway in Harbor City, a neighborhood of small one-family homes that had once been prosperous but was now mainly inhabited by people just off the bus who didn't know any better or people who couldn't afford to move out. All the windows were dark except for an occasional night owl up clipping coupons or crocheting a doily that couldn't wait for morning. He pulled into the driveway of the kind of bungalow that you could buy out of the Sears catalog. It had a small front porch, four small rooms on the first floor, and one small room upstairs. I knew that without going in. I'd been in houses like it. There was a Ford that had to be at least ten years old parked in front of him. No lights were on inside. I continued past, pulling along the curb almost at the end of the block.

I watched in my mirror as Rosenkrantz got out of the car, walked around the backside of it and went up the path to the door. He opened the screen and then let himself in with his own key. Maybe it was a bungalow he kept to do his writing in. Maybe he was an insomniac and could only write at three in the morning, with a pitcherful of liquor inside him. Maybe. I figured I'd give him a few minutes, and then I would go back over to Soso to finish the job I had been hired for. I could always come back and investigate the house during the day.

Less than a minute later Rosenkrantz burst out the front door and bolted to his car. The screen banged shut behind him. I heard the engine catch and then he backed out of the driveway fast enough to make the wheels scream. I waited a minute to see if anyone would take notice of the noise. The neighborhood was silent.

I got out of my car and walked to the house. On the way, I shined the small pen flash I kept in my pocket into the Ford, looking for the license holder, but I couldn't see it. I went up the walk, and pressed the doorbell. I could hear it buzz inside. Rosenkrantz had left the door wide open, and through the screen I had a dim view of the stairs to the second floor and a small entryway. No one answered the buzzer. I opened the screen door and went in.

I listened, but heard nothing. I swung the door closed and found a switch that turned on an overhead light. It lit the rooms to either side of the entrance enough for me to see old furniture in both, respectable but worn, and none of the pieces matching. I crossed into the living room and turned on one of the lamps on an end table. It was painted gold, but the gold had flecked in places revealing white ceramic beneath. There was a couch upholstered in tan, two chairs upholstered in different shades of blue. The floor was hardwood but a cord rug took up some of the space between the couch and the chairs. It had no doubt been advertised as a furnished house, and maybe it even commanded a few extra dollars for that.

I continued through the living room towards the back of the house where an open door let into a bedroom. The smell hit me before I turned on the light. I felt for a light switch beside the door, but didn't find any, so I got my pen flash again and waved it back and forth, painting the room with light. She was on the bed. The blood was from her neck and thighs. I forced myself to cross the room to the lamp on the bedside table. I turned it on, and recognized the face from that afternoon: Mandy Ehrhardt. A thin wool blanket had been pulled down to the foot of the bed and hung over onto the floor. She had bled out, and the sheets were sodden. This hadn't happened in the last five minutes. Which left Rosenkrantz in the clear. The rest of the room was a mess, clothing on the floor trailing out of the closet, a pile of shoes beside the bed, drawers left slightly open in the dresser, but it was the mess of a careless woman living in a room. There hadn't been any struggle. The room hadn't been searched.

I opened the drawer of the bedside table. It contained a comb and a brush, both with hair clinging to them, a small green jewelry box with a few inexpensive pieces of jewelry, a compact, and a makeup kit. I checked the dresser and the closet, but there was nothing but clothes. Miss Ehrhardt might have been in pictures, but she wasn't living the life of a star. I set everything as it had been before. When it looked right, I turned off the light. I went through the living room, past the front entrance into the dining room. The table was littered with movie magazines, some movie ticket stubs, used dishes, a glass with dark lipstick on the rim, bills, flyers. Her purse was there as well, but it contained nothing more interesting than her bedside table. Same with the kitchen.

I went upstairs. This room smelled dusty. There was a bed with a dropcloth over it. There was a stack of boxes, the lower ones caving in from the weight of the ones above. There was a roll-top desk and a swivel chair. There weren't any lights that worked. I went back downstairs, and turned off the lights there. Back in the vestibule, I thought about what reason I could give for being here. There wasn't any, except if you counted the truth. If I told it straight then I was Rosenkrantz's alibi, and maybe this could all stay away from his wife. On the other hand, if I called it in anonymously, my name would probably come into it anyway and then the cops would want to know why I had called it in anonymously in the first place. They didn't like an outside operator operating outside the role they gave to him. Knox wouldn't like it either. I cursed myself for being curious. I could have been sleeping in my car ten minutes away. I picked up the phone and dialed the police.

NINE

The cop who got it was a Harbor City homicide detective named Samuels. I didn't know him, but he took my story at face value and I liked him for it. He was a redheaded Irishman with piercing blue eyes and a spate of freckles from his hairline all the way down into his collar. His coat hung limp, like there wasn't much for it to hang on, but from watching him move it was clear that there was a lot of wiry strength there. He smoked cheap cigars that came in cellophane which he cut open with a pocketknife, putting the cellophane back in his pocket. I liked him for that too. We stood in the dining room while the medical examiner and the photography boys took care of the body. He spoke quietly but forcefully.

"These Hollywood investigations are a farce. The studio will shut it down when they get wind of it tomorrow. Today, I guess."

"There are still a few hours before they have to hear of it," I said. "And it is murder. There's only so much that can be kept under wraps in a murder."

"Yeah, just who was murdered, and who did the murdering."

"The studio really has that much on you boys? I thought the law was untouchable in this town."

"Go on and laugh. Of course the studios can't order us to stop our investigation, but it seems that the bosses have a way of making it so that it should be a low priority with even a lower profile."

"The bosses," I said.

"The bosses." He smoked his cigar as the medical examiner, a young man with an expression of sobriety twice his age, went towards the front door with his bag. "You got anything for me, Doc?" Samuels said.

"She's dead," the ME said with his hand on the screen door's latch.

"That your professional opinion?"

The doc made a straight line of his mouth. "It was within the last six to eight hours. The cuts are all deep and inelegant."

"So this guy didn't know how to use a knife?" Samuels said.

"No, it looks more like he didn't know his own strength. The cuts are deliberate, no hesitation."

Samuels nodded and blew a plume of smoke.

"I'll have the rest once I get her on the table." And with that he went outside.

The sky might have been brighter out there or maybe I just hoped it was. "She have any family?" I said.

"An aunt and a grandma out in Wichita," Samuels said, flat.

"Isn't it always Wichita?"

"It always is." He paused. "You got any ideas you might be thinking of looking into on your own?"

"I was thinking of looking into a shower and then into my bed, but maybe into a liquor store first if I can find one that's open this early."

"Cut that and tell it to me straight, like you've been doing up until now."

I sighed and shook my head. "I've barely been on this thing longer than you have. This is just on the side of my job."

"The job that is why you were following Rosenkrantz."

"Yeah."

"So it must have been a divorce job?"

I smiled but didn't say anything.

"You sure you can't tell me?"

"Not unless you can make me understand what it has to do with this murder."

"How can I do that unless I know what the job was?"

"I guess you can't."

He squinted at me then and bit down on his cigar. "The tech get your prints?"

"You've got them on file."

He nodded. "You can go then. Just don't leave town, the usual story."

"I'll be right where you expect to find me."

"Yeah, well. Good night."

"Good morning, detective." We shook hands. I went out the screen door into the chill of the morning. The sky was starting to show purple at the edges, like a bruise. I'd be able to see the sunrise if I could find a place to watch it from.

My car had the bottled-up smell of sweat and stale smoke. I rolled down the windows to let in the cool air while it lasted, and started the engine. I had been hired to babysit a paranoid prima donna, and I had ended up finding a dead woman cut almost to pieces. For some reason, I felt as though I hadn't done a very good job.

I could at least try to make up for it. I pulled away from the curb and instead of heading back to Hollywood I took the turn at Montgomery.

TEN

The Rosenkrantz house looked undisturbed. I parked in the same spot I had the night before and killed the engine. The police would have to make a stop here later to get Rosenkrantz's testimony, but they weren't here yet. I got out of my car and walked up the middle of the road to the house. At the end of the drive, the garage doors were open and both the tan Buick and the maroon LaSalle were in their spots. I could check the house for signs of forced entry, but I didn't see the need. It was just a sleeping house in a sleeping neighborhood. There was nothing to see and no one had missed me. I went back to my car and leaned against the hood as I lit a cigarette. It took three tries to get the match going.

The Mexican arrived on foot just before seven wearing the same ill-fitting hand-me-down jacket of the day before. He saw me and came over.

"How was your night?" he said.

"Hot."

"Mine too."

We both let the silence take a turn. "My name's Miguel, by the way." He nodded toward the house. "I've got the dayshift now. You don't have to wait around."

"I'm just finishing my cigarette," I said, and took a drag.

He turned and crossed the street, on his way to his little castle where he got to protect the princess and there was trouble around every corner. I watched him go around to the back of the house. I waited another ten minutes to make sure he didn't come back out again with news of some tragedy, or at least a tragedy I didn't already know about. He didn't. The cops still hadn't shown up either. I finished my cigarette, got in my car, and pulled away.

In Hollywood, I stopped outside of the Olmstead without putting my car away in the garage. My apartment was just one big room with a private bathroom and a small kitchenette in a closet. I had done what I could to give each corner of the room its own purpose. There was a Formica table with two chrome chairs just outside the open kitchenette closet. There was a twin bed with a standing lamp and a night table just outside of the bathroom. There was my one good reading chair with another standing lamp and a stack of books on the floor over in the third corner. The only window was in the bathroom and it was made of pebbled glass.

I took three fingers of bourbon before my shower and another three after. I looked at the time and thought I ought to be hungry, so I went out again and stopped at a counter diner I liked and ordered a couple of scrambled eggs, hash browns, bacon, some well-burnt toast, and coffee, but the whole time I was working on it, I was thinking of a girl with her neck open and her thighs gouged out. I got down about half of my breakfast and left a good tip. I picked up the morning papers outside, but there was nothing in either of them about the Ehrhardt killing. It must have gotten called in too late.

The lobby of the Blackstone Building was empty. I took the automatic elevator up to the third floor. The hallway there was empty, too, and I was willing to bet that my office's unlocked waiting room would be empty as well. I was wrong. It had two too many people in it.

Benny Sturgeon stood as I came in, his hat held in both hands in front of his stomach like a shield. He was tall, but no taller than me. Up close there were flecks of white in his hair that made him look distinguished instead of aged. He wore a pair of glasses with circular frames that I had not seen on the set the day before. He was in shirtsleeves and a vest, and there were deep lines across his forehead and at the corners of his mouth.

Al Knox was already on his feet, pacing, a lit cigarette in one hand. His eyelids were heavy and his shoulders tilted forward as though his back couldn't support the weight of his stomach. He looked exactly like a man who had been woken early in the morning with bad news. I looked over at the standing ashtray covered in a fine layer of dust and saw that there was only one new butt. He hadn't been there too long.

"Now, Mr. Foster—" Sturgeon began.

"Dennis," Knox said.

"Mr. Foster, I must insist on seeing you first," Sturgeon started in again. He spoke with the conviction of a man used to giving orders that are obeyed. Only the way he held his hat ruined the effect. "I've come with a job of the utmost importance. It's imperative that we act right away."

I quieted him with a look I only took out on special occasions. "Al first, then you."

I stepped across to the inner door, unlocked it, and let Al into my office. I went around to my side of the desk and he sat down on one of the two straight-backed chairs on the other side. His lip curled.

"You're a bastard, you know that?"

I raised both my hands. "Al, I was following a legitimate lead…"

"They want Rose for it."

"What?" I felt as though someone had cut the cables on the elevator I was riding in.

"They want Chloë Rose for Mandy Ehrhardt's murder."

"Who do?"

"The cops. Who do you think?"

I leaned forward in my chair. "Al, I was at the scene. That was no woman's killing. Certainly not a woman of Chloë Rose's size. Can't the studio quash it?"

Al shook his head and ran a hand along his cheek, letting it slide off his chin. "She had the motive. Ehrhardt was sleeping with her husband. And thanks to you she doesn't have an alibi, but her husband does. The mayor doesn't like that the press says the SAPD turns a blind eye to the movie people. They don't like it in Harbor City much either. They're going to make an example of this one. There's no way they would convict a woman with Rose's looks, or one as famous as her—she's not even a citizen, for Christ's sake. So the press will feel they can ride it as hard as they want without anybody getting seriously hurt."

"Except for Mandy Ehrhardt, whose real killer walks away."

"And Chloë Rose's career, and the studio's bank account."

I sat back in my chair and lit a cigarette. "What do you mean she's not a citizen? She's married to Rosenkrantz, isn't she?"

"Resident alien. They met when he and his first wife were living in France. You ever hear how old she was?"

"How old?"

"The official story is eighteen. Unofficially, I've heard everything from seventeen to fifteen."

"So what? She's over eighteen now."

"So everything. It's all going to come out, how old she was or wasn't, and that story about what happened to her with some prison guard…"

"What prison guard?"

Knox waved a hand angrily. "I don't know, it's all rumors, but they're pretty nasty rumors. Mix that in with a murder trial here and see what you get. I'm telling you, there's plenty to feed the headlines for weeks. Months, maybe."

I shook my head, trying to reconcile the small, vulnerable, beautiful woman I'd seen the day before with the brutal mutilation and killing I had come across that morning. "It's all circumstantial."

"That's all they need. She's not supposed to hang for it. They make a big splash of her arrest, and if it never gets to a conviction, who cares? Only, we do care. We care plenty."

I just shook my head again.

"You really screwed up," Knox said.

"You came over just to tell me that in person?"

"That, and this: You're fired." He reached into the inside pocket of his jacket, and pulled out an envelope. He tossed it on the desk. I left it there untouched.

He shook his head sadly. "I'm sorry, Dennis, I know we go way back, but—"

"You can skip the old friends bit. I heard it yesterday. I didn't like it then, and I like it even less now."

"Fine. Then just take the money and be glad you're not in deeper than you are." He mashed out his cigarette in my ashtray and stood up. He pointed at the door. "And if Sturgeon tries to get you to—"

"Oh, don't worry. I'm off the case."

At the door, Knox turned back with his hand on the knob. "We're not public servants anymore, Foster. We're not supposed to deal with this stuff anymore."

"We all serve someone," I said.

"I wish like hell I knew who you thought you were serving last night," he said. And he left the office, leaving the door open to the reception room, and slamming the outside door to the hall.

ELEVEN

I would have liked a moment to collect my thoughts before dealing with Sturgeon, but he was already in the open doorway. His hat was in one hand down at his side now. He had his chest out with his chin raised in a caricature of defiance. He was directing himself and he had lost the ability to realize he was hamming it up. When he started, his tone was stern. "Mr. Foster, I have a job for you."

I indicated the chairs across my desk. He sat on the one Knox hadn't.

"I assume Mr. Knox told you that they suspect Chloë of…" He took a deep breath. "Of what happened to Mandy."

I still had half a cigarette left, and I drew on it. "He did. What's that done to the picture?" I asked. "You're not filming today?"

He watched me smoke, but it was unclear if his expression was distaste or desire. I didn't offer him one. "With Mandy's death, and this business with the police and Chloë…I was forced to suspend filming for the morning. I'm shooting B-reel this afternoon."

"So the movie'll go on?"

"Mandy's parts were mostly finished. We'll just get Shem to rewrite the few remaining scenes, and it should be fine."

"You mean Mr. Rosenkrantz, whose lover was killed last night, and whose wife is suspected of the killing. I'm sure he'll be eager to get to a typewriter."

His face showed his distaste. "Yes, I mean Shem Rosenkrantz.

Now, what's with all the questions? I came to hire you. Don't you want me to let you know what the job is?"

I went on. "It must be a relief to you, that the picture will still get finished. You need this movie, don't you? Your career depends on it. Or was I misinformed?"

"What are you suggesting?"

"I'm not suggesting anything. Only that you have a pretty good reason not to want Chloë Rose to be on the hook for Miss Ehrhardt's murder. Especially if you were finished with Miss Ehrhardt anyway."

He stood. "I'm repulsed by your implication."

"What was my implication?" I said. "I must have missed it." Then I gave him the five-dollar smile.

Grudgingly he sat back down. "Don't you want to at least hear about the job?"

"You want me to prove that Chloë Rose did not kill Mandy Ehrhardt."

He tilted his head and gave a single downward nod. "That is correct."

"Well, I'm sorry, but I can't," I said.

"You can't? Mr. Foster, you're part of the reason she's in this mess, don't you want to get her out of it?"

"I just promised your chief of security that I was off this case. I don't want it anyway."

"Knox made you promise not to take my case?"

"Knox didn't make me do anything," I said, standing. "This whole thing was wrong from the start. All of you Hollywood people may be used to using each other like props, but I'm not a prop. I'm an honest guy trying to make a living. This story doesn't need me. My part was written out."

"You can't allow Chloë to have her career ruined, her life—"

"Skip it. Your picture'll get finished, and it'll even make a few extra dollars because it's got a dead ingénue in it. So don't start crying crocodile tears. My answer is no. Now if you don't mind."

He tried to push his chest out again, but it didn't work with me standing over him. He got up himself, to even things out. "I do mind," he said. "I'm willing to pay you quite a bit of money." He started fumbling at his pocket, at last coming up with a tan goatskin billfold. He took out a handful of bills.

I waved them away. "If you don't put that away, I might have to do something we'll both regret."

He stood there with the money in his outstretched hand just long enough to feel foolish. He put it away with one quick motion.

I picked up the envelope Knox had left on my desk and went over to the safe with it. "Had Miss Ehrhardt been in many other pictures?" I asked, just to be saying something.

"No, this would have been her first one, other than a few jobs as an extra."

I nodded as though that meant something to me, deposited the envelope in the safe, and locked it. Then I went over to the door and gestured for him to vacate my office. "You're welcome to use the reception room, but I've got work here."

He regarded me for a moment, deflated, and then stepped by me as though I were wet paint he had to worry about getting on his clothes. I pushed the door shut and locked it.

I listened, waiting for his exit. After a minute, I heard the outer door open and his footsteps grow faint in the hall. I could just make out the chime of the elevator when it arrived.

I looked around my office. I didn't have a damn thing to do. If I sat around long enough, maybe a client would come in, a fat heiress with a kidnapped dog, or a kid sister looking for her missing brother.

I hadn't decided about the check in the safe yet. It felt dirty
to me. Studios didn't usually hire private investigators to follow
their stars. The stars might themselves, but not the studio. And
with the murder added in, the whole thing seemed like a setup
to me. But who was getting set up? The obvious answer fell too
close to home, but I couldn't figure it. There would have been
no way to predict that I would have ended up in Harbor City
last night at all. Something was wrong with this thing, and I
wasn't going to figure out what standing around here.

I paced over to the safe and then back.

It's none of your business, Foster. You got paid off to let it drop.

Yeah, but the patsy costume doesn't quite fit right. It's too tight
in the neck. And I'm not actually paid until I cash their check.

You're a damn fool, Foster.

That one I had no answer to. The only kinds of people in this
business were fools who could admit it and fools who couldn't.
I could admit it, but it didn't change what I was.

I started to unlock the door, but before the knob turned, the
phone on my desk rang. I hesitated a moment, not eager to add
whatever headache was on the phone to the ones I had been
handed in the last five hours. But it rang again, insistent and
impossible to ignore. I went back to my desk, and watched it
ring a third time. I picked up from the client's side of the desk.

"Foster."

"Mr. Foster, we met yesterday." The voice was deep and
charming and expertly controlled. "Do you know who I am?"

"I met a lot of people yesterday," I said. "So many that some
aren't even alive today."

"This thing with Mandy is horrible," the voice said and I
thought it sounded almost sincere. But who was I to judge?
Maybe he was really shaken. Maybe he'd cried all morning.

"It's also keeping me busy. What do you want, Mr. Stark?'

"You do remember me! I suppose remembering people is important in your line of work." He paused to give me a chance to reply, but I didn't say anything. How many people forgot meeting John Stark? He went on, "I'm calling because Greg Taylor is missing. My…kitchen help. He answered the door for you yesterday."

"Yeah, I remember him too."

"I'm calling to see if you think you could find him. But you say you're busy…"

"How long has he been missing? He was there yesterday afternoon."

"Since shortly after you left. We had a fight, you see. He didn't like how you'd treated him and he thought I should have defended him better. Or that was the excuse for the fight. It had been almost two months since our last quarrel. It was bound to happen sooner rather than later. Anyway, he left, stayed away all night. He'll do that, but he always comes back in the morning. And with this thing with Mandy…I'm worried."

Now he sounded it.

"Why don't you go to the police? I'm sure for you they won't notice that it hasn't been twenty-four hours. They have a whole operation for this kind of thing."

"When Greg goes off like this, a lot of the things he does are not strictly legal. If he were in a compromising situation, I wouldn't want the police to be the ones who find him…"

Knox wanted me off the Rose/Ehrhardt case, and anything I had had in mind to do there was going to be strictly on my own time. Things weren't so good that I could turn away business.

Stark spoke into the silence, "I'd rather not go into more details over the phone."

"Of course you wouldn't," I said. "I take it you can't come to my office?"

"I was hoping you would come here."

"Right."

"They'll expect you at the door," he said, and he hung up.

Everyone wanted to keep me in this movie business. Everyone but the person who got me into it in the first place. I went through the routine with the lock and took the stairs so I wouldn't have to wait for the automatic elevator.

TWELVE

A proper butler opened the door at Stark's this time. He was bald with a horseshoe of hair around the back of his head, a pencil mustache, and a tuxedo with white gloves. He led the way across the marble entry hall, back through the same set of rooms I had seen the day before, and out onto the same verandah where Stark was in the same position. He was reading a different script, though, because only a few pages of this one had been turned back. Or maybe he was rereading his lines.

"He hasn't come back," he said, and tried his million-dollar smile, but his face looked pinched, and his eyes were afraid. He set the script down. "You will find him, won't you?"

"I charge twenty-five dollars a day plus expenses and I get one hundred dollars up front as a retainer."

His face lost any pretense now. He was very troubled. "That won't be a problem. That doesn't matter. He doesn't even need to come back. I just want to know that he's all right."

"You said he's done this before when you've fought. Where did he go?"

"He never gave me specifics. That was part of our unspoken arrangement. He could go on an occasional bender but we would act as though it hadn't happened. I know that he would get high, shoot up."

"H?"

"Morphine, I think. Maybe it was heroin. His eyes were always glassy. Sometimes he'd end up with bruises on the insides of his arms. He's very delicate."

"Any friends, family he might have gone to?"

"I don't think so. Definitely no family. Greg isn't from San Angelo. Maybe friends, but I never met any. I know he would go to the Blacklight, Choices, all those Market clubs. If he was feeling lucky, maybe the Tip. He knew people who went there."

"Who?"

"Well, me, for one."

The Tip was Gilplaine's club. Of course it had to be the Tip. I didn't know the other places, but I wasn't the type who would know them. "Clubs close. He would have had to sleep somewhere."

"I told you. We never spoke about details."

"Do you have a photo of him?"

"No."

There was a sound at the door and I turned to find Vera Merton standing there in a bright red blouse with an oriental pattern and a muted red skirt that stopped just before the tops of her brown calfskin high-heeled boots.

"I step out for a moment, and I miss everything."

She touched my shoulder as she went past me and I caught the scent of cinnamon and cloves. She went around Stark's chair and settled herself in the one beside him, putting her boots up on the wicker ottoman.

"This is Mr. Foster," Stark said. "He's here about Greg."

She smiled, and her smile had no concern dampening it at all. "I think maybe we saw one another yesterday. Is that right?"

"Yes," I said.

She bit her lower lip and then said, "This has been a horrible

horrible day." It sounded like the sort of thing she might say on a day when it rained too much.

Stark said, "I know that I'm not giving you very much information, but it's all I've got. I met Greg when he was nearly just off the bus and since then he's been living here. He didn't have much of a life outside of the house."

"And you never went out in public with him," I said.

He stiffened and said, "Not never. But rarely. I'm sure you'll understand, and you'll understand why this matter has to be kept private. If the studio hired you, I know you can be trusted."

"The studio doesn't feel that way this morning. I was the one who found Mandy Ehrhardt."

Miss Merton winced, almost as though she were remembering the ghastly scene herself.

Stark said, "I didn't know."

"Why would you have?" I said.

"Was it awful?" Miss Merton said, and now her face was pale and her voice unsteady.

"It always is," I said.

"Hey, Johnny," a man called from inside, and then appeared at the entrance to the porch. He was tall with dark hair, wearing dress pants and shirtsleeves, very neat, but the back of his shirt wasn't tucked in all of the way. He stopped short when he saw me, and ran his hand through his hair. I'd seen him yesterday, too.

"Tommy, this is Mr. Foster," Miss Merton said. "He's a private eye. Daddy hired him to look after Chloë."

"Oh?" Tommy said.

"But now I'm working for Mr. Stark," I said.

"John," Stark said, almost on reflex. "Please."

"Smashing," Tommy said. Up close, his breath carried a hint of gin on it as he exhaled. "I hope it all works out." He darted glances at each of us in turn. "Well, everybody...I need to see a man about a horse." And he gave a little bow with his head. As he walked, he faced backwards, pointing at Stark. "Don't you go anywhere, Johnny. We need to talk." Then he slipped inside the house.

"Is he always like that this early in the morning?" I said.

"What do you mean?" Miss Merton said.

"You know what I mean."

"Excuse me," Stark said. We both looked at him. "Can't we please get back to Greg? I'm concerned that he might have done something to hurt himself. With drugs or..." He shook his head and made a distasteful face. "I just want to make sure he's safe."

"And to get him to come back."

"If he wants to," Stark said. "But finding him is what matters. At least you've seen Greg, which is a place to start from."

"If you'll allow me to be blunt, John, that's nothing to start from. And if you'll allow me to be even blunter, all you've given me is that he's a queer dope user. Well, I guess that narrows it down a little."

"There's no need to be nasty," Stark said, and he seemed genuinely hurt.

"I'm not being nasty, I'm just making sure I've got the facts since it seems some of them have only been implied and I don't want to work from the wrong implication."

Stark nodded. "You have the facts right."

I said nothing.

Miss Merton said, "So where will you start?" The color had come back into her face.

"I'll start with the crime blotters to make sure he wasn't picked up on a charge or thrown in the drunk tank or any other reason that the police might have gotten involved."

"I should have thought of that," Stark said.

"You wouldn't have gotten anywhere and might have caused yourself some embarrassment. I can call people I know and can keep your name out of it. If those calls are a washout, well, I suppose I can try Hub Gilplaine. He and I are old friends these days."

Stark nodded. He looked satisfied. "Potts can give you a check on the way out."

"Don't worry about it. I know you're good for it."

There was an awkward silence in which Stark looked out at his lawn, Miss Merton looked at her feet, and I watched the two of them.

"You're sure there's nothing more you can give me?" I said.

He shook his head.

"I'll call you when I've got something to report. It might not be today."

Stark looked up, shocked. "What if he's on the street?"

"It's warm out," I said. "You do understand, you've given me basically nothing to go on."

He returned his gaze to the horizon. "Of course," he said.

Miss Merton said, "We're all just so shaken by Mandy Ehrhardt's death."

Maybe she was and maybe she wasn't. Stark was shaken all right, and probably had cried all morning, but not over Mandy Ehrhardt.

I left them to commiserate, and let myself back into the house. The butler met me before I got out of the music room.

"Is there anything you require?" he said.

I didn't stop, and he fell in beside me. "Is Mr. Stark good friends with Miss Merton and her brother?" He didn't answer at first and I could see him try to think of a way to reply. I turned to him. We were in the main entrance. There were blinding patches of white on the marble floor in line with the windows. "Mr. Stark just hired me to find Greg Taylor. I think that he would want his staff to be cooperative, so that I can conduct my investigation."

The butler still hesitated, but said, "Yes, Mr. and Miss Merton are regular guests here. Their father, too. Many people from the studio are."

"They would all have known Mr. Taylor?"

"Yes."

"How about you? How well did you know Mr. Taylor?"

A disdainful expression came over his face. "We were hardly fraternal," the butler said.

"Of course," I said, and walked away from him, my shoes echoing in the hall.

THIRTEEN

I was just getting into my car when the front door opened again. "Mr. Foster!" Vera Merton ran on her tiptoes like a ballerina. "Wait."

I waited and she stopped short on the other side of the car. If she had been upset inside, she didn't show it now.

"Mr. Foster," she said, and then decided that she didn't like having the Packard between us. She came around to my side, the better to show me her legs. They were lovely legs. She could have been in pictures. Nobody would have complained about paying to look at her. She pulled at her lip and put her eyes in their corners so they weren't on me. Indecision didn't look natural on her.

"Am I supposed to guess what you want or are you going to tell me?"

"I just can't stop thinking about Mandy Ehrhardt," she said. "Do you have any ideas? About who did it?"

"I haven't been asked to have any. In fact, quite the opposite."

"How'd you come to find the—her?" Her eyes darted to my face and then went back to their corners.

"About the same way I found you and your brother yesterday. I just happened along at the wrong moment."

This time her eyes went right to mine. She tried to cover her nervousness with a smile. "So you weren't supposed to be, I don't know, following Mandy, or something?"

"Didn't you just get finished listening to Mr. Stark talk about how respectful I am of people's privacy?"

"Yes, but Daddy would want you to tell me. It's all right."

"If that's how he feels about it, he can tell me."

"Well, what were you doing at the studio yesterday?" she tried.

"I knew then, but I don't know now."

She pouted. "You're making this very difficult."

I gave her a knowing grin. "Sorry."

"I know that Daddy hired you yesterday and I know that you found Mandy's body. I'm just trying to understand." She paused for a second and decided she needed to add something to that. "It's all so horrible."

"Look, Miss Merton. I was hired by Al Knox, the head of security at the studio. If you want to take this up with Al, go ahead, but I've got work to do." To make it convincing, I should have gotten in my car, but I didn't.

She took a step closer and reached out to play with my tie. "You don't like me, is that it?"

We both watched her hand toy with the silk.

"You think my family are awful people."

"Miss Merton, I don't think of your family at all."

"Not even now?" She had found more inches to eliminate between us. Her perfume made me think of homemade cookies, which soured both her and the cookies.

"I'm trying harder to forget your family every minute."

"I just worry about Tommy. And Daddy," she said. "They need a woman around but all they've got is me, which isn't much of anything."

"You're definitely a woman."

She raised her head the right angle. "I knew you could say nice things."

"I can say all kinds of things."

"Why did Daddy hire you? Was it about Tommy? You can tell me."

"I told you before, your father didn't hire me, Al Knox did. If you think your father was behind it, you'd better go ask him. Whatever you and your brother do is no concern of mine. Though from what I've seen, your brother does altogether too much of whatever it is he does."

She stepped back then, all of her charm withdrawn. "How come you found Mandy?"

"It was an accident. It had nothing to do with anything."

"That's the best you can do?"

"I could do better, but you wouldn't like it."

She screwed herself up to say something more, but thought better of it and walked back to the house instead. She was a girl too used to getting what she wanted. Knox had warned me about her and her brother the day before, and now I could appreciate better what he'd meant. Poor Daddy. Running a movie studio wasn't all it was cracked up to be. You might give people orders, but that didn't mean your kids wouldn't run all over town getting into trouble. In fact, it probably ensured it.

I got into my car and rolled down the hill again. This missing person job seemed like only slightly more of a case than protecting Chloë Rose. It must have been my advertising: give me your money, no satisfaction guaranteed.

FOURTEEN

I was too close to the Rosenkrantz house to resist a visit. The way I figured it, I was owed the audience with Chloë Rose that I had been denied the night before. Knox may have thought that he could just throw me off of this thing, but the police wouldn't let me go that easily. With my name already in, it was for my own good that I meet the other person at the center of the storm. Anyway, Chloë Rose and Stark were co-stars, perhaps she knew Taylor, too.

Soso in mid-morning was a collection of geysers and waterfalls sprinkling the various lawns. It was the Rosenkrantzes' front lawn and flowerbeds that got the treatment this morning, requiring me to run a gauntlet to the front door. I timed it so I got the minimum shower. A faint shimmering rainbow appeared on the outer edge of the fan of water. It held a beautiful mystique, but collapsed before it could be properly admired, and then threatened to damage my suit a moment later.

I glanced back. There was a car parked out front. It was unmarked, but it said police anyway. It didn't fit with the neighborhood.

The door again opened before I could ring the bell. This time it was Detective Samuels and another plainclothes cop. Miguel was visible beyond them, wringing his hands like an old maid.

"Don't you sleep, Foster?" Samuels said.

"No, I'm a vampire, didn't I tell you."

"Vampires can't go out during the day," the other cop said.

"Go on, you know all about it," I said.

The other cop looked away, embarrassed.

"I know you're not here about that murder," Samuels said. "Right?"

"You know, I heard a funny story about that," I said. "It had something to do with Chloë Rose being a suspect in your investigation. It was so ridiculous it made me laugh." I showed him how it made me laugh.

He was unimpressed. "This is a police investigation. You played it straight with me this morning, and I'm grateful for that. But I don't want any private dicks chasing my tail."

"And I'll do whatever I need to, to protect my client." If I could get her to be my client.

"Except provide her with an alibi. You still claim it wasn't a divorce job?"

"I don't do divorce."

Samuels cocked his head to his partner. "Come on, McEvoy. We've got work."

They waited for the sprinkler to finish its cycle, and then hurried down the wet path to their car.

Miguel came forward to stand in the doorframe. He greeted me like a long-lost cousin, stopping just short of giving me a hug. "That was the police," he said.

"I hadn't noticed. Were any others here?"

He shook his head. "No, just those two."

"When did they get here?"

"Maybe an hour ago. Maybe a little more. They talked to both Mr. Rosenkrantz and Miss Rose."

"About what?" I said.

He averted his eyes. "I wouldn't know. They were private conversations."

"You can skip that bit. What did they say?"

He bobbed his head to show his reluctance, but then opened up as though he couldn't wait to tell somebody. "About a murder. Another actress in Miss Rose's movie was killed. They asked Mr. Rosenkrantz about his relationship with this actress, when he had seen her last, did she have any enemies, was she afraid of anything."

"Sure, I know the drill. And Miss Rose?"

He shook his head. "They kept asking her where she was last night. They would talk about something else, and then they would ask her again if she was sure she had been here the whole time, and had she made any phone calls, and had nobody seen her? She got very upset. She had to lie down. What about you, Mr. Foster? Where were you last night?"

"Out gambling. Where can I find Miss Rose?"

He waited. I started around him. He thought about trying to stop me, but it was only a thought. Instead he led the way. We took the squared arch to the right, entering a dining room with a heavy wooden baroque dining set. We went through a door on the opposite side into a poorly lit antechamber in which hung a portrait daguerreotype of a cat. This opened into the library, which was arranged like a sitting room with Louis XV loveseats facing each other over a delicate Chippendale table. The fireplace was large enough to stand in, but it didn't look like it had been used anytime during the current administration. The built-in shelves housed richly bound volumes in matching sets. Everything in the room looked like it belonged in a museum.

Chloë Rose was on the loveseat facing the entryway when I came in. If Vera Merton was one kind of woman, then this was the other. She had the kind of beauty that made you nervous you were going to do something that would break it. She wore no makeup, and her eyes were red from crying. She had on a simple navy ankle-length skirt and a white-on-white patterned blouse.

I took off my hat, and gave her a moment to collect herself.

"Your colleagues were just here," she said. Her accent was faint but it was there.

"I'm not the police, Miss Rose. I'm the private investigator that was hired to protect you yesterday." I got out one of my cards. She made no motion to take it, so I left it for her on the corner of the table.

"So you know," she said.

"I found the body."

Her tears threatened to fall again, but she held them back. "They said you were supposed to be here last night. It seems that the fact that you weren't is not in my favor just now."

"No, it's not," I said.

"Shem and Mandy were sleeping together. It wasn't any secret. Everyone knew."

"It didn't bother you?"

She looked at me with eyes that were suddenly indignant. "Of course it did. It killed me. But what could I do?"

"You could have left him."

"Oh, it's so easy for a stranger to stand there and say I should have left him. You come in and you know: leave him!"

"I didn't say you should have, I said you could have. And I didn't say it was easy."

She collapsed back on the loveseat again. "What does it matter? Mandy killed. Why does any of it matter?"

"I hope that's not what you told the police," I said.

She shook her head, her voice growing pinched again. "No. They just wanted to know where I had been, over and over. I said here. But I can't prove it. I'm a suspect in a murder. Oh, God! I thought I was finished with the police. Finished with prisons, finished with the police, a new life here in the saint's city."

She sounded as though she was just barely keeping hysteria at bay. I remembered Al Knox's original description. And now I could see the capacity for panic, for melancholy. I took a step forward, but resisted the urge to put a hand on her shoulder. "You're not going to be arrested. We just need to figure out what really happened. Then you'll be in the clear."

She looked up at me and it was almost as though she noticed me for the first time. "Mr. Foster? What do you want? What are you doing here?"

"Protecting myself as much as you. The studio fired me this morning. I don't know which of us is being set up here, or maybe it's both of us, but I needed to talk to you before figuring out what to do next."

She looked frightened. "I don't know what you're talking about."

"Don't worry," I said. "That's my job, not yours. Can you tell me what's this about prisons, and police? Is it connected to something that happened to you in France...?"

I thought she was going to start crying again, but the spell had passed. Now her delivery was cold, her accent heavier than when she had been taking pains to control it. "My father was a safecracker." She rubbed the heel of one palm against her eyes as she spoke, first the left, then the right. "He was killed in prison many years ago."

"The police questioned you about his death?"

She turned her look on me. "It was many years ago."

All the same, I could see how it could play into Samuels'

circumstantial case, if she'd been questioned once about another murder. But I didn't say anything about that to her. "There's nothing you could do to document your time last night?"

"I was asleep in bed," she said.

"Your husband's son? He's staying with you, isn't he?"

"Shem sent him back east yesterday afternoon, before all of this."

"The neighbors, then? Maybe they could confirm you never went out."

"They could say they saw my car still here, but there was enough traffic on the street last night, no one could say I didn't get a ride. Anyway, our nearest neighbors were out late to a gala."

It was still all circumstantial. They didn't have the murder weapon, they couldn't have her prints in Ehrhardt's house, and they didn't have a witness. But people went to jail on circumstantial evidence. They certainly went to trial.

I had another idea. "Let's go back to the man you thought was following you. Was Miss Ehrhardt always there too, when you saw him? You told Al it was usually on the studio lot, right?"

She looked frightened and the pitch of her voice went up. "Why does that matter?"

"Because maybe the man following you was also following her."

She knitted her brow in thought, shaking her head back and forth. "I couldn't say, not for sure. Probably yes, she was there, but…" Back and forth, back and forth. "I don't know about at the first fitting. And I thought there might be someone following my car once or twice; I was alone then." The memory seemed to trouble her. Her eyes were wide now with fear. She shook her head even faster.

"Miss Rose?"

She sat up rigid. "No, it couldn't be that he was following Mandy. He's following me."

"Don't get excited."

"No, no, no."

I reached for her, but before I could get to her Miguel was there with a drink on a tray. "Try this, Miss Rose. Try this."

He managed to get the glass into her hand, and she raised it mechanically, still shaking her head. The liquor went in, she shuddered, and fell back. Miguel grabbed the glass from her hand before the last sip could spill. He looked at me, imploring, and then left the room with the tray tucked under his arm and the glass in his hand.

"You don't have more on the description of that man," I said, a fighter kicking his opponent when he's down.

She said nothing.

"Okey," I said. "I'll show myself out."

That didn't get any reaction either. She just lay there, collapsed, her beautiful face miserable in a way that the public never got to see on screen. It was disconcerting, like seeing the skull beneath the skin.

I made my way back to the front hall. Miguel was waiting for me.

"You see how fragile Miss Rose is?"

"Yeah, I see. Did she pull the same act with the police?"

"Nearly."

"Samuels can't want her for this. He'd see right away she's no good for it. Unless he tries to play her as crazy." It was my turn to shake my head. "Listen, I didn't get a chance to ask Miss Rose. Are she and John Stark close? Would she know his friends?"

"Not that I know of. Miss Rose keeps to herself."

I nodded. "Thanks." I put on my hat and took a step towards the door. "Call me if there's an emergency. I'm not wanted here otherwise."

"Actually, Mr. Rosenkrantz would like to see you."

I turned back. "And how would Mr. Rosenkrantz know I was here?"

"He saw you come in." He indicated the stairs and said, "If you'll allow me."

I thought about how it was really not my business. I thought about how little I had to go on. I thought about how the studio and the police had told me to clear out and stay clear.

"Lead the way," I said.

FIFTEEN

The room was supposed to be a study, but the same person who decorated Hub Gilplaine's office had decorated this room too. Every visible surface except for a small path from the door to the desk was covered in books and papers. There were unfinished shelves screwed into the length of one wall, bowing under the weight of the books piled on them. One shelf had ripped out of the wall and fallen onto the books on the shelf beneath it. That one only held because of the piles of books on the floor propping it up from below. The papers were strewn about in inelegant stacks, the edges curling. There appeared to be a green imitation-leather easy chair in one of the corners, but there was no way to get to it now. By comparison, the surface of the desk was relatively tidy, dominated as it was by an Underwood typewriter. There was a bottle of vodka that had had a good deal of its contents acquainted with a glass, and an already empty bottle on the floor beside the desk chair. The place smelled of alcohol and old paper.

Rosenkrantz turned to face me. He looked pale and his eyes were dilated, but he had no trouble sitting up straight or tracking me. When he spoke, it was surprisingly clear, the sign of a practiced drinker. "You followed me from the Carrot-Top," he said.

It didn't require an answer so I didn't give him one.

"You saw what they did…"

"What who did?" I said.

"This goddamn life. This goddamn city. These goddamn people."

For a great writer, he seemed awfully hung up on one word. "Had she any enemies?" I asked.

He looked up again. "What are you, the police? They were already here."

"Okey. Then what did you want to see me about?"

"They say Clotilde did it."

"They do."

"She didn't."

"I know."

He nodded, satisfied with the work that had been done so far. We had who didn't do it established beyond a doubt. He shook his head as he reached for the bottle and brought it to the rim of his empty glass. He didn't have any trouble with the maneuver. "Mandy didn't have any enemies. No one she'd fought with. Nobody she was scared of. Nobody who cared either way."

"Friends?"

"I know that she made friends with a few of the girls that worked in the club where she was waitressing, but just to go out and have a laugh with. Maybe some of the valets too. She was new to San Angelo."

"And the name of the club?"

He lowered his head and looked at me out of the tops of his eyes.

"The Carrot-Top."

"No, but close enough. The Tip. That's where I met her."

"You said you could put her in movies."

He shrugged, raising his glass in a toast. "And I actually did." He drank the whole thing down in two gulps.

"I guess there's a first for everything," I said.

He raised his empty glass again. "Hear, hear."

"Well this is lots of fun. You could probably charge a door fee. You might need to share the alcohol though."

"She was a swell kid, Foster. I didn't love her. In fact we fought just as much as we laughed. But she could really lay into you, and always made it good afterward. She was a swell kid."

"Sure. And she had a heart of gold. And she never would hurt a fly."

His face clouded and he looked up at me. "Ah, go to hell." He grabbed the bottle for a refill.

"Should I send Miguel up with another bottle?"

"Why weren't you here last night doing your job!"

"I know my place," I said. "I know I'm not supposed to say, why weren't you here with your wife, or why weren't you at Miss Ehrhardt's place to protect her. Because if we always ask ourselves why then pretty soon we can make anything our fault."

"Especially when it is."

I nodded. "Then too."

He sneered and shook his head. "God, the people in this town will cut your throat and tell you they're giving you a shave. They're not people, even. They're money, with no eyes and no heart, or they're raw desire hidden behind bulletproof glass. You can see them, but you can't touch them. Either you go through the system until you're just money, too, or you find out that your bulletproof glass wasn't as bulletproof as advertised. If at any point you remember you're a person, you better watch out, you're halfway on the bus home."

"I hate to interrupt the great American man of letters while he's being insightful, but you'll have to excuse me."

"You'll go and talk to Hub now, won't you?"

"I'm no longer working this case."

"That's why you came here. Because you're no longer working on it."

"Just some matters I wanted to tie up."

He considered me for a moment. "When you go see Hub, ask him about Janice Stoneman." He waited for me to write it down. I didn't. He refilled his glass and downed it without preliminaries, then sat staring at it. "Huh." He looked up from his empty glass. "In my books, the characters always have a moment of realization, some object or event that crystallizes their very being. Not the trash I write for Gilplaine, my real books. But who really recognizes the moment that his life changes? At the time, I mean. Maybe later, but not at the time." He shook his head and sighed. "I was wrong, what I told you a minute ago. It would be bad enough if it was those Hollywood bastards that cut your throat. But no, you cut your own throat. Up until the moment it's done, it's not done, but once it is done…" He opened his hand in front of him as though letting a lightning bug go.

"Tell Hub I don't ever want to see him again." He picked up the bottle, but I didn't wait for him to refill his glass.

Downstairs, there was no sign of Miguel. Miss Rose must have required his further assistance. If I'd been smart, I would have counted myself lucky that my own assistance was no longer required. But like the man said, you don't know you're holding the razor until after it's too late.

SIXTEEN

It was a little after noon. The Tip served lunch, but Gilplaine probably didn't come in until mid-afternoon; part of his job was to be seen by the night people. I stopped at the lunch counter in the hotel across from the Blackstone and had a melted cheese sandwich with a slice of bacon as its backbone. The coffee had grounds in it, but I drank it anyway. The mid-day paper was out and there was now a small piece buried on the last page of section one, no more than four inches, about a waitress killed in Harbor City. I wondered how Rosenkrantz would take that. They cut your throat even after they've cut your throat.

Back in my office, I picked up the phone while walking around the desk to my chair. There were any number of cops I could call to look over the morning report for me, some who might even do it. But if I was going to end up in Harbor City again, it was best to maintain good relations. Samuels picked up on the third ring. "Shouldn't you be out investigating something?"

"Who's this?"

"Foster. I was wondering if you could give me a little information."

"Try the operator. I'm busy."

"You get a chance to glance over the morning report? It's out already, isn't it?"

"You think I have time for that kind of thing? I'm working a murder. What are you doing? I told you to cool it."

"New case. Missing person. Wanted to relieve you of any concern about my intentions with regard to your murder."

"Okey, funny man. You've got five minutes. Who you looking for?"

"Name's Greg Taylor. Blonde male, clean-shaven, early to mid twenties, last seen wearing pale blue pants and a white shirt with no jacket or tie. Real pretty boy."

A moment passed while Samuels flipped through the list of the night's crimes. After a minute, he said, "Nothing. No luck. Now is there anything else I can get you, your majesty?"

"No, that's about what I expected. Thanks, Samuels, call me if you need me."

He hung up without a reply. It was good for him to think that I owed him something. He'd be more likely to keep me informed that way. I checked my watch. Just after one. It was still a little early for Gilplaine to be at the Tip. I found a rag stuffed in the back of one of my file cabinets and gave the office the once over. It probably only kicked up more dust, giving it a chance to redistribute, but at least I didn't feel as much like an embarrassment to my profession. I threw the rag back where it had been hiding. I couldn't think of any other stalls, so I locked up the office and headed for the Tip. If Gilplaine wasn't there yet, I could at least feel out the other employees without his interference. It was the best lead I had.

The lunch crowd at the Tip was just finishing. Still, everyone looked up when I came in, to make sure I wasn't someone important. I wasn't.

The room was smaller than it looked in the newspapers. There were maybe twenty circular tables in the center of the room around the fountain. Some were large enough only for two, some for up to four. They were each draped with two tablecloths, one white that hung to the floor, the other small and black that hung over the edge of the table just enough to form isosceles triangles at each place setting. The tables were bunched close together, with hardly enough room for the tuxedoed wait staff to fit between the patrons' chairs. There were circular booths lining the two outer walls, four to a side, and a staircase just inside the door led to an open balcony with three more booths that had a view of the whole room. The centerpiece was the fountain, an imitation Roman marble with Cupid sitting at Aphrodite's feet, shooting a plume of water from his bow and arrow into the well below. Or maybe it wasn't an imitation. I wasn't an expert on Roman statues.

All of the tables were filled. The noise was distracting. The kitchen was in the back, and there was another door in the back wall labeled *Private*.

The maître d' was a thin man in his late fifties. He combed his scant hair over his balding crown for the maximum effect. He unwisely sported a Hitler mustache, and both the mustache and the remaining hair were pitch black. He adjusted the leather reservation book on the podium in front of him with both hands and looked at me down his nose with borrowed superiority.

"Do you have a reservation, sir?"

"I'm not here to eat," I said.

There was a spark of recognition in his eyes. "Of course not, sir. Police, then."

"Private. Work here long?"

"Only six months, sir. I used to be at the Haviland on Seventh. May I ask what this is regarding?"

"Do you know Mandy Ehrhardt?"

"Should I, sir?"

"You can stow the sir, and stop answering my questions with questions. She used to work here."

"No," he said, pausing to pretend to think about it, "I don't believe I know anybody by that name. Now you'll have to tell me what this is about or I'm afraid I'll have to ask you to leave. This is a private establishment."

"Yeah, private. Where everyone can see everyone." I handed him my card. "I want to see Gilplaine."

The maître d' sucked in his lips and held my card away from him by its edges. "Mr. Gilplaine is not here at the moment."

I had expected Gilplaine would be out, but I recognized that 'not here at the moment.' Not here for *me*. I pushed. "Why don't you show him the card and let him decide if he's in or not?"

He seemed to be deciding whether it would be safe to throw me out or if I actually had some pull with the boss.

"And tell him I expect to get that card back. He already has one, and they cost."

"Yes, *sir*," he said.

He turned on his heel and crossed the room to the aisle that ran along the booths on the right, then went through the door marked *Private*. Nothing happened except for servers trailing in and out of the kitchen, giving quick glances of a white well-lit place through the swinging door. The noise in the restaurant remained constant. It didn't matter what anyone was saying; it all sounded the same. Cupid's stream was never-ending.

It was no more than two minutes before the maître d' appeared again, walking quickly towards the front with an excellent display of good posture. When he regained his place at the podium, he said, "Mr. Gilplaine will see you in his office. Take the door by the kitchen, and you'll see his office at the end of the hall."

"It's a good thing that Mr. Gilplaine just got back in time to see me," I said.

No one looked at me as I crossed the room. The door marked *Private* led to a small corridor, no more than ten feet with two doors to the left and one straight ahead. That door was open. Gilplaine was behind a desk that could have been a twin of the one at the Carrot-Top Club, but the desk was the only thing about it that resembled the office at the casino. This was a pristine environment with no boxes piled up and nothing on the desk other than a bronze souvenir ashtray from Tijuana, two black telephones, and a small clock that was turned to face Gilplaine. There was another desk in the corner, a smaller metal one with a typewriter on it and two neat stacks of paper. The walls were hung with framed photographs of Gilplaine with one movie star or another. They were all autographed as well. Leaning up against one wall was the big boy from the night before, grinning like I was a long-lost friend.

I came in and closed the door behind me.

"You have one minute to say something interesting," Gilplaine said.

"Interesting to who?"

Instead of answering, he turned the clock on his desk so that we could both see the thin red second hand sweep around the dial.

"I'm looking for Greg Taylor," I said. There was no reaction at all. "I was told he comes here. I thought maybe you or someone on your staff—"

"I won't have my staff harassed by some snoop who's decided to pester me."

"If you call this pestering, I'd like to see what you consider being friendly."

"Your minute's going fast, Foster."

"This guy is young, early twenties with sandy blonde hair and fine features. He's just the kind of pretty boy that makes the queers go gaga when he bats his lashes. He hangs out with movie people."

Gilplaine sat back in his chair. "Whatever game you're playing, you can stop it."

"This isn't a game. I call this work."

"What's it have to do with Chloë Rose?"

"I didn't say it had anything to do with Chloë Rose."

"So you haven't come to ask me about Mandy Ehrhardt's death?"

"I'm no longer involved with the Rose case, and Mandy Ehrhardt's something else altogether."

"You just found the body."

I said nothing to that. I certainly didn't ask him how he knew. A man like Gilplaine had a way of knowing things. He and the police were best friends. Drinks on the house anytime.

"Edwards said you asked him about Mandy," he said.

"He also said you weren't here. I don't think his word is to be trusted. Anyway, I told you, it's not the same case."

He turned his clock back to face him. "Time's up, friend."

"I'd like to ask your bartender whether Taylor was in last night or not."

"The police already wasted an hour of his time. That's like wasting an hour of mine."

"The cops came here?" I said. "Did you forget a payment or does your arrangement with them not cover Harbor City murders?"

He snapped his fingers over his shoulder and said, "Mitch." His man came off the wall and stepped forward.

I stepped back. "Okey. I'm going."

Gilplaine watched me as I stepped back again, my hand now on the door handle. His expression was the same one the tiger gives you at the zoo: forlorn frustration that he was prevented from ripping you limb from limb.

He had given me nothing when I had asked for little more. It was out of a need to strike back that I said, with one foot on the threshold, "Just out of curiosity. What can you tell me about Janice Stoneman?"

His eyes narrowed at that, his lower jaw jutting out from under his upper. I like to throw peanuts at the tigers too. "Who?" he said.

"I thought maybe she worked for you. Like Mandy. I haven't started asking around yet, but if she did, I'm sure people will remember—"

His expression grew more thoughtful. "Did you say Janice?" he said. He smiled widely, showing off his dental work. "We did have a Janice working here some time ago. Haven't seen her for months, since December at least. She had to go back to her folks in Kansas or Oklahoma or one of those places these girls come from. We owed her some money. Tried to get it to her, but with no luck. Is that what this Taylor business is about? I'd love a chance to get Janice her money."

I had been shooting in the dark. I never expected him to get loquacious. I kept playing it by ear. "When did you say you saw her last? There's some confusion about the date she left. Some say it was at the beginning of December, some say the beginning of January. The police aren't much better."

"Who'd you talk to at the police?" he asked through his smile, which wasn't so wide anymore.

"You'll understand, I can't say."

"I think it was just before Christmas," he said. "I seem to recall she was going home for the holidays." He shrugged and frowned. "Never came back."

I nodded as though that meant something to me. "You know, it's kind of funny, two women who worked for you, and one's dead and the other's missing."

He couldn't keep up his smile through that. "Who said she's missing? Just because I couldn't find her."

"I'd think you'd be able to find anyone you wanted."

He shook his head. "These kids come through here. They work a few weeks, a month, it's always temporary. If a couple of them disappear, wind up in bad situations, well, that's just what happens. It's San Angelo."

"It is San Angelo." The subject appeared to be exhausted. Mitch, meanwhile, looked ready to go nine rounds. I turned to go.

"This Taylor," Gilplaine said, slowly, as if just remembering. "Is he a junky? Hangs out with John Stark?"

I didn't say anything.

His smile came back, as comforting as the Cheshire cat's. "A lot might go on in my clubs, but not the sort of thing you're thinking about. Not what this Taylor kid was after. I suggest you go down to Market Street in Harbor City. You might do better there."

"I thought you didn't know him."

He shook his head a little bit yes and a little bit no. "I know a lot of people. I can't always remember all of them."

"Sure," I said, "you have a memory like a goldfish." I nodded to both men and shut the door behind me.

At the maître d' stand, I asked Edwards, "Were you on the door last night?"

He shifted his weight.

"Oh, come on, you can tell me that much. I could find it out from almost anybody."

He looked behind him as though the answer would be there. He was no gangster, just a dandified waiter.

"Look," I said. "I was just making conversation before. This is serious."

"Yes, I was on the door."

"And did you see a young blonde man, very slight build, medium height, maybe high on heroin?"

"No I did not," he said in a way that made it clear that he regretted saying anything and that he wouldn't say anything else.

"Thank you," I said, and left the club. I got in my car and sat for a moment behind the wheel. Gilplaine literally wouldn't give me the time of day when he thought I was looking into Mandy Ehrhardt's murder, and Taylor meant even less to him, though he did know who he was. But when I added Janice Stoneman in, he was quick to give me an answer that would keep me satisfied and working on something else. I sat for five minutes thinking, maybe ten. There was nothing more to do on Taylor until Market Street opened for the night. I started the engine. As I eased away from the curb, a sand-colored coupe pulled out of an alley along the side of the club and fell in behind me. Gilplaine was telling me too much.

SEVENTEEN

The main branch of the San Angelo Public Library was in an art deco building that had been built by workers in the W.P.A. Its façade made gestures towards grandeur, but inside it wasn't much more than a warehouse. The coupe parked half a block behind me, but I wasn't too worried that one of Gilplaine's men would take a step into a library.

I went to the periodical department and got out the bound volume of the *S.A. Times* for last December. I scanned all the way through the paper from December 20 onward, including every advertisement and job posting. I found nothing of interest the first three days. Then I started on the issue for December 23. It was at the bottom of page three. They probably hadn't wanted to spoil anyone's Christmas; otherwise it would have been a front-page piece. An unidentified woman's remains had been found on the beach in Harbor City. Her throat had been slit and her thighs had been gashed open. I flipped through the next few days' papers. The story moved to page six on December 24 and wasn't mentioned again after that. The woman still hadn't been identified as of Christmas Eve. Clearly Gilplaine thought that it had been Janice Stoneman.

I placed my hand on the fold in the page and looked around. There were only a few other men in the room, all engrossed in their reading. I coughed and tore the article out. I returned the volume to the periodicals clerk and started for the front door, but stopped just before going out. As long as I was here, I might as well look into everything.

I went to the circulation desk. A plump woman wearing a lily-patterned tea-length skirt over a pink silk blouse smiled as I came up. She had prematurely silver hair streaked with white, which she had braided and wrapped around her head like a coronet, holding the whole thing in place with a box worth of bobby pins. Half-lens reading glasses hung from a cord around her neck, but she hadn't been using them to consult the volume opened flat on the counter in front of her. It looked like a dictionary.

"May I help you?" she said.

"Yes," I said. "I'd like to find some information about a horse called…" I pulled out the sheet I'd torn from the notepad in the Rosenkrantz home the night before. "Constant Comfort," I said.

The librarian frowned. "I don't approve of horseracing. I voted no in that election."

"I did too. Horseracing is dreadful and only dirty and dangerous people go in for it. This isn't about racing. A friend of mine just got this horse, but he thinks he might have been cheated. He just wants to see who owned it before him to make sure he got the right one."

"I'm sure I don't know about that. Would City Hall keep those kinds of records?"

"I don't know. That's why I asked you."

"I'm sorry, I have no idea." She pulled her lips in, causing little wrinkles to erupt around her mouth. Those were premature too.

I knocked on the counter twice. "You know what? Never mind. Thank you for your help."

So much for Constant Comfort.

I went outside. A bank of phone booths stood against the wall of the building. A broad-shouldered man in a navy blue suit and no hat leaned against the nearest booth. His hair was slicked back and his brown brogues were freshly polished. But he wasn't there for me. He held a racing form folded into a rigid rectangle about the size of a closed street map, in case anyone might be confused about what he was doing there. He looked up at me as I came down the steps, then looked back at his paper when he saw that I wasn't a customer. I went into the booth furthest from his, and pulled the door shut. The overhead light turned on and the exhaust fan in the ceiling began whirring. It didn't help. The booth was still stifling.

I dropped a coin in the slot and dialed. It was answered after one ring. *"Chronicle."*

"Pauly Fisher, please."

The line began to hum, and then there was a click, and then Pauly's warm voice came on. "Fisher here."

"It's Dennis Foster."

"Foster. What you got for me?"

I cracked the door just enough to get some air. "Maybe something. Maybe nothing. You remember a murder in Harbor City just before Christmas? Jane Doe, slit throat, carved-up legs?"

"Maybe. I don't know. What about it?"

"You only get the news that's in the paper or do you get the real stuff?" I wiped the back of my neck with my handkerchief.

"What? You're thinking of this starlet that got herself cut up yesterday?"

"Sounds like they were cut up in the same ways."

"Sounds like a coincidence to me."

"Well, can we find out if it's been a coincidence any other times?"

"You must be kidding."

"What?"

"You know what I'd have to go through to find that out? I hope you don't need it this week."

I tried to entice him. "I think I've got a name for Jane Doe."

"Nobody came looking for her. It's not news."

"Don't you find that odd? You'd agree that a cut throat and carved-up legs normally is news, right? Especially when it's a nice-looking young woman on the receiving end."

"Yeah."

"Then why was it buried on page three? And a dead story two days later?" I heard the faint electric whistle along the phone line that passed for silence. Now I had caught his interest. I sweetened it. "What if it wasn't a coincidence? What if there were other women?"

"You been reading about Jack the Ripper again?"

I waited.

He sighed. "Okey. But it's going to take me a while."

"Try my office first. If I'm not there, try the apartment. Oh, and Pauly, one more thing, do you know anything about a horse named Constant Comfort?"

"I know about horses as much as I know about Einstein."

"All right. Thanks." I hung up. I opened the door and stepped out of the phone booth. There was one man around here who'd know more about horses than about Einstein. He was in the same spot I had left him, still holding his little folded racing form. I walked down the bank of booths.

He saw me coming and he tucked the paper under his arm and held out his hands, palms up. "I'm just waiting on a call from my aunt to tell me my uncle's out of the hospital."

"What's he in for?"

The man readjusted his stance. "Appendicitis."

"Next time try he was in a car wreck. Sounds better."

He tilted his head and squinted.

"I'm not a cop," I said. I held up a five-dollar bill. "What do you know about a horse named Constant Comfort?"

"You're sure you're not a cop?"

I crinkled the money. "Private."

He checked to see if he needed a shave. He did. He probably needed to shave after every meal. "Comfort doesn't race anymore. He won a couple of pots last year. Out to pasture now."

"You know who owns him?"

"He was in Daniel Merton's stable when he was racing. I don't know about now. Why? You in the market for a horse?"

"Nah, your horse might have appendicitis."

I held out the bill to him, and he snatched it away as though he expected me to do the same. He pocketed it and made a big production of taking the racing form out from under his arm and finding his place. He leaned back against the booth again, but his eyes weren't moving across the page. He was waiting for me to leave.

At the curb I got back in my Packard. Daniel Merton was one of the founders and owners, and the current president, of Merton Stein Productions. If he had owned the horse before and Chloë Rose owned it now, he must have given it to her. But he was also the man she worked for, which made him the one the mystery man on the phone had been calling on behalf of. Why would Merton want to buy back a horse he'd given her?

I started the engine. None of this was my business. I had a client, and he probably expected me to work for my money.

I checked the time. Almost five. It was too early for any of the right people to be on Market Street in Harbor City and too late to go sit around the office. I decided to go home, and wait for Pauly Fisher's phone call. The sand-colored coupe decided to join me.

EIGHTEEN

I didn't bother locking my apartment door. If Hub's men wanted to get in, they'd get in, the only question was whether I'd have to deal with a busted doorframe afterwards.

I took up a position so I'd be behind the door when it opened. I stood there and nothing happened. I kept standing, feeling like a fool. But in the last thirty-six hours I'd had a gun pointed at me, been threatened by gangsters and by the police, and found a mutilated body. I waited.

The knock came, three heavy thuds made with the meat of a fist. I stayed quiet. We all listened to the floorboards. The knock again, more insistent, and this time, "Come on, Foster. We know you're in there. We just want to talk." It was Mitch's voice.

I heard a hand on the doorknob, and then the door swung towards me, but faster and harder than I'd expected. It slammed into my hip, sending a sharp pain up and down my side. I must have cried out, because Mitch hurled his full weight against the door, pinning me behind it. I tried to lean forward but my shoulders were pushed together, my arms in front of me like a fighter trying to protect his middle. I was stuck.

Mitch peeked around the door, still holding his weight against it. At the sight of me, he eased the pressure for a moment only to fall back against the door, shooting pain along my shoulder blades.

A second man appeared, rail thin and well over six feet tall, wearing a gray suit with a black vest underneath. He patted me down to see if I had a gun. I didn't. He took the newspaper article I'd stolen from the library out of my pocket. Then he nodded at Mitch.

The weight fell away from the door and I staggered forward. "What do you two want?"

The tall man unfolded the newspaper article, glanced it over, and looked back at me. "For somebody not working on a murder, you have an interesting choice of reading material."

"I just ripped that out for the crossword on the back."

He held up the backside, which wasn't a crossword. "We were told to give you a chance. We were told to use our discretion."

"I told it to Gilplaine straight. I'm working another job."

"Then how do you explain this?"

I couldn't explain it. I couldn't even say why it was important. I didn't know anything other than I was a damn fool for having gotten mixed up with this business in the first place.

"Mr. Gilplaine finds your explanation unconvincing," the tall man said. He turned to Mitch, who was jumping lightly in place on the balls of his feet, like he was warming up. "Leave his face alone. This is only a warning."

I tried to dodge to my left in an attempt to get out the door, but Mitch barreled into me, slamming me back up against it. Holding me there, he punched me in the kidney. One would have been plenty, but he did it again and then a third time, so that my legs went watery and tears pushed out between my squinting eyelids. A fire lapped around my midsection. He let me go since he was sure I wasn't going anywhere now. Before I could collapse, he propped me up and punched me just once in the stomach. I doubled over, throwing my upper torso into Mitch's waiting fist. The dull ache of my pectoral met up with the fire in my side, and I fell back against the door, trying to draw breath and failing.

Mitch stood up, his breathing only slightly heavy. "He doesn't look too good, does he?"

The tall man made no comment. We could have been reading the stock prices. He was bored.

Mitch jumped in place again. "I think I better even him out." He twisted his torso, bringing his arm all the way back. He was going to show me that fist long before it was going to get to me. I couldn't move anyway, and he barreled it into my other kidney. I fell forward onto my knees.

"He's blocking the door."

"You're in the way," Mitch said. He shoved me over with the toe of one shoe. I didn't resist. I couldn't have if I'd tried.

"I think we've made our point," the tall man said.

Mitch kicked me in the stomach once more for good measure. Before I could catch my breath, he bent down and snaked a thick arm around my windpipe, his hot breath up against my ear. "Just because I'm not supposed to mark up your face don't mean I've got to leave you conscious, you flatfooted…"

Whatever it was that he called me was lost to the ages. There were more interesting things to command my attention, black splotches appearing before my eyes intermixed with white flashes, and then the black beat out the white and then I was drifting above the floor, high up near the ceiling, and then I wasn't.

The black-and-white flicker of a movie screen came on in front of me, the test strip counting down five, four, three, two, one. Chloë Rose lit up the screen, a radiant aura around her. There were quick cuts and there was a knife and there was a gun, and then there was a body floating on a pool of blood. Chloë Rose came back again, and she was screaming. She was beautiful. Then there was a man seen from behind. It must have been the star of the picture. John Stark or Hub Gilplaine. He came to a mirror and I saw that it was me. But I'm down there with the paying marks in the cinema seats. How could I be up on the screen? The image flickered past. There was a lanky brunette stuffing a body into a car. There was another body floating in a pool of blood, but this time the blood was mixed with white foam. It was on the beach, and the waves were lapping away at the black blood, white, black, white, black, a gaping throat. A gunshot. And they're off. The horses pounded around the track. Cut to the stands. Chloë Rose. The horses rounding the far turn. Cut to the stands. Mitch and the tall man and me holding our tickets. The horses are coming around. Cut to the stands. John Stark holding hands with Greg Taylor. The photoflash! It hurts my eyes. And then the horse race was a prize fight and Mitch was in the ring with me and the bell was being rung...

And then suddenly it was a telephone ringing.

A voice said, "Turn off the lights."

I took a deep breath and immediately started coughing. Every part of my upper torso ached, except when I moved, at which point the ache was replaced with shooting pain.

"It's too bright," the voice said. "Turn off the light and bring me a drink."

No one answered, and it's a good thing, because I was alone.

I looked over at the phone, but it had stopped ringing. If it ever had been ringing. Maybe it had just been my head.

I put my hand against the wall. It was a good wall. It stayed where you left it. Not like my breath. I gasped to draw it in, my throat getting tight, but in it went, and I exhaled with the only consequence being more throbbing and jabbing along my ribs.

The wall helped me to my knees and even held me when I fell against it. Like I said, it was a good wall. I was able to reach up and flip off the light.

Now it was too dark. Whatever little light was supposed to come from the window in the bathroom wasn't there, so I'd been out at least a couple of hours.

Okey, Foster, one step at a time. That's the way. Hands and knees. Now just knees. What do you say about feet?

One foot was under me now, and then with the help of the doorknob I got up onto both feet and stumbled across to my chair and fell into it. The newspaper article was sitting on the bed. That was nice of them. They were solid people who wouldn't steal a newspaper clipping from an unconscious man. The library should hire those two. They'd never have any late returns again.

I rested for some amount of time, re-learning how to breathe. I got so I was pretty good at it. I could even do it with my eyes closed. When I had gotten that under my belt, I figured I might as well try for that drink. I got to my feet, and this time it wasn't like riding a bicycle with a bent wheel. I made it to the liquor, poured a stiff drink, and drank it off in one gulp, enjoying the only burning inside of me that I had put there. While I poured another one, the phone began to ring again. Or maybe it was the first time. I looked at it way over on the side table. It was probably Pauly Fisher. Anything he had to tell me, I didn't want to know just then; he could call me at the office tomorrow.

I made my way back to the light switch with the second drink in my hand, the phone still ringing. The lights came on and I squinted, holding up my hand as if to ward off a blow.

I drank the second drink. I could see then. The clock on my nightstand said it was almost half past eight. It had been just about five when I'd left the library. I'd been out for three hours, assuming it wasn't the next day.

The phone was still hollering at anyone who would listen. Pauly Fisher wasn't that persistent, but I didn't want to find out who was. It was still plenty early for Market Street—in fact, it might still have been too early. But it was time to go either way. Because that was my job. All of this other stuff was just a side-line, a hobby.

I looked at the newspaper article again. Gilplaine had done me a favor in his own vicious way. He'd told me this dead woman was much more important than I'd known. That seemed like a mistake a man like Gilplaine wouldn't make. Maybe someday I'd know why.

I thought about a third drink, but left my glass on the table and went to the door instead. I got it open without any problem. No one was waiting outside. It was just me and the hallway. They seemed pretty confident I'd gotten the message. I'd gotten it, but it might not have been the message they intended.

I locked up behind me and leaned against the wall. Behind my door the telephone was still ringing. That was an awfully long time to let a phone ring. Maybe it was important after all.

But getting out of there was important too. Whoever it was could call back.

I went down the hall, took the automatic elevator, and found my car just like a man who had all of his organs in the right place.

NINETEEN

Market Street in Harbor City meant Market Street between Fifth and Sixth, a rundown block of seedy bars that had been glamorous at some time but no one could remember when. Among the fairies it was known simply as The Market. If you were a pretty boy on the prowl, The Market would be one of the first places you would go. In its heyday, neon signs and flashing lights had gone up all along the length of the block, and the signs had survived the block's decline, making for a rather bright underworld now. All the light didn't make it look any better than the rest of the neighborhood. It just made it easier to see how shabby everything was.

I parked three blocks away on Second Street, where the storefronts were mostly covered with yellowing newsprint or plywood. As I walked up Market, the stores began to look like they had some daytime trade, even if there were bars on most of the windows. One doorway was being used as a bedroom by a man wearing paint-spattered overalls and no shirt. He was laid out on a cardboard mat he'd made by cutting open a batch of fruit cartons, and he slept like a corpse at a wake.

The Blacklight was on the corner of Market and Fifth. To distinguish itself from its competitors, the front was completely dark. No neon. No lights. The windows had been painted over black. The only sign was an unlit naked light bulb over the door. This unassuming front, coupled with its location at the end of the block, helped make the Blacklight the favorite of S.A. queens who wanted to go slumming but be discreet about it.

Inside, the lighting wasn't much better. After passing through a second door, I found myself at one end of a fifteen-foot bar, which ran along the close wall all the way to the back. The bar top was painted red but had been scuffed to white in some places. A padded black leather armrest lined the side of the bar where the drinkers sat. On the bartender's side there was a door with a brightly lit square posing as a diamond that must have let into the kitchen. Next to an out-of-order phone, another door led to the toilets. They were still marked 'M' and 'F.' On the opposite wall was a row of booths with black leather cushions, some of which were intact, some of which had been repaired with tire patches, and some of which had bits of their yellow stuffing spilling out. A narrow row of two-top tables divided the bar from the booths. There were maybe a dozen patrons spread out across the room. I sat down at the closest stool.

The bartender came over with his arms crossed over his apron. They were big arms and tattooed, and they went with the rest of his physique. He looked like a boxer who no longer fought in the ring but stayed in shape because it was all he knew how to do. They come in all sizes, I guessed, but maybe he wasn't like that and just worked there. Maybe he had been here from before it turned into a queer joint. Maybe he couldn't stand his job but it was a job and who could argue with that? Right now his brow was pulled into an angry V. He hated somebody.

I put a five-dollar bill on the bar and ordered a gin and tonic. His look grew nastier, but he made the drink and set it on a paper napkin in front of me with a scowl. He didn't touch the five-dollar bill. He watched me sip my drink. Then he said, "We're paid up for the month."

"I'm not a cop," I said.

"You sure look like a cop. And we're all paid."

"I'm not a cop," I said again, and took another sip of my gin and tonic. Just a sip, because I didn't know how many drinks I was going to have to order in how many bars before I got something. "I'm looking for Greg Taylor. Does he come in here?"

"I wouldn't know," the man said, his arms crossed again. There was a nervous quiet among the other patrons, but I didn't look to see if they were watching.

"Would you know the names of any of your regulars?"

"No. I'm not too good with names."

I leaned in, pressing myself against the bar, ignoring the complaint from my bruised ribs. "Look, I'm not a cop, I'm a private detective. The man's family is worried about him. I'm just trying to find where he is and if he's okey."

"I don't know any Greg Taylor."

"I thought you weren't good with names. You remembered that one all right."

He didn't have an answer to that other than to shift his weight from one foot to the other.

"Look, I'm not trying to stir up any trouble. My client doesn't want that either. Could you just give me a yes or a no if he comes in here? He's a pretty man, about my height, tan skin, light hair, small, feminine features, couldn't weigh more than one-thirty, probably less."

His face grew even emptier. "I don't know," he said pointedly, giving each word its own time in the spotlight.

I did look around at the other patrons then. Greg Taylor wasn't among them. No one appeared to be giving our conversation too much attention. Just a group of men enjoying their beer. To anyone who didn't know better it looked like a regular crowd of steady drinkers. I brought my eyes back to the bartender, but I said in a louder voice, "If you hear anything about Greg Taylor, you let me know."

I left the rest of my drink when I got up and put my card on the five-dollar bill. The money hadn't bought anything but you never knew when a five was going to be remembered at the right time. I glanced over the patrons again, but no one seemed to have reacted to my announcement. "Don't think too hard," I said.

"Don't come back," the bartender said.

"You must get a lot of repeat business talking that way," I said. He didn't care to respond. I went out through both of the doors and back into the glare of the street.

There was a group of three streetwalkers on the opposite corner now. I crossed and they saw me coming and started in with their propositions until they got a good look at me and turned away as though they were waiting for a bus. They all looked young, no more than twenty-five but probably younger. One of them was dressed in women's clothing, a long, slinky kimono wrap with matching slippers that weren't meant for wearing out of the house. His makeup made it almost hard to tell he wasn't a she, but only almost. The other two wore suit pants that were too tight on their already thin frames and un-tucked white shirts with the top three buttons left open and shoes that needed polishing. One had sunken cheeks and pallid skin with a slight sheen to it in the streetlight. I made him for a junky. None of them had hats.

"Can I buy anyone a drink?" I said. All three heads turned studiously away from me, doing what they could to catch the shadows from the next block. "I just have a few questions. The people on the block don't seem very friendly."

"We got nothing to say to you, copper," the he-she said, still with his head turned.

"I'm not a cop," I said. I was starting to wonder if I was, I had to say it so much. "I'm just looking for someone who I was told comes down here. For his folks."

The he-she turned then. "Peeper, huh?" he said. There was a reedy lilt to his voice and a softness around the edges, but it wasn't fooling anyone. "We've got nothing to say to peepers either. Unless you're looking for a good time."

I ignored that, took out my wallet and brought out another five. I held it where they could see it. "All I'm looking for is the whereabouts of a particular person. Easy money." I waited, but none of them made a move for the money. The two dressed in regular clothes shifted on their feet and looked up and down the block. They couldn't talk. Most of their customers had a wife and kids and a whole ordinary life in the city. The boys who worked in The Market were partially paid for confidentiality. I put the money away, and said, "Fine." I started to turn around, and one of them spoke.

"What's the name?" It was an unsteady voice. It came from the junky. His companions eyed him with upper lips curled in disgust.

I turned back and watched them as I said, "Greg Taylor." There was no flash of recognition. Just the same shiftiness. I was making them nervous. "Fine," I said again and went across the street and into the bar next to the Blacklight, a place called Jillian's. Stark had mentioned only the Blacklight and Choices by name, but that was because those were the bars that someone of his caliber might know about. I had a feeling that

Taylor was just as likely to be known at any of the places along the block.

Jillian's was no different than the Blacklight. The tables were up front and the bar was in back and the lighting was better and there was a small platform in one corner with a drum kit, a standup base, and a trumpet beside a stool, but it was the same anyway. The same eyes looked at me. The same eyes made sure to look away. The bartender gave me the same business. I looked around, but nobody dared a second glance in my direction. As I watched, three Negroes came out from the back and went to the stage, resuming their positions at the instruments. The trumpet player counted a beat with his foot, and they all started together, a fast number that the patrons shouted over to be heard. The band didn't need the audience; they were making music. I left another five. No Greg Taylor. No anything. I didn't even touch my drink.

I went outside. It was getting later and there were more men on the street now. Different music could be heard coming from a few of the joints, clashing in the night. A faint breeze stirred the air, carrying the briny smell of the Pacific from only a block away, but it didn't make the night any cooler. As people passed me they hardly noticed I was there. They didn't like my look and I didn't like theirs. Only two of the whores were standing on their corner. I was probably wasting my time out there, but I didn't have a better idea, and the thought of going home to lick my wounds made me feel sorry for myself, and I didn't like feeling sorry for myself.

At the third bar, after going through the same routine with a blond-haired bartender wearing a too-tight shirt, my eyes caught on a face as I made my quick survey of the place. It was the junky from outside. He drew a few knowing glances from some of the men at the tables but he kept his eyes on the back of the bar, heading for the toilets. As I watched him, his eyes flicked at me and then away just for a moment. He went into the bathroom. I nursed my gin and tonic. The bartender had gone to the other end of the bar, finished with me. After ten minutes the junky still hadn't come out of the bathroom. I pushed off of the bar and went to the front door. If the junky wanted to find me, he would find me once he had worked up his nerve. For all I knew, he was just getting high.

The storefront next door was an all-night liquor store without any customers. I skipped that because Greg Taylor had not looked like the kind of man who ever bought his own liquor, and because when you go out at night to get back at your lover, you don't do it with a bottle bought at a liquor store.

The next bar was Choices. It was more of a dance hall than the other places. A five-piece band was playing fast numbers in a corner under a palm tree in a pot. The dance floor took up the center of the room, lit with spotlights recessed into the ceiling that made white shiny spots on the wooden boards. There were several couples dancing and I wondered how they knew who should lead. The tables nearest the dance floor were filled, but the ones further out were empty. The bar was a classy thing with a gilt framed mirror along the back and lights under the glass shelves where the liquor was kept so that the various bottles shone and were reflected and shone some more. I didn't bother to try my line on the bartender over the sound of the band. Instead, I waited at the bar and watched the dancers. They could really dance.

After a minute or two, the junky streetwalker came in through the front door. He saw me looking at him and I smiled and he immediately looked away. A man at a nearby table called to him and he went over and let the man hold his hand, all the while looking at a spot on the table that was a thousand miles away. I watched them for a moment, the seated man pulling on the junky's arm, waving at the chair across the table from him, the junky just standing there with his head bowed and no expression on his face. I didn't want to watch anymore. There was no reason I had to. I turned my back and drank my drink all the way down. The liquor spread out in my body, reminding me that life was just life and it wasn't good or bad. I turned around again and the junky was now sitting at the table. He wouldn't stay long. I needed some fresh air. It was getting stuffy in there.

Outside, I smoked a cigarette, and when I'd finished with that one I lit another. Down at the end of the block, only the man dressed in pants and the unbuttoned shirt was standing under the streetlight. Maybe the getup with the kimono was good for business. I had started my third cigarette when the junky came out of the club. He stopped short when he saw me standing there. "You can follow me around all night and not get anywhere or we can just talk now," I said.

He looked down the block where his companion was standing watching him back.

"We can go somewhere else," I said.

"Meet me on Seaside at Sixth," he said without looking at me.

"You've got something to tell me?"

He didn't answer, already walking back down towards his street corner.

I turned in the other direction, making it quick to get to the end of the block and turned right on Sixth towards the ocean.

TWENTY

He came up on Seaside walking along the closed-up shops, well out of the glow of the streetlamps. He kept his head down, shooting occasional glances behind him as though he were afraid of being followed. When he was three feet away, he stopped, glanced up at me once, and then back down at the sidewalk. He was even younger than I had first thought, probably no more than eighteen. He looked sickly and every half a minute he would shiver as though it wasn't seventy-five degrees out. He was a real nervous one. I wondered how he got any business.

"You have something to tell me?" I said, trying to make him look me in the eye.

"Where's the money?"

I got out my wallet and took out the five-dollar bill I had shown them on the street corner, or one exactly like it. "This isn't for nothing," I said, not yet holding out the bill. "You've got to have something to tell me."

"I've got something. Now give me the money."

"What's your name?"

His expression turned suspicious. "Why?"

"So I have something to call you by. Just a name. Your street name."

"Rusty," he said, the name foreign on his tongue.

"Okey, Rusty." I held the bill out to him and he snatched it away faster than I thought he could move. It disappeared.

"How long did it take you to learn to get the money first?" I said.

He looked up at me with his eyes without moving his head. He didn't like me very much. Even if I had given him the money. His eyes went back to the street. "I know Greg from a while back," he said.

I waited for him to say more. When he didn't, I said, "And?"

"We had the same dealer. A guy named Renaldo who works on the boardwalk. I can take you to him."

"When was the last time you saw him? Taylor, I mean."

He shrugged and tilted his head. "Six months. Maybe eight."

"But you can take me to the guy he used to get his junk from maybe eight months ago?"

He bobbed his head emphatically. "Yeah."

"That doesn't sound like five dollars to me."

The eyes flicked again. "Look, man. If anyone's gonna know anything about Greg, it's going to be Renaldo. Anyone who's gonna tell you anything anyway."

Junkies will scam you any way they can to get a buck. But I didn't have a better lead. "Well. Let's go meet Renaldo."

He bobbed his head again, rocking on his feet as well, and then stepped off the sidewalk into the street. It was only after he stepped off that he looked both ways. Seaside was deserted at that time of night anyway. You would never know that just around the corner was a burgeoning nightlife.

We stayed on Sixth, going the half a block that ended at the boardwalk in a sandy cul-de-sac. A wooden lattice blocked off the black space under the boardwalk. There were stairs on either side of the street, each step with a bar of sand on its back edge. I could hear the ocean now and the salty smell was stronger. We took the stairs on the south side of the street and as soon as we stepped out onto the boards, we were met by a cool, steady wind. There were no lights on the boardwalk or stores or concessions here. It was just a raised set of boards with a railing on either side and steps down to the beach. At regular intervals were wooden park benches. There were silhouetted figures on most of the benches, standing out against the darkness that was the ocean and the sky.

Rusty turned north and I followed alongside him. Neither of us spoke. He seemed less nervous, less jumpy, but it could just have been that it wasn't as obvious when he was walking. The wind blew my tie, making it flutter up against me and over my shoulder. My coat rippled and I had to put my hand on my hat a couple of times. As we walked, the sounds of couples on the benches came as a soft murmur, and then there were the occasional loud voices lost in the darkness of the beach. In the distance, the nighttime lights of Harbor City's commercial boardwalk shone like a mirage for the night traveler, the rides stretching away from the land almost all the way down to the water, a flashing neon peninsula. There was a lot of darkness between The Market and the lights of the tourists' playland.

We had gone maybe five blocks when Rusty made a move for a street-side stairwell. We were still at least ten blocks away from the carnival lights, a good walk, but not an impossible one. This location would allow Renaldo to service customers from either community. We clopped down the stairs, grains of sand crunching under our heels. In the darkness of the corner made by the staircase and the wooden lattice stood a man in a sharp blue suit with a purple shirt and a purple tie. He wasn't Mexican, as his name had suggested, but rather a pale and doughy-faced man with deep-set eyes and a cocky smirk that looked like a permanent fixture. The clothes were expensive and unnecessarily flamboyant, an affectation like the name, but maybe good for business, like the whore's kimono.

"Hey, Renaldo," Rusty said as we came up to him.

Renaldo's eyes ignored Rusty and held my own. "Can I help you?" he said. His voice left no doubt that he was in charge or at least thought he was. He probably had a piece tucked under his arm. That made him invincible.

"Yeah, five dollars," Rusty said, the bill magically reappearing in his hand. His voice was wrought with eagerness.

"Can I help you?" Renaldo said again, his eyes still on mine.

"Oh, yeah," Rusty said, half turning towards me. "This guy's a dick. He's looking for Greg."

"Why would you come to me?"

"Yeah, I don't know," Rusty said. "But I've got five dollars. That's enough for plenty."

I decided it was time I spoke for myself. "I was hired by Greg Taylor's family to make sure he's all right. He doesn't even have to go home. I just need to talk to him."

"Again, why would you come to me?"

"Once a junky always a junky," I said.

He laughed, one short bark. He liked that. It was amusing to him. He liked me now. "All right, peeper. That's rich."

"I don't care what you're doing here. I just need a line on Mr. Taylor."

"You've got nothing?" His eyes were lights in the shadows.

I held out my hands to show just how empty they were.

He thought about it. Then he gave a half-shrug. "Greg came by last night, as a matter of fact. He was with some guy. Tall, good-looking guy. I don't know him."

"Did you hear a name?"

"John, or Tim, or Tom. Something simple like that."

I nodded to show I was listening. "What time was this?"

"Late. Maybe three in the A.M. They bought some stuff, and went up on the boards."

"Did they say where they were going?"

"Didn't have to say. I could hear them under the boardwalk. Must have gone there to get high and get cozy. Certainly sounded like it."

"Sounded like what?"

He just smiled. "Sounded like *it*, shamus." He unleashed his bark again. Rusty was almost hopping from one foot to the other now. "That's all I know."

"They didn't come back out?"

"Not that I saw, but that doesn't mean anything. They could have come off of the boardwalk at any of these streets."

I nodded.

"Who'd you say you were working for? Greg doesn't have any family."

"My client would prefer to stay anonymous."

That warranted a bark as well. I was a funny man. I was really cracking him up. "I like you, dick."

"Renaldo," Rusty said. "Come on."

Renaldo continued to ignore him. "I hope you know this isn't all free," Renaldo said.

"It's not much. You're going to get my five in a moment."

"That's his five. And five doesn't sound like a lot right now."

"What makes you think it's worth more?"

"You had nothing and now you have something. You gave this junky five bucks just to bring you to me."

The man had a point. And anyway John Stark was footing the bill. I brought out my wallet and dug out a ten. He took it from me and then turned to Rusty to conduct his business. I was dismissed. I wasn't anywhere. I had nowhere to go. I had let an innocent woman get turned into a murder suspect and now I was letting my one remaining client down. I wouldn't hire me. I took the stairs back up to the boardwalk and then the ones across the way down to the beach. I don't know why. It was something to do.

TWENTY-ONE

From the beach, the carnival lights took on a sad, hopeless appearance. They were insignificant when compared with the dark surging body of water churning and crashing and whispering some forty yards away. There was just enough light to make out the water's movement but little else. The spot at which the ocean ended and the sky began was lost to the darkness.

My shoes slid on the sand and sank, and I could feel wet grains pour in around the sides of my feet. I hobbled awkwardly around the stairs with the grit weighing me down. The wind from the shore chilled me.

On the beach side, there was no wooden lattice blocking entry to the black space under the boardwalk. I got my penlight out and used it to paint the space between two support beams right in front of me. It allowed me to see only about six inches ahead. But the ground was more even there, and there was enough room to stand up without crouching. I walked forward slowly, my light pointed down with an occasional sweep upwards to be sure I wasn't about to knock my head against a support. I didn't know what I expected to find. The sand was littered with empty cans, crumpled newsprint, and candy bar wrappers, along with shells, rocks, and some scrub brush. There were also empty paper envelopes, discarded needles, and plenty of cigarette butts, showing that the spot under the boardwalk where Renaldo sold was a popular place for those of his customers who couldn't wait to get indoors for their fix.

I walked straight back until I was at the lattice that separated me from the street. Renaldo was standing on the other side, leaning against the stairwell, smoking a cigarette. The syrupy flavor of the smoke told me it wasn't tobacco he was smoking. I played my flash on the ground in either direction, but there was nothing to see. I was searching just to be doing something, to convince myself that I wasn't entirely useless. I'd do better at home in bed. My head hadn't touched a pillow in nearly forty-eight hours. My little nap courtesy of Mitch hardly counted.

I picked my way back towards the beach. The debris crackled under my feet and my shoes now felt as though they weighed an extra two pounds each. I had veered off to the right in the dark, and was coming out under the stairs. I started to correct my path when the edge of my penlight beam caught the scuffed sole of a man's shoe. That didn't surprise me. It was just one more thing that might get discarded under the boardwalk. But then I traced my flash up a little more and saw that the shoe was still attached to a leg. It was attached to a leg wearing familiar pale blue suit pants. I crouched as the stairs came down above me and my penlight lit up the pile that was wedged under them. A man could have decided it was an out of the way place to spend the night. He probably wouldn't sleep face down though.

I knew who it was but I had to make sure. I lifted his head by the hair enough to see his face. It was a pretty face, a strange, half grown, boyish face. Mr. Greg Taylor was never going to fight with Stark again. He was never going to fight with anybody.

I let his head drop, hiding the face back in the sand, and I felt my way along his body, training the flash on my hand. There was nothing in his pants pockets and he didn't have any others. He could have been robbed, but it was just as likely that he had

had nothing in his pockets in the first place. His was a nameless body and would have remained such if found by someone who didn't know him. That would have set the police back days and whoever did it would have plenty of time to distance himself from the crime. Assuming there was a crime, and he hadn't died of a self-inflicted overdose. Even then, his companion, John or Tim or Tom, would want to have been somewhere else when it happened. Especially if "John" was John Stark and this whole case was a preemptive ruse.

I came out from under the boardwalk and stretched in the open air. I made my way back up the stairs, pushing away the idea of what was underneath, and then crossed the deserted boardwalk and came down the other set of stairs to the street. At the bottom, I leaned against the railing and emptied first one shoe and then the other, adding my share to a little mound of sand where other people had done the same. I walked back around to Renaldo. Rusty was long gone.

"You have anything else to add to the noises you heard last night?"

"Just noises, peeper," Renaldo said and let out a laugh filled with smoke.

I looked back along the street to Seaside and the block beyond. This was a commercial district. It probably closed up at six o'clock just when the boardwalk was starting to draw business away for the night. "There a phone nearby?" I said.

"At the end of the block. Who do you need to call?"

I looked at him. "Let's just say you might not want to hang around here to find out."

He straightened up. "Why do you want to do that?"

"Take a peek under those stairs on the other side of the boardwalk and you'll see."

He spat a word that conveyed the full range of his feelings.

"I'll leave you out of it by name," I said, "but I can't promise to leave you out completely. I guess the police will still know who I mean."

He spat the word again, and then said, "I hate junkies," only he included the adjectival version of his new favorite word there too.

"Don't worry too much. The police won't be too happy to see me again either."

He nodded ruefully. "You too, huh? You too."

We turned to go then, and walked the half-block together without speaking. At the corner, Renaldo pointed out the phone in silence, and then turned north on Seaside and walked briskly away.

The phone booth was wood without a door. The inside surface had been carved with any number of names, initials, suggestions, and complaints. I picked up the receiver and dialed a number. I ran my hand over the booth's wall, feeling the scrape of the cut words.

A voice came on the line. I was surprised that it didn't sound sleepy. In this deserted part of town it felt like the dead of night.

"Mr. Stark, please," I said.

"Mr. Stark is no longer receiving calls this evening," the voice said. It was the butler who had opened the door that morning, a lifetime ago.

"Tell him it's Dennis Foster about Greg Taylor," I said.

There was a moment's hesitation, and then the voice said, "Please hold the wire."

I held the wire.

"You found him," Stark's famous voice said after several

minutes. There was the sound of another extension being hung up. "I knew you were good. I have a sense for these things."

"You may not think so when you hear the rest of it."

A note of caution entered the baritone. "Go on."

"He's dead."

A sharp intake of breath sounded over the line. There was a moment in which he collected himself, preparing before going on. When he spoke, his voice had lost its usual tone of command, but there was nothing else to indicate that he was upset. "What happened?"

I told him. I left out that Greg had been seen with another man.

There was a pause. At last, "Did he suffer?"

"I'm not a doctor, but it didn't look like it."

"Good," he said.

"I need to call it in, and I want to know what you'd like me to say. I'm down in Harbor City and the police are going to want to know why."

"I don't know," he said.

"Where were you last night?"

"Home. Why?"

"Anybody with you? Was anyone else in the house last night?"

"My butler was in. I asked him for some coffee at, I don't know, ten o'clock, maybe later. The maids were in also. They'd all vouch for me. But why does that matter? Wasn't it the drugs? We'd fought about that so many times; Greg always promised to quit." His voice had grown tight and risen half an octave. "Damn him. It was an overdose, wasn't it?"

"I don't know."

"So you think I'm a suspect?"

"No, but the police are going to. Did Greg know Mandy Ehr-hardt?"

"They might have met once or twice. Why? Does this have anything to do with that?"

"No. I can't see how it does. I'm just thinking of ways to leave you out and I don't see any."

"That's all right. You do what you have to. The police have always been kind to me before."

"These aren't S.A. cops. They're Harbor City cops. They don't tend to be kind to anybody. You told me Greg was on your payroll. Was he really or was that just a story?"

"He is. He was. He always claimed he didn't like it, that it made him feel like a kept man. I always thought it was a good precaution."

"It was. People will guess the truth, there's no avoiding that, but it should mean that everyone keeps to the story officially at least. I can't speak for Parsons and Hopper."

"I can't worry about that," he said. He paused. "Thank you. For finding him."

"I'll call tomorrow if I know any more. The police may be there tonight. This phone call never happened. They don't like me very much already. I don't need to give them another excuse. Your butler…?"

"Nothing to worry about," he said without any hesitation.

"I'll call tomorrow," I said, and hung up. I picked up the phone again and called the police.

TWENTY-TWO

It was only five minutes before a prowl car pulled up alongside me. In this neighborhood at night they probably had a black-and-white every ten blocks, so I wasn't too impressed with the timing. They popped the spotlight on. I hadn't finished my first cigarette yet, so I let them watch me smoke it. The passenger door opened and a uniformed officer stepped out. "You call the cops?" he shouted from behind the safety of his open door.

"Yeah. That was me," I said.

He looked in the open car and said something and then he shouted over at me again, "Where's this body?"

"Under the boardwalk," I said, and started down the block without waiting for them.

The door slammed behind me and there were rapid footsteps and the sound of an engine being gunned. The car lurched ahead of me, pulling to a stop at the end of the block where Renaldo had been standing ten minutes before. I hoped the smell of his marijuana hadn't lingered. The cop who had called to me came up behind and said, "Stop right there."

I stopped. His partner got out of the patrol car and went over to the wooden lattice at the end of the street. The spot from the car was still on, and he peered through the holes trying to make out Greg Taylor's body. I finished my cigarette and threw away the butt.

"There's a body all right," the partner called.

"Turn around, buddy, and give it to me slow."

I turned around and said, "If you don't mind, I'll wait for the homicide boys. I hate to repeat myself."

The cop was young, at the utmost twenty, and the attempt at swagger in his posture was laughable. He wore his hair in a military crew, which made his hat fit him loosely. He had his hand on the butt of his gun and looked a little too eager to draw.

His partner came up. He was older, thicker in the gut but more comfortable in his own skin. He wore wire-rimmed glasses with round lenses. "How'd you find him?"

"He don't want to talk," the younger one said. "Wants to wait for the homicide boys."

"I just don't want to waste any of our time," I said. "You know in five minutes you won't have anything more to do with this."

The cop in glasses shrugged and started to walk back towards Seaside Avenue. His partner stepped to the side so that he was within his partner's path but still had his eye on me. "Carter, we need to watch this guy. What's he doing out here at this time of night?"

Carter didn't stop. "He's a dick, wetbrain. He's out here because he's snooping."

The younger cop trained his eye back on me, and I gave him a smile and reached for another cigarette. His hands jumped to his gun again until he saw the cigarette and matches in my hand. "You're a dick?" he said to me, jutting his chin to show he was in control.

"You want to see my license?" I said.

"Yeah," he said. So I got out my license and held it out to him. He stepped close enough to read it and then stepped back. "What are you doing out here?"

I didn't say anything. An unmarked car pulled up alongside

Carter, who took a step back on the sidewalk. A short man in plain clothes got out the passenger side and started in our direction without waiting for his partner. He wore a brown felt hat with a yellow feather in the brim. His face was a closed fist. He had a pocket notebook out and was writing in it with a pencil as he approached. Carter fell in beside him. His partner brought up the rear. He was broad at the shoulders and not much narrower below. His blue shirt required quite a lot of yardage and even so there wasn't enough at the collar for him to close the button comfortably. His knotted neckie rode halfway down his chest. The three of them walked past without a glance at me or my young interrogator. They went up the stairs to the boardwalk and then were out of sight. A moment later a flash could be seen under the stairs.

I smoked my cigarette. The young cop watched me smoke it.

Eventually the other three came back. Carter went to his patrol car and got in it. The small man and his broad-shouldered partner came up to me. As they approached, the short one said, "Where's Renaldo? Make sure they bring him in." The big man nodded. Then the small man addressed me, "I'm Captain Langstaff, this is Detective Graham. You are?"

"He's a private dick from S.A., Captain."

The captain looked over at the kid, and then back at his notebook. "Graham, show Officer Stephens how to get into his cruiser. Maybe he and Carter can find Renaldo."

Graham stepped around and the kid actually took a step back as though he expected to be punched. He then walked in a wide arc around all of us and went back to the cruiser. He opened the passenger door still looking back at us as though we were planning to attack him. He called, "We'll find Renaldo," and then he climbed into the car.

Graham walked back, stopping when he was just behind my shoulder, visible out of the corner of my eye.

The captain left his eyes on his notebook. "Private dick from S.A."

"That's right. Dennis Foster. Do you want my story?"

"Hmm-mm," Langstaff said.

"I'm working a missing persons job. A fairy, so I went to The Market to ask around. Nobody knew anything, naturally."

"Naturally."

"But then a junky said he knew where my man scored his dope. He brought me here."

He nodded, writing in his notebook the whole time. "You talk to Renaldo?"

"I didn't ask him his name."

"Doesn't matter." Langstaff looked up. "And the body, is he your man?"

I nodded. "Greg Taylor."

"Who are you working for?"

"I'd rather not say."

The folds in his forehead deepened.

"But I won't insult your intelligence. It'll take you ten minutes to find out. John Stark."

"The movie actor?"

I nodded again.

Langstaff said something under his breath. I couldn't make out the words, but I got the idea. He nodded to Graham. "Check his license. Get his info." He looked at me. "Is there anything you're not telling me?"

"Nothing that I think is relevant."

"It's not your place to make that decision, Mr. Foster, but honestly, some fairy o.d.ing that's going to be covered up anyway,

I don't really give a damn." He walked back towards the beach again, and started up the stairs.

"You're his new favorite person," Graham said behind me. "Let's see the paperwork."

I got out my wallet again and handed the whole thing to him. He took out his own notebook and wrote down all the details in careful tight letters.

I threw away my butt and waited for Graham to finish. The night was cooling off, especially near the water. My chest hurt when I breathed, and the exhaustion of the last two days had finally hit me. My knees were suddenly unsure if they wanted to keep working in my employ.

Graham tapped the wallet on my shoulder and I reached up and took it. "Got a car?" he said. He was a gentle giant. He was a pal. Don't believe what they say about cops. They're there to protect and to serve.

"On Second."

"Okey, get going. We'll call if we need you."

The meat wagon pulled up then, taking the spot where the black-and-white had been parked. A wizened looking man with a large black leather case got out and started for the boardwalk stairs.

I bowed my head and left.

TWENTY-THREE

It was almost two in the morning when I stepped out of the automatic elevator onto my floor in the Olmstead. The injuries from Mitch's thoughtful beating had settled into one continuous ache that covered my body from my neck to my hips. I pulled out my keys, and separated the apartment door key from the others on the ring. Halfway down the hall a phone was ringing. Its shrill insistent call was the only sound on the floor, a nasty, unwelcome sound at this time of night that could only mean bad news, somebody died, you're wanted at the hospital. When I got closer, I could hear that it was my phone. It was the same noise I had walked away from nearly five hours ago; as though it had been ringing the entire time I was gone.

I got the door opened and crossed to the phone without turning on the lights. "Foster."

"I've been trying to get in touch with you all night." The accent was thicker in his panic.

"Well you have me now, Miguel. What is it?"

"Miss Rose, she's not well."

"Was she ever?"

"No, you don't understand, she wants to die. She cut her wrists."

I let out my breath like I'd been thumped on the chest, and I didn't have to imagine what that felt like either. "When did this happen?"

"I tried calling you many hours ago. At dinner time at least."

"Why didn't you call the police?"

"She wouldn't have wanted…" He trailed off.

No, she probably wouldn't. They couldn't have helped much anyway, and they might have taken the act as an admission of guilt. But surely someone could have helped. Anyone could have more than me. "How is she now?" I asked

"She's sleeping. I gave her some pills. I've been keeping her pills away from her for many months now. The doctor didn't think it was safe for her to have them. But I didn't know what else to do…" He was getting worked up again.

My mind was racing. Something wasn't making sense. "Keep an eye on her. I'll be right there."

"Thank you. I'll leave the door unlocked so you don't have to ring."

I hadn't had to ring once yet, but I didn't bother pointing that out. I hung up and went back out into the hall.

The streets were mostly empty at that time of night. The city's neon still flashed and blinked, reflected in chrome façades and plate glass store windows, even as the stores themselves were dark. In the residential district, all of the house lights were out, giving the impression of an abandoned city whose traffic lights flashed red and green for no one. I made the turn onto Highlawn Drive and parked in the driveway this time. Unlike the neighbors, the Rosenkrantz house was lit up with what appeared to be every light they had.

Once more Miguel opened the door for me before I could reach for the knob. "She's sleeping still, upstairs in her room."

"Where's Mr. Rosenkrantz?"

Miguel shook his head. "I don't know. He hasn't been home since morning. At dinnertime, Miss Rose started to get very excited. I tried to call you. Where were you?"

"Out. Give me the rest."

"She started shouting. Then she locked herself in her room. After a time, she quieted down, and at first I thought this was good, but when I stopped hearing any sounds at all… I went in with another key."

"Did she know you had another key?"

"Yes."

"Then what?"

"She was on the floor in the bathroom with her wrists cut. There was blood, but not so much. I bandaged her arms and carried her to her bed, gave her the pills, and I've been calling you ever since."

"When was the last time you checked on her?"

"Every ten minutes."

It sounded believable. It also sounded like a headstrong movie star who needed drama in her life as well as in her pictures. Knox had mentioned that she was prone to moods, and I had seen that. But no one had said anything about suicide.

"Take me up," I said.

We went up the staircase opposite the one that led to Rosen-krantz's study, along the catwalk hallway, past two closed doors to a third that had been left ajar. Miguel knocked enough to satisfy propriety and then opened the door the rest of the way.

The only source of light here was a pair of wall sconces made to look like lit candles in brass candelabras. There was one to either side of the four-poster bed. The soft glare from each shone on the green patterned wallpaper, turning the wall at those spots yellow. There was a nice chandelier in the center of the ceiling that wasn't doing anything but looking pretty. An open door just past the bed was the bathroom.

She was on the side of the bed nearest us, propped up on

throw pillows of varying sizes, all with gilt tassels and somber colors except for the pillow just below her head, a normal pillow in a normal white pillowcase, good for sleeping no matter your station. The bedclothes had been pulled back on that side of the bed to form a nice triangle of exposed sheet. She hadn't pulled the covers back over herself. Her right hand lay on the white cloth. A handkerchief had been wrapped around her wrist, and I had no doubt there was one on the other wrist as well. The whole scene looked like a sick room out of a movie, and I wondered if wherever Chloë Rose was it always looked like a movie.

Miguel went to her side. "Miss Rose, Miss Rose, it's Mr. Foster. He's here to help." She didn't stir. He looked back at me with open honest eyes filled with worry. It was plain that he was in love with her. It was a bad thing for him to be.

I stepped past him and took her right hand. I turned it over and unwound the white handkerchief from her wrist. Either she hadn't been very serious about dying or she didn't know what she was doing. There were two jagged cuts across her wrist, not up it, and they intersected as though she had been unsure of the first one and tried again. They were more than superficial, but they wouldn't need stitches. The blood had already clotted, and there was hardly more than a small rusty stain on the handkerchief. I reached across her for the other one just to make sure. It was the same.

As I replaced her left hand, her eyes flickered, and she said something in French in the dull dreamy voice of the drugged. She said a little bit more, and then opened her eyes again, this time enough to maybe see me. She switched to English then. "I'm not dead."

"Did you hope to be?" I said.

She closed her eyes and licked her lips. "Could I please have some water?"

Miguel went around the bed to the bathroom. There was the sound of the sink going on and then off, and he brought the glass to her. He had to put it in her hand, and once he did she just held it, resting the glass on the bed, making no effort to actually drink.

"If you want to kill yourself by slitting your wrists," I said, "you need to cut along the veins up your forearm. That's how you'll bleed out. Slashing across your wrists will just hurt more than anything else."

"I wondered," she said, "why there was so little blood."

"Why do you want to kill yourself? Because you've got an alcoholic husband and some policemen weren't very nice to you?"

Miguel shifted behind me, and I knew that he wasn't happy with the way I was talking to her. Well, he had called me, so I was what he was going to get.

She shook her head back and forth on the pillow, slowly.

"You want to go to a hospital?" I said. "You think that'll get you away from all of this?"

"I don't want a hospital," she said, a petulant child. "I don't want anything. I don't want to be alive."

"You can quit playing Madame Bovary," I told her. "Nobody really thinks you have anything to do with this murder. The police just want to catch a few headlines."

"It's not about the police." Her voice was stronger now. It sounded more like a cornered animal than an injured one.

"Maybe at Merton Stein they like it when you pull your prima donna act, it makes them feel like they've got a real star, but out here, it's not getting you anything."

"You think this is an act?"

"Mister Foster," Miguel said behind me.

"Yeah. I think you're feeling upstaged by a dead starlet who was having an affair with your husband. You've got to remind everyone you're around, but all you got was a Mexican and me."

"Mister Foster," Miguel said again, putting his hand on my elbow now.

"No," Chloë Rose said, throwing the water glass. She only had enough strength to get it a foot or so away from the bed. The water splashed my pant leg. She was shaking her head. "No. No, no, no. I have no one anymore. My mother…my father… Now my husband, too. I have nobody! Nobody wants me."

Miguel left then. Probably going back to his stash of medicine.

"What about your adoring fans? Hell, I'm waiting for your next picture."

She just kept shaking her head.

Miguel was back then with another glass of water and some pills cupped in his palm. I held up my hand to prevent him from going forward. "She's had enough of that."

She pushed what covers were on her off and stood, but she was unsteady on her feet and she fell against me. "Hold me," she said. I put my arms around her. It hurt like hell.

Our faces were inches apart. Her eyes were desperate, urgent with need. Did she want me to kiss her? With her husband missing and her doting houseboy watching?

I held her away from me, one hand on each of her arms. "I know a private place," I said. "The Enoch White Clinic. I had some dealings with them a year or so back when I was working a missing persons and the missing person turned up…unwell. They're good, professional, real doctors."

"You think I need to go to hospital?"

"You think you're fine here?"

She rested her head against my chest. "I'm not fine anywhere."

"I'll ring them right up. They've got people on call any time of the day or night. I bet they can be here within the hour."

She looked back up at me, and now she was scared.

"It'll be all right," I said, although I didn't know if it would.

"But what happened to Mandy..."

"The police are looking into it. Sometimes they surprise you and do their job."

"You said the police only want headlines, not killers."

Throwing my own words back at me. I was as crazy as she was to go on talking to her. But up close like that she smelled so nice. A man could get distracted by that.

She straightened a fold in my shirt, studying the weave intensely. "If you would look into it, I would feel so much better. Everyone else seems out for themselves. I'm frightened."

"I've been warned away from this thing by more people in more ways than I would care to list."

She looked up at me without moving her head. Her eyes glistened, just like they did at that crucial moment in all of her pictures. "Please," she said, breathing the word so I could feel it on my lips.

I bent down and mashed my lips against hers. It wasn't right, but I did it anyway, and I won't say I'm sorry. When we broke apart, I said, "Why does Daniel Merton want to buy your horse?"

Her brow crumpled, and she took a step back, both hands still on my chest. "What does that have to do with anything?"

"I don't know. That's why I'm asking you."

She shook her head, confused, and I could see the hysteria setting back in.

Miguel said, "Mr. Foster, I think you should leave."

We ignored that.

"When did he give you the horse," I said.

She still shook her head. "Four months ago, maybe five."

"Does he often give you things like that?"

"On occasion. When a picture does well. He does it with all of his actresses. It doesn't mean anything."

"Has he ever asked for a present he's given you back before?"

She pressed her lips together, and shook her head. Maybe this time it meant no. "I don't understand, why are you asking me these things?"

"Miss Rose," Miguel said.

"Forget it," I said, and then I leaned in, and she met me, and I kissed her again, smelling flowers and something behind the flowers that was really her.

This time when we parted, she said, "Promise me you'll help Mandy."

"I'll try," I said, because I was a fool.

She collapsed in my arms, going limp, and I struggled to hold her. I leaned her back so that she sat down on the bed, and then I turned back to Miguel, indicating that he should step in and take over. He wouldn't look at me. He took her arm and leaned down for her legs, helping her back onto the bed. There was a phone on the night table and I picked it up to call the clinic. They did the bulk of their business giving people the cure, booze and dope, but they handled all variety of mental disorders. I couldn't tell if Chloë Rose had a problem beyond an artistic bent, but if she was suicidal, she needed more than a Mexican with a pill bottle and a stack of handkerchiefs to sop up her blood. The nurse on the phone assured me that they'd be right over.

Miguel had gotten her back in the bed, and was holding a

new glass of water to her lips. I didn't see if he had given her the pills too. I went back out into the hall, feeling that I had done what I could and a lot that I shouldn't have, and wondering how I had put myself back into this thing right when I should have been walking out. Miguel joined me in a moment.

"Don't be sore at me," I said. "I didn't mean for any of it to go that way in there."

"We're all doing our jobs," he said.

I was too exhausted to fight with him.

"These doctors that you called? Will they call the police?"

"No. And they'll do all they can to keep the police from her— to keep everyone from her, really."

He nodded as though that was satisfactory. We went back downstairs and smoked cigarettes in silence while we waited. When the men in white came, they were quick, cool, and professional. We watched Chloë Rose, the great star, led into the back of the white van that read "Enoch White Clinic" in red with a caduceus along the side. They pulled away with her.

"Tell Rosenkrantz where she went, if he ever comes back," I said. "He can call me if he wants to."

Miguel didn't say anything. I didn't care. I set a brisk pace to my car, got in, made it to my apartment building, and fell on the mattress without taking off my shoes.

TWENTY-FOUR

I missed the sunrise and missed most of what people call morning. I had to get undressed before I could get dressed again, which only hurt a little. No more than getting gored by a bull. I decided that I needed a proper breakfast. I brought out most of what was in the refrigerator and fried it in butter while the coffee brewed and then ate the whole mess in a little less time than it took to cook it. It was eleven o'clock. I had the vague sense that at some point the previous night, I had promised Chloë Rose that I would find Mandy Ehrhardt's killer. I distinctly remembered getting thrown off that very case by no less than three people, some more emphatic than others. And I didn't know if Greg Taylor's death tied in to all of this, but with Chloë Rose and Stark in the same picture, it felt a little too close for comfort. When you added that all up, I guessed there wasn't much to do except to go see if any more paint had peeled off of the walls in my office.

The waiting room at my office appeared empty when I opened the door. The standing ashtray had the usual number of butts plus the one that Knox had added the day before. The layer of dust on the rough burgundy upholstery was undisturbed. It was the appearance of no business, which was business as usual. I closed the outer door and turned to face the space behind it.

"That's far enough," Benny Sturgeon said, holding a .32 automatic in his right hand. The barrel pointed at me.

"When you want to hide in doorways, Mr. Sturgeon, it's best to leave off the aftershave," I said, like I was an expert at hiding in doorways.

He took a quick step towards me, but when I didn't move, he stepped back again. "I'm the one who's going to do the talking, you get me?"

I laughed, and the hard expression on his face turned to pained confusion.

"I've got a gun here," he said.

"You've been watching too many of your own movies."

I turned away from him to go to my office door.

"That's far enough," he said.

"You said that already," I reminded him while getting the key out and fitting it into the door. "When you want to threaten somebody, it's best to have the safety catch off. It makes the whole thing more effective."

He moved behind me, but I ignored him. Hollywood. The talent was crazy and the people behind the scenes were crazier. I opened the office door, and flicked on the overhead light.

There was a man standing against the opposite wall with his arms over his chest. He looked familiar, but I couldn't place him.

"Who the hell are you?" I said.

"My partner," a voice said behind me. "McEvoy. You met yesterday."

"How do you do," McEvoy said, bobbing his head.

"Samuels," I said, and turned to see him. "You couldn't wait out front like a civilian would? You've got to break into my office?"

"It's not breaking in when there's probable cause," Detective Samuels said. "You're suspected of interfering with a police investigation." He looked over at Sturgeon, who had come in, his gun still outstretched. "You can drop that, Sturgeon," Samuels said.

"Don't mind him," I said. "It's just a prop. You've got blanks in there, don't you, Sturgeon?"

His hand dropped to his side and he was the same ineffectual man who had tried to hire me the day before. "Yes. They're blanks."

"And the safety's on," Samuels said.

"Okey, the damn safety's on!" Sturgeon said.

I nodded my chin at Samuels. "You mind if I sit down? I've kind of been running around the past few days." I went around my desk, pulled out the chair, and sat down like I was all alone, bringing my hands up behind my head and resting it on both of my palms. Samuels was still staring at the director. "What are you doing here?"

Sturgeon looked around at each of us like he was going to ask for directions.

"He came by yesterday," I said. "He wanted to hire me to work the Ehrhardt murder. He had this crazy idea that you wanted Chloë Rose for the spot. I told him I'd already been warned off of that case and anyway I've got a job going and I only work one job at a time. So he came back to change my mind."

"You know, I never saw his lips move," Samuels said, eliciting a choked-off laugh from his partner.

"Is that what it was all about?" Samuels said to Sturgeon. "You thought you could scare the peeper into working this case?"

Sturgeon nodded. "Yes. It's all exactly as Mr. Foster says."

"What, you don't trust the cops?" McEvoy said.

"Do you?" I said.

"Okay, enough from you," Samuels said. "You know, Foster,

the other morning I liked you all right, and I'm not a man who likes peepers."

"You're not alone."

He ignored that. "You played it straight with me. You didn't hold anything out." He looked at me sharply. "Did you?"

"No," I said, leaning forward in my chair and resting my hands on my desk.

"You see? He didn't leave anything out," Samuels said across the room to McEvoy as if they had been arguing about it before I got there. Samuels looked back at me. "So how come I find out you're working the Ehrhardt murder when I told you not to?"

"Who says I am?" I said, squinting.

"I say it," Samuels said. "And an informant who I won't mention. You'll understand."

"Did you find everything you needed in here, or do you need me to get out any other files for you?"

"This one's a real riot," McEvoy said.

"Who asked you?" I said.

"Enough. Just tell me what you found out, Foster, and then that's the end of it for you. Understand?

I nodded over at Sturgeon. "Do we want company while we talk?"

"Sturgeon, you wait outside," Samuels said.

Sturgeon slumped his shoulders, and went back out into the reception room. Samuels closed the door behind him. I listened for the sound of the outer door, but it didn't come. Sturgeon was waiting.

"So my friend at the *Chronicle* ratted me out," I said, taking a cigarette from the pack on my desk.

"Why do you say that?" Samuels said.

I waved out my match. "Only person who could have talked."

"You think what you want," Samuels said. "Just spill."

"I'm guessing you already know everything I know. There was a woman killed the same way as Ehrhardt back in December, just before Christmas. Found in Harbor City, never identified. So naturally I got to thinking that maybe they were killed by the same person. You see why I might have thought that?"

Samuels pressed his lips together and squinted. He saw all right. But it looked like it might have been the first time he saw. Maybe it hadn't been Fisher who had ratted me out after all.

"So who was the Jane Doe?" Samuels said.

"Never identified," I repeated, slower than before. "You can find everything I know in the *S.A. Times* for December 23."

"Fine," Samuels said. "What about this man under the board-walk in Harbor City last night? Or did you think I hadn't heard about that?"

"A different job."

"He's connected to another actor in Ehrhardt's movie. I don't like that."

"You saying there's a connection between their deaths?"

"Am I?"

"Don't let me be the one to tell you," I said.

Samuels took a deep breath then and let it out. His whole face went limp. "Look, Foster. I don't mean to give you a hard time, but you know how it is."

"Yeah, I know it," I said, and held back a sneer. At least, I thought I held it back.

"Peepers," Samuels said and stood up.

"Yeah," McEvoy said, dropping a heavy hand on my shoulder. "Peepers."

"Here's a little advice, Foster. Don't find any more bodies in Harbor City."

I smiled.

Samuels opened the door to the reception room just as the phone rang. He and McEvoy both turned back to look at me. The phone rang again.

Samuels said quietly, "Well, aren't you going to answer it?"

TWENTY-FIVE

We all looked at the phone. I let it ring one more time, and picked up. "Foster."

"Foster, you bastard, you're a real pain, you know that?" It was Pauly Fisher at the *Chronicle*.

"Some people were just reminding me of that."

"I don't have anything for you on any other murders yet, but I found out who buried the story about the Jane Doe."

"Yes," I said, noncommittal. I looked up at the officers. Sturgeon was standing behind them, and all three of them were watching me. I gestured that it was nothing and that they should go, which worked about as well as I could have expected. I turned away in my seat a little, so that I wasn't facing them. "Go on."

"You okay, Foster?" Fisher said on the phone. "You don't sound like your usual self."

"I'm fine," I said.

"You're not alone, is that it?" Fisher's voice lowered as though the people in my office could hear him.

"That's right."

"Okay," he said. "I'll keep it quick. That article you mentioned was by Ronald Dupree, a guy I've known for a thousand years. So I called Ron and asked him why the story had been buried. He was cagey at first, but I pushed and finally Ron told me the story was quashed by none other than Daniel Merton."

I turned farther in my seat, so I was facing the grimy window behind my desk, the cord of the phone dangling over my shoulder.

"You there, Foster?" Fisher said.

"Did your friend have any idea why?"

"No. And after he told me, he tried to make out like it was just a rumor, and there was probably nothing to it. Which tells me it's the truth."

Someone cleared his throat behind me. "Yeah," I said. "Listen, thanks. I mean it."

"Like hell you do," Fisher said. "We'll talk later when you can talk." He hung up.

That was the second time that Daniel Merton's name had come up, first with the horse and now this. Why would the head of one of the studios, one of the richest men in California, want to keep the murder of an unidentified woman in Harbor City quiet?

I turned back and cradled the phone. "My dry cleaner. My other suit is ready."

"Cut the comedy, Foster."

"All right, it was my guy at the *Chronicle*. I'd asked him to look for more murders that matched the pattern, and he was calling to say he hadn't found any." I looked Samuels in the eye. "That's the truth. Now if you boys wouldn't mind clearing out, I have some real work to do." I opened one of my desk drawers as though I were looking for a file.

"If I find out that you made my job harder," Samuels said, "I'm going to come down on you with everything I've got."

"Doesn't look like you've got too much," I said, "if you can waste your time hanging around a peeper's office, listening to his phone calls."

Samuels tapped a forefinger against my desk. "If your friend calls you with anything," he said, "you call me with it. Otherwise, you stay away from my case."

He stalked out of the office, leaving the door open behind him.

McEvoy tipped his hat to me with one finger, nodded at Sturgeon, and then walked out. He pulled the door shut.

Like Gilplaine before them, they were telling me too much. They were telling me they didn't want this case solved by me or anybody, that there was something to hide. That was okay with me, it could stay hidden for all I cared, only there was the matter of a broken movie star and whether my word was worth a damn thing.

I looked at Sturgeon. "You, too," I said.

He raised his shoulders and pushed out his chest. "Now, look here, Foster. I'm prepared to pay you a lot of money—"

"That tune again," I said, standing up. "You can't decide if you're sticking me up or bribing me." I grabbed the edge of the door, preparing to close it. "Besides, you heard the detective, I'm not allowed anywhere near this case."

"Now, see here," Sturgeon said, "he has no right—"

"Neither do you," I said, and I shoved him gently with the heel of my hand. When he'd cleared the threshold, I swung the door closed. I stayed close, listening, waiting for him to leave. There was no sound at first. He just stood there, trying to decide what to do. Then after another minute came the sound of his footsteps crossing the floor, followed by the outer door opening and closing. I listened for his steps in the hall to be sure he hadn't doubled back. They were faint and grew fainter.

That should have been the end of it. There was nothing that made staying in it make any sense. But there was nothing about any of it that made any sense. And even telling myself that

Chloë Rose had been out of her mind when I had seen her last, and heavily sedated to boot, did nothing to quiet my conscience. My word was my word, and I'd given it.

I went to the safe and got out the envelope with the check in it that Al Knox had given me the day before, and put it in my pocket, still sealed. Then I stepped into the waiting room, and locked the office behind me.

Downstairs I got my car out of the garage and took it around the block, watching my rearview to make sure that neither Samuels nor Sturgeon meant to follow me. No car stayed with me the whole way, so I completed my loop out onto Hollywood Boulevard, and started for Daniel Merton's movie studio.

TWENTY-SIX

The kid at the gate wasn't Jerry, but it might as well have been.

"I'm sorry, sir, your name is not on the list," he said, holding up his clipboard. "You're going to have to go through the gate and turn around and come back out again. There are people behind you."

I put on my most charming smile for him. "I was hired two days ago by Al Knox. You know Al Knox?"

The kid nodded. "He's my boss."

"Well, why don't you call Al, and tell him I'm here. Dennis Foster. He'll tell you to let me through."

Somebody behind me let go with their horn and held it down. I checked my rearview. There was a black coupe behind me and a truck behind that. It was the truck driver who was honking.

The noise startled the kid, who ducked back into the box and picked up a phone. He came out a moment later.

"I'm sorry, Mr. Foster," the kid said, back at my window. "Mr. Knox wasn't in the office just now."

"Well, did you ask anyone else if they knew me? I was just here the day before yesterday."

The truck horn had not let up.

"Look, call the office back, tell them I'm coming in, and open the gate before that truck driver ruins the soundtrack on all of the pictures being made."

"I don't think I can do that, sir."

"I think you can. Just step back inside and try."

He blinked, looked back at the truck driver, and waved his hand. "Would you quit it?" The horn kept blaring. The kid looked all around again and shook his head. "I'm sorry, sir. You'll have to come around."

He hit the button that made the bar go up and then stepped in front of my car, guiding me, forcing me to turn around unless I wanted to hit him. From the other side of the booth, he triggered the exit gate, and I pulled back out onto Cabarello Boulevard.

The studio wall continued along Cabarello until the next intersection, where it turned right, maintaining the perimeter. I followed it until the next opening, a smaller gate just large enough to be used by one vehicle at a time. There were large wrought-iron gates that opened inward and would be shut at night. A heavy chain was suspended across the opening with a sign hanging from the middle that said, "Private. No Trespassing." The security officer here was an older man with a soft belly, no doubt one of Knox's retirees. I pulled up to the gate as another car was turned away.

"Any chance of getting in here today?" I said.

"About as good a chance as any other day," he said.

"I should be expected."

"Believe me, they all should be expected. You got a screen test with DeMille or Hughes or some other director that doesn't even work at our studio but across town at the competitor's? Or are you good friends with Chet Gelding or John Stark, or maybe it was Layla Carlton?"

"Al Knox hired me a couple days back to work a private investigation. I'm just trying to get in to see him, but the boy at the front gate couldn't get Al on the phone."

"Where do they find these kids?"

"Will you at least call Al?"

"You a cop?"

"Not anymore."

He nodded. "What's your name?"

"Foster. And if you don't get Knox, I actually *am* friends with John Stark," I said, and smiled.

"You can leave that one in your hip pocket. I'll get Knox. Just a matter of knowing where to reach him. Hang on."

He went over to the side of the gate, opened a little panel there and brought out a phone receiver. He talked a few moments, waited, talked a bit more, then hung up and closed the little panel. He unclipped the side of the chain nearest him, and walked it across the opening, clearing the path through the gate. He waved me on. As I pulled up, I said, "Thanks."

"I guess it was about time for my daily exercise anyway," he said.

I pulled in to the studio. Security wasn't as useless as Knox had made it out to be. It might not have been impossible for a strange man to appear on the set of one of their movies, but it would take a little doing.

I followed the streets as best I could coming from the side entrance. I passed through the shadow of two soundstages and arrived at the four-story administrative building with the parking lot out front. I took a spot between what appeared to be an Army truck and what was for sure a Rolls Royce. I wasn't too concerned about whether Knox was available or not; I hadn't come to see him. Still, it was his house. I crossed the parking lot to the door on the end of the building with chicken wire glass, where three security golf carts were parked.

The officer on secretary duty today looked up as I came in. "Mr. Knox just got back in the office. I'm sorry about Billy. He's just doing his job."

"Aren't we all?" I said, and continued past him and on into Al's office.

He was on the phone. "No, damn it. This has nothing to do with my department or anybody else at the studio. It was an unfortunate but unrelated event." He gritted his teeth and shook his head at me. "There will be express instructions as always to allow no member of the press on the lot. And you're not to bother any of our actors either. You say whatever you damn please, but we'll sue you for slander if you get a word of it wrong." He slammed the phone and a ghost of a ring hung in the air between us.

"Dennis, what are you here for?" Knox said. His cheeks were red, and perspiration made his forehead shiny. He took out a handkerchief and wiped his mouth and then put it back in his pocket. "I don't have time for anything but business. This Ehrhardt-Rose thing is a twister just waiting to happen."

"Fine with me," I said. I pulled out the envelope and tossed it on his desk, much the way he'd tossed it on mine the day before.

He looked at the envelope. Then he reached for it, his eyes searching for an answer in mine. "What's this?"

"Something you left in my office. I'm returning it."

He puffed out his upper lip and looked up at me. "You know, sending Rose to the nut house was a fine idea you had there. Now *everyone* thinks she killed Mandy."

"No they don't," I said.

"All right, no they don't." He held up the envelope. "You really should keep this. It would make me feel more comfortable."

"Who asked you to hire me?"

"I hired you, what do you mean? Look, I don't have time—"

"Then don't waste it repeating yourself. Who asked you to

hire me? It wasn't your idea. I've seen Sturgeon in action, it wasn't his. All I want to know is, who wanted me—or some other sap like me—following Chloë Rose around?"

"Dennis…"

"I don't get paid off. I get paid to do a job. And I definitely don't get paid off when I don't even know who's paying me off and what they're paying me off for. I got hired to do a job. I didn't do it. So I don't get paid."

Knox's face sagged. "I was doing you a favor, goddamn it," he said. "I was throwing a bone your way. Why the hell couldn't you just take it and chew on it?"

"Because I'm not a lapdog, Knox. I don't fetch, I don't heel, and I don't roll over."

We stared at each other then. Taxidermied deer couldn't have done it better. Knox tapped the unopened envelope on his desk. Someone in another part of the office yelled, but I couldn't make out what it was about. Outside, the whole engine of Merton Stein Productions chugged away. Take an actress, an actor, and one of those scripts they were forever carrying back and forth out there. Slap some film in the camera. Plug in some lights, pay a violinist or two to add background melodies, and presto, you've got yourself a product you can show at theaters around the country, or drive-ins if it isn't good enough for the indoor crowd. Then do it again. Fifty times a year. A hundred. No slowdowns along the line. One part in the machinery is broken? Get another. Mr. and Mrs. America need their Sunday double feature, otherwise it would be nothing but newsreels, and we need morale to be high. Leave your dime at the door.

Knox set the envelope down. "Mr. Merton gave me the order personally. He said I should hire someone who could do a simple job, and I picked you. Okey, you bastard?"

I nodded. "Okey."

"You're not surprised."

"I can't say that I am."

He watched me. The voice down the hall yelled again, a happy sound. "I'm working with children here," Knox said.

"I'll leave you to it." I started for the door. Behind me came the sound of his chair creaking and then an exhalation as he pulled himself out of his seat.

"Now wait just a minute, Foster. Do you have something on this you want to tell me?"

"No, like I said. I got the message from you yesterday. I did a bad job. I'm fired. I even worked another case since then. Fastest P.I. in the west."

"Don't be like that, Foster. We're all acting stupid around this. Damn it, I went into this security detail so I wouldn't have to deal with this kind of thing anymore. I'm tired of blood."

I softened and leaned in toward him. "The police put me off of this thing too. Nobody wants me in it. I don't want me in it."

He waited for more. When I didn't say anything, he said, "Well, why are you here?"

"To see Mr. Merton," I said, and headed for the door.

He caught me by the shoulder. "You can't just go see Mr. Merton. You need an appointment."

"I don't think he'll make one for me, do you?"

He didn't stop me when I turned to go that time.

Merton wanted someone to follow Chloë Rose, he wanted Chloë Rose's horse, which used to be his horse, and he wanted a Jane Doe story to go away. Probably this Mandy Ehrhardt story, too. And Mr. Merton was a man who got what he wanted. So what else did Mr. Merton want? I figured I'd ask him.

The exterior walkway on the second floor cast the ground

floor walk in shadow. The main entrance was a pair of double glass doors that entered into a wind block, and then another set of doors. The Merton Stein crest hung on the wood-paneled wall behind the front desk, and there were two secretaries at the desk who looked more severe than any of the security officers I'd seen so far. But I walked as though I belonged, waving and nodding to both of them, and went straight for the stairs. They might have called out after me, but I didn't wait to find out.

Upstairs, I was in another reception room almost identical to the lobby below. There was no avoiding the secretary here, a middle-aged woman with the lined face of a gorilla, her hair pulled back into a tight bun.

"May I help you?" she said. Her voice had the sandpaper rasp of a lifelong smoker.

"I'm here to see Mr. Merton," I said. I had my wallet out, already reaching for one of my cards. I held it out to her, and she looked at it without making any move to take it. Her expression did not change.

"To see Mr. Merton, you must have an appointment."

"I think if you check with him, I have an appointment."

"I make Mr. Merton's appointments," she said. She was annoyed with me, but not so annoyed that it was worth exercising a facial muscle over.

"Mr. Merton had me hired the day before yesterday. Last night—"

"I know who you are," the secretary said.

"So do I," said another voice, much friendlier, though no less stern.

I looked up. She stood in the entryway of the massive double doors just to the left of the secretary's desk. She wore a blue

blouse with a red ascot tied around her neck and a tailored pair
of khaki pants that ended mid-calf. Her open-toed brown heels
showed that her toenails were the same color as her lips, rose
red. The last time I had seen her, she had offered me those lips,
and the time before that she'd been stuffing a drunk into the
back seat of a car. Yeah, she was a girl that could make life very
pleasant or very difficult, sometimes both at the same time.

The secretary's annoyance deepened then. "Miss Merton, I
have already asked you to return home and wait for your father
there." Including me she said, "Mr. Merton isn't here right
now. As you know all too well, Mr. Foster, he is quite busy today
handling the situation."

"That's grand, Mr. Foster, isn't it?" Miss Merton said, still from
the doorway. "The 'situation,' " she mimicked.

The secretary turned white.

Miss Merton nodded her head into the mysterious dark between the doors, and said, "Come on in, Mr. Foster. We can
wait for Daddy together." She passed through the doors without
waiting to see if I would follow. I guess they always followed. I
smiled my charming smile at the secretary and it got about the
same response it had with the kid at the front gate. I walked
around her desk, and let myself into Daniel Merton's office.

TWENTY-SEVEN

The lights were off and the curtains drawn, giving the room the oppressive tone of sick days in bed. Mr. Merton's desk stood by the windows, its footprint smaller than Al Knox's office downstairs, but not by much. Beside the desk there was a small school chair with attached writing surface where the stenographer would sit when Mr. Merton wanted to write something down. There was a long boardroom table off to one side with high-backed leather chairs all around it. A clutch of cozy couches in burgundy upholstery with buttons on the cushions surrounded a glass coffee table on a zebra-skin rug.

Vera Merton had chosen the couch with its back to me so that I had to walk around to the other side if we were going to talk. When I did, the shadows cut her features sharper. It didn't hurt her any. Her legs were crossed at the ankles and extended under the coffee table where I could see them through the glass. She was a lifetime of getting what she wanted when she wanted it and no realization that that wasn't true for everybody. Chloë Rose made you want to protect her. This one made you hope someone would protect you.

"There's a bar hidden away in the wall over there, if you'd like a drink." She didn't have one. In fact, it was unclear what she had been doing all alone in the dark. "I knew you were hired by my father," she said as I sat on the edge of the opposite couch.

"Only I didn't," I said, leaning forward on my thighs, my hat in my hands. "Daddy can't pay the electric bills?"

"Sometimes I like sitting in the dark. It helps me think," she said.

"And what do you think about?"

She cocked her head. "If I'm not mistaken, that was a personal question. Did you just ask me a personal question?"

"I don't know. Sometimes in my business I get personal when I'm not supposed to. Do you ask all the men that happen by to palaver in your father's office?"

"Only ones that work for my father," she said.

"So I guess around you that's all of them," I said.

"If you decide to be fresh with me, I might decide I don't like you."

"You liked me all right yesterday."

"That was yesterday."

"Well, take your time. I don't need an answer today."

She laughed at that, though it sounded as sincere as an acting class exercise. "Are you auditioning for a part? You're like a man out of my father's movies."

I smiled along with her, but said nothing.

She turned the laughter off but left the smile on. It was a perfect smile, barely a crease showing around it on her face. And it was a perfect face, a young girl's face, nineteen, maybe twenty.

"You have a knack for finding bodies, it seems," she said.

"You were there when Stark asked me to find Mr. Taylor. I didn't promise I'd find him alive."

The smile went away.

"Do you remember the question I asked you, and you told me to go ask Daddy? That's why I'm here. But Daddy's not here and you are."

"A coincidence. What was your question?"

"You're getting personal again."

"Sorry. I'll try to cut it out. What was your question?"

"What did my father hire you for?"

"Maybe that's personal," I said.

"Maybe, but you're going to tell me anyway."

"I will?"

"You wouldn't yesterday, but you will today. He hired you because of my brother, didn't he?"

"I wouldn't know," I said.

"Oh, I'm sure he told you to be cautious, he probably even had a cover story prepared for you. Was it that some crank was claiming that he had the exact same story idea as our most recent picture and that he sent it in two years ago, and now he was threatening Tommy over it?"

It was fascinating watching her guess as we sat there together in the dark. Even if she was young, she wasn't stupid; even if she was wrong, I had the feeling she might be groping in the right direction. "No," I said, "that wasn't it."

"It's got to be my brother. That's the only reason Daddy would handle something as menial as hiring a detective himself. It's the only reason he would have hired somebody instead of using someone that already worked for him."

"Sure, you're too smart for me," I said. "You knew all this days ago. You knew it before I was hired even." I nodded my chin at her. "What's with your brother that he needs a detective?"

Her confidence slipped as she realized that she might have spoken out of turn. She looked away from me, her eyes darting down and then across the distance to the blacked-out windows. "Nothing," she said. "Gambling." She looked back at me, proving that she could meet my look. "Gambling, women, too much room for blackmail." She said this last as if she didn't expect me to believe it.

I felt sorry, so I said, "I was hired on studio business. It was Al Knox, head of security who actually did the hiring. The word just came down from your father."

She didn't look relieved or placated.

"That's all I can tell you," I added.

"No, of course," she said, lifting her head up and with it her shoulders. "I try not to know anything about my father's business. When your father's a magic maker it takes all the magic out of life, because you've seen all the tricks."

"Unless he learns a new one."

She smiled, and it was her award-winning smile again. "Old dogs, Mr. Foster. Or I forget, did you say to call you Dennis?"

"I didn't say either."

She waved that away, and let her arm fall limp beside her.

"You know why I was hired. All of that business about your brother, that's just your protective side coming out."

"Let's forget about that," she said quietly. "It's in the past now."

"That doesn't always mean it goes away," I said.

Our eyes met, and I held hers. We measured our stares. One of us had to be the first to look away, and in the end I did it. I didn't want to stay any longer. "Enjoy the dark," I said, standing.

"My father's probably at the track." She didn't look up at me, but spoke straight ahead. "He's been nearly every day since the law went through. He put up the initial money to build the place before it was even legal."

"Santa Theresa or Hollywood Park?"

"Hollywood Park, of course."

"Then who runs things around here?" I said.

"Younger men," she said. Her eyes were gone.

I put on my hat and left before she had fully convinced herself that she had the right to feel sorry for herself.

TWENTY-EIGHT

In the outer office, the secretary didn't pause in her typing, even when I stood right up against her desk. "Is there a public phone around here?"

"Are you sure you don't want to just use mine?" she said in exaggerated indignation.

"No, I'm afraid the call's private."

"There's one downstairs to the right of the door."

"Thanks," I said, and tipped my hat. She never looked up.

I went downstairs and crossed the lobby to the payphone. It wasn't in a booth, just bolted to the wall. I had the operator put me through to the *Chronicle* and asked for Pauly Fisher. There was a long pause during which I watched the flags dangle listlessly on their poles, and then Fisher came on. "I've got news for you," he said.

"Give."

"I talked to a friend in the Harbor City police department, a real veteran. You talk to them down there?"

"I don't think we're friends right now."

Fisher snorted. "Well, there's at least one other case, a few years back. Same thing. Cut neck, cut thighs."

My pulse went up. "Name?"

"A Drusila Carter. She was working as a temp in a cleaning service. No record, family in the Midwest. They never even brought in a suspect."

"Anything else?" I said.

"My friend on the force said he thought he remembered the case being made a low priority. What are you onto here, Dennis? Should I be checking other parts of the city?"

"No," I said. "I just want to see things that aren't there."

"Like hell they aren't there."

"Thanks, Fisher," I said in a voice to end the conversation. Then before he could hang up: "Hey, you know anything about Merton's kids?"

He wasn't fooled by my attempt at sounding casual. "Is that what this is about, Merton's kids?"

"I don't know," I said. "Maybe."

"Well, I can't say I know much about them. Just what's in the society pages. The girl's a knockout, she's got brains, they gave her an east coast education, but she has a tendency to get lonely and to get photographed when she does. Twenty? Something like that. The boy's a few years older and there's got to be something wrong with him because for a few months he'll be all over the movie scene and then for a few months he's gone. I'd guess it's dope. All those rich kids are users."

"All right," I said. "Thanks again, and call if you get anything else."

"This better be as good a story as I think it is," Fisher said. "And you'd better not give it to anyone but me."

I made noises he could interpret however made him happy, then hung up.

I crossed the lobby to the exit. He was opening the outer door as I was opening the inner door, and I hurried two steps and slugged him on the chin with all of my one hundred and eighty pounds. It was like punching a bag of unmixed cement. Mitch stumbled backwards, holding onto the door handle to keep from falling, although he wasn't really in any danger of it until I took advantage of his momentary imbalance by throwing myself against his chest. He went down and I rushed past him out the door.

The sand-colored coupe sat at the head of the circular drive with the tall thin man at the wheel. He stood on the gas when he saw me. I ran along the building back towards the security office and my car. The Packard started without any trouble, and I was able to pull it out and make it to the first intersection before the coupe appeared in my rearview mirror.

The way I had come into the studio would require the guard to unlatch the chain again, which would take too long, so I turned left towards the main entrance, where I could ram the wooden gate if I needed to. I pushed the car as fast as I could between the soundstage buildings, causing people to jump out of the way and one car to swerve and honk furiously. The coupe stayed behind me, but gaining.

As I reached the front gate, a blue Lincoln was just pulling out. I gunned the motor, slipping under the black-and-white gate arm as it began to close. It banged off the back of my car. My front bumper bottomed out, scraping against the road as the shocks absorbed the decline to the street. I took advantage of the blocked lane of traffic trying to get into the studio and turned right onto Cabarello.

I went through one light and then a second with no sign of pursuit, and then the coupe appeared several cars back and one lane over. Either it wasn't so essential that they keep me in sight or they were confident they could catch up later. The traffic on the main thoroughfare acted as a barrier, but it also prevented me from getting away. I wove my way between the cars, changing lanes frequently, and made a sudden left turn at Underhill without signaling, earning me more angry honking.

I stepped on the gas, shifting up to third gear, and then to fourth, going much too fast in too highly populated an area. The coupe was behind me, doing the same, and it appeared to be gaining again. I pulled up the hand brake and jerked on the wheel, making a hairpin turn onto a residential street, then released the brake and flooded the engine as I sped down the block. I repeated the maneuver at the next corner, slamming my tail end into a telephone pole, almost losing control of my spin, until I managed to pull the car straight again. I was moving parallel to Underhill, still heading south, in the direction of Hollywood Park Racetrack.

I eased up on the speed, downshifting as my rearview stayed empty, and then brought it down to twenty-five, watching the mirror more than the road. When the street I was on hit California Avenue, I turned left and joined the traffic at a normal speed. It was only four blocks later that the sand-colored coupe was visible, weaving between the cars, two blocks behind me. I increased the gas, and made the turn onto Amity that would descend into the Valley, going through undeveloped rock formations before bottoming out in Hollywood Park. The winding road was clear of traffic, and I continued to increase my speed as best I could as the road switched back and forth, all the while descending.

The view behind me at first remained clear as well, but soon the sand-colored coupe would appear just before each curve, playing peek-a-boo behind the rock walls. Each turn, the coupe would stay in sight just a little bit longer, and soon they were taking one turn just as I was taking the next. We passed a produce-and-flowers shack built on a sandy lot where the space beside the road jutted out far enough. Around the next bend, there were more buildings on the left. Soon the rock wall would fall away from the right as well, and we would be back in a residential area. It would be better for me then.

But an explosive crack caused me to jerk the wheel, veering into the oncoming traffic lane, while looking behind me to find that the coupe was no more than thirty yards behind. There was another crack. Mitch was leaning out the passenger side window, trying to steady a gun as he aimed at me. Neither shot had cracked my windows, so I decided he must be aiming for my tires. I pulled onto the right side of the road, and another car flashed by, the sound of its horn dropping through the registers. As it passed the coupe, the thin man pulled into the oncoming traffic lane and gunned his car, bringing it within a few feet of my left taillight. Mitch shot again. The bullet pinged off of the body of my car. The sky grew to the right, the rock receding and houses appearing below. The sand-colored coupe's front right wheel was even with my back left wheel. I took my foot off of the gas and jerked the steering wheel hard to the left. I slid along the front seat from the impact, my bruised ribs bringing my stomach up to my throat and the taste of vomit into my mouth.

The coupe veered off to the left while its driver tried to regain control. A red car, maybe a Chrysler, maybe a Pontiac, appeared, nosing out of a residential street ahead. The coupe slammed into it, causing the red car to spin ninety degrees, and bringing the coupe to a stop after a forty-foot skid that left a trail of burnt rubber on the pavement. I managed to maintain control of my Packard and I continued on, watching the rearview for two more blocks, unconvinced that the coupe was out of commission. But they remained where their car had stopped.

I wondered if it had been Knox or Merton's secretary who had called them in, or if maybe I had been followed this morning without noticing after all, but in the end I decided it didn't matter.

There was a siren already in the air. I put all my weight down on the gas pedal.

The racetrack was only another ten minutes away.

TWENTY-NINE

The Hollywood Park Racetrack was on a large stretch of land south of Hollywood that had been fields five years before. The parking lot was a patch of dirt outside of the grandstand, a three-story high, shingled edifice painted white. It shone in the California sun and blocked the view of the track from the lot. People had been opposed to the legalization of horse racing in the state, afraid that it would bring with it organized crime, more alcoholics, and debt-ridden gamblers. They were right; it had brought those things. But the main investors in the track had not been gangsters. They were the Hollywood brass. The head of just about every studio had put money into the Hollywood races, and they came to watch as often as possible.

Inside the grandstand was a crowd of men who had nowhere else to be in the middle of a weekday afternoon. They lined up nine and ten deep at the twelve brass-barred windows where tellers took the money eagerly pushed through the bars and handed back slips of paper. Drifts of spent papers littered the floor, kicked and crumpled underfoot, ignored. There were large windows looking down into the horses' stables so you could get a good look at the contenders. A large mechanical letter board of the kind used in train stations took up part of an enormous wall to the right of the tellers' windows. It rattled through the names of horses, showing that day's previous races in first, place, and show, with spots for the upcoming races left blank. Most of today's races were already finished. Another board beside it showed the names of the horses in the next race and the odds. A chalkboard with the same information was posted in the tellers' room, kept up to date by a small man in a gray suit. Ceiling fans worked at stirring the air overhead.

I looked at the harried tellers behind the counter, and took one step in their direction. I got dirty looks from no less than three of the marks, who didn't want anyone getting in the way of their emptying their wallets. I turned and went the other direction, through one of the large open archways that led out into the stands. There was a lot of well-tended dirt in an oval around a lot of well-tended grass. The starting gates were being rolled into place. Several horses carrying bright-colored jockeys were stamping the track behind the gates. An amplified voice kept up a running commentary, listing the names of horses and the names of jockeys, goading people into placing bets. The grandstand was just under half full, the crowd thick down near the track and then spread out all along the upper seats. Above that, there were large windows open to the air. The V.I.P. section. I went back inside.

A white-haired Negro custodian in a blue uniform shirt and matching pants was using a rake to gather up the slips of paper on the edge of the crowd. He had a garbage can on wheels just behind him. He was unconcerned by the frenzy, and showed no resentment when a mark walked through his carefully collected pile. I pulled out a five as I approached, but then a second mark kicked through the Negro's work and I switched it to a ten. I held it down near where his hands were on the rake so he would see it. He stopped scraping and looked up, causing creases to form in stacks on his forehead.

"Now I know you know I don't take bets, officer," the Negro said.

I didn't correct him. "Show me where the V.I.Ps sit, the owners, the studio brass. Upstairs, right?"

He turned his eye to my outstretched hand, still holding the ten, still without taking it. "The stairs are right over there," he nodded. "I know that's not worth ten." He looked back up at me again, waiting for me to say what it was I wanted.

"I need in. I was told Daniel Merton was here. I need to see him. Is that enough?"

He nodded his head and took the bill. "You'll need another one of those for the boy upstairs," he said.

I nodded. He led the way across the room. A race had started and the space around the teller booths was nearly empty. The door to the stairs was underneath the big board. It was a narrow steep set of wooden stairs that were painted green. The heat was bottled up inside and I began to sweat before we'd even climbed halfway. "You ever find a winning ticket in all of that mess?" I asked him.

"I never have," he said without turning around.

There was another door at the top of the steps under a naked light bulb. He went through, holding the door for me. We were in a kind of vestibule open to the air on both sides. I could tell by the sound that the race was already over. He went and talked to an identically dressed young Negro standing guard outside a set of double doors opposite the door we'd come through. The youth looked at me and then back at the old man and shook his head. The old man said something more and the youth shook his head again. I walked up. "What's the problem?"

"Damn fool don't know where his mouth is to feed it," the old Negro said.

The youth turned to me. "I can't let anyone through these doors that's not a founder. There's no way to get in other than past me. I'd lose my job. What sense does that make, old man?"

I reached into my pocket and brought out another ten, my card, and a pencil. I turned the card over and wrote three names on the back. I held the ten and the card out to the youth. "Take this to Daniel Merton. Tell him I'm outside and that I'd like to talk to him. He'll tell you to let me through."

The youth looked at the ten and looked again at the old man. Then he took the money and the card. "Don't let anyone past," he said, and slipped through the door, which closed behind him.

"Kids today," the old man said, and headed off through the door to the stairs.

The echoing voice of the announcer continued its pitch. Better keep the patrons' anxiety running high, right up to the last race. It was near on dusk now and the track would be shutting down soon. Then all of the winners and losers would cross to the strip of bars across the street, whether in celebration or to drown their defeat.

The door opened and the young Negro gestured me inside. "It's the last one," he said stepping past me. He closed the door without even looking back.

It was a long narrow hallway with painted green doors every five to twenty feet. A brass number marked each door starting at one. There was no way to tell if any of the other boxes were occupied. I figured they were probably filled about as much as the grandstand, just below half. There was an unpainted door in the middle of the hall with no number that must have been the janitor's closet. The last door was numbered fifteen and it had been left open.

It was a small booth. Just four chairs along the short wall at the front. The entire track could be taken in at one glance. There were telephone extensions on both sides of the booth at seat level for calling in bets. Merton was alone. He sat in the chair all the way to the left. He didn't turn around.

I stepped between the two chairs on the right so that he could see me.

"Have a seat," he said, still without looking at me.

I left a seat between us. In profile he looked like a Roman emperor on an ancient coin. He wore a dark three-piece suit with a starched white shirt. The shadows were deep enough that I couldn't see very much of him. The family clearly had a predilection for sitting in the dark.

He didn't say anything. Neither did I. The announcer's quick patter announced that the last race of the day was about to begin. The horses were already at their starting gates. There was a moment of anticipation and then the sound of a pistol and the announcer cried, "They're off." His voice then droned like a dentist's drill, telling us what we were seeing. Merton kept his eye on the race but with an expression of indifference. I couldn't tell if he had bet on it. The horses pounded around to the far side of the track, turning into miniatures. Then they came back around the bend, the clatter of their hooves only just audible over the crowd and the announcer. A red jockey and a green jockey were out a length ahead of the pack, which was bunched close enough that show could have gone to any of them. They barreled past where the gate had been. The red jockey eased his horse out ahead of the green one and they came into the finish that way, the third horse still half a length behind. The people in the grandstand started filing back towards the doors. There was a sense of deflation in the announcer's voice.

Merton spoke then. It was the measured voice of a powerful man who had not yet decided to use his power. "What do you want?"

"Your boys followed me from the studio, but they didn't quite do their job, did they?"

"Hub's boys. Hub gets overexcited sometimes."

"Well, when his instructions are to put a stop to all unnecessary inquiries, I could see how he might get confused."

He ignored that, and said again, "What do you want?"

"To not be played for a fool, first off," I said.

"You are not a fool. Al Knox made a mistake there."

"Did he say I was?"

"No. I couldn't imagine that he would know anyone who wasn't."

"You should try sitting down in the stands sometime, then maybe you wouldn't be so surprised by what the rest of us are like."

Merton held up a hand, his five fingers spread to silence me. "What do you want?"

"Well, since I found you where your daughter told me you'd be…" That got me nothing. "…I guess I want to talk to your son."

"That's not possible."

"Do I work for you or do I work for the studio?"

"That's the same thing."

"No, it isn't. Not when I go to the cops with everything I've got. I've left some of it out until now, but I can't do that forever, and I need to know which parts need to be told which way."

"Just the other day I read a story in the paper," he said. "I thought at first I'd try to make a picture out of it, something mysterious and catchy." He held his outstretched hands in front of him, framing an invisible marquee. *The Great Unknown.*"

He paused a moment and then dropped his hands. "Then I saw there's no commercial appeal. But the story still grabs me."

"I think it would be best if I talked to your son before talking to the police or the press—"

He went on talking over me. "Apparently there are people living in South America in the middle of the jungle who have never seen a white man. These people still live in a pre-literate, prehistoric state. They hunt, and they gather their food. They wear almost no clothing. They live like our ancestors did thousands of years before us. They don't know we exist."

"Then how do we know they exist?" I said.

"Stories told by other tribes. Careful anthropologists. They exist," Merton said. "I don't doubt that." He glanced at me for the first time, but my face must have been just as hidden by shadows as his was to me. "These people have never seen a movie. They don't even know that movies exist. They don't know that cameras and film exist. They don't know that artificial light exists. They can't even imagine them since they have no frame of reference. No guns, no airplanes, no cars. We know these people exist, but for them, *we* don't exist." He paused, stilled by his own revelation. When he spoke again, it was with unguarded wonder. "Should we contact these people?" he said. "Are they better off knowing less? Without our wars and our diseases and our entertainment?"

"I don't know about them, but from where I'm sitting, sometimes I think it would be nice if this city didn't exist."

"If no one knows about something," he said, "then it doesn't."

I saw where he was going then. "But I know. I know you wanted someone to take the fall for Chloë Rose's murder. Only she wasn't the one who got murdered, Mandy Ehrhardt did. But I'm not going to take the fall for that one either. Not when it's your son that killed her, and at least two other girls that you covered up for him. Now, Mr. Merton, I need to speak to your son."

His voice was measured, calm, dispassionate. "We never thought you'd really take the fall if Chloë was killed. Hell, we didn't want Chloë to be killed, she makes too much money for the studio. But if it happened—if your presence didn't prevent it—you'd have provided some cover. Some delay."

"That's what you say now," I told him. "If it had been more convenient to make it stick to me, you'd have done it. Circumstantial doesn't mean a thing in this town if the right people are involved."

He waved his hand in a noncommittal way.

I stood. "I think I'll see the police now."

He dropped his hand and spoke without tearing his gaze from the empty racetrack. "1313 West Market Place in Harbor City," he said. "Too many people have been paid off over this; too many people who want to protect themselves. You were just insurance."

I nodded, but he couldn't see me. "That's fine. I just need to make sure I'm protected too." I pulled open the door, and then stopped. "Why'd you want to buy the horse back?"

"I love that horse," he said, matter-of-factly. "I couldn't let it go to that idiot Rosenkrantz if Chloë were to die."

I had nothing to say to that.

"My boy won't talk to you," Merton said.

I left the room.

THIRTY

I stopped at a bank of payphones and put a call through to Samuels at the Harbor City station. I checked the time. Nearly 6:30.

The officer who'd answered came back on the line after setting the phone down for long enough that I'd had to deposit another nickel. "The detective's not here."

"Is he working tonight or did he already go home?" I said.

That earned a sigh. "Mister, I'm not in charge of where everybody is around here. I'm not even in charge of where I am around here. I just answer the phone."

"Will you take a message or is somebody else in charge of that?"

"You know how many years I had to train to answer this phone? Two years, and that's not counting kindergarten. And you know how many years I've had to answer this phone? Five years, and that's a quarter of the way to my pension. So you want to tell me what it is you've got to report or can I go back to waiting for some other slob to make the thing ring?"

"How many years did you train to talk like that?"

"Ah, go to hell."

"What's Samuels' home number? Maybe I can get him there."

"Mister, I'm going to hang up now."

"Hang on," I said. "Here's the message. Tell Samuels that Dennis Foster called. Tell him to meet me at 1313 West Market in an hour." I looked at my watch again. "Make that an hour and a half. Tell him it's important. You got that?"

"I got it. An hour and a half. 1313 West Market. Shake a leg. It's beautiful. It's a poem."

"It's a message, and he'd better get it."

"I get it, it's a message. Maybe someday someone'll take a message for me."

"A man can dream."

He hung up.

I went to my car and was out on the road in under a minute. It was downhill from Hollywood Park almost the entire way, and I had to keep reminding myself to lay off the gas a little. A minute would go by and I would remind myself again. The closer I got, the more I started to feel that something was not right. Merton had not acted defeated when he gave me the address. There was something I was missing. I noticed my speedometer again and eased off.

The neighborhood wasn't about to be written up in any magazines. These were rows of small houses, each one only slightly larger than a shotgun shack. Many of them were unpainted, hard to see in the dark. The bathmat of grass in front of most of the houses was bordered with chain link fencing. I watched the stenciled numbers on the curb to find which one was 1313. It was painted at least, white, and caught whatever light there was, but there were no lights inside. I pulled up to the curb halfway down the block and walked back. Families were sitting out on their front stoops, trying to get whatever relief there was to be had out in the evening air. The sound of children playing in the dark came to me softly from the end of the street. I kept my eyes forward and my head down.

Some of the shingles at 1313 showed the wood through in the

centers and some were replacements, unpainted altogether. The lawn had been hacked at without achieving a positive effect. The push mower leaned beside the front stoop. I mounted the three steps and knocked on the wooden edge of the screen door. No answer. No lights. No sounds. I knocked again. The door rattled in its frame. The latch was off. I waited another moment, and when there was no response, I opened the screen door and tried the doorknob inside. It opened, swinging in.

Inside, the smell of alcohol was strong. I closed the door behind me and listened for any sounds. Still nothing. I found a switch by the door and turned the overhead light on. It was one large room with an open door at the other end that led to a kitchen. The floor was bare wood without a rug. The living room furniture consisted of a couch and matching armchairs upholstered in peach-colored leather. It had been expensive when it was bought, but the years had worn away the stain in the places people would sit, and there was a ragged gash in the back of one of the armchairs. There wasn't any other furniture and I figured the couch for a convertible. The rest of the floor was strewn with clothes and trash with no attempt to separate the two. It was the sign of a most slovenly bachelor.

He was sitting in the other armchair, facing the door. His clothing was not at all slovenly, but instead an expensive tailored blue suit of the kind that was necessary if your friends were of a certain caliber. The coat was draped over the back of the chair behind him. That left him in a monogrammed off-white shirt with the sleeves rolled up. The monogram was TOM. He had thick dark hair that he wore pushed back from his forehead. He might have had something nice he called a face, but his head was hanging down at an awkward angle, hiding his features. He could have been asleep or passed out or maybe nodded out on morphine if it wasn't for the blood. His wrists had been cut lengthwise along the veins, and the blood had stained the arms of the chair and dripped in long strands down the sides. There was no knife in his hand, but there were a couple of empty liquor bottles at his feet. Judging by the smell, most of the alcohol had gone into the floorboards and not into Thomas Oliver Merton.

I crossed to the couch, not touching anything. I bent down and looked under the couch and chairs to see if the knife he had used was anywhere to be found. What I found instead was two glasses, one by the leg of the couch the other near Merton's feet. The glass by the couch still contained two fingers of what smelled like bourbon. The glass at Tommy's feet was nearly emptied. There was a hypodermic needle. There was no knife.

My mind went over it even as my thighs complained about squatting so long. The police wouldn't trust a suicide without a weapon nearby, it was always hard to believe the dead man had gotten up to put it away before he died. The scene could play suicide or homicide, depending on which facts the police were convinced to ignore. The hypodermic could be the last ounce of courage to go through the business with the wrists or it could be an overdose to make it easy for someone else to make the cuts. Merton Senior must have known that his son was dead when I saw him at the races. He wanted it to go murder to avoid the scandal of suicide in the family. He'd played me for a fool again when he'd given me the address. If a recently hired private dick was found at the scene, it was good for the murder rap. The police would be there any moment, no doubt. But Merton hadn't counted on me calling my own police too. That hurt his frame and meant the police would like someone else for the murder. Suicide would be better for everyone.

I stood and crossed back to the door and killed the light. Lights from other houses on the street provided a weak orange glow through the windows. I gave my eyes a moment to adjust and then made my way back to the couch. I took out my handkerchief and picked up both glasses. It was better for the police to think that Tommy had been alone, and two glasses would put someone else in the room, at least at some point in recent memory. I went into the kitchen and dumped their contents in the sink and then set the glasses in the basin. There were other unwashed dishes there. No one would notice a couple more. Tommy Merton hadn't been big on cleanliness.

I got out my penlight and started going through drawers. The drawer closest to the back door was a junk drawer, filled with unmatched buttons, broken springs, a screwdriver and a hammer, matchbooks, string, the kind of things people kept around just in case. The three drawers below it were empty. The house was clearly just a place for when Tommy couldn't make it home or to his father's office, or maybe when he wasn't welcome at either. Maybe he didn't have any silverware besides what was in the sink.

I crossed to the set of drawers on the other side of the sink, between the stove and the icebox. There was loose silverware in the top drawer, but nothing sharper than a butter knife. The next one down had the carving knives. I picked a knife that wasn't long enough to be unwieldy, but was sharp enough to do real damage. It could have been the knife. There wasn't any reason to say it wasn't. Except if the knife was wrong the M.E. would know, because one knife doesn't cut the same as another. But I had the feeling the M.E. wouldn't be as diligent as he normally was. The police like a neat suicide to keep their murder rate down, and there might be somebody exerting pressure to not look a gift horse in the mouth. I held the knife handle through my handkerchief and shut the drawer.

Before I could take a step, the front door opened and closed with a click. There was the sound of the switch and then the light in the front room went on, spilling a rectangle onto the kitchen floor.

THIRTY-ONE

I stood still and listened. There was no audible reaction to the sight of the dead man. The police would have knocked first and there would have been at least two of them, but no one spoke. Footsteps crossed the floor and stopped right about where Merton's body was. They were high-heeled footsteps.

I stepped into the doorway. Vera Merton was standing in front of her brother. She was wearing the same clothing I had seen her in that afternoon. She reached into a small clutch purse, her head down, her hair hiding her face. When her right hand withdrew from the bag it was holding a silver-plated .22.

"You won't need that. He's already dead," I said, stepping into the room.

Her head jerked up. Her eyes were red despite an expert attempt to hide the signs of crying with makeup. The hand with the gun in it jerked up too, drawing a bead on my chest.

"And you might want to turn out the light. Anyone can see you from the street through that window."

She didn't look behind her to see which window I meant. She steadied the gun. "What are you doing with that knife," she said.

I reversed my hold on the knife so that it was not threatening. "Knife's missing from the scene. I was just going to add it in. It'll look more real that way. You really don't need the gun."

She didn't lower it. "What are you doing here?"

"Your father sent me. I think he meant for me to take the fall for this."

Her face broke a little then, and no makeup could hide the pain in it. "He called me and said that he was going to call the police. I was just going to make sure…I knew Tommy was…"

"I'm taking care of it. Put away the gun and turn out the light. We haven't much time."

She lowered the weapon then, but she didn't move. Instead her eyes went back to the body, and her head and shoulders fell. She might have been crying.

I went and turned out the light. "How'd your father know what was here?"

"He came by this afternoon."

"Your brother gets a lot of visitors for a dead man."

I stepped around her, wiped the knife clean with my handkerchief, pressed it against his fingers, and then put it on the floor below his hand.

She spoke behind me. "Father wanted to talk about Tommy's options. As if Tommy had any options."

I checked the window. There was no sign of the police. Even with the lights out, we could probably be seen from outside. I took her arm. "We have to go. Where'd you park your car?"

She didn't move. "There's something wrong with us, isn't there?"

"Nothing a little hard work wouldn't cure."

She looked up then, her eyes hidden in the dark. "Hard work!" There was a note of hysteria. "Do you know what Tommy did? What we let him do again and again?"

I took the gun out of one hand and her purse out of the other. I put the gun back where it had come from and held onto both. "Yes. I saw his work yesterday and it was much worse than this."

She looked back at her brother. "He had no more options."

"Maybe he did and maybe he didn't. Maybe he would have

gone to the police or gotten some help. Maybe he would have snapped out of it. It doesn't matter. He has no options now."

"I had no more options. And now…"

"Don't say it. Don't say anything else. I'm working for your father, so I'm helping you out of a jam, but if I were to know otherwise we'd have to have some law in it. You understand?"

She nodded her head.

I checked the window again and saw a black-and-white parking silently across the street. I pulled her arm again. "Come on. We're out of time."

There was the sound of car doors slamming. She was pliant now, and I dragged her into the kitchen, her high heels clicking on the floor behind me. When the police walked in, they would see a poor slob who had written his own ticket. Merton could fix anything else that needed fixing himself. Except for Mandy Ehrhardt. She had been a cold one, but that didn't change what happened to her. It was better that Tommy got his own.

We went out the back door in the kitchen. I pushed her ahead of me and closed the door behind us. The backyard was a slab of concrete with overflowing metal garbage cans tucked up against the house. A small chain fence enclosed the slab with an opening that let into an alley. When they got no answer, one of the cops would come back here. I wanted to be out of the alley before then.

I hurried us down the narrow path between the slabs of concrete. There were fences all the way, creating a wall that separated people's private garbage from the public trash. "Where's your car?" I asked again.

"I parked on Front Street, one block over." There were no tears in her voice now, and some of her self-assurance had returned.

I let go of her arm and she stayed with me. "Good. Go to your car and get out of here."

"What are you going to do?"

"Does it matter?"

She didn't answer. We were at the end of the alley now, stepping onto the adjoining street. She took her purse from me, and left without a word. I went the opposite way to come back around to West Market. I crossed the street and hurried along to my car. If I were just getting here, I would be coming from my car.

THIRTY-TWO

Both uniforms were still at the door. Or maybe they had already checked the rear and had come back around to the front. They pounded on the door again, loud enough that I could hear them halfway down the street. The summer night sounds of the neighborhood had died away, killed by the police cruiser.

Once they went inside, I could pull away. But before I could get in my battered Packard, an obvious unmarked pulled up and double-parked along the marked car. I waited a moment and then started up the middle of the street for it. Samuels got out. He was by himself. He saw me coming and said as I reached him, "You call the law?"

"No," I said. "Just you."

"What's going on?"

"I think this guy is your man. Other than that I don't know any more than you do."

Samuels led the way up the walk. We were friends again. "Officers," he said to the other cops, "Detective Samuels with Robbery/Homicide. What's the trouble?"

"Call about a possible prowler. Nobody's home."

I liked the call about the prowler as much as I liked having my teeth kicked in.

"Step aside," Samuels said, and stepped between them and banged on the door with his fist. He turned back to me, still standing on the path. "How sure are you about this?"

"Sure," I said.

"We'll get a warrant later," Samuels said, and opened the screen door and tried the knob, which opened for him as well as it had for me. He stepped inside and the lights came on. The officers followed after him, and I followed behind. The scene was just as stunning the second time. "Damn it!" Samuels said. He turned on me. "Okey, spill. Wait a second." He turned to the officers. "This was your call. You call it in, and wait outside for the dusters to get here." Once the two policemen, one ashen faced, the other red, were gone, Samuels turned on me again. "That's Daniel Merton's kid. You going to tell me something now?"

"Remember the other case, the one before Christmas? Merton had the story quashed. There's another one a couple years back. Merton probably killed that one too, because it never went anywhere. When I looked into it, a couple of Hub Gilplaine's stooges used me for a punching bag. They tried to prevent me from seeing Merton earlier today too. I'm guessing Gilplaine was blackmailing the old man, and it wasn't worth anything if other people knew. I managed to check in with the old man anyway and he gave me this address. I called you and you know the rest."

He looked at me with narrowed eyes. "I don't like it."

I shrugged and kept my mouth shut.

"You're claiming that Thomas Merton killed at least three girls and that his father has covered it up for him? Do you know who Daniel Merton is?"

"Sure," I said.

He looked back at the stiff. "I don't like it. But I guess I'll take it. What did Merton senior say when you talked to him?"

"He said that it was okay if his kid killed a couple of girls as long as nobody noticed. I guess killing a girl who's going to be in a picture gets noticed. And so we have it."

"He told you that?"

"Not in those words."

"Well, you keep a lid on this thing. We'll figure something out."

"You always do, detective," I said.

He gave me another squinty-eyed look and then dismissed the comment with a wave of his hand.

"There's more," I said.

He shook his head without even looking at me. "You're going to tell me this other stiff under the boardwalk was Merton's too."

"You're pretty good at this," I said.

"I'm also good at using my gun as a club without knocking it out of line. You want me to show you that trick too?"

"You said you like it straight."

"Like it? I don't like it one bit." He sighed. "Give it to me short. We'll go back to the station and you can tell it as long as you want."

"Tommy and Greg Taylor were friends. They were both out, looking to get high. I'm guessing Tommy killed Ehrhardt on the way. When he realized Taylor could be a witness, he took care of him also."

He looked at me. "This isn't the world we were born into," he said. "It wasn't like this when we were kids. If a man killed you, he did it looking you in the eyes and he had a good reason, and everyone slept all night."

"You believe that?"

"Not for a second," he said, and went back outside.

I followed, leaving the door open.

THIRTY-THREE

At the station, I gave the police my story, leaving out Daniel Merton at Detective Samuels' suggestion. I then went home and gave the story, leaving in everything, to Fisher. Then I collapsed on my bed. When I came to, the sun was shining, and I went out for a newspaper in the same clothes I had on.

There was no mention of Merton on the front page—not the father, not the son. I took the paper back home and read through every article, but there wasn't one on the Mertons or on the Ehrhardt killing. I went back down to the newsstand at the corner and bought three other papers and took those back upstairs and read through every article in those too. Nothing. The fix was in. That left me a loose end.

I considered the house visits I needed to make while deciding if I should change my clothes. In the end I left without changing. At the studio, my name was on the list. When I got up to the secretary's desk, she picked up her phone at the sight of me and had it back on the receiver by the time I was in front of her.

"You're to go right in," she said, without a hint of expression.

I went through the door. The curtains were open this morning. It made the office feel grand and light. Merton was at his desk with a folder open in front of him and three more to the side. Two telephones had appeared on the desk as well. Maybe he locked them up at night.

He looked up. His face was stern.

"Aren't you in mourning?" I asked.

"I still have to eat," he said.

We looked at each other, holding eye contact for half a minute before I decided there was nothing in it and looked away.

"I hope you know I didn't expect that murder rap to stick on you," he said.

"Sure, suicide plays just as well, and it's easier to keep it out of the papers."

"I can keep anything out of the papers I damn well want to."

"I've noticed that."

He leaned back in his chair and the bluster drained away. An old man looked back at me. "It had to stop. He was getting too hard to control."

"I've got no problem with what you did."

"Not me," he said.

And then I flashed on it. That's why she had been sitting in the dark.

"Some family you've got," I said.

"It'd make a great picture," he said. "Too bad I can't make it." Then he leaned back over the open folder. "My secretary has a check for you. I filled in an amount, but if it's wrong, she can write you another one." He turned a page in the file. I was dismissed.

The secretary gave me my check without any comment. It was for $2,500. I considered tearing it up and walking out, but that wouldn't do anybody any good. I went down to my car to make my final stop.

The Enoch White Clinic was housed in two adjoining mansions and five outbuildings that had been built by oil men in the years before the pictures came to southern California. Signs along the long drive pointed the way through the acres of grass and trees to a parking lot that had been poured in front of the eastern of the two main houses. The door displayed a brown placard with businesslike letters that read RECEPTION.

The front hall was two stories high, a large bank of arched windows at the rear displaying the grounds behind the house. It was a peaceful view that suggested that the city was far away or maybe that there was no city at all. It was the kind of view that you could grow to love until it made you lonely and became stifling. The reception desk was to the right facing away from the window. I had to sign my name on a clipboard and they asked me to take a seat in one of the chairs that were provided for visitors. I was the only one there. The house was silent. They kept the crazies under wraps here. Screaming was bad for business.

When a nurse came to get me, I followed her down a wood-paneled hallway that had large gilt-framed portraits showing men in collars and robes in between every two doors. At the end of the hall, we turned into another hall just like it. Shem Rosenkrantz was leaning against a doorframe, drinking from a flask.

"I ought to kill you," he said.

The nurse looked flustered and turned and left without saying anything or pointing out which room belonged to Chloë Rose. I think I had an idea.

"The doctors say Clotilde is sick. They won't let her go. They say she's got a nervous constitution. That she may never be able to leave. They say she's a danger to herself. They know her better than I do. They know her better than she knows herself."

"It's a private clinic. You could take her out of it at any time."

He brought up the flask, but it didn't make it to his mouth. His face collapsed and a sob escaped him. "She wanted to die. She wanted to leave me."

"And you didn't give her any reason."

The anger took over again. "I was all she had and she was everything to me."

"You had a funny way of showing it."

"You don't let up, do you? The only reason I don't sock you is that you're right." He drank then. "You bastard." His eyes were red. "You can go in," he said.

I walked around him and opened the door. She was sitting in a cane rocking chair by the window, looking at the same beautiful view I had admired in the front hall. She didn't turn when I walked in. She kept her eyes forward. She rocked herself ever so slightly with her slippered foot.

I went around the bed and put myself in front of her, but she didn't look up. Her eyes were glassy, the reflection from the window casting them white. She was well drugged. They had taken a pretty French girl and put her in the movies to be in all of our dreams. Now she was tucked away in her own dreams. The life in between was nothing but infidelities, lies, heartache, and death. The solution was the same for the victim as it was for the perpetrator. She had just gotten the order reversed: cut her wrists first, and now she was getting high.

I left without speaking. Rosenkrantz was crying into his flask. At the front desk I asked for a pen. I brought out my check from Merton and I wrote it over to Chloë Rose. She must have had money in the bank, but that money would run out with no more coming in. I handed it to the nurse, and told her to credit it to Chloë Rose's account, and to make sure she wasn't taken out of there before it ran out.

Outside in the sun, I watched the gardener play with his flowerbed, cutting away dead stalks and weeds. I went to my beaten car and got in, thinking that the casualties are often bigger than could be understood. That's why the movies never made any sense. The screen's not big enough to hold everyone in it.

POLICE at the FUNERAL

A HARD CASE CRIME NOVEL

in memoriam J.T. *with apologies*

I.

I sat on the edge of the hotel bed trying to convince myself that I didn't want a drink. The argument that it had been three months since my last drink—and that had only been one Gin Rickey—and almost seven months since my last drunk wasn't very convincing. I tried the argument that I would be seeing Joe for the first time in four years, and Frank Palmer, Sr., the lawyer, and probably Great Aunt Alice too, so I should be sober when I saw them. But that was the reason I wanted a drink in the first place.

I glared at the mirror attached to the front of the bathroom door. I knew it was me only out of repeated viewing, but now, about to see my son, I saw just how broken I looked. My hair was brittle, more ash-gray than straw, and my face was lined, with crow's feet at the corners of my eyes, sunken cheeks, and broken blood vessels across the bridge of my nose. I looked worse than my father did when he died, and he was almost ten years older then than I was now.

"You don't want a drink," I said to my reflection. Then I watched as I sighed, exhaling through my nose, and my whole body sagged.

Why the hell was I back in Maryland, I asked myself, back in Calvert City?

But I knew why. It was time to pay Clotilde's private hospital again. And I owed money to Hank Auger. I owed money to Max Pearson. I owed money to Hub Gilplaine. And those were just the big amounts, the thousands of dollars. There were all kinds of other creditors that wouldn't be too happy to know I was three thousand miles from S.A. There had to be money for me in Quinn's will. Otherwise Palmer wouldn't have called me.

The door from the hall opened in the front room. It crashed shut and Vee appeared in the mirror, framed by the square arch that separated the rooms. "Don't you just love it?" she said.

She was in a knee-length sable coat with a collar so big it hid her neck. She wasn't bad to look at normally, deep red hair, unmarked white skin, and what she was missing up top was made up down below. In the fur and heels she looked sumptuous.

"It's the wrong season for that," I said.

She came forward. "He'd been saving it."

"I hope he's planning to p—to give you more than a fancy coat."

"He's paying for the suite." She opened one side of the coat, holding the other side across her body, hiding herself. But I could see that she wasn't wearing anything underneath anyway. She slid onto the bed behind me, putting her hands on my shoulders. In the mirror, a line of pale skin cut down her front between the edges of the fur.

"He didn't wonder why you weren't staying with him?"

She faked shock, raising a hand to her mouth in the perfect oops pose. "I'm not that kind of girl," she said, and then she made herself ugly by laughing, and flopped back on the bed, her whole naked body exposed now, her arms outstretched, inviting me to cover her.

"You were just with him," I said.

"But now I want you. That was just business anyway."

I shook my head, my back still to her, although I could see her in the mirror.

She dropped her arms. "What's wrong with you?"

"I want a drink," I said.

"Then have one."

"I can't."

"Forget what the doctors say." She was losing her patience. "You'd feel a lot better if you took up drinking again instead of always whining about it. Now come here. I demand you take care of me."

I looked back at her. She should have been enticing, but she was just vulgar. "I've got to go." I stood up.

"Like hell you have to go," she said, propping herself up. "You bastard. You can't leave me like this."

"The will's being read at noon. As it is I'll probably be late. That's what we're here for in the first place, remember?"

"You pimp. I'm just here to pay for you. I should have stayed with him upstairs. At least he knows he's a john, you pimp."

"If I'm a pimp, what's that make you?"

"I know what I am, you bastard. You're the one with delusions of grandeur."

I could have said, that's not what she thought when she met me, but what would be the point? I left the room, going for the door.

She yelled after me. "You'll be lucky if I'm here when you get back."

I went out into the hall. I should have left for the lawyer's before she got back. I had heard her go through that routine more times than I could count, but it was the last thing I needed this morning. No matter how much she got, she couldn't get enough. An old man couldn't satisfy a woman like that. But when I first met her, I hadn't felt old. She'd made me feel young again, and I hadn't realized what she was until later. I wasn't any pimp,

I'll say that, but a man's got to eat, and she was the only one of the two of us working.

I took the elevator downstairs to the lobby. Instead of pushing through the revolving doors to the street, I went into the hotel bar. The lights were off since enough sunlight was creeping through the Venetian blinds to strike just the right atmosphere. It took my eyes a moment to adjust. When they had, I saw that I was the only person in the bar other than the bartender, who stood leaning against his counter with his arms crossed looking as though he was angry at the stools. I went up to the bar. "Gin Rickey," I said.

He pushed himself up, grabbing a glass in the same motion. He made the drink, set it on a paper doily, and stood back as if to see what would happen.

I drank the whole thing in one go. I immediately felt light-headed, but it was a good feeling, as though all of my tension was floating away. I twirled my finger, and said, "Another one."

The bartender stood for a moment, looking at me.

"Room 514," I said. If Vee's "friend" was paying for the room, he could afford a little tab.

The bartender brought my second drink. "Don't get many early-morning drinkers," I said, picking up the glass.

"It's a bad shift," he said.

"And let me guess. You worked last night too."

"Until two ayem."

I tipped my glass to him and took a drink. He watched me like we were in the desert and I was finishing our last canteen. I set the glass down, careful about the paper doily. "If you came into big money, I mean as much money as you can imagine, what would you do with it?"

He twisted his mouth to the side in thought. Then he said, "I'd buy my own bar."

"But this was enough money so you didn't have to work again. You could settle down anywhere, or don't settle down, travel all over."

"What would I want to leave Calvert for?"

"Get a new start. You said yourself you were miserable."

"I said it was a bad shift."

"Aren't they all bad? Every last one of them."

He put his big palms down on the bar and leaned his weight on them. "No, they're not. Are you finished with that? Do you need another?"

I waved him away. "When you're a kid, you know how you dream you'll be a college football star or a fighter pilot? How come you never dream of just being satisfied?"

"I like tending bar."

"Right." I drained the last of my drink, and felt composed, at least enough for the reading of the will, even with Joe there.

"Kids don't know anything anyway," the bartender said. "What do you do, mister?"

"Nothing anymore. I was a writer."

"Anything I would have heard of?"

"Probably not," I said.

"You need another?"

I shook my head. I had a soft buzz on, and it felt good. It felt better than it should have. "Put the tip on the tab," I said. "Whatever you think's right."

"Thanks, mister."

I shrugged. "I just came into some money."

"Well, thanks."

I waved away his gratitude. It was making me feel sick.

I walked out of the bar and pushed my way through the revolving door in the lobby onto Chase Street. The August heat
and humidity had me sweating before I got to George and turned
south towards downtown. Calvert hadn't changed much since
Quinn and I lived here in 1920. Or was it '21? The Calvert City
Bank Building over on Bright Street that now dominated the
skyline hadn't been there, and there had been more streetcars
instead of busses, but overall the short and stocky buildings of
the business district were the same. I remembered when those
buildings had seemed tall, after *Encolpius* was published and I
suddenly had enough money to marry Quinn. Now Quinn was
dead and *Encolpius* and all my other books were out of print
and even Hollywood had thrown me out and my life would never
be as good as that day here in Calvert thirty years ago.

I was one poor bastard. If I had known how much of our married life was going to be screaming at each other and trying to
outdo the other with lover after lover, pill after pill, drink after
drink, I would have—at least I hope…yeah, I would have called
it off. Quinn knew how to make me jealous from across the room.
It was only natural when I started stepping out. And there were
the two miscarriages and then Quinn started bringing a bottle
to bed and finishing it in the morning, so of course I did the
same. It got to the point where I couldn't think without something to get me going. We tried the cure, once in New Mexico,
once in upstate New York, but it didn't last long, and when we
got to Paris, we didn't care anymore, it was all-out war.

And then I met Clotilde. She set Quinn off more than any of
the others. And when I began to sober up for her, Quinn left
me. She told me I had a kid only after the divorce had gone
through. Then Clotilde and I married and we were happy for a

while at least, until we went to Hollywood, or maybe it was still in France… Anyway, she got famous, with thousands of men after her, and the public had forgotten me, so who could blame me when I had a girl or two on the side? No one. But Clotilde ended up in the the madhouse, and I was broke, and I borrowed from everybody who I knew even a little, and now all I had was Vee.

As I walked and felt sorry for myself, my mood sank lower and lower, and the effect of the alcohol wasn't helping it any. How could Quinn have left me any money after all these years? Maybe Joe had asked for me to be there, but had been too ashamed to contact me directly. I was his father after all. I passed the C&O Railroad building, and turned into the Key Building where the doorman, with a big servile grin, followed me inside, skipping ahead to reach the ornate brass elevators before I did. "Good morning, sir. Where are you off to?"

"Palmer, Palmer, and Crick, to see Mr. Frank Palmer the senior," I said.

He pushed the elevator call button and then pushed it again repeatedly. "May I ask your name, sir?"

"Shem Rosenkrantz. Do I need to be announced?"

His eyes flicked over, and he smiled and waved at someone who came in behind me. "Morning, Mr. Phelps."

Mr. Phelps started right for a door that must have led to the stairs. "Sam," he said with a single nod, and disappeared through the door.

Sam beamed back even as the door shut. How could a guy like that be happy, with a job pushing buttons and kissing ass? I guess some guys have to be that way, making everyone else feel bad because they feel so goddamn good. He turned his attention back to me. "Mr…"

"Shem Rosenkrantz." The sweat was streaming down my face. The hand of the floor indicator swung counterclockwise, counting down the elevator's progress.

Then he answered my question from before. "No need to be announced. I just like to keep track of who's in the building. For security reasons."

The elevator bell rang and the heavy doors rolled back. A man and a woman stepped off. Sam had fresh smiles. "Mr. Keating. Sally."

They smiled and nodded and hurried to the door. I started to walk around Sam to get at the elevator. He moved out of my way, nodding his head. Then he leaned into the elevator reaching around to the control panel and he hit the button for floor eight, the top floor. He gave me one last smile, and I almost told him Quinn was dead to knock that smile off his face, but I didn't. "Eighth floor," he said, and the elevator doors closed.

2.

The elevator rolled open on the eighth floor revealing the reception room of Palmer, Palmer, and Crick. The place had been redecorated since the last time I'd been there, brought into the 1950s, the walls paneled in dark hardwood, the floor a tawny deep-pile wall-to-wall carpet, and the clutch of waiting-room furniture upholstered in maroon patent leather. The two secretaries behind the high front desk wore headsets. The one on the left was talking into hers, while the one on the right offered me a professional smile.

"How may I help you?"

I stepped forward, not bothering with a return smile. It wouldn't have looked right given the occasion, and there was no use wasting it on one of those office girls. They probably got the sweet talk from the janitors on up. "I'm here for the reading of Quinn Rosenkrantz's will. Shem Rosenkrantz."

"Yes, Mr. Rosenkrantz. Mr. Palmer is in the conference room just through these doors to the right."

I drummed my hands on the top of the desk, then gave an awkward nod, and headed through the door. It had been maybe twenty years since I'd been to those offices for the divorce. Palmer's son had still been in law school then, and now he was a partner. Crick had had only four other shysters under him and half of the eighth floor instead of the whole thing. I guess some people have to come up in the world while the rest of us go down.

The conference room was poorly lit. The same paneled wood
from the reception room covered the walls, with gilt-framed oil
portraits of the senior partners at regular intervals along the
inside wall, each lit by its own arc lamp attached to the frame.
The other walls were devoted to glass-fronted bookcases with
uniformly bound sets of law treatises. I felt the moment of distraction I always get in a library, the need to look at the titles, to
flip through a volume, to search out my own books amidst the
stacks. But I knew that these books were dry lifeless things that
held no interest to anyone but lawyers, which was perhaps more
interest than anyone had in my own work anymore.

"Shem, Shem, I'm glad you're here." It was Palmer Senior,
now almost seventy-five, crossing the room ramrod straight with
the vigor of a man half his age. He took my hand in both of his.
"I'm sorry it's under these circumstances," he said, and held my
hand a moment longer than was necessary, trying to be discrete
about smelling for liquor on me. So what if he did?

"Mr. Palmer."

He gave my hand one more squeeze and let it go. "Frank.
Please, Frank. And you look well," he said, which wasn't true.
Then he stepped back and indicated the conference table.
"Please, take a seat. We'll start this shortly. It won't take long."

I stepped up to the table and put my hands on the back of
one of the oversized leather armchairs. There he was, Joseph
and a young woman whom I took to be his fiancée, next to each
other on the far side of the table. They talked in a subdued
whisper, Joseph purposely ignoring me, and that hurt. It wasn't
right, and it hurt.

It had been three years since he and I had spoken, four since
I'd seen him at his high school graduation. He'd grown up;
lanky limbs fleshed out, broader face, the hint of a beard or at

least the five o'clock shadow that stood in for a beard. If I hadn't known who he was, I would have said he was one of those angry young men who want something they're never going to get and are just realizing they're never going to get it, so they're going to make the world pay for it. You see lots of those guys hanging around the corner or at the pool halls or the garage. But usually they're not sitting on a couple of million dollars like Joe.

His fiancée—I'd forgotten the name she'd given on the phone two weeks before when she called about Quinn…that she… about her dying—the fiancée was a prim blonde, with an aura of wispy down over lightly tanned and freckled skin, a soft woman with which to make a wealthy life. She hazarded a look, and when our eyes met, she smiled despite herself, and that made up for Joe some.

In the back of the room, in the corner, not even at the table, sat Connie, Great Aunt Alice's Negro maid. A stocky woman now in her late forties or early fifties, she held her large trapezoidal purse in both hands on her lap. She gave me a polite nod when I caught her eye.

"Now I've asked you all to be here," Palmer said, taking the chair at the head of the table, "because you or those you represent are mentioned in Mrs. Rosenkrantz's will in one way or another." He took a machine-rolled cigarette from a silver case and lit it with a paper match. He waved out the match and tossed it in a brass ashtray, then slid the folder on the table closer to him. He opened it, and talked down into the will, and I sat down.

"I'm going to read the will aloud straight through, and I ask that you hold any questions until the end. We can go through it line by line after that, either together or individually. I want to urge all of you, no matter what has happened in the past, not to get excited here and make any decisions. These things can take time, and there will be time enough for any unpleasantness later." He looked up at us without raising his head like a judge handing down a sentence. "Not that I expect any unpleasantness. This is a simple will, and to my infinite sorrow, there aren't many Hadleys left as you can see here today." He picked up the papers, and tapped them on end to straighten them.

Joseph sat hunched in his seat, his nostrils flared, a scowl cutting valleys that joined his nose and mouth and pushed dimples into either side of his chin. His bride, turned sideways, held his clenched fist with one hand and his forearm with the other, her entire attention on him.

Palmer started, "I, Quinn Rosenkrantz née Hadley, being of sound mind and body, do solemnly swear that this is my last will and testament signed on this Thursday the 12th of June 1941, containing instructions for the dispersal of my estate, both real and liquid, and personal effects. This will is to make null and void all previous wills and agreements..."

It went on like that for several pages, Palmer intoning the words in a rapid-fire monotone. There was an outdated section regarding Joseph's custody should Quinn die when he was still a minor. I was named fourth in line after Quinn's grandmother Sally Hadley, who had since passed away in '45, then Great Aunt Alice, and then Connie Wilson, who shifted uncomfortably when that part was read, for it was surely meant to be a jab at me.

All cash, stocks, bonds, insurance policies, and other liquid assets—in short, somewhere around two million dollars—were to pass into Joseph's possession if he was of age, and into a trust overseen by Palmer and the elder Hadley women if he was not. The house was also Joseph's. Its contents, however, were his only after Great Aunt Alice had selected any items of importance to her.

As Palmer had stated, a simple will. Except for this. Should Joseph predecease Quinn, the estate would be dispersed as described, but with me in his place.

"…pursuant to the laws of the great State of Maryland and the United States of America. Signed, Quinn Rosenkrantz, Thursday the 12th of June 1941, witnessed by Frank Palmer Sr. and Frank Palmer Jr., Thursday the 12th of June 1941."

Palmer cleared his throat and ran his hand across his lips. He took a drag from his cigarette and gathered the papers. There was a palpable and awkward silence. I was stunned. That Quinn might award me anything had been a shock; but that I had been in line for everything—it emptied my mind. But then, Quinn had all the reason to believe that Joseph would survive her. So maybe my place as the next heir in line was meant as no more than a gesture, a way of being the better party and lording it over me. And this was why Palmer had gotten me all the way out from the West Coast? He should have saved me the trouble.

The silence continued. There was an understanding that the cue had to come from Joseph. He had just been awarded a tremendous amount of money. But he sat with the same scowl on his face, his eyes straight ahead, not focused on anything, no doubt fuming at my position in the will. The fiancée, Connie, and I all shifted in our seats, and Palmer cleared his throat again, which turned into a barking cough, and then he stood, picking up the folder in one hand and his cigarette in the other. I stood as well, and Joseph's gaze remained steady, now somewhere around my belt.

"My secretary can have copies available for any of you later this afternoon," Palmer said, and he walked around and put his hand on Joseph's shoulder, which elicited no reaction. He leaned down, and I heard him say, "Joe. Are you okay?"

Joe said nothing. Yeah, he was a hard boy now.

"Joe, we should talk about a will for you at some point."

Still nothing. Palmer appealed to the fiancée with his eyes, but she shook her head primly. He said, "Joe, we can do it right now, if you want, or you can set up an appointment with my secretary, but it's important you have a will."

Palmer looked across the table at me, and that woke me up, and I started to leave. As soon as I made it through the doorway, I heard Joseph say, "Not now. Maybe after we're married."

He wouldn't even talk when I was in the room, my own son. I didn't care what he thought I had or hadn't done—and I'm not saying I hadn't done anything, because you can ask anyone, I'm the first to admit I've done something wrong—but to not even talk in front of me, that just wasn't right.

"Joe, a will…"

"When we're married," he repeated, and then I was in the reception area out of hearing range.

Palmer came out a moment later. "Shem." I turned and he shook my hand again. "I'm sorry about all of this," he said.

"Sorry about what?"

"Quinn's dying. I'm not supposed to see you people dying. You're supposed to bury me."

"I'll have someone remind you of that at my funeral."

"It was spiteful what she did about Joseph's custody. I advised her not to do it."

"It's a moot point now."

"I still wanted you to know, it wasn't the right thing to do. But you couldn't have expected to come out any better from this thing financially."

"I didn't expect to have come out at all."

"Like you didn't come out for the funeral?"

I smiled and said nothing to that. So that's why he got me out here, out of spite.

He gripped my upper arm. I could tell he smelled the alcohol on me. But so what? Can't a man have a few drinks every now and then? "She loved you still, you know."

"Thanks for thinking that."

He looked back in the room. "I'll be in my office. I'm available to you for the remainder of this hour. I'll have those copies prepared." And he strode out of the room, his cigarette perched in his mouth.

I shuffled my feet, sort of just standing there. I figured I better get a copy of the will or Vee would think I was holding out on her. In the conference room, the fiancée was leaning right into Joseph's ear. The sight caused a pang of jealousy, not so much about this particular girl, but just the idea of a girl whispering earnestly in your ear. Vee wouldn't ever have done that unless she planned on shouting next, to break your eardrums, her idea of a joke.

Connie came out of the conference room and slid up to me then, her purse still gripped two-handed and held at her waist. She nodded. "Mr. Rosenkrantz."

I forced my face to stretch into a wide, charming grin, a skill I had learned in the wilds of my youth with Quinn when charm mattered above anything else. "Connie, how long have you known me? Shem, please."

She hunched her shoulders, and backed a step away from me

into the shadows of a five-foot ficus tree. "Mr. Rosenkrantz. Miss Hadley expects to see you while you're in town. You will stop by the house later?"

The last thing I wanted just then was to see Great Aunt Alice. She had a famed reputation for not pulling her punches, and in the state I was in, there were plenty of punches to throw. "Well, Connie, I don't know if I can," I said, still displaying that dapper grin.

"Tea is generally at two-thirty."

I checked my watch as a stall. Just one now. "I don't think that's going to work for me." Connie's whole body fell in disappointment, as though inviting me to tea was the real reason she was there, the reading of the will just a coincidence. "You'll send Aunt Alice my best, of course."

She took another half-step away from me. Then, "I'm sorry for your loss."

I sighed through my nose. "Thank you, Connie."

She waited another half beat and the fiancée appeared beside me, her brow wrinkled, her lips puckered ever so slightly. Connie ducked and said, "Thank you," and hurried to the elevator where she pushed the call button and watched the row of lighted numbers above the door.

I turned to the fiancée, who looked a little lost, and renewed my smile. "I'm sorry, but I don't remember your name," I said.

She looked at me, confused, as though she didn't expect that I could speak. "Yes, of course," she said, "Mary O'Brien." She held out her hand, and I took it, turning it so I could hold it in both of mine.

"Joseph is a lucky man."

She looked at her hand in mine, but seemed unsure how to reclaim it. "Yes, well…"

"I thought Quinn always wanted a daughter."

"She was very kind to me, even while she was sick."

It was hard to reconcile the phrase "very kind" with Quinn, but I nodded as though I knew just what she meant. "Perhaps we could mend things now. I would very much like to have a daughter as well."

"I thought Joe needed some time to himself," she said. She had exquisite cheekbones and small bright eyes and her unease and the wrinkle across her brow were precious.

"Of course."

"He's upset. He's not himself."

I still held her hand and it grew warm in mine. "Of course."

"I've read your books," she hurried.

I felt my own face falling, the charm slipping. "Thank you."

"Joe didn't want me to, but I needed to. You do see why? Don't you?"

I felt strained, tired.

"You will be my father-in-law, even if... Well you understand."

Joseph appeared then, still stormy, and upon seeing me clutching his future wife's hand, he sucked in his lips to try to control himself as he took her by the elbow. "Come now, Mary."

She drew her hand back as though she'd touched something hot and he steered her towards the elevator. It was a move I had used many times myself on his mother—but never on Clotilde —and I knew Mary was in for a talking to on the way home.

"I was just saying you're a lucky man, Joseph," I said, keeping pace, but maintaining a distance of several feet. "I wish you'd give me a chance to make things right with us."

He kept his eyes on the numbers above the elevator, his back to me, not even allowing the possibility that I might come into his line of sight, and whose fault was that? My own son! He kept a firm grip on Mary's elbow. I knew my face had grown plaintive, and it made me sick at myself.

The elevator came, the bell dinged like the end of a round, and I watched them get on. Just before the doors closed, they turned, and Joseph gave me a withering look of pure hatred, a look that hurt more than any words could have, used to, as my years of drunkenness had made me, declarations of disgust, pathetic amusement, consternation, pity, and sadness. I didn't think I'd ever be able to pick up my feet to walk a single step. And my empty stomach was much too hollow.

3.

I got my copy of the will and went back to the hotel. Vee was sitting in front of the vanity in her slip, making up her face. She turned in her chair when I came in. She had only done one eye so far, so the right eye looked wide and innocent while the left was hard and mean. "Well?" she said.

I threw the will onto the vanity in front of her, and sat on the bed in almost the same position I had been in that morning. "I thought you weren't going to be here when I got back."

She had snatched up the will and was skimming through it, flipping pages. "Tell me. I don't understand this stuff. What's the number?"

"Nothing."

"Nothing? What do you mean nothing?"

"Just that. I didn't get anything. It all goes to my son."

She threw the will at me. It bounced off of my arm, fell onto the bed, and then slid over the edge, fluttering to the floor. "Then why the hell did we come out here?" She turned back to the mirror on the vanity, and went to work on her other eye.

"I'm mentioned. If Joe had died before Quinn, it would have gone to me."

"Well, a lot of good that does us."

I wanted to say her anger didn't do us a lot of good either. But why bother? She was like that. It didn't matter that I was feeling just about as if getting up to go to the bathroom was too much effort, she was laying into me.

"You better get ready to spend a long time here," she said, applying her makeup with hurried, jerky strokes. "Because you can't think I'm going to get Carlton to pay for your ticket back to S.A. You were a deadbeat loser out in Hollywood and you're a deadbeat loser on the east coast too. When will I ever learn?"

When would either of us? "You didn't think that when you met me. You threw yourself at me. You loved my books. You were a fan. It was such an honor."

"And didn't you eat it all up. I'd read some of your books. A big-time writer. I didn't know you were broke." She started putting away her brushes, gathering tubes, pencils, closing various compacts, and stowing them in her makeup kit. "All you care about is that somebody's read your damn books. Well nobody has."

She said that just to hurt me. And it worked every time. We were like a broken record, having the same fight over and over, and still each word squeezed me tighter and tighter. "Where are you going?"

"Carlton put the wife on a plane to Palm Beach this morning. It's just the two of us for the next few days." She snorted. "And you." She got up and crossed the room to the armoire on her side of the bed, and pulled out a black sheath dress. She held the hanger above her head to examine the sheer fabric.

"Are you going to be back tonight?"

She bunched up the dress to get at the hanger. "Wouldn't you like to know?" She had the dress over her head.

My chest squeezed even tighter, and my anger turned into anxiety. I hated her one moment, and I couldn't live without her the next. "Vee, please. You've got to come home tonight. I don't know if I can take being alone."

"Then don't take it." The dress fell down the length of her

body. "Go out. Go find some floozy, or go jump off a bridge, I don't care." She straightened the dress, and then turned her back to me waiting for me to zip her up.

I got up, came around the bed and gripped the zipper. "I'm serious, Vee. This thing with Joseph…" My eyes stung, and I tried to swallow the lump in my throat. "I don't have anyone anymore, and my own son…he's my own kid, and he won't even talk to me. You don't know what that's like."

"I don't even know where my kid is," she said, waving her hand over her shoulder, hurrying me.

I zipped her up. "That's different. You gave your kid away. Joseph… He wouldn't even look at me."

"You know what?" She picked up one foot and slipped on a heel, and then the other. "If he's hurting you so badly, I'll tell you what to do. Kill him. That way he's out of your hair, *and* the money is yours."

The idea was so startling that I didn't know what she meant at first. "Money?"

"From the will," she said, fully dressed now. "How do I look?"

"What are you talking about? How could you even say that?"

She rolled her eyes, and shook her head. She pulled a small black sequined purse out of the armoire, and went to the red handbag on the bed. She started pulling things out of the one and putting them into the other, her wallet, a small vial of perfume. "At least you're drinking again. Thank god for small favors." She pulled out her gun, a pearl-handled two-shooter that Carlton had given her.

"Why do you need that thing?"

"Carlton doesn't like it if I don't carry it. Where are my keys?"

"Vee, Joseph—"

"It was a joke. Relax." She threw the red handbag down.

"God damn it, where are my keys?" She stood up and stared at the vanity, shook her head, and clipped her purse closed. "It doesn't matter. I don't need them anyway."

With every further preparation, my throat got drier, and the muscle in my cheek spasmed. The thought of killing Joseph made me nauseous. Vee leaving made me weak. I started thinking about what drink I would order downstairs when she left.

She expertly stormed into the living room towards the outer door.

I called after her, "I love you."

She called back without turning around. "I told you about saying that." The door opened. "It's not true anyway." The door closed behind her, and I was alone, and I couldn't figure out where to go, or how to even take a step.

What I wanted was to go down to the bar. I knew it was a bad idea, but that's what I wanted—a Gin Rickey. It sure sounded good. But I was on the wagon again, I told myself. That morning had only been an exception. I couldn't have another drink, it was the last thing I should do.

But, I thought, maybe I could go see Joseph again. Give it another try. He might just see me. That girl of his Mary seemed open to smoothing things over, a nice girl and she liked my books. When a guy's dame got involved, anything could happen. He might… But I knew he wouldn't. I wasn't kidding myself. Joe would just see it as a grab for Quinn's money, and he'd probably be right.

The money! What was I going to do for money? We were counting on that inheritance. Vee would leave me here, she really would. There was a time when I just had to cable that I had a story written—not the story itself, just that it was written— and a magazine would cable $1000 just like that, and that was during the Depression, too. But nobody would give me money now. They couldn't even pretend it was an advance at this point. I hadn't written a single sentence in years. But if I did write…

If… Ha!

But if I did… Then they'd have to send me money, Auger or Pearson, somebody. Maybe I *should* write. That's what I could do. Then I'd get some money, and then once one story was written, I could write another, maybe even take on a novel again. There was no reason I couldn't! A publisher would love to have a new Shem Rosenkrantz book, a triumphant return.

I looked around for the pad a good hotel like the Somerset always provided. It was on the telephone stand in the living room. I picked it up, and underneath there was a room key attached to a plastic diamond that read "Suite 12-2." It had to be the key Vee was looking for. Without thinking, I slid it in my pocket and began to look around for a pencil. There wasn't one on the stand. I opened the drawers of the desk, then both bedside tables. There wasn't anything to write with. I even checked the bathroom.

I stood in the center of the living room, tapping my foot, and scanning the suite to see if there was someplace I had missed. I could go down to the desk to get a pencil, but that seemed like too much effort. And as I thought further about it, I got more anxious, and the idea of writing began to seem insurmountable. I didn't know what to write anyway. I didn't really want to write either.

I stepped to the phone, picked up and asked for a long distance connection to California. It took almost a full minute, but then I was through to the Enoch White facility on a shoddy connection. "Yes, this is Shem Rosenkrantz. I'd like to speak to my wife." It was mid-morning in California, and it was likely Clotilde was outside on the grounds if the weather was nice. But it wasn't more than two minutes until her voice came through to me, and the connection improved.

"Shem?" she said.

I grew weary, her voice an excuse to let go. She'd make it all better. "Clotilde…"

"Have you been drinking?" she said. Just like that. One word and she knew.

"We didn't get anything from Quinn," I said. "We got nothing."

There was a pause. When she spoke again, her French accent was thicker than at first. "Director Philips has been very good to us," she said. "I'm sure he'll understand."

"I'm not sure he will," I said. The director had made himself quite clear on my visit the previous week. We had to the end of the month, and then they would either release Clotilde or transfer her to a state hospital.

"But I'm Chloë Rose," she said, the name one she hadn't used in ten years. "I'm…it's good for their advertising, no?"

"I'm not sure it matters anymore."

Her voice grew tight and I started to pull myself together. I couldn't hope that she could take care of me; I had to take care of her. "I can't leave here," she said, and then switching to French, *"Je n'ai pas—"*

"English, Clotilde. My French is no good anymore."

"Shom, it's not safe for me to leave. It's just not safe."

I couldn't tell if that was a threat, that she would kill herself if forced to leave, or if it was part of her paranoia, her paralyzing fear that she was going to be attacked at any moment.

"It's not safe, Shem."

"I know, sweetheart."

"You can talk to Director Philips."

I sighed. "I will."

"Shem, I can't leave."

"Calvert's nice," I said, trying to put cheer in my voice. "You remember that time we stopped here, it must have been '36, '37, before the war? We picked up Joe?"

"Shem. Don't let them make me leave."

I forced a smile. "Don't worry, honey. It's going to be all right."

"You'll talk to Director Philips?"

"Put him on," I said, and immediately there was a clunk as she put the receiver down. She would go find a nurse who would transfer the call back to the front desk who would then transfer me to the director's office. She could never figure out how to transfer me back to the desk herself. While I waited, listening to the faint shush of the open line, I thought again about my options. Maybe I could ask Joe for a loan. He could afford it now. Or maybe Vee could get some actual cash out of this hood Carlton. My chest tightened as I ticked off each option, knowing that they weren't ever going to be.

Director Philips came on the line, all business. "Mr. Rosenkrantz."

"Director Philips, I just wanted to assure you, I'm in Calvert, things are working out, it's just going to take a little time, I'll be able to pay you some of our arrears."

"That's great news. Thank you for telling me."

"I just want to make sure there are no preparations for Mrs. Rosenkrantz to be moved. It upsets her very much."

"Of course. We know how to take care of our patients, Mr. Rosenkrantz. That's why we cost what we do. Just wire the money as soon as you get it, and there won't be any trouble."

"Of course, as soon as I get it."

"Good day."

"Yeah. Goodbye." I set down the receiver, but left my hand on it. I felt worse than before I had called. Now I really needed a drink. But first, maybe I'd call Auger or Pearson. If I told them Clotilde was going to be thrown out... But I'd called so many times, the secretaries knew not to put me through. Maybe I could send a telegram. I hadn't asked them for money in...it had to be three months. No, it must have been more. If I told them I was writing again, maybe that would force me to actually write. It was a chance.

I threw the pad onto the couch, and went out into the hall and to the elevator.

Downstairs, I hadn't gotten two steps from the elevator when somebody said, "Mr. Rosenkrantz."

I turned. It was a young man, about twenty-five, maybe a little younger, about Joseph's age. His face was long and narrow. He wore wire frame glasses and a gray felt fedora with a red feather on the band. He was brimming with excitement, shuffling his feet as though he might have to run after me at any moment.

"I..." He started to pat his jacket. "I—if you...just one moment." Pat, pat, pat. "Here..." He reached into his inner coat pocket and came out with a pad. "If I could..."

I saw then, and I shook my head. A reporter. "I'm not interested. No comment." I headed for the front desk.

As expected, he jumped after me. "Mr. Rosenkrantz. Sir. Please. I am a reporter. I cover the city council for the *Sun*. But I just...I mean, I'm a fan. I'm a writer too—"

That was even worse. I turned, about to lay into him. I could feel it rising, and I wasn't going to be able to stop it. But he was leaning in towards me, with a stunned expression on his face, an expression I hadn't seen in a long time. And I paused. "What do you write," I said.

"Well, for the paper…"

I waved him on.

"I had a play produced last year at the Everyman. *Spook*. My first. It got some nice notices."

"And you are…how did you find me?"

He looked down as though he were ashamed of doing what reporters do. "I knew your wife's will was to be read. Your ex-wife's, excuse me. I waited outside the building where it was to be read, you understand, and when you came out—I knew it was you from the pictures on your dust jackets—I followed you, but I didn't have the guts to say anything. And I nearly didn't just now either."

"So you're a fan?"

"Yes, sir."

"What's your name?"

"Taylor Montgomery, sir."

I held out my hand. "Nice to meet you." He shook it with wide-eyed wonder. That was how it should be. That was how it was at one time. If only Joe had met me like that. I'm his father, he should have given me that look. He should have given me a hug, you know, like roughhousing, but it's a hug. "Buy me a drink," I said.

"Oh, no, really…"

"Look," I said. I was starting to feel bad for the kid. Nobody should be that paralyzed to talk to me. And suddenly everything seemed better. Of course Auger would send me money. How couldn't he? I was his client. I made him a lot of money back in the day. Yeah, he'd wire money, and then Vee would come back west with me, and it would all be okay. I might even get a $400 week at one of the studios if I begged hard enough. "Look," I said again. "You go to the bar. Order yourself a drink. I've got to send a cable, and I'll meet you in there. And if you're not there, then I understand that too."

"Oh, I'll be there," he said. "Thanks. Mr. Rosenkrantz. Yeah," and he stepped backwards, and almost tripped into somebody, said "Excuse me," righted himself, gave an embarrassed smile, and headed for the bar.

If only Joseph had met me like that. That was the way it was supposed to be. I had worshipped my father. I would never have turned my back on him, even when he said all of those horrible things about me becoming a writer. He took it all back when I sold my first book too. But Joseph shoots daggers at me, and this kid Montgomery treats me right.

I started for the front desk. A tall man in a three-piece suit said, "How can I help you, Mr. Rosenkrantz?" Don't you love that about hotels? They always make you feel important.

"I need to send a telegram."

"All right." He reached down and came up with a telegram form. "Do you need a pen?"

I waved at him impatiently, and he handed one over. I wrote Auger's name and address on the top, and then I wrote:

IN CALVERT STOP NEED MONEY STOP PLEASE WIRE $200 OR WHATEVER YOU CAN TO SOMERSET HOTEL ROOM 514 STOP

I paused for a moment, and then added:

AM WRITING AGAIN STOP I THINK I'VE REALLY GOT SOMETHING STOP

Then I crossed out that last line, reread the whole thing, and crossed out the line about writing too. I pushed it across the desk, and the deskman, who had been standing off to the side ignoring me in order to give me privacy, came alive and took the telegram and the pen.

"Charge it to the room, sir?"

I grinned. "Yes. Charge it to the room." And then I thought, if Carlton's paying for it all, I should really send one to Pearson too. Maybe the publishing house could spare a little petty cash. "Actually let me have another." I wrote out the same message, handed them both over, and then headed straight for the bar. This was good news, and it deserved a celebration. I was still on the wagon, of course. This morning's drink was for courage, and no one would begrudge me a drink to good fortune.

4.

But as I crossed the lobby, the anxiety began to creep back in. Pearson had told me never to cable him for money again. He said he didn't think he'd publish me again even if I ever wrote anything. And Auger had always been nice to me, but he would only go so far. And Vee was out with another man, and Quinn just teased me with her will to get me in a tight spot, no doubt, and Joseph wouldn't even look me in the eyes.

I went into the bar, and Montgomery was sitting on a stool near the entrance with an untouched pint of beer in front of him. He was jiggling his foot on the lower rung of his barstool. Here was a young man who had read my books. I could still reach out and touch someone half my age, younger. There was that. Maybe everything was fine, and I was just worrying for nothing. I came up behind him, put my right hand on his back and leaned into the bar. It was the same bartender from this morning. I caught his eye, and he nodded and then brought over a Gin Rickey.

"So, you're a fan," I said, taking a deep gulp from my drink.

Montgomery shrugged sheepishly, but once he started talking, he was full of passion, like I had been once, when the writing was still fun. "I read *Sweet as Summer* when I was fourteen, my uncle who lives in West Virginia gave it to me, and when I finished it the first time, I just turned it over, and read it again."

"You like that one? It didn't sell too well, but it got some good reviews."

"Yeah, I like it. But my favorite's *Only 'Til Seven*, but everyone probably says that. I've read all of your books, most of them more than once."

He was starting to come on a little strong, and he ducked his head, realizing it, but I liked hearing it anyway, so I didn't stop him. Before I knew it, I had finished my drink and the bartender was setting up another one. "So what was this…play you wrote? What'd you say it was called?"

"*Spook*."

I raised my eyebrows and circled my hand to say, come on.

"It's just about a former slave who lives over on the west side, and there's a ghost living in the house that is actually a white slave owner, and they talk about slavery, and freedom, and really everything. About being a man."

"And that's it?"

"That's it." He looked down at his beer, which he still hadn't touched. "It makes more sense when you see it."

I swallowed half of my drink, and patted him on the back again. "Drink up, drink up." He picked up his glass and took a tentative sip. "So you work for the newspaper. I was never quite able to do that. I did some reporting for a small town paper for maybe it was a year, and that was enough for me."

"A man's got to eat."

I nodded, and drank the rest of my Gin Rickey.

"There's no money in the theater unless you make it to New York, and even then…" he said.

"Yeah?"

"You can make some real dough in the theater in New York. If you're lucky. Or you know the right people."

I waved to the bartender. "I know the right people, I think, but I'm not lucky." The bartender set down my third drink. There was a part of me that was saying I should take it slow, but there was another part of me that didn't care. "You know, I wrote a play once."

"*In Justice.*"

I frowned and nodded my head, impressed. "You *are* a fan. I didn't think anyone read me anymore."

"Sure they do."

"Who?"

He paused.

I smiled and shook my head, and then threw an arm around his shoulders. "It doesn't matter. You read me. You know *In Justice.*" It felt good to be taken seriously. I'd almost forgotten what it was like to have somebody's respect. It didn't make it all better, but it sure helped a lot. Or maybe it was only the alcohol. In either case, I felt at ease. I raised my glass. "My wife probably doesn't even know *In Justice.*"

He looked into his drink again, remembered he was supposed to be drinking it, and picked it up in both hands like it were a mug of hot cocoa, and took a sip. He knew about my books, so of course he knew about Clotilde. Everybody knew about Clotilde. I wished I hadn't brought her up.

I kneaded his shoulder, and slapped his back. "But go on, tell me. You're going to write another play."

That brought him back. "I'm working on something. It's just an idea really."

"You knew about *In Justice*," I said, shaking my head. "What do you think of that? Did you like it?"

"Oh, sure. It was great to read." He looked to see if he had insulted me. "I mean, I've never seen it done. I've only read it, but I'm sure it's great on stage too, is what I mean."

"What's the new play about?" The bartender set another drink next to the one I hadn't even finished. I guess he'd decided I was a big spender. And why not? All thanks to Carlton. Or to Vee, my girl. I pointed at Montgomery and called to the bartender, "He's on my tab too."

"Oh, thank you, Mr. Rosenkrantz. I couldn't…"

"Of course you can. We're celebrating. To my only fan." I raised my drink, and he raised his. We tapped our glasses and both drank up.

"Mr. Rosenkrantz, sir, could I maybe interview you?"

"Maybe later, kid. Your editor wouldn't want to run it anyway. Besides, I thought you said you were on the city desk."

He shrugged.

"What's this new play about?"

He took another drink. Now he was loosening up. And it was about time, since I already felt as though I couldn't stand. "It's called *The Furies*, and it's based on this story I did a little ways back, about a family out in the county, a mom and her three kids. Her husband, if he was her husband, had run off. Her little boy got hit by a tractor one day, crushed his leg, but when she went to the hospital they kept taking other people and so she went home, but the leg rotted and the kid died. So she went back to the hospital with her other two kids and she cut their throats one after the other right there in the emergency room, saying that it was no different than what they'd done to her little boy."

"That's all true?"

"All up to the killing her other kids. I embellished it a little. The one kid died though."

I shook my head. "Nah. No, you can't kill two kids on stage like that. No one would come. No one would put it on. What if she's about to kill them and the action stops and the Furies, the actual Furies from the myths came down, and..."

He was leaning forward on his stool. "And what?"

"I don't know maybe they take her around and show her it's wrong."

"Like *A Christmas Carol*?"

"I don't know. It's your play. You write it. You don't have to listen to advice from a washed-up old man like me."

"No, I like it. The Furies come down, they take her to—"

"Isaac on the rock," I said, and punctuated it with a drink. I was sweaty now, that uncomfortable hot feeling that makes you sick to your stomach.

Montgomery was looking at me even more amazed than when he first found me. "You wouldn't...I mean, you must only be in town...You wouldn't want to write this play with me?"

"No, son, no, you don't want to do that."

He leaned forward. "I do."

I considered him. Having a young, hungry, energetic writer alongside of me might be just what I needed to get me going again. I wished I'd left the sentence about the writing on the telegrams after all, because I could see it might just work. It wouldn't even take long, no more than a week in all likelihood. Hell, I must have written a dozen screenplays in less than a week.

I slapped him on the back and pulled him close, my arm around his neck, stopping just short of tousling his hair—a man didn't deserve that kind of disrespect no matter how young he was. I held onto him to prevent me from keeling over, and said, "Why don't we give it a try? Who the hell knows, maybe we'll get something. At least we'll have a few laughs."

He went to his pocket and produced the reporter's pad he had brought out before and a fountain pen, and he started to write. "So they go to Isaac on the rock." He looked up. "Wait, how do the pagan Furies get to the Old Testament?"

"Once the Furies come in, the audience is either with us or not, so what does it matter if we mix and match a little."

He could see I was right, so he nodded, and started writing, and I started talking and it just came out of me. I don't know how, but on and on, the two of us throwing ideas back and forth, the bartender setting up drinks, and Montgomery was drinking right alongside me now. We were matching each other drink for drink—he'd switched to rum and Coke—and from what I could tell, he could hold his liquor. I reached that familiar plateau where my mind focused, and my body let go, and some of my best work was in that state. No, all of my best work was in that state. Inebriation. What a wonderful word.

And it wasn't just me. Montgomery also. He really had an ear for dialogue. I'd just need to suggest a scene, and in no time, he had it all marked out, and the characters sounded just as natural as we were talking. Every now and then I thought, I should stop drinking. I needed to go to bed. I needed to find some way to get out of here tomorrow. But the idea of the empty hotel room, of what Vee was up to, was too much, and I knew I shouldn't be alone. This thing with Joseph would start to eat me up if I went upstairs alone. So we kept talking, fleshing it out. And who could blame me if I kept tossing down the drinks. I was in a bar after all. What did anyone expect?

After a while, I started to notice that Montgomery was slowing down, and was a little green in the gills, hanging over the bar like all he could think about was keeping his head up. And his eyes kept darting to the clock behind the bar. Of course it was ten minutes fast, but that didn't change that it was almost eight o'clock and we'd been there nearly six hours.

"Son," I said, patting him on the back. "It's time for us to recess. We can resume our composition tomorrow."

He tried to shake his head, but it hurt him to do it. "No."

"Don't you have work in the morning?"

"Work in the morning?" he said as though it were a new concept. As if he had never thought about what it meant to work in the morning. As if he didn't remember that there was anything outside of that bar.

"Come on, up." I pulled him to his feet by the arm. I was steady on my own feet, because like I said, I was in that magic alcoholic plateau where I could function normally, but clean, without the anxiety, without the bothersome thoughts that never seemed to go away, that never let me do any little piece of work or pull myself together, get a job of my own, even if it was washing dishes. It would be a comedown, but I was still a man, after all. Who was that doctor to tell me if I drank much more it would kill me? I knew what would and wouldn't kill me.

Well, I had him to his feet, like I said, and I brought him out to the curb, and he was hanging off of me completely now, and maybe I felt a little guilty, but only a little. We'd had a good time.

The bellman called a cab, and got the back door open for us. I poured Montgomery into the black plastic seat. "Where do you live?" I said.

"My notebook."

"I put it in your pocket. Tell the driver where you live." I called to the bellman, "Is there a way to put the cab on my room?"

"Certainly, sir, I'll work it out." He went around to the driver's side, and the driver rolled down his window.

Montgomery said something about Tudor Street and I felt

fairly certain that he would get home all right. I said to the driver, "If you can't get him to tell you where he lives, bring him back here." He nodded, and turned back to the bellman. I closed the back door, and went back inside.

But then that empty hotel room began to loom up again. And there was a twinge, and only a twinge thanks to the alcohol, of the panic about the telegrams and Vee leaving me here. But that was silly, I told myself. Someone had recognized me, and worshipped me. If this kid reporter could, then why couldn't Joseph? But the answer was easy. He could. He just needed a chance to calm down. That was all. And he'd had a chance. All those hours, all afternoon. And it wasn't too late. Eight o'clock was early for a kid his age. That was just the start of the evening.

I turned around and went back out the revolving door. "Cab," I said, and the doorman whistled. He opened the door for me like he'd done before, and closed it when he saw I was settled. The driver had his head cocked, waiting for directions. I gave him Quinn's address—Joseph's address—and we pulled out of the circular drive onto Chase Street.

5.

The old Hadley mansion was in the neighborhood of Underwood, in the northern part of the city, just above the university. The whole area had been owned by one family up until about sixty or seventy years ago, and when they started to parcel it off and open it to development, the Hadleys took their umbrella fortune and built a four-story brick edifice into the side of a slight hill. There were pitched awnings over all the windows that made the place look like a hotel. A steep multi-tiered set of stairs rose from the street to the main entrance, while the garage and the servants' entrance was at street level in the back.

Half the lights in the house were on when the cab pulled up front. I got out and paused for a moment with the cab door still open. I turned to ask the driver to wait, but in the end I closed the door and the cabbie pulled off before I had stepped away from the curb. I started up the steep stairs, which proved to be more difficult than I expected. I mean I had had a few drinks, but it had been over a lot of hours, so there was no reason for it but I leaned a lot of my weight on the iron pipe of a railing.

Just when I was at the next-to-last landing, the front door opened, and out came Mary O'Brien and behind her Connie, both of them with their heads down, looking for the first step. I wanted to go up to meet them, but I had had enough, so I waited for them to come down. Mary saw me first, from about halfway down the top set of stairs. She caught herself up, and said, "Oh."

Connie looked up, but the light was too poor to see her expression, her black features like a shadowed mask.

Mary started down again. "Mr. Rosenkrantz, you gave me such a start." She picked her way down to the landing. "What are you doing here so late?"

I could have asked the same of her, but she was his fiancée, and she had Connie with her, no doubt as a chaperone, and hadn't it been such a tough day and all, with the will being read, and Joe becoming a millionaire. He must have needed the company to bolster his strength. "Thought I'd see Joe. Didn't realize it had gotten so late."

Her face took on a pinched look. She probably smelled the alcohol, but I tell you, I really was fine, only I guess she didn't know that. "I'm glad you're here," she said. "I was very much hoping to get a chance to talk to you."

"Well, here I am." I nodded to Connie, who said, "Mr. Rosenkrantz," and I said, "Shem, please."

"Joe was very upset," Mary said. "I mean at the—earlier. Before. He didn't...oh, you do know what I'm trying to say, don't you?"

"Yeah. Sure. It's awfully nice of you to say even if it isn't true."

"Oh, but it is. I mean, well, ask Connie. That's the only reason we're here so late. This has all been so hard on Joe. He needed me—us, somebody with him, I almost don't like to leave him now. Miss Quinn was really all he had," and realizing what she'd said, "I mean...of course he had you too—"

"And you, and Aunt Alice, and Connie here, right Connie? And any number of other people, but sure, yeah, I know what you mean. Quinn was his mom, of course he's upset. I'm here to take over for you guys. It's my shift." And I tried that dapper grin of mine, but it was probably sloppy, I was feeling a little green.

"Oh, but, I don't think now is the right time. I mean…"

"Mary," I said, "Can I call you Mary? You're doing a lot of oh-but-ing and I-mean-ing. Take a breath and just relax. If Joe's not up to my visit tonight, for any reason, sure, that's okay. I'm disappointed, but it's okay. Right?"

She took a deep breath, and when she let it out her face looked lighter. It really did. "Joe said you were so unreasonable, and really…" She turned and looked at Connie. "Connie, could you go down. I'll be right there."

"Yes, ma'am," Connie said, and stepped around her, but to me she hazarded a look and said, "Miss Alice was quite disappointed you didn't make it to tea."

"Well, Aunt Alice can add it to the list of ways I've disappointed her," I said.

Connie cringed, and really I didn't have to be so tough with her. She was just doing her job. Sometimes it was hard to remember that, it was so much like she was a member of the family, even if she was a Negro. And how awkward must that be for her, family yet not family, employee and confidante?

"Listen, Connie, I'm sorry, but you know—" I started, but the light in the front room went out just then, and we were plunged into a deeper darkness. I looked up at the windows to see if Joseph was standing there watching us. I couldn't tell, but I figured he probably was. We all paused while our eyes got used to the dark.

Then Connie said, "I'll be sure to send her your regards, Mr. Rosenkrantz." She started down the steps, leaning even more heavily on the railing than I had, dropping one foot onto the step below her, and then limping the rest of her weight after it.

Mary and I watched her for a moment, and when she was nearly to the next landing, Mary turned to me. "Mr. Rosenkrantz…" I had to resist making the wisecrack, 'Call me Dad,' but she was trying so hard, it wouldn't have been fair to her. "I know you and Joseph have had a hard time in the past."

"A hard time's hardly saying it. Last time we saw each other he took a swing at me, and that was his high school graduation."

"Yes. Oh." He hadn't told her that one.

"Look, Mary, I appreciate what you're trying to say. It was stupid of me to come up here. I've been sober for months up until today."

She gave a start at that.

"I guess this whole thing with Quinn is getting to all of us, and I…" I felt like I was maybe going to cry. I didn't, you understand, but I felt like I *might*.

She nearly put her hand out to comfort me, but thought better of it. "Maybe we can meet tomorrow," she said. "I meant to call on you at your hotel earlier, but somehow the day has slipped past. I've never been here this late, and if Connie weren't with me, my parents would have had the police out. They probably have anyway. You're…we're all tired. Can I call on you tomorrow?"

"Of course."

"I just think it would be best if we spoke tomorrow. Things aren't so simple."

"Of course, of course. A pretty girl like you? You can call on me anytime you want."

She looked down and I knew I'd spoiled it with that comment about her being pretty. She was trying, but she'd no doubt heard all of Joe's stories about my sleeping around—never mind that Quinn did too—and here I sound like I'm trying to pick her up.

"Any time after breakfast, let's say. At the hotel. We can get a cup of coffee in the hotel café."

I was starting to sweat heavily then. The cloying heat and alcohol were getting to me and I felt as though I were going to be sick. It didn't help knowing Joe might be up there watching me talk to her.

"Yes, I'd like that," she said, and ventured a look at me, and then she sighed in relief and even smiled, and pretty wasn't really strong enough for what she was. Like I'd said before, Joe was a lucky man.

"After you," I said, and held my hand out to the steps in invitation. She went down before me, and I looked back up at the looming house again, but it was still impossible to know if Joe was at one of those windows. All of the other lights in the house were still on.

At the bottom of the steps, I was breathing heavily and the sweat was making me irritable, so I just said, "Ladies," and turned south on foot before they could offer me a ride or inquire after my health. Wouldn't that have been rich?

I made it to the end of the block, and I turned in, and was immediately sick on the foot of a tree. The heaves were strong enough to make my sides sore. Tears pushed out of my closed eyes. I pressed my forehead against the bark of the tree, both hands bracing me on either side, but it was only later that I felt the pain of the sharp bark cutting into me. I heaved again and the taste of alcohol and acid burned the back of my nose, and I felt chill even as the sweat poured off of me. I heaved and I heaved. A part of me marveled at the volume, but soon there was nothing coming up, and the sour smell of my vomit was sickening in its own right. I brought my forearm up, and leaned my head against that on the tree. The sweat soaked into my sleeve. I was lightheaded and I shivered as a pang went down my sides. I shivered again. And then I seemed to be finished. There was the taste in my mouth, but nothing was rebelling any longer.

I pushed myself up, and wiped my mouth with my handkerchief. Great job, I thought. A really classy guy. What would Montgomery think if he saw me now? It's not enough I owe money all over the country and depend on the whims of a hard-boiled whore, I've got to drink myself sick a block from Joe's house when I've got the crazy idea about making it up. Yeah, I was nothing but a poor bastard, like I said before, and I deserved everything I got, but don't let me catch you saying it.

Once I felt sure on my feet, I stepped into the near-black street, crossing to the other side. There, a recessed footlight in a brick retaining wall revealed the vomit on the toes of my shoes. I stopped, pulled out my already soiled handkerchief and, leaning against the wall, lifted one foot, wiped it off, and then the other. When I was done, I threw the handkerchief into the gutter, and started south towards the less residential part of the city near the university where I'd be able to find a cab.

The lights came first, and then the lawns ended, and there was a five-story apartment house visible across University Avenue. If I looked straight down St. Peter's Street, I could see the lights of the skyscrapers all the way downtown. The roads were empty, and the traffic light went through its pattern needlessly as, still shaky, I crossed University into George Village. Quinn and I used to hang around George Village to be with people our own age, and she knew some men at the university. Not much had changed in the intervening years. The row homes hidden by overgrown trees looked broken down and abused, which they were, rented short-term to college men who took the job of being college men very seriously.

When I got to the block where the George Village Pub was, I still hadn't run into a cab. I was starting to feel a bit hungry, my stomach now empty after my little spell. I pushed into the stale smoke of the bar, and was comforted to find that I didn't look too out of place. The students were away for the summer, so the only people in the bar that night were some loud and coarse citybillies and a few grad students trying to keep their heads down. I ordered a Gin Rickey. The bartender sighed and took his time getting to the hard stuff. In a place like that the only kind of orders they get are draught and the bartender gets lazy. But he made me the drink.

With the first swallow, I felt calmer. I pushed the whole pathetic incident, the talk with Mary, the puking, pushed it all away, and my mind turned to the play Montgomery and I had been working on that evening. And just like the old days, the thought of having to write more tomorrow clenched my heart in a vise. I didn't want to; I couldn't; the burn of vomit in the back of my throat made my stomach turn; I'd just tell Montgomery to forget it, I was too busy.

Then all of a sudden, something clicked: the Furies in our little play could die, be killed themselves, that is. The vise relaxed, and I took another drink. It's like that sometimes. An idea at the end of the night hits, and you feel, at least I've got somewhere to start tomorrow. Well, I felt good about that idea, less anxious about the next day, and after two more drinks, I started to think about visiting Joe again. The idea of my hotel room didn't strike me as any more appealing now. If he threw me out or took a swing at me, it'd still be better than the hotel.

I thought about another drink, patted my pockets for a little cash, but of course I didn't have any, so I went out back where the bathrooms were. I pushed my way through a door marked "Exit," and found myself in the alley behind the bar. I ran as fast as my aching body would let me back up to the next block, and when I came out in the street, I walked one block east to Caroline Street in order to make my way back to University.

6.

Nothing had changed in the hour since I'd been turned away. The little sprint from the bar had me sweating worse than before, and I was angry, no, irritable, eager to get in where it was air-conditioned at least. I pressed on the buzzer when I got to the top of the stairs and took off my jacket. I mopped my forehead, my face, the back of my neck with the sleeves of my shirt. The whole idea of being there in the middle of the night struck me as crazy again. How could I expect that he would open the door? I mean, I probably could have walked right in, they never used to lock their doors in that neighborhood, but that wouldn't do. I pressed the buzzer again, figuring just the last time, and the door swung open immediately. He must have been standing right on the other side.

"What do you want?" he said. He was still dressed, but his collar was unbuttoned and he wasn't wearing a tie.

"Joe, I—" I hadn't thought of what I was going to say to him if he did answer. "Can I come in?"

"What do you want?"

"Can't I just come in?"

"*What do you want?*" He was sneering, but he hadn't closed the door.

"To talk," I spat out. "To talk. Come on, Joe, we should be friends. We should…now, you know—if we're all that's left… Can't I just come in?"

He took a step back, and I thought he was going to slam the

door, I really did. And oh, if he had… Well I wouldn't be where I am now, would I? But he took a step back and said, "Do what you want." And walked away from the door, leaving it open.

I stepped inside and closed the door behind me. I hadn't been in that house since I don't know when. They'd pulled up the Persian rug that used to be in the front hall, revealing the black-and-white chessboard tiles. The grandfather clock was also gone, replaced by a wall-mounted brass starburst with no digits and a long pendulum. Joe had gone into the further room to the right, the dining room, where he stood at a glass-topped brass refreshment cart. He was pouring a brandy. There was a glass on the dining room table with melting ice and an amber residue in it already, so at first I thought he was making me a drink, but he brought the glass to his own lips. It was then that it hit me he was drunk too, drunker even than I was.

"Joe, what can I do to make it up with you?" I said, the table between us.

"You can't."

"Well can you at least tell me what it is I'm supposed to have done? How can I try to explain myself, if I don't even know what it is I have to explain?"

"You don't have to explain yourself. I know already. I was here, remember? I was the one who had to watch Mom suffer. You were off with, who is it now? Are you and Chloë still married even? I can't remember. Not that it would matter to you."

"You just wait until you're married," I said, angry now myself. Somehow the air conditioner wasn't doing its job. "You don't know."

"I know I would never do to Mary what you did to Mom."

"You think I planned it? I didn't plan it."

"But you did it."

"Come on. What is this? You're twenty-one—"

"Twenty-two."

I wished I hadn't gotten that wrong. But I went on, "Right, twenty-two. You're just a kid. You'll learn that when you're older—"

"I am older." His glass shook in his hands. "I'm not a kid anymore."

"No, you're not a kid. I don't mean to say you're a kid. I mean things just look different when…" I took a breath. "You know I wasn't the only one being unfaithful. Your mother was there right along with me."

His lips were quaking despite his efforts to maintain control. "You would speak on the dead."

I lost it for a moment then. "Listen, you— Just shut up and listen. All of this, this crap you're on about, it all happened before you were born, so what do you know about it anyway? You weren't there!"

He raised his voice too. "And you weren't here for the last twenty-two years, so what do you know about it! Mom was… she never…she was…you had Chloë Rose, not that she was enough for you either, but Mom just had, she only had…" He brought the glass to his lips and it was shaking.

I steadied myself on the back of one of the chairs. "Joe, what's this really all about? This is all ancient history. Let's forget all of that. I'm here now to try and make it different."

He took another drink from his glass. The ice clinked. There was nothing left in the glass to drink.

"You know, I met a guy today, about your age. And he, well, he just about thinks I'm the greatest thing on two legs, and I thought, why couldn't my boy feel that way? Why couldn't Joe feel that way? And I thought, sure he could. There's no reason he couldn't."

He took another drink from his empty glass, his lip still trembling and his hand unsteady.

"I'm not all bad," I said.

"What you did to Mom—"

"Oh stop it," I spat. "You don't know a damn thing about it. You don't know how often she'd be out and I'd be in one hotel or another all by myself, or even worse, when she would come back to the room with someone and it didn't even matter I was there. Don't go on about how Quinn was some kind of martyr. She kept me on the hook for alimony and child support the whole time too, even though I couldn't pay it and she didn't need it. She wanted me to know she could send me to jail any time she wanted."

"Of course it's about the money with you. That's why you're really here."

"Damn it, Joe. You say you're grown up, but you're acting like a brat."

"Tell me you don't want the money. Tell me that you weren't drinking yourself dumb today after you got nothing in that will."

"Forget the damn money. This isn't about the money. What do I have to say to prove it to you? Your mother cared more about the money than I ever did."

"Mom suffered. She, you don't know—she wasted away. Her body, it just, it fell off her somehow. She lost a lot of her hair." There were tears falling down his cheeks, but he hadn't given in to them. He wasn't all-out crying just yet. He swallowed and shut it down. "I had to face that alone, just like always. I had to help her to the bathroom. I had to sit in the hospital waiting for it. It was me. And her life was just, it, she wasn't, it could have been so much more. I could have done more." This last line came out in a squeak, and he shook his head.

"Joe…"

He shook his head more, and he turned and walked through the swinging door back to the kitchen. He'd been all over the place, I had cheated on Quinn, I wanted her money, I didn't know what her death was like. It didn't matter what I said, he was poisoned against me, and in his eyes, there was nothing I could do right. But still I followed him.

He was at the sink with his back to me, but I could tell he was crying. "Joe?"

No response.

"I loved your mother. I—"

He spun around and flung the glass at me. It went wide and hit the wall, spraying melted ice water in a splatter along the paint. The glass broke neatly in two.

We both waited, shocked by the violence. Joe cried and fought crying at the same time, which only contorted his face worse than if he'd let go. I tried to count to ten, which I'd never done before, but I was with a girl for a little while who did it all the time and swore it worked. I couldn't make it all the way to ten, but when I spoke, I felt steady and I didn't yell.

"I loved Quinn very much, more than anyone except for Clotilde maybe. I can't even believe that she's dead. She was out there for so long…"

"Like you," Joe said, not able to fight the crying anymore. Standing there with his fists clenched, crying openly, well it was enough to bring tears to my eyes too, and that meant I loved him too, right? I mean, of course it did. "When I was a kid, I worshipped you," Joe said, his voice erratic as he sobbed. "You meet some kid in a bar and you feel important because he looks up to you. As a writer. I worshipped you for being my father."

I waited. Let him get it out.

"It was hard living with Mom. And Grandma and Grandpa. Knowing you were out there, though, that you were famous…" The crying renewed itself. "And those times I flew out to California, and you couldn't be bothered with me, and you were loud and drunk and you fought with Chloë, with everybody. What do you think that did to me?"

I just shook my head.

"Even after the first time and after the second time, it got harder and harder. It took me a while, but I figured it out, that I meant nothing to you and you weren't so great, in fact, you were pretty terrible."

"I'm sorry."

"That doesn't mean anything."

I stepped forward, reaching out for him. "I'm sorry. I was, when I was drinking, horrible."

He snuffed at that. "*When* you were drinking?"

"You can ask anybody, I've been sober for months. This… well, like I said, I loved Quinn, and I don't have to tell you." I nodded at him.

"No. Because I don't care."

"You're the one who's crying."

"You betrayed me."

"By being different than something you made up in your head?" I said, my voice rising again.

"By everything!" He started forward, but he had to pass me to get to the door. I reached out to stop him, and he jerked away, and lashed out with his arm, striking mine away, but I managed to stay between him and the door. "Stop it! Let me go!"

"Joe, I'm your father," I said, reaching out for his shoulder again.

"No!" He fought me, and our arms got tangled, and he landed a few accidental blows and I'm sure I did the same, and then he pushed me away and turned to the refrigerator and pulled from beside it an ice pick and then swept around at me, brandishing the ice pick as a deterrent only I'm sure.

I pulled back. "What are you doing?"

"Get out," he said, panting. His eyes were red from crying, but he wasn't crying anymore. His face was pure malice.

"You're not going to—" I said, walking towards him again. And don't ask me what I was going to do. I was going to hug him, I guess, even though it sounds kind of sappy. But when you spend too long in Hollywood, what do you expect? You turn sappy. So I took a step towards him, and he lunged.

The ice pick struck me a glancing blow, tearing my shirt, a hot flash crossed my bicep. And I guess I threw my arms up, or pushed, or something, we were so close together at that point, and I think I was probably just trying to knock the ice pick out of his hands, but instead, he tripped and he fell backwards and there was a clunk, like the sound of a grapefruit dropping, as the back of his head hit the edge of the counter, and his chin raced against his chest and he fell to the floor in a heap.

I had my right hand over the cut in my left arm, the pain like a paper cut multiplied by a thousand if you can imagine that. And there was blood dripping down my sleeve from between my fingers, and I know from later that some of it dripped on the floor.

Joe was unconscious. That's what I thought. But I probably knew.

"Joe," I said.

He didn't say anything.

"Joe? Are you all right?"

I kicked his foot, lightly, to try to wake him, but it just jostled his leg, and he didn't move. Fear started racing up my arms and into my jaw. I bent down. The back of his head didn't look too bad, what I could see of it, although the hair was matted from the blood, and his head was at a funny angle. "Joe?"

I didn't try to touch him, because by then I knew. Maybe it was the bump on his head or maybe he had broken his neck. The ice pick was on the floor only a few inches from his hand, the end spotted with blood. I was shivering all over, still gripping my cut arm, and if I hadn't vomited so much before, I would have vomited then, my throat constricted, my mouth dry.

I wanted to cry, but instead my heart was racing.

I don't know how long I crouched there. My thighs started to burn. But it was the sound of the telephone ringing that jarred me out of my stupor.

I stood up, and I don't know why I did it, except maybe that a phone rings and you answer, so I answered.

7.

"Joe? Are you still awake?" It was a whisper.

"Who is this?" I said.

The voice on the other end got tight and a touch louder. "Who is this?"

It was Mary. How could I talk to Mary now? "Joe just went out to the bathroom, and then I'm going to get him in bed, I promise," I said, it just coming out natural like that.

"Mr. Rosenkrantz?"

"I got to thinking I should give Joe a try anyway, and I'm glad I did, because we had a swell time. I'm just about leaving. Should I have Joe call you when he gets out of the bathroom?"

"No, no, it's late," she said. And lucky for me she did. What would I have done if she'd said yes? "I'm glad you're there. I was really worried. He shouldn't be alone."

"He's feeling better now."

"Good. Very good. I'm so glad things worked out." She did sound glad about it, relieved almost. "We still have our date for the morning though?"

"I wouldn't miss it," I said, and I was even grinning my patented grin, even if my throat was dry. You can hear someone smile over the telephone.

"Good night."

"Good night," I said and hung up.

Then I was alone with my son again. Alone with his corpse. I had killed my son. I didn't mean it. Nobody could say I meant it. He had attacked me. The blood was trickling down my arm. My son was dead. I needed to go. I needed help. If I were writing a movie, what would I have the murderer do? I didn't know. I never got the hang of those murder stories. That's why nobody in Hollywood would hire me.

All this time I was trying to look everywhere but at his body, but then I saw him again, and the lump in my throat was a baseball that was choking me. Vee would know what to do. Vee was...

I needed a drink. I needed to get out of there. That was definitely what I needed to do. As soon as the thought occurred to me, I went into action. I went back through the swinging doors, through the dining room, grabbing my coat, over the chessboard floor and out into the night. I took the stairs two at a time.

The heat was oppressive. But I was nearly running, and I went like that the whole mile and a half or so back to George Village. The pain in my arm had dulled, maybe from the exertion, but I could see from the streetlights that it was still bleeding. I stopped to put on my coat. It was like a razor searing my arm as I slid the coat sleeve over the cut and twisted to get the other arm in. The renewed pain throbbed before settling back to a dull ache. Then, luck would have it, a car turned onto University from Caroline, heading towards me as I crossed University at St. Peter's. The headlights resolved themselves, and I saw it was a cab. I flagged it down, and ran up to it even as it was coming to a stop in the southbound lane on St. Peter's. The cabbie was a rare man—a driver who didn't try to talk your ear off, so I didn't have to try at small talk I was in no state to conduct. With no traffic, it took only ten minutes to get back to the hotel.

Then I was in the room. The window air conditioners had been on full blast, and the place felt like a refrigerator. It made the hairs on my arms stand up, and sent a shiver across my shoulders, which shot pain through my arm. I slipped out of my jacket, pulling the right sleeve off first and then gingerly sliding the coat off my left arm. The bleeding had stopped. My shirt-sleeve was stuck to me with dried blood, and I pulled it free, a satisfying little tug, and tried to see the cut. It wasn't anything serious, not much more than a scratch, and I guess that was something to be happy about. Yeah, thank God for the small things, never mind the—well, just never mind...

I checked my jacket. The blood hadn't soaked through. I turned the sleeve inside out. There was a slight black smudge there, but that was all right. I righted the sleeve and tossed the jacket at the couch, missed, and left it there.

I kept standing there in the center of the living room with that whooshing hiss of the air conditioners deafening me as I tried to make sense of the suite. The maid had made up the bed and vacuumed the carpet and the place was so clean it was anti-septic, with that unreal sense of domesticity that hotels have, the furniture set up like someone were living here but without any of the telltale signs—a lamp off center on a side table, stubs and ashes in the ashtrays, a book laid out, hell, any books at all.

And, of course, Vee wasn't there.

The sweat had dried on me, a salty skin that made me feel unclean. I started nodding my head, just nodding. At what I do not know, but nodding all the same. Joe was gone. I had killed him. I had killed a man. I was going to go to prison. Did they have the death penalty in Maryland? I couldn't remember. I thought they did. I was going to go to the electric chair. Or maybe it was the gas chamber. And Joe was dead. I had killed him. I had killed a man? I was going to go to prison. And around and around like that for who knows how long, but you get the idea.

Then I thought I should really get some sleep. I had a meeting with Joe's fiancée in the morning, and I was supposed to see the Montgomery kid too. I needed to be rested. And I know it was crazy to be thinking about things like I'd be able to keep my appointments, but *you* kill a man and tell me you don't think crazy things. I started unbuttoning my shirt, but I hadn't made it two buttons when the image of Joe lying there in the kitchen came back to me strong and I rushed for the bathroom, because this time I thought I would throw up again. But when I was on the floor in the bathroom with the cold porcelain in my hands, I only gave one belch that was half cough, and then just stayed there with my head hanging down near the toilet water and the cold of the tile floor bleeding in through my pants.

The cold woke me up again. I couldn't go to prison. Who would look after Clotilde? I had been living in the YMCA so that the last of her movie money could go to keeping her in the hospital, but the money was running out, and I couldn't let Clotilde go to a state hospital; they butchered the patients at those places, all of them walking around like empty spirits, drool hanging from their lips, a bunch of drug addicts and maniacs. That was why I was out here in the first place, grasping at straws, because while Vee had rescued me from the Y as a charity case, I needed to come up with Clotilde's hospital money myself, and I couldn't do it in prison. I had to do something. I had to—I didn't know. I couldn't think of anything, not one thing.

But Vee would probably know. Vee's friend Carlton would definitely know. He was a gangster, wasn't he?

I reached my hand into my pants pocket and clutched the hotel key with its plastic diamond tag that read "Suite 12-2." They were sure to be able to help me. I didn't need to go to prison. Nobody needed to know at all. It could have been an accident. It was an accident. I just needed somebody to show me how to…how to make it all okay.

I was up and moving then. I went out in the hallway, forgetting that I was wearing a torn and bloody shirt, that was how out of it I was, and I went to the stairwell because it was closer than the elevators, and so I had to climb I can't tell you how many steps, but it was a lot of steps. The stairwell wasn't air conditioned, of course, and the sweat was pouring off of me. I kept taking breaks at the landings, checking the cut to make sure it hadn't started bleeding again. Finally at the twelfth floor, I pulled open the door. My heart was pounding, and I was out of breath, and I was overheated and dripping, and it all put me in more of a panic.

There were only four suites on the twelfth floor. These were the luxury suites. The grand suites. Vee had said that Carlton kept Suite 12-2 in perpetuity even though he had a house uptown and one on the Eastern Shore and spent maybe three weeks worth of nights at the hotel in a year, if that.

The door to Suite 12-2 was twenty feet from the stairwell with maybe another fifteen feet between the door and the elevators. It was very quiet. The eternally burning hall lights felt defiant so late at night, almost as though they were saying they didn't need people, they could do fine on their own, thank you. See, I told you I was screwy.

I stood in front of the suite door. My heart was pounding, my arm was aching, I swallowed but my throat was dry. I raised my hand to knock, but managed nothing more than a tap, so of course there wasn't any response. My nerves grew shakier. I couldn't bring myself to knock again, and I couldn't keep standing there in the hallway with a bloody shirt and a glistening brow. So I took the key, which was still in my hand, slid it into the lock, and opened the door.

8.

There was a light on. I could see that before I had the door open enough to see anything else. There was a galley kitchen immediately to the left of the door that ran for several feet, and there was a bank of mirrored sliding closet doors to the right. The light I had seen was a reflection in the mirror; the entryway was actually quite shadowed.

I stepped past the kitchen into a big open space with a dining room table to the left and living room furniture a little further on. The furniture was organized around a glass coffee table, taking full advantage of the large windows that offered a wide view of the city. In the far corner there was an armchair lit by a standing lamp, and in the chair, a book closed over one finger on his lap, was an enormous man—it was hard to say just how big with him sitting. He wore a pair of blue-and-white striped pajamas with a mauve silk robe over it and a pair of leather slippers. He looked at me with open amazement.

"Who—the hell—are you?" he said, almost biting off each word, his amazement turning fast to anger.

"I'm sorry, I—"

He raised his bulk and he was big like a gorilla. "Who the hell are you." He let the book fall to the floor, and it lay open in the middle.

"I just…Mr. Carlton."

"Mr. Carlton? Mr. Carlton?" He was advancing on me. I thought I was going to cry. I really did. How would that have been, me crying in front of a gangster? "Those who address me," he was yelling, "address me as Mr. Browne, but that's just those who address me." There was still half the room between us. He was livid, but he wasn't too concerned about getting at me. "You better talk or you won't be able to talk no more."

Vee appeared from the hallway at the left in a short robe. "Shem!" she said. "Carlton... I mean Mr. Rosenkrantz, what's going on?"

Carlton; Mr. Browne—how was I supposed to know Carlton was his first name?—Mr. Browne yelled without turning around, "You know this man, Victoria?"

"No," she said, looking at me with complete shock. "I mean, yeah. He's my cousin."

"What's your 'cousin' doing in my suite at nearly two in the goddamn morning?"

She started across the room then. She had her face in a pretty good imitation of honest confusion. "I saw him this afternoon. I lost my key. Shem, you should have just left it at the front desk with a note."

He grabbed her by the arm and pulled her around.

"Oh, Carlton!"

He must have squeezed tighter, because she winced.

"Carlton...please."

"This is your cousin? How old is he?"

"Oh, I don't know." She was struggling to keep her face composed. "Shem...?"

I held the key out, like that was going to make it better. This was a man who wanted his girlfriends to carry guns and was just about breaking Vee's arm. "I'm sorry," I said, and I *sounded* like I was going to cry. "It's just that I killed him, and I didn't know what to do."

He took a step towards me, pulling Vee with him. She was looking at me with terror, trying to shake her head so that I'd see but he wouldn't.

"Excuse me," he said.

"He's dead," I said, still holding out the key.

"Carlton, please..." Vee said. He threw her to the side and she tripped but caught herself against the wall so she didn't go down.

"I'll tell you what," he said, and he was smiling as he said it, which was much worse than when he was angry. "I don't feel much like ruining this robe, and I just had a manicure this morning, so I'm going to go back in my room for my baseball bat, and if you're still here when I get back, I'll show you what to do when you kill somebody."

Vee took a step towards him, "Carlton—"

He punched her in the face and her head swung around and she fell into a dining room chair and then sat on the ground. "That goes for you too," he said to her, walking away from us.

Vee looked up at me from the ground. There was a large red blotch on the left side of her face that was already becoming puffy. "You bastard," she said, and started to try and pull herself up with the help of the chair she had fallen into.

"Vee, I didn't know what else to do. I killed Joseph, and—"

"Stop saying that!" She grabbed onto me to steady herself. "Come on, or are you really that stupid?"

"You're not wearing any—"

She pushed me back towards the hall door, got it opened, and went right for the stairs, dragging me along. "I could kill you. I should kill you."

We were in the hot stairwell. The room key was still in my hand, and I slipped it back into my pocket as Vee started down ahead of me. "I told you I was only joking," she yelled back up at me, her voice echoing. "You weren't supposed to go and do it."

And it hit me that she had told me to kill him this afternoon. And had that been in the back of my mind when I went to see him? Had I killed him because I actually wanted to? The money would be mine now—he wasn't married yet, he had no will, I was his closest living relative. I realized just how much trouble I was in, because nobody would believe it was an accident now, even if I tried to say it was. I had too good a motive. But I hadn't meant to kill him. It had been an accident.

Vee was a whole level below me. She pushed out onto our floor, and the door had already closed behind her when I got to it, but she had to wait at our room, because I had the key. She had her arms crossed just under her breasts as though she was cold, but really she had caught an unnatural case of modesty. She shoved me aside once the door was unlocked and was at the armoire already by the time I made it into the bedroom. She took out a skirt and a blouse and flung them on the bed.

"You're really crazy, you know that? He could have killed us both. He probably will kill me. What am I to him? I'm just another whore." She was getting dressed, not taking the time to hide her nakedness now. "He's not so foolish to think I'm with him alone, but to have another man show up in his room. Like Samson and Delilah." She had the skirt on now, and was zipping it up. Then she pulled it around so the zipper was in the back. "We need to get out of here."

"Vee," I said, and I don't know what was in my voice, but she stopped and looked at me.

"What the hell happened to your arm?"

"Joe stabbed me with an ice pick."

She got very calm. "You're serious? You really killed him?"

I just nodded. I couldn't talk then.

"S—t! S—t, s—t, s—t."

"It was an accident."

"Who saw you?"

I shook my head. "When?"

"When! When! Now, you idiot. Who saw you? Who'd you tell? What happened?" She started putting her blouse on, but her fingers were shaking so much as she tried to work the buttons that it took several attempts with each one.

"I don't think anybody saw me. It was at his house. It was an accident."

"Like anyone will believe that."

"It was!"

"All right! Don't yell at me about it. I believe you it was an accident. But who else will believe you!" She had her shirt mostly buttoned. Her face was bruising.

"I ran out. It was dark. I took a cab here, and I don't know. I guess I came through the lobby."

She gestured at my bloody arm with her head. "With that?"

"I had my jacket on."

She paused. "Can we get back in the house? Is it locked?"

"I don't know. I don't think so. Probably not. It never used to be."

She went past me, finishing the last button and picked up the phone. "Yes, could you have Mr. Browne's car around front please?" She paused. "Thank you, I'll be right down."

"What are you doing?" I said.

She picked up my jacket and pushed it at me, pushing me towards the door at the same time. "You go down the stairs and out through the back. Make sure no one sees you. Wait around the corner and I'll be there to get you."

"What are you going to do?"

"Fix it. That's what you wanted, didn't you?"

"Vee, are you okay?"

Her face was purple and black, her eye had red in it. She looked like she was going to claw me. But instead, before I could say anything more, she was off to the elevators, striding away from me with all the assurance in the world.

I felt exhausted all of a sudden, and slumped against the wall. How could I get up? How could I ever walk again? My eyes closed and my head sagged. Quinn, I thought. Clotilde… Again the sight of Joe's head flopped over on his neck came before me, and it made my stomach turn. But it got me going. I went back to the stairs, and went down, down in the fiery heat.

9.

Vee was angry. She kept her jaw set and her eyes on the road. We only spoke enough for me to give her directions. The city was asleep and we had the road to ourselves. "Are we close?" Vee said up around the train station where a handful of cabs sat out front waiting for a late train to come in.

"About halfway," I said.

"Let me know when we're close. We can't park nearby."

She was like that, all business, and I got the feeling that she wasn't angry that I had killed Joe, not the killing itself so much, but angry at the annoyance of it. And of course she was really angry that I had gotten her in dutch with Carlton. Browne. Whatever his name was.

At the university I told her we were nearby and she pulled off on 34th Street, went over to Caroline, and turned the car back south. She found a spot about midway up the block. We got out and she came around the car. "Take my arm," she said. "We're just coming home from a night on the town."

I led the way and the sweat was pouring off of me again. It had been a relief of sorts when Vee took over—that *is* what I had wanted—but now the idea of having to go back into that house again, of having to see him again, I wasn't sure if I could do it. Things could be that way, a place you went to every day, so often you didn't even see it anymore, you knew every inch of it so well, a place like that and a little time goes by, or something happens…well sometimes a place that was like home could suddenly feel like the strangest place in the world. And I started to feel that way as we were walking in the dark, in the shadows of the trees along the road with the lights out in all of the houses and not a single car on the street. It started to seem like I'd never been in Underwood before, hell, like I'd never been to Calvert City before.

But I had been. I'd been there nearly every day for over a year and more besides when I was courting Quinn and then after we were married. And it wasn't the time. It was the thing. I had better look at it because I'd have to look at it soon enough. It was Joe being dead. It was why Joe was dead.

I must have faltered in my step, because Vee's hand on my arm tightened to where I could feel her fingertips digging into my arm through my jacket, and she kept me moving. "Oh no you don't," she said. "You're going through with this now or you don't want to know what'll happen."

Yeah, I was going through with it, because I had already, hadn't I? I'd gone about as far through with it as you could, and it was my deal. The whole neighborhood looked foreign to me, but I knew right where I was going, and I'd better get there.

"Can we come up from behind the place? That would be better."

I didn't answer, but I took us around the block where we would come up on the side of the house near the driveway and the servants' entrance. I didn't know that it would be open, but when we tried the door it was unlocked.

It was dark inside, but we only needed to make our way up the stairs, and then… I was more lost in the house than I had been outside. It somehow felt as though it were expanding and contracting at the same time if you can imagine that. Like the house was the whole world, so huge I couldn't ever hope to get through it in a hundred thousand lifetimes, but also so small that I was trapped inside, unable to move, the very walls crushing in on me, choking me, my throat, my shoulders, my chest, my heart, all of it pulling in. This wasn't Quinn's house. This wasn't the place where I once walked around completely naked, the time the Hadleys were off on a cruise and Quinn and I crashed on our way to New York or from New York or somewhere anyways. This wasn't the place where old man Hadley had put his arm around me in his office and told me that he didn't trust me but that his daughter was sure stuck on me and so he couldn't but give us his approval. No, this couldn't be that house, because this was the house in which Joe and I had fought. This was where I chased him and then he tried to push me or I pushed him or, somehow I got cut, and I, or Joe, yeah, this was where it happened, so it couldn't be that other place from long ago.

"Come on," Vee said, pushing me from behind. "We don't have all night. The faster we are the better. And keep away from the windows."

I started forward, although I don't remember moving, and I took her into the kitchen and nothing had changed, he was lying there on the floor with his head bashed in and the ice pick near his hand. I went numb. Vee ducked down, squatting, and hissed at me, "Get down."

I did, and I didn't have any trouble after that. I was shut off. I was a million miles away.

"You got some blood on the floor here," Vee said, on her hands and knees. "Wipe it up." She went over to where his body was, and that's all it was now, just a thing. "We've got to wipe the ice pick and put that back." She looked back at me. "Well, hurry." I must have looked confused. "Use your sleeve." I started to reach. "No, your shirt sleeve. The one that's already got blood on it."

I took off my jacket, and I bent down to wipe up the spot of blood. I wouldn't have even noticed it, it was so small. It had dried so I wet my finger with spit and then rubbed at the spot until it was gone and wiped my finger on my shirtsleeve near the cut. Vee handed back the ice pick and I did the same with that, wetting it and rubbing it on my sleeve, wetting it and rubbing. It was a tedious job and I thought, why couldn't I just use the sink. That's really what I was thinking. Not that I was cleaning up my blood, because I couldn't think of that, you see. But why couldn't I use the sink. Of course, Vee was probably right about the windows.

While I was doing that, Vee was looking around, examining everything. She tried to lean Joe forward, but the body was already set up some, and it was heavy, so it just sort of slid to the side. She looked at me, and I was just watching her. "Well, are you finished? Put that back, and come over here and wipe this counter and cabinet. We don't want any blood down here."

Down here? Where else were we going? But I crawled over to the refrigerator and slid the ice pick back where Joe had taken it from as nearly as I could tell, and then I crawled over beside him and Vee. If a place turns all funny once you've killed a man, just try crawling around in one. It's a whole new room.

"Couldn't I use the sink?" I said, looking at the few smudges of blood.

"Just hurry." She was exasperated. And her face really looked terrible, the bruise spread now from over her eye all along the side and across the cheekbone. It must have hurt to talk. "Take a picture, why don't you? I should have come done this myself, but I wouldn't be able to carry him alone."

So I reached up to the sink, still on the floor, and wet the edge of my sleeve, and then I wiped up the blood on the edge of the counter and the front of the cabinet. There wasn't much, like I said, and I had that pretty much cleaned up, and Vee started tugging on Joe's body, getting him over on his side. The sound of his shoes scuffing on the floor was about one of the worst things I'd ever heard. Because I'd seen a body in worse shape once, although I didn't like to think of it, but the sound of the shoes, that was, well, that was sort of normal, and nothing about any of this was normal, so it kind of got to me. Maybe I was just loopy, so you can't understand, but that's the way I felt, I'm telling you.

"Turn off the light," Vee said, "and then help me with this."

I crawled over to where the light switch was, and I saw the broken glass that was still on the floor against the wall, so I went over towards that, figuring we ought to clean that up too.

"What are you doing!" Vee snapped. "I said get the light."

"But the glass—"

"Leave it. That's a good thing. See, he was drunk, right?, and upset. So he threw his glass at the wall, right? So when he passes out with a lit cigarette in his hand, it makes it look better."

"What do you mean with a cigarette?"

"Would you just turn out the light? You think the sun's going to stay down forever? How long do you think I can have Carlton's car out? Now move. Can you do that? I need you to move."

So I moved. I got the light out, and Vee stood up immediately, and went around the body. "You get him under the arms, I'll get the feet."

We tried it like that a couple of times, but it wasn't going to work. His body was in a weird position, which threw the weight off, and Vee wasn't too strong. So at last, I pulled him up as best I could and flung him over my shoulder in a fireman carry. I staggered and started to feel lightheaded immediately, but I had him up.

"Do you know which one's his room?"

"I think," I managed.

"Okay," Vee said and started out ahead of me. Only, wait, she must have picked up my jacket, yeah, because she gave it back to me upstairs. But I wasn't really seeing where we were going or even thinking much about what we were doing anymore. I was just trying to get one foot in front of the other and not drop him as I held my breath under the exertion, only able to take quick pants every few seconds or so.

Vee turned off the lights ahead of me as we went, asking, "This way? This way?" And I would just nod, and she would turn off a light, and we got to the foot of the stairs, and I said, "There's a light up front."

"Leave it," she said. "Only the ones going up to the bedroom."

The stairs were brutal. I staggered to get my foot up on the first step, and I almost dropped him and I banged into the banister, which gave a little under the weight but held. So Vee rushed back around behind me, slipping past in the tight space, and she pushed me up from behind, and that actually did the trick, taking just enough weight off of me so that I could manage one step at a time, resting for a minute against the wall at each step. Vee kept saying, "Okay? Okay?", nervous, but I needed to take a rest. I wasn't sure if I was even going to make it at all.

We got to the top of the stairs, and I almost dropped him then, but managed to say between my teeth, "I can't hold it much longer." I took a few rushed shuffling steps into the room immediately to the right at the top of the stairs and was relieved to find that it was still Joe's room. It didn't look that different from when he had me up in it as a boy once when Clotilde and I laid over in Calvert on a trip to France.

I staggered across the room, and the light went out when I was only halfway to the bed, and then I dropped him there, the bed creaking and banging against the wall at the headboard. I fell down on the bed on top of him for a moment, and it was all I could do to breathe, there were black-and-white stars before my eyes and my head felt so heavy, and there was a pain in my neck and the cut on my arm.

Vee pulled at me, trying to get to Joe. At last I was able to focus enough to realize I was lying on top of a dead body—on top of my son's dead body!—and my stomach turned over and I rolled off of him onto my back and tried to get to my feet, but had to just lie there.

Meanwhile, Vee went through his pockets. "Where does he keep his cigarettes? Help me."

I started to roll to my feet, trying to remember if Joe smoked, but she didn't need my help by then. She had the cigarettes and was looking for the matches, running her hands over his body in the dark, with just barely some light coming in from outside, or maybe my eyes had just gotten used to the dark.

She felt her way along the bedside table and then opened the top drawer, and I could hear her messing through various things, scraping the wood in the drawer, and at last the sound stopped, and there was a flicker, and her face was suddenly illuminated. It was a Zippo. The light went out. I was blinded again. She turned the pack of cigarettes over in her hand, got one out, put it in her mouth, and the flame again.

She stood there, crouched, smoking for a moment.

"What are you doing," I hissed, although there was no reason we had to worry about being quiet.

She whispered back, "It's got to be smoked down a little. You never know how much things are going to burn."

"Burn?" But I guess I sort of got what she was planning then, and it didn't seem too crazy. It seemed like it just might work. Because why couldn't I have left, and then a couple hours later, Joe throws a glass against the wall, goes upstairs, turns off the lights as he goes—he's drunk so he leaves lights on in the other rooms—manages to light a cigarette and then pass out, and then the bed catches fire. You hear about that all the time, why they're always saying you shouldn't smoke in bed, and every time you do it, you think, that's never going to happen to me.

Vee put the cigarette near Joe's hand, still burning. Then to make sure, she took the Zippo, and held it to the comforter near the cigarette, waiting for it to catch. It flared up almost immediately, and then died down a little, and we stood there watching it, the orange glow of the flames lighting the room immediately and then growing, and soon there was some heat you could feel too.

Vee wiped the Zippo against the bed on all sides and then holding it by her fingernails, she tossed it at the bedside table where it struck and fell on the floor. That seemed to satisfy her. She turned. "Come on."

But I stayed still, watching. I hadn't really known this man. I'd known him as a boy, or at least had an idea of him then when I'd see him every few months. Okay, at least once a year. But he had been right. I didn't know him. And so, in some ways, it was like being at a funeral for a stranger. You felt crummy, but you didn't really care all that much. No, that's not true, because I cared way the hell too much. I cared so much that I didn't care.

The flames had really spread, and there was smoke in the air. Vee yelled, "Shem! Come on. Now!"

She grabbed at my shoulder, and I let her pull me away. We went back the way we had come, down the stairs, down the back stairs to the servants' entrance, out into the hot night, and back around the corner, and Vee had her arm looped in mine, and was setting a leisurely pace.

"You don't have to worry," she said, and she sounded relieved herself. "It'll be fine now." I didn't say anything. And then she hit my arm, a slight slap. "You goddamn bastard. You rich goddamn bastard. Two million dollars!"

And I was confused. What two million dollars?

"I could kill you though. Ooo, my face hurts something fierce, you goddamn bastard pimp. Carlton could have killed me." She slapped me again. "He could have killed us both. And he doesn't need to burn a house down to get rid of a couple of bodies, let me tell you." She was almost laughing now, she was so relieved. "Two million dollars! I knew there was a reason I got mixed up with you. I'd started to wonder, but I knew. I'm a smart one. I always know."

We were across University in George Village. A streetlight must have caught us, because I could feel that she was looking at me, and once we were in the shadow of a tree, she pulled around so she was standing in front of me.

"Oh, baby," she said, and she reached up and brushed my face and I could feel that it was wet. "Oh, my poor, poor baby."

"What…"

But she pulled me in to her, and pulled my head to her shoulder. She put her hand on the back of my head and ran her fingers in my hair and held me, and it felt good, because my shoulders were shaking, and my face was wet, because, I'm not afraid to say it, I was crying.

10.

In the morning I woke up in the hotel's queen-sized bed next to Vee, and at first I didn't remember anything about the night before. My head hurt and my mouth was dry and I had a real stiffness, an ache, in my arm, but as hangovers go, this one was mild, and it was kind of nice being there in that bed with a warm body next to me. I pulled back the covers and swung my feet onto the floor. Behind me, Vee rolled from her side onto her back, and I looked at her, her right arm flung over her head, her hair a pool beneath her, her beautiful breasts exposed. And half of her face like a giant blackberry.

It came back to me then all right. It was like all of the air had been sucked out of my body. I remembered the teardrop of fire that Vee had set down on Joe's bed, and it made me shudder. I got up and stumbled into the bathroom, turned on the cold faucet in the sink as far as it could go, cupped my hands beneath it, and brought them to my face. The water hit the basin with such force that it splashed my chest as well, getting my undershirt wet. I repeated the process over and over, cupped hands, splash on the face, until my fingers were numb and my shirt was soaked. I turned off the water, and used the sink to prevent me from collapsing.

In the mirror I watched the water run off the end of my nose and chin. My eyes were frightened. I looked haggard, but I had looked that way plenty of mornings in my drinking days. Hell, I still looked that way most mornings. But my eyes... I made myself look even closer, to see where it was written that I had killed a man, my own son, and burned his body. All I saw was the fear, and that I needed a shave.

I stood up and pulled the wet shirt over my head, using it to wipe off my chest. The room around me had receded, my insides felt shrunken, my hearing was muffled. I needed to get out. If I stayed in the room, I'd just stew. If I woke Vee, she'd be no comfort, just pissed off that I had woken her. I went back into the bedroom and picked my pants up off the floor where Vee had left them when she had undressed me the night before. They were still weighted down by my wallet and keys and the belt threaded in the loops. I pulled them on, and went out into the living room where I had hung my clothes in the coat closet. I found a new shirt, and put it on without an undershirt, and dug out some fresh socks from my duffel bag, got my shoes on, and went out into the hall.

The light in the hall was the same, the eternal non-day of electric lights lit twenty-four hours. I needed coffee. I needed a drink. I needed both. I took the elevator down, and stepped into the lobby, where somehow a normal morning was progressing, people coming out of the dining room, checking out at the desk, the doorman helping an elderly woman into a taxi-cab out front, some men sitting with the morning paper and a cigarette in a clutch of couches and easy chairs. I felt as though I were watching a play I didn't care for. I wanted to scream at them, to tell them they were banal, that their lives would end, and what meaning did they have? How unnatural to sit in a building thirteen stories high made out of materials we couldn't name and couldn't say how they were made, in a block of pavement and concrete that someone had had to lay down, where once there had been only nature, and the few people hunting and fishing, just getting by. And sure, having wars. They killed each other too. But they couldn't conceive of this, a hotel in a city. Yet somebody had, and it was so audacious as to be beyond comprehension.

But I had to look normal. Natural. A little disorientation was okay; I had a hangover. But nothing was terribly out of the way. I'd feel better once I had some coffee anyway. And the thought made me think about money, how to pay, and I remembered the telegrams I had sent yesterday—could that have been only yesterday?—and I thought I'd better check to see if there'd been any reply, that's what I would normally do. Right? Of course it was.

I went to the front desk. The concierge was helping with the morning checkouts, so he was the one who said, "Mr. Rosenkrantz, good morning." His eyes flicked behind me for a moment, at least I thought they did, and he made this odd little nod.

"Morning. Do I have any telegrams waiting for me? I'm expecting a couple."

His eyes looked at something behind me again, but he had a broad smile on, and said, shaking his head, "No. No telegrams, sir."

It was bugging me the way he kept looking behind me, like I wasn't interesting enough to hold his attention, so when I turned around and there were two men in dark suits almost right behind me, I was surprised. I really was.

"Mr. Rosenkrantz," the one on the left said. He was heavyset, a bit of a potbelly, rounded cheeks, with tufts of orange hair showing beneath his hat.

"Yes?" I said, looking back at the concierge as if for help.

"Sir, I wonder if you would come with us?"

My stomach dropped and my headache started pounding. It made it really difficult to think. "I don't understand," I said.

"We have news," the other one said. He was like a movie star, strong jaw, dark brow.

"We're Calvert PD," the orange-haired man said, and I hoped my face didn't show anything, even as my whole body felt deflated.

"If you'd just step to the side here, Mr. Rosenkrantz. We want to have a little talk."

Just to the side. They weren't taking me to the station. They weren't arresting me. "I don't understand. What's going on?" I wanted to stall. As long as I was near the desk, the concierge was still part of this, and it couldn't be too bad.

"Mr. Rosenkrantz, please." The heavyset man took a step back and held his hand out to indicate that I should go ahead.

I went. I didn't like to, but what else was I going to do. They stayed behind me, but the redheaded man stayed a little to my side, so I could see him out of the corner of my eye.

"This is fine," he said, as we came to a support pillar with a large potted plant beside it, and we stopped and I turned towards them.

"Sir," the redheaded man said. "I'm Detective Healey and this is Detective Dobrygowski."

I looked from one to the other, unseeing, but at the same time hoping that I looked appropriately responsive, the way an ordinary person would if confronted this way.

"It is with great reluctance and sympathy that I have to inform you that your son has passed on."

"What," I said, blinking rapidly. "What do you mean passed on? I saw him yesterday."

"I'm sorry, sir, it's always the hardest thing to tell people."

"I don't get it," I said, shaking my head, floored. I mean, I knew it before he said it, but hearing him say it was a whole different thing than carrying Joe's dead body up the stairs. It made it impossible to deny. "What happened?"

Dobrygowski started, "We won't know for certain until after an autopsy—"

I cringed at the word.

Detective Healey took over. "It appears as though he fell asleep with a lit cigarette and the bed caught fire."

As he said it, he watched me carefully, and that made me shudder, but I figured that was okay. When you lose someone close to you, people act in all kinds of crazy ways, so I figured I was clear no matter what I did, but that didn't stop it from worrying me. Still, Vee's plan had worked. That was some relief.

"We were wondering if you could maybe fill in a little of what happened last night, just for our records," Detective Healey said.

Dobrygowski pulled a pad out, and I shivered again.

"I don't…"

"You were there last night. At the house, weren't you?"

"Yeah, sure. I mean, I got to the house, but Mary," I looked him in the eyes, "she's Joe's fiancée, they're getting married," his lips turned down ever so slightly at the present tense, and that was good. "Mary was leaving, said Joe didn't want to be bothered."

"So you didn't go inside? You didn't see your son?"

I shook my head, stalling for time, while not exactly saying no. My heart was going fast, and my headache was pounding, making the whole room look dull.

"Because Miss O'Brien said she called your son around

midnight, she thought…" Healey looked at Dobrygowski, who nodded, and then Healey looked back at me. "She said you answered the phone."

I froze. I'd forgotten that call. I hadn't even told Vee about that call, and it's a good thing I hadn't, because she would have left me to rot.

"Mr. Rosenkrantz. Isn't that right? Didn't you pick up the phone when Miss O'Brien called?"

I didn't like the way he said that, like I'd been caught in a lie. But I nodded and hoped I still looked shocked, not frightened. "Yeah. I did. I went back. I didn't go into the house that first time, but I went back, maybe an hour later."

"So that was around midnight?"

"If you say so. I didn't look at the time. I was drunk." And I looked down, as though I were sheepish about admitting I'd been drunk.

"So you got there around midnight, and you left?"

"I don't think I was there more than half an hour. But why is this important?" And I was surprised to suddenly find tears in my eyes.

"We just like to establish a timeline. It won't take another minute. Can you go on?"

I blinked my eyes and swallowed. I was really tearing up. And it's a good thing I was, but to think that I had more crying in me. I nodded.

"So you went to see your son, but Miss O'Brien was there, so you left."

"She said he didn't want to see anyone, and I walked down the steps with her. We left at the same time," I said as a tear fell down my face. I pulled out a handkerchief and wiped my face.

"I'm sorry to put you through this, Mr. Rosenkrantz," Healey said.

Dobrygowski didn't look sorry. He just had his pencil poised over his notebook.

"No, it's good, I understand. I want to know what happened too. That's my…Joe's…it's my only child." I hoped that wasn't laying it on too thick, but it was true, and I was really feeling it. I really was.

"So you went back around midnight…"

"I went back. We talked for a little bit, drank. He was drunk, I was drunk, and I left."

They didn't seem particularly impressed with this story.

"If you want to know the truth, he sort of threw me out," I said. "Our relationship wasn't always very good. He blamed me for the divorce always. From his mother."

"No, we understand. That's all the same as Miss O'Brien said. I'm sorry to even have to put you through it at a time like this. It really makes us heels, and I hate to do it."

"It's all right."

"It's not all right, but it's the way it is."

I nodded.

Dobrygowski spoke then. "But why did you say at first that you hadn't gone into your son's house?"

Healey gave him an angry look, but somehow I got the sense that it was a staged look, that I wasn't quite out of the woods yet. Maybe I wasn't even close to the edge.

"I didn't say I didn't go in. I said I didn't go in that first time. I went in the second time, like I told you."

"It just seems a little weird to me that you would say you didn't go in, when you did."

"I said I didn't go in that first time," I repeated. My tears were gone. I felt worn.

"Leave it be, Pete. Man just lost his son."

Dobrygowski closed up his pad and put it in his inside pocket. "Of course, I'm sorry. Just the detective in me."

"You don't think that there's any…I mean, that somebody… did…something?" I said.

The question actually seemed to relieve Healey. I guess that's the kind of question people ask right up front in cases like these.

"No, no," Healey said. "Forget Dobrygowski. We know you didn't mean anything. But, one last thing. Miss O'Brien said you were here, but you're not registered. I was just wondering…"

"I'm staying with…a friend."

"Yeah, it was just odd when you weren't registered, that's all."

I burst a little then. "Why's it odd? I'm a well-known writer. Sometimes it's better if people don't know where I'm staying. There are some crazy people out there."

Healey paused before responding. "You don't have to tell us. We didn't mean anything by it."

"I just don't like the way this one's asking me about whether I went into Joe's house or not when I said I did. And Joe was fine when I left. Drunk, but fine."

Healey held out both his hands to calm me. "We didn't mean anything by it. We know this is a tough thing. We just like to make things clear."

I knew I had tripped up then, getting angry like that, but you don't know what it's like when you have the police there and they're asking questions just about something you don't want them to know. "Well, I don't like the implications that you think I'm lying or hiding something. My son just died."

"We know, Mr. Rosenkrantz. We're sorry."

I rubbed my head, trying to push out the headache. "And you ought to be."

Dobrygowski said, "You'll stay in town until after the funeral now, I take it."

Healey looked at him like he could kill him.

"What are you suggesting," I started, both hands to my temples now.

"Mr. Rosenkrantz!" A woman's voice, and we all three turned. It was Mary, and as soon as her eyes met mine, her face crumpled and she started to cry. I stepped forward, and she was in my arms, her own arms wrapped around me, crying into my chest.

I looked at the detectives over her head, and even Dobrygowski looked embarrassed. They walked away, and I brought my lips to the top of Mary's forehead, kissing her, letting her know everything was all right.

11.

We held each other for a full minute, which was long enough for me to think about the fact that we hadn't known each other until the day before, and then—and yeah, I feel guilty about it— that her small young body felt good against mine.

"Those were the policemen who came to our house this morning," she said, still pressing her head against my chest.

"It's a hard job," I said.

"Mommy and Daddy were just impossible, bringing me tissues, and a glass of water, and looking at each other over my head, and walking around like I was going to break, I just had to get out of there."

I ran my hand along the hair at the back of her head. "It's okay."

"I knew we had plans for this morning," she said, her voice cracking, becoming almost a whisper. "I wanted to make things all right with you for Joe." The crying got worse again, but she was able to pull herself together quickly this time, even if she still held on to me.

If you think you've ever been in a tough place, you can't even imagine what it was like holding that little girl, as beautiful and sweet as anything, knowing I had murdered her true love. You can't even know.

She pulled back a little, just enough to raise her head so she was looking up at me, but I still had my arms around her, and I was starting to feel excited about her, so close to me like that.

"Don't say I have to go back to them, Mr. Rosenkrantz. I can't stand another minute of pity, not today. I just need to grieve without feeling like I'm putting on a show."

"Sure. You can stay right here with me. Or go anywhere you like."

"It's just that I knew you'd be grieving too. It's different when the other person is grieving too." The tears filled up her eyes. "Oh, damn me. All that time this week I tried to be there for Joe while he was mourning. No wonder he was angry. He probably hated me every minute."

"Of course he didn't. Hey, how could he hate you? He was going to marry you."

"Yeah." Her eyes turned down. "I know. It's only just that it didn't *feel* like he was going to marry me anymore. You know? It was kind of like I'd lost him already when Quinn," her eyes darted to me to see how I would take that familiarity, "when she died. And now I know why."

I pulled her against me again and patted her back. "Shhh."

"I'm sorry. You're grieving too."

"Shhh. What do you say to some coffee? Do you want to get some coffee, maybe something to eat?"

She shook her head, rubbing her face on my chest.

"Should we go somewhere? You need some air."

"I just need to lie down."

"Okay," I said. "Sure. We can go up to my room if you think that's okay. I just need to go up and...see that everything's all right."

She wiped her cheeks with her hands.

"Can you wait for me a moment? Will you be okay?"

She nodded, blinking her tears away. "I don't know why Joe was so angry at you. I told him I was sure you were perfectly nice, that it was a misunderstanding. I just knew you were. Anybody who's read your books can see that."

I'd felt guiltier and guiltier as she spoke until she went and ruined it with that last bit about my books. Why'd she have to do that? I wasn't my books. I wasn't even the person I was when I wrote those books.

"I'll be back," I said. "You wait right here."

She nodded again, and I crossed the lobby to the elevators and hit the call button. The dial over the door began to run counter-clockwise. Away from Mary, my own grief came rushing back in, and I felt my knees give way; I had to hold out my hand to lean against the wall. I had grieved before. When my parents died. When a girl I knew, an actress in Hollywood, was killed. That had torn me apart, the violence ripping her away from me. God, the same thing had almost happened to Clotilde back in France when a man had surprised her at home. I couldn't even bear to think of that; I wouldn't have survived if... And sure, I grieved when Quinn died. But this was different. The guilt echoed over the grief, the two trading off of one another, and it was all I could do to get on the elevator and hit the right button for our floor. I leaned against the wall inside, and let myself be carried up.

Upstairs, I stepped out of the elevator, and turned towards our room—Vee would understand if I brought Mary up even if she didn't like it—but ahead of me in the hall Carlton Browne stepped out of our room, stopping, stepping out of the way while looking back, and then Vee stepped out in a red dress and sunglasses. I dropped back, and managed to catch the elevator door just as it was closing. I stepped inside, hit the button for the lobby, and then jammed the button to close the doors repeat-edly until the doors slid shut, and with a gentle jerk, I started down again.

My heart was pounding. I didn't know why exactly. I was sweating. And it dawned on me, I was afraid. I was scared to death of this gangster Browne. I didn't know how much more my nerves could take, between Joe and Browne and Vee and Mary and now the police and even Great Aunt Alice who was no doubt still waiting for me to drop by, maybe now more than ever since Joe was gone.

The door opened and I hurried to Mary, putting my arm around her before she could even say anything, and leading her back to the elevator. With luck we wouldn't have to see Browne or Vee at all. But the counter for the elevator I had gotten out of was climbing, while the other counter fell, paused for a moment, and then fell again.

I pulled Mary closer to me as the doors opened, and Browne and Vee stepped out right in front of us. Vee was hidden behind those sunglasses, which covered most of her bruise, but certainly not all of it; I couldn't make out her expression. Browne saw me, and his lip curled in a snarl at first, but then he laughed, and put a hand on my shoulder.

"Vee, look, it's your cousin." He looked at Mary. "With his very lovely young friend. You making this girl cry, cousin?"

Vee took his arm before I could say anything. "Carlton, please. You promised."

"I'm just saying hi," he said back at her. He gave Mary another hungry look. "You do okay for yourself, bud." He looked back at Vee to see how she was taking this, and laughed again, a mean laugh. Then he gave my shoulder a painful squeeze, and walked past us, Vee trailing him. She didn't even look at me, which was good.

I ushered Mary into the elevator. I exhaled. I had been holding my breath, it turned out, and I felt lightheaded. The doors closed, we started our ascent, and all of a sudden I felt as though I were going to cry.

I must have looked it, because Mary put her hand to my face. "I'm so thoughtless, doing all of the crying."

I pulled my face away from her, and shook my head with my lips pressed tight, holding in my tears. I would have them bring me up a bottle of whiskey, damn sobriety, my son had just died.

She drew her hand away, uncertain of herself, and then the elevator door opened. I led her down the hall to Vee's and my room. We went in, and I guided her to the couch, where I sat her down. "Wait," I said.

I went to the door and put out the Do Not Disturb sign, and then I went into the bedroom where the bed was still unmade—had Vee and Carlton only just gotten out of it; I pushed the thought away—I went into the bathroom, ran the tap until the water ran cold, filled the glass and brought it back to her. I handed it down, standing over her while she drank, like a parent tending to a sick child. When she'd finished, she handed it back to me, looking up at me with timid eyes, and I set it on a glass coaster on the coffee table.

She turned to her clasp bag, which I hadn't even noticed until then, and then stopped and looked up, and said, "Is it all right if I smoke?"

"Of course," I said. "You want a drink too?" I picked up the telephone receiver.

She shook her head, got out a cigarette packet, pulling the box of matches she had stuffed in the cellophane wrapper and then shaking out a cigarette and placing it between her lips.

The desk picked up. "Could you send up a bottle of whiskey? Any kind is fine. Thanks." They'd probably send me the most expensive bottle in the place, all hotels are chiselers, but that was all right with me. If Vee and Browne were all patched up, then the whiskey was on Carlton. I'd like a good whiskey. And just the thought of the alcohol coming on up relaxed me.

Mary blew out a stream of smoke. "I was so happy last night when you answered the phone at Joe's and said you'd made it up."

I nodded, trying to remember if I had said that.

"Why had you fought? Joe never wanted to talk about it. It just made him angry, so I tried to not bring it up."

"Why are you here instead of with your parents? With some stranger."

"You're not a stranger. You're Joe's father."

"But I am a stranger. You don't know me from anyone else. And I could be just as horrible as Joe thought, couldn't I? Sure I could. You don't know. So why are you here instead of with your folks?"

"I told you I couldn't stand to be with them right now." Her voice was flat, and she took a jerky drag off her cigarette.

"But why?"

"I just— They were on my nerves. I— Oh, do we have to talk about them?"

"Yeah, well I guess that's the same reason Joe hated me."

"He didn't hate you."

"Sure he did. Did it hurt? Of course it did. But I had to get used to it. I had to like it."

"But you made it up last night," she said, and pulled on her cigarette for punctuation.

"Right. Of course, we made it up last night," I said. Well, we had certainly ended it, whatever it was.

She stared straight ahead, smoking. "He was the most caring

boy I ever met." She shook her head. "He had a temper. He'd get mad real fast, but he never got mad at me. For me, he was more defensive than I was for myself."

I listened, and the pit in my stomach grew, every word pulling my throat along after it.

"He was so faithful. He lived for his mother. She could do no wrong. She was the ideal everyone had to live up to. And for some reason he thought I did. When he talked to me, when he would tell me he loved me, it was almost like he was describing someone else, someone I didn't know. It was like he was making me up, and I liked who that girl was. I wanted to be that girl."

I jiggled my knee, and couldn't get it to stop. She was conjuring him now, someone I had never known, and it was making me sick.

"He wrote poetry. He'd probably be angry at me for telling you that. He didn't want anyone to know. He assured me it was okay, because it wasn't fiction, he was so afraid of being at all like you. He never drank, too."

There was a knock at the door. I went for it, relieved at the interruption. A bellboy stood there with my whiskey, a brand I didn't recognize. I found a quarter in my pocket and gave him his tip. He was a professional, and made no indication as to what he thought of the amount.

I brought the bottle of whiskey back to the couch and pulled the glass I had served her water in closer to me. "It's the only glass," I said by way of explanation as I twisted off the top, and sloshed out a good dose of alcohol. I held it out to her, but she just shook her head, blowing out smoke, her cigarette more than halfway gone, so I downed the whole thing in one burning go. It sat heavily in my stomach, but it warmed me up, and I felt easier immediately. I refilled the glass, and sat back, taking more reasonable sips. If Mary hadn't been there, I probably wouldn't have bothered pouring it into a glass.

"Does it stop?" she said.

"No. But you think about it less. And the edge gets dulled."

She shook her head. "I'm so tired."

I sighed, and drank.

She looked at me. "So very tired." Her face was completely drained of color.

I drank some more. "You should sleep then," I said.

She ground out the stub of her cigarette in the ashtray on the table beside her. "No…"

I stood up, indicating the couch. "Come, lie down. Sleep. You'll feel better."

"I couldn't sleep last night I was so worried." There was a break in her voice, the tears about to come again. "He… We were going to be married." And a sob escaped her.

I felt as though I had been stabbed. The searing pain of the night before when Joe stabbed me with the ice pick flashed through my chest even as the pain in my arm was nothing more than a soreness now. I could have killed myself right then. All the guilt I'd ever felt over the years had never been like this. I thought of the policemen's suspicions this morning—but had they been suspicious? was it just in my mind?—and I wanted to come out and say it. To say that I had killed him. That I should be punished. But of course I didn't. And I wouldn't. I was too much of a coward.

I picked up the bottle, poured myself a glass, and tossed that one back too, pouring the next one while still swallowing. It was helping calm me at least. "Lie down," I said.

"No," Mary said, while lying down anyway.

I brought her a blanket from the closet, and draped it over her.

She reached out with a hand and pulled it closer to her chin, rocking once back and forth. "You look so much like him," she said, looking up at me.

I smiled. "Thank you."

"How am I going to live?"

I could ask myself the same thing. But I said, "Close your eyes."

She did, and she was asleep within moments. I sat and drank and made an active effort to think of nothing but pouring the liquid from one container to another and then into me. It was a lucky break, Carlton seeing me with Mary and thinking she was a girlfriend. I don't know if Vee knew who Mary really was or not, but I hoped if she was angry, she was at least a little relieved at being in the clear with Browne. That wouldn't help her face, she would have told me, and I wouldn't have had anything to say to that, but it was something.

I thought of Mandy. She was the girlfriend in Hollywood who had gotten killed. We'd been…dating, we'll call it, for a few months when it happened. We fought all the time we weren't in bed, although I couldn't tell you what we fought about. And it had Clotilde out of sorts with me too since I was never too good at keeping anything secret. (Only I'd have to keep this secret, Joe, this one thing.) Then Mandy was murdered by some madman they never even found, and I discovered her body all cut to ribbons, blood everywhere. It was the worst thing I'd ever seen, and I'd dreamt about it a long time after. Was this going to be like that?

Clunk—he went down—clunk—he went down—clunk.

Of course it would.

I poured another drink, and drank it down. My stomach began

to feel full, but I was calm, able to think on it and stay calm. Mary slept silently on the couch. She slept with such trust, I wanted to get her up and get her out of there, to tell her to stay far away from me, that I was no good, she didn't need to know why, but Joe was right, I was a terrible person, and she should keep away.

It hit me that Joe had been visiting when Mandy was killed. No, wait, that couldn't be, because I'd really gone on a drinking binge after that, enough so I remembered it. And that was when Clotilde...when she first went to the hospital. So Joe hadn't been there. But he'd met Mandy. I'd practically handed him off to her like she was a babysitter. And Quinn let me have him at all. I was no good even then. Yeah, he had been right to hate me. Here's your kid. Why don't you leave him with your mistress so you don't have to stop getting drunk? I could have killed him any number of times, I was so irresponsible. But he had been the one to hit me at his high school graduation. Hell, he had stabbed me last night. But...

Clunk—he went down—clunk—he went down—clunk.

I needed to do something. The whiskey was good, and it helped, but I needed to do something. I couldn't just sit there thinking about it, not if I didn't want to go crazy. Mary slept on. Should I leave her? Where should I go?

And I don't know why it came to me. You probably won't believe it if you try. But I thought, I should write something. I should do some writing. I hadn't done that in who knows how long. That was what I needed.

I retrieved the pad, and this time I found a pencil in the back of the desk drawer. It had gotten lodged in a small space between the back of the drawer and its bottom, so it hadn't rolled around when I opened the drawer the day before. I took the pad and the pencil back to the easy chair I had been sitting on. I balanced the glass of whiskey on the armrest, and I sat staring at the page.

Clunk—he went down—clunk—he went down—clunk.

And I started writing, whatever came into my head. I wrote and wrote and wrote, and I filled up most of that pad, and I finished the bottle of whiskey. I wrote, but don't ask me what I wrote, because I don't know. It probably didn't make any sense, but I wrote it all down anyway, and I think there was something about Joe in there, and I don't know what else.

Mary slept, and I wrote, and Joe was dead.

My hand started to cramp and I wore out the pencil's lead and had to find another, which took me a few minutes, but then I found one just under the edge of the couch, where it must have rolled off the telephone stand. But I filled up pages like I hadn't been able to in years, just pouring it all out, the anger at being washed up, the hate for the people who had done it to me, the fear for Clotilde, and all the goddamn YMCA rooms, and living with a whore, and just all of it, all of the meanness that had settled inside of me since Clotilde went away, hell, maybe before then, maybe from when Quinn and I started fighting. Yeah, I'd always gotten a raw deal, and I was too pathetic to do anything about it, and I hated myself for that. I hated myself and every goddamn one else, every last one of them.

12.

It was only when I woke up that I knew I had fallen asleep. Someone was moving in the bedroom, and the sound of drawers opening and slamming shut had seeped into my dream and woken me. My watch said two o'clock. Mary was gone. She had draped over my legs the same blanket that I had draped over her that morning. The pad I had been writing on was still in my lap under the blanket, but the pencil was gone.

I listened to the hurried sounds in the other room for another minute, working up the energy to get up. I knew it was Vee and I had a pretty good idea of what she was doing and I wasn't ready to deal with it just yet, to deal with her after last night. My shoulders and back ached from sleeping in a chair for too long, and when I stood up, everything went black for a moment and I thought I'd lose my balance, but the black resolved itself to white patches, and then the room came back into focus.

I stepped over to the entryway into the bedroom. Vee was stuffing things into a suitcase with bitter violence. "Vee," I said, my voice coming out in a croak.

She yelped, and brought her hand to her chest. "Jesus H. Christmas, Shem, you scared the bejeezus out of me. What the hell's the matter with you?"

"What are you doing?"

She went back to it. "What does it look like I'm doing?"

"Where are you going?"

She stormed around the bed to the vanity where she started

collecting her makeup and perfume. "Carlton wants me upstairs in his suite. He wants to keep an eye on me, no thanks to you."

The makeup was zipped up in a carrying case and brought over to the suitcase on the bed.

"You better start packing too," she said. "You're thrown out."

My lingering exhaustion deepened, my shoulders sagging. "Where am I supposed to go?"

"I'm lucky he hasn't killed me," she said, pulling some shirts on hangers out from the armoire. "I just wish he'd send me home. I'm not too keen on sticking around."

"Where am I supposed to go?" I said again.

She looked up at me. "Quit whining! You start whining, I'm going to beat your head in myself, getting me mixed up in a murder, getting me in hot water with Carlton…" She was so angry, she didn't even know how to finish. She stuffed shoes into the suitcase, forcing them into a corner on top of some clothes. "I don't know why I even helped you," she said, and paused in her packing, sneering at the suitcase. "I'd say something about love, if I didn't know that was just a crock."

I felt sick to my stomach, or I had heartburn, or both, and I was suddenly very hot and clammy.

"Why aren't you packing!" she yelled. "Start packing. You've got to be out of here toot sweet."

"I feel sick," I said. How had I looked with loving calm on this no-good woman only that morning as she slept?

"What does that have to do with the price of tea in China?" She was trying to close the suitcase, leaning on it with all of her weight.

I retrieved my duffel, my mind dead as I did it. In the mirror on the front of the bathroom door I looked like I had a hangover and had slept in my clothes, which was how I should have looked, and it wasn't any great surprise, I'd looked that way plenty of times before.

"Vee," I started, but she cut me off.

"Don't say 'I love you,' I just told you love's a crock, and only foolish little girls believe any different, and I'm not a foolish little girl, so you can just hold any sentiment, it's not going to buy anything with me." She crossed her arms over her breasts, and her face grew narrow. "Besides, you love Chloë, and you always have and always will, calling every day to check on her, begging me to take you across the country so you can pay for her precious hospital. You sponger, you bastard, don't you dare say anything to me."

Her suitcase was still open, and she hit it, and said, "I hate this thing."

I knew I needed to say something, but my mind couldn't catch on what it was I was supposed to say. "I guess I'll stay with Great Aunt Alice," I said.

Vee stamped her foot, and then clopped around the bed, heading past me to the bathroom.

"Vee, I'm sorry," I said, panicked all of a sudden that she wasn't just leaving me until we could get out of this situation, but that she was leaving me for good, and I couldn't live with that. I grabbed at her shoulder, and she shook off my grip, but didn't go into the bathroom. "Please," I said.

She turned, and said, "No, you comfort me this time," and she fell into my arms.

"Shhh," I said, and patted the back of her head. It was the second time that day that I'd found myself in that position, a girl in my arms, but I still didn't know what to say, so I said, "It'll be okay."

"No it won't. Carlton's going to kill me," Vee said.

"He's not going to kill you."

"He's not, huh?" She pulled back so I could see her bruised face. "This was just a love tap?" And then she put her head back on my chest. "You better be getting a good share of that money now, with your son out of the way."

I stiffened.

"You talk to the lawyer yet?" she said.

I pushed her away from me, and turned to get my clothes out of the closet in the living room.

She followed me. "Oh, I repulse you now? I'm a gold digger?"

I didn't say anything, but walked around her and stuffed my clothes into my duffel. I don't know why I was angry at her for asking about the money. I certainly had no right to be.

"Well, did you go to the lawyer?" she said, putting her hands on her hips.

"No."

"You better."

"I will."

"You better, that's all."

"Didn't I just say I will?" I said, spreading my arms in defiance. "How long are you going to be staying with Carlton anyway?"

"I don't have much choice in the matter."

"Damn it, how long are we going to be *stuck* here?"

"Do you get the money?"

"I don't know."

"Then I don't know how long we're going to be here. Until Carlton gets bored with me, I guess. That's usually four or five days. Don't you have to go to the funeral anyway?"

The funeral? What funeral? Oh, right, Joe's funeral. "I guess I do," I said, and dropped my duffel on the floor.

"I guess I do," she mimicked. She went back to her suitcase

and started to struggle with the zipper again. I came around to help her, and she stepped back, and let me take over. I put my weight into it, and the zipper started to move. I had to switch hands to get it to go all the way around, repositioning the pressure from my other hand as I went. It closed and I straightened up, a fine sheen of sweat on my forehead.

I turned to go back around the bed, but Vee stopped me. "I'm just scared," she said.

"Of what?"

"Of Carlton and of getting caught."

"I'll go see the lawyer," I said. "Then we'll get out of here."

"We better get that money."

"I'll call the lawyer," I said again.

She picked up her suitcase, staggered under the weight for a moment, and started across the room. Without looking back, she said, "The room's already checked out. You just have to vacate."

She went out the door. My neck and back muscles were all tensed, and I tried to relax them. I'd fought with a lot of women, but none who could hang a murder on me, only that part I didn't figure out until later. For now, I was thrown out without any money, and nowhere else to crawl but Great Aunt Alice's, and that wasn't the best position to be in, believe you me. There are always ways in which things can get worse.

13.

Great Aunt Alice's house was one of the old mansions in Washington Hill facing north on the eastern square. There was still a marble stone at the curb from the time when such a step was necessary to descend from a horse-drawn carriage, as there was a wrought-iron boot scraper at the foot of the stone-carved stairs that led to the front door. The house was a three-story townhouse built of Cockeysville marble, the first floor one and a half times as high as the second and third floors, which allowed for large wooden pillars and a small portico above the door. Narrow black shutters framed each of the four windows across the second and third floors, held in place by hammered iron S's.

I had stopped on the way there to get one drink, which had turned into two, and I wondered how long this bender would last. I mean, I was still on the wagon and this was a temporary setback due to circumstances. But the alcohol had bestowed on me a general lightness that allowed me to think it wouldn't be so bad to see Great Aunt Alice, it might even be nice to see a familiar face, and one who called you family even when you weren't. She had always remained a friend to me, remembering me at Christmas and my birthday, and unashamed at chiding me for what my life had become. She was sure to take me in, and could be just what I needed to pull myself together. I pressed the button for the bell, and deep chimes played an eight-note melody somewhere inside, real classy.

Connie answered the door in a frilled apron tied over a black ankle-length skirt and a deep blue blouse. She didn't seem surprised to see me standing there with my duffel bag in hand, some shirts hanging on hangers over my shoulder, she just took it in stride. "Mr. Rosenkrantz. You come in now, come right in."

"Connie, you see," I said, stepping inside, "I was wondering if…"

She closed the door behind me and took my things. "Miss Hadley in the conservatory," she said. "Tea's as soon as I get it heated up. I'm a have to make up a second plate."

"Great, Connie, great, thank you," I said, and smiled my charming smile. "I know my way."

But she'd already turned to take my things up to one of the guestrooms.

The house had the sweet smell of lemon-scented dust cleaner. There were fresh flowers in a brass vase on the marble side table, and the exposed hardwood floor in the hall to the kitchen reflected white patches of light streaming from the back of the house.

I went through the front sitting room, the small dining room, and the sewing room to the open glass door to the conservatory, which ran along the back of the house. Great Aunt Alice sat in a white oversized wicker chair that faced the window to the garden. She had a large open book propped on her lap and reading glasses that she wasn't using hanging from a chain around her neck. At the sound of my entrance, she laid her book flat on her legs, and looked up. "Ah, Shem, Shem. You come to see an old lady, what a life saver."

"Great Aunt Alice," I said and bent down to kiss her on the cheek.

She frowned. "Not sober, I see."

"Not drunk either," I said.

She shrugged, and pointed with an arthritis-bent finger at a round glass-topped table in the corner. "Bring that here, will you, Shem? Connie would do it, but you're here, you can at least make yourself useful."

I went over and lifted the table in both hands and set it down beside her. She worked the book in her lap onto the table, leaving it open at her place. "Sit down, sit down," she said pointing again at another wicker chair. I pulled it a little closer and sat down. "I hope you're prepared to talk about books. I could use a little conversation. Connie and I don't have too much to say to each other. And I absolutely can't get her to read. I try and try, but she just won't touch a thing."

I nodded, Mr. Debonair Literary Lion, the charming smile creaking on my face.

"But first, this horrible business about Joseph. Quinn was enough, but we were expecting Quinn. But Joseph, I'm trying to recover."

I tried to produce the appropriate expression, but I didn't know what that was, and just hoped I looked like a father in mourning.

"I understand you were the last person to see him alive."

I shifted in my chair. "I don't know—"

"Yes, yes," she said, nodding. "Mary told me. What a good girl that Mary is. It's a shame, oh, it's a tragedy, that poor little thing. She comes and visits me once a week you know."

"I didn't," I said.

"You know her?"

"We just met."

"Oh, a wonderful girl. She'll be by this afternoon, I'm sure. So unfortunate. But you were the last to see Joseph."

"I guess I was." Why was she harping on that? It made me nervous, like maybe she suspected something.

She gave me a contemplative look. "You're not fooling me. You're tight. I thought you were supposed to be a teetotaler now."

"I am. I am. This thing with Quinn and Joe…"

"Nonsense. That's no excuse. You look terrible," she said.

"Thanks."

"Well, you do." She gave a single satisfied nod. "So what did he say? Last night?"

"Who?"

"Joseph."

Connie came in then carrying a tray with tea, both hot and iced, and cucumber sandwiches, crackers, and pâté. I took the opportunity to collect myself. Of course Great Aunt Alice wasn't suspicious. Why would she suspect something? It was that kind of paranoia that would get me caught. She was just being Great Aunt Alice.

"Thank you, Connie," she said. "You can just put that over there. Shem will take care of it." She turned back to me. "Well?"

"He was drunk. He…was upset still about Quinn, and angry at me, but I don't know what about."

"You should never have split with Quinn in the first place."

That hadn't taken long. "Are we going to go over this now?"

"Joseph needed a father. A boy should have a man around."

"Thanks for the compliment, but I'm hardly a man."

She nodded. "You said that. I didn't say that. I'm not letting you off any hook." She pointed at the tray. "Hand me that, darling, won't you." I got up, and poured her some tea. "And a lemon slice. Yes, that one." She took the cup and saucer from me, and I sat back down. After a sip, she said, "The whole thing's so terrible. And with you right there." She shook her head again, "No," and took some more tea. "What's happening with that wife of yours, that movie star? She still locked up in the loony bin?"

I gave up pretending and let my face fall. "She is."

"Why is that again?"

"She has psychotic episodes and she's suicidal."

She shook her head again. "You should never have split up with Quinn. And you need money, I can tell that."

I had forgotten just how acerbic Great Aunt Alice could be. But I couldn't help but feel as though I deserved to be put on the spot. "It'll work out."

"If you mean it won't kill you, you're absolutely right. These things happen. There are good times and there are bad times, and when you have a bad time, you just hold your head up and remember that tomorrow's another day, it can always be better tomorrow. Now what do you want? Go on and ask it, if it isn't money."

I ran my hand over the stubble on my face, and crossed my legs. "How do you know…"

"You aren't taking any tea. I'm not going to eat all of those sandwiches."

I leaned forward and made myself a plate.

"Well?"

"I need to stay here for a few days." I looked up to see how she was taking it. "Until the funeral at least," I added. "Then I'll be going back to S.A."

"But you'll need me to pay your airfare for that."

I bit into a sandwich. It was cool and refreshing.

"Of course you can stay. Stay as long as you like. We'll have Connie make you up a room. Maybe if I can watch over you,

you won't get into any trouble, and I can browbeat a novel out of you."

My body deflated, I wasn't able to stop it, I collapsed under the weight of it all.

Great Aunt Alice shook her head. "Poor Joseph. Poor poor Joseph. And that girl of his. She won't get anything, since they weren't married."

I hadn't even thought about that part of it, and I had a fresh pang of guilt, but I pushed it away. I needed the money more than Mary did. She would find a new beau in no time, but this was my last chance to settle my debts and start anew. And it had been an accident. I hadn't killed Joe for the money. You could hardly say I killed Joe at all.

"You didn't know him well enough," Great Aunt Alice said. "He was really a sweet sweet boy. You didn't know him, and now it's too late for that, no thanks to you. You're a real bastard, Shem, don't think I ever forget that, but a helluva writer, what a writer."

"I don't know what to say to that."

"Don't say anything. You'd only screw it up. Ask me what I'm reading."

And I did. And she talked nonstop for over an hour. She didn't need my conversation at all. She just needed someone to talk at. Joseph dying didn't change it one bit. I was as good as anyone else no matter what I might feel, and of course I couldn't fool her about anything. She knew how much and what I felt. And this was my price to pay. For staying here, for not staying in touch, for not writing, for running around on my wife, for every wrong I'd ever done. Great Aunt Alice managed to remind me of all of it without ever saying a word. She was the mirror of truth. She was what laid bare my conscience and made it impossible to ignore, because I was always going to be inadequate as a man in her eyes even if I was 'a helluva writer.'

After about two hours of that, it was getting up near dinner time, and Great Aunt Alice said I'd have to excuse her, she needed some time to get ready for dinner, and I should go up to my room too. The alcohol had long worn off, and I felt groggy, wiped out, a diffuse headache sitting on the top of my head like a newsboy's cap.

I went up to my room. It was on the second floor in the rear of the house, canary yellow wallpaper with a pinstripe pattern, a bed with a white duvet and yellow accent pillows, a nightstand, and a bureau. Connie had hung my shirts and pants in the closet, and emptied my duffel bag into the bureau. The sight of the bed hammered me with exhaustion. I was still working off of a sleep deficit, even with the nap earlier, and suddenly the idea of dinner with Great Aunt Alice, of the hours ahead of me, made it hard to even stand.

I sat down on the edge of the bed. There was a telephone extension on the nightstand. I remembered telling Vee that I would call Palmer to see about the will, but I knew that calling Palmer was exactly the last thing I should do, since it would make it look like I was so anxious to get the money I didn't even care that Joe had died. That was the kind of misstep that someone like Vee would make after they killed somebody. I was proud of myself for thinking of it, and refraining from making the call. Instead I picked up the phone and dialed the long-distance number to the Enoch White Clinic. My heart rate went up, and I started to sweat. I thought, as I did every day, if I could just hear Clotilde's voice…

It was Nurse Dunn who answered. I called often enough that I knew all of the nurses' voices. "Enoch White."

"Yes. This is Mr. Rosenkrantz. I was hoping to speak to my wife, please."

"It's lunchtime. The patients cannot take phone calls. Phone calls can only be received between two and four in the afternoon."

I looked at my watch. About four-thirty, which made it one-thirty in California. But I needed to talk to Clotilde. I couldn't tell her anything, but it would help me just to hear her. "It's only a half hour," I said.

"Mr. Rosenkrantz, I'm sorry."

"Well, can I talk to Director Philips?"

"He's at lunch too. I can take a message."

I sighed. "Yes, I just wanted to let him know that the legalities are being worked out here, but I will have the money. He shouldn't do anything until I get back to California."

She intoned, "Right. I'll pass it on." She'd taken the same message from me countless times. They all had.

"Goodbye," I said, not wanting to get off, not knowing what I'd say.

"Goodbye," Nurse Dunn said, and rang off.

I replaced the receiver in its cradle, and sat with my head bowed and my hands between my legs. I tried to elicit some emotion by forcing myself to think of Joe's head—clunk—hitting the counter, but I was already too beaten to feel anything about that. Great Aunt Alice had taken it all out of me. Instead I fell back on the bed, and slept through dinner, through the night, and well into the next morning, and even then I was exhausted and didn't want to get out of bed. But Connie knocked at the door to tell me that the police were here.

14.

It was Detective Healey and Detective Dobrygowski, and I don't have to tell you I wasn't happy to see them. Connie was hovering nearby as though she expected the cops to steal something if left unguarded. They were smiling and making an attempt at small talk. I stood for a second on the top step and swallowed. If they were coming to arrest me, they wouldn't be trading pleasantries with the maid. They'd told me yesterday it was an accident, and for all they knew it was an accident. They didn't suspect me of anything. I forced a smile, and started down the steps.

"Mr. Rosenkrantz," Detective Healey said. And with concern, "Are you all right?"

So much for my smile. "I just need something to eat."

"Don't let us stop you." But they didn't move any, and neither did I.

I looked at Connie, and they did too, and she got flustered and turned back towards the kitchen.

Healey craned his neck to peer over my shoulder. "Should we follow?"

"Is this going to take long?"

"No, not long, not long," Healey said.

"We don't want to put too much strain on you," Dobrygowski said, "given your loss."

They both regarded me with blank expressions. There was no

way to tell if their sentiments were genuine. I gave up any attempt to hide my exhaustion. As Dobrygowski said, I was in mourning. I should look exhausted and done in.

"Nice place," Dobrygowski said. "Must be better than staying in a hotel." That was meant to be a question, but I wasn't biting.

"The hotel said you gave this as a forwarding address." Healey's brow creased again. "Are you sure you're all right? You don't look so good, Mr. Rosenkrantz."

Dobrygowski added, "Tough night? You sleep okay?"

"I slept too well."

"One of those nights. Sure. You want to shut things out, you just keep to bed so long, dead to the world, as long as you don't dream."

"But you always dream," Dobrygowski said, also looking straight at me.

"Not always," Healey said. "But, yeah, usually. Usually you dream. Did you have any dreams, Mr. Rosenkrantz?"

I didn't say anything. Their whole tone was different from yesterday. If they came by just for amusement, I didn't need to amuse them.

Healey got a guilty look on his face. "I'm sorry, Mr. Rosenkrantz. I know you just lost your wife and boy."

"My ex-wife," I said. I don't know why I felt I had to add that. It was comments like that that would get me in trouble.

"Sure, you lost your ex-wife and son. You've got a lot weighing you down. Sleep like that, it's a blessing. It's nature's way of protecting our sanity when things get to be too much. There are plenty of nights where I wish I could sleep right through, dead to the world."

"How long did you sleep?" Dobrygowski cut in.

"Is that really why you're here?" I said. "There's so little for the police to worry about they have to worry if I had a good night's sleep?"

"No, of course not. We've got some other things to talk about, but when we see a man looking down and beaten, we worry. We just want to help out. That's a policeman's real job anyway. To help out."

We all let that sit for a moment to see if any of us believed it, but none of us were that stupid.

"But you must not have gotten much sleep the night before last, right?" Healey went on. He reached into his inner coat pocket and came out with a policeman's notepad. He flipped it open, paging through. "You said you were at your son's house around midnight, that you were there maybe half an hour, and then you went back to the Somerset. So you didn't get to bed until at earliest one, one-thirty?" He looked up at me with a furrowed brow.

"That's what I said." This was starting to make me nervous. Why were we going back through my statement? That couldn't be a good thing. That could only mean they suspected something. But it was hard to think, tired and hungry as I was.

"That seems about right, the man on the desk that night said you came in around 1:15, so that's about what it would be, right?"

"I don't understand," I said, hoping my expression showed confusion, not fear. "We went over all of this yesterday. What's going on?"

"Why'd you leave the hotel?" Dobrygowski said.

So they did suspect something. "Aunt Alice offered to put me up."

"Aunt Alice. But she's not your aunt, is she?" Healey said.

"Quinn, my ex-wife's great aunt, her mother's mother's sister. Why is this important? Gentleman, I'm really—"

"And she just now decided to put you up?" Dobrygowski cut in. A real bleeding heart, that Dobrygowski. This guy just lost his son; we better grill him.

I didn't say anything. I was sick to my stomach, that ambiguous feeling that could mean hunger or could mean heartburn. I needed to eat, and I needed a drink even more.

"We're just trying to get things straight," Healey said, the good cop.

"I'm sorry, gentleman, but Joe got killed two days ago. I just can't go through this again right now."

"It's funny how you say Joe got killed," Dobrygowski said, jumping on me. "Because if it was just an accident, falling asleep with a lit cigarette, I would have thought you would have said that Joe died, not that he got killed."

"It's just a way of talking," I mumbled.

Healey sighed. He looked at Dobrygowski, but when he spoke it was to me. "The M.E. says that it looks like your son may have been murdered."

And there it was. A punch in the stomach. It couldn't have hit me harder than if they were putting the handcuffs on me right then. Then I'd know at least. I almost retched, but managed to turn it into a burp, covering my mouth. I tasted stale alcohol.

Dobrygowski reached out as though he were going to brace me.

"Are you okay?" Healey said.

I coughed and swallowed, and shook my head, waving my hand to show I was all right, just give me a second, I'm all right.

"I'm sorry to have to bring you more bad news," Healey said, and I could tell he really was. He wasn't a bad guy at that. He really cared. And my reaction had been the right one, it turned out. He thought I choked out of parental horror. I choked because I felt the noose tightening. "It's not definite," he said. "He had a pretty severe skull fracture at the back of his head. It's possible that he just fell, and it's even possible that it didn't kill him, that he still made it to his bed and lit a cigarette. But it looks suspicious, and so we have to look into it."

"Is that why you're checking my story with the deskman?"

"I'm sorry about that. It's no good. It makes me sick. But we had to come at you with this to see how you took it."

"Well, how am I taking it," I said, angry now. Angry that I was so relieved they *weren't* putting me in handcuffs. And angry because it meant I had been much more frightened than I had thought.

"I'm sorry," Healey said again.

"So what happened? Joe was murdered?"

"We didn't say that. We're not saying that. We're just saying that it's something we need to look into."

So they were just double-checking my story. They didn't suspect me of anything. I was just the last person to see him alive, as they always say in the movies. Didn't mean I killed him. He was my kid. How could I have killed him?

"I'm really sorry we had to ruin another morning for you," Healey said.

"So am I." I said it with a little heat behind it. I was entitled to some anger now.

"You will contact us if you think of anything else?"

I sneered. "Oh, you don't have to worry about that."

My tone seemed to pain Healey, but it made Dobrygowski

examine me with more intensity. "Right, then. I'm sorry again," Healey said, putting his pad back in his pocket. "We'll let you know if we find anything."

"You know where to find me," I said, showing that I had nothing to hide. I was right out in the open.

Healey opened the door, and I stepped forward and held it as they both filed through, and then I closed it behind them. When I turned around, Connie was right there, creeping down the hall from the kitchen.

"Someone killed Mr. Joe?" she said.

"That's what they're saying," I said.

"It sounded like they was giving you the third degree. If I'd a known that, I'd a said you weren't here, the no-good police hassling a father in mourning. They should be ashamed." Her indignity was enough for the both of us, hands on her hips, lowered brow, and pushed-out lips. "Well your breakfast is all fixed, so come on back and get something inside you now."

In the kitchen, she took a plate out of the oven with a towel, and brought it over to the small kitchen table. "You don't mind eating in the kitchen here, do you? Miss Alice takes all her meals in here with me now. The dining room's only for company."

"That's fine, Connie." And it was fine. Scrambled eggs, a link of sausage, hash browns, grits, and a toasted English muffin with a container of jam on the side. It was the kind of meal a man deserved on a morning he was hassled by the police. My stomach was still boiling, but I figured it would calm down once I got some grub in me. I dug in, and Connie went about her business cleaning up, not saying anything. She and Great Aunt Alice could probably go whole days without saying a word to one another.

I ate with relish. Once I got the first taste of egg, I knew that my discomfort was more hunger than heartburn, although there was still some of that too.

I reviewed my interview with the police. I had been by turns exhausted and angry, but I didn't think I'd made any big mistakes. Aside from one or two glances from Dobrygowski, and that crack about me saying 'killed' instead of 'died,' it seemed like what they said it was, a routine double-check of my statement now that they were approaching it as a murder and not an accidental death. And they said they weren't even sure if it was a murder, they were just looking into it. No, I was fine. They didn't suspect me of anything. Why would they? I was Joe's father. I ran through it again, and I still couldn't find any other mistakes. I was okay.

I wanted to call Vee, though, or to see her. I wanted to let her know what was happening. But it was exactly the last thing I should do, and she would be mad as anything if I did get in touch. It would call further attention to our relationship than we wanted. For all I knew at the moment, they didn't even know about Vee, and it was better all around if it stayed that way. Still, I really could have used her reassuring voice.

I finished my meal. Connie had left the kitchen, presumably to check on Great Aunt Alice. I knew I should probably do the same, but even fortified by the food as I was, I didn't have it in me for another long session in the conservatory. I couldn't call Vee, and what I'd really have liked was to call Clotilde, but it was too early on the West Coast. The hospital would never put me through to her even if I claimed it was an emergency. Especially if I claimed it was an emergency. They wouldn't want to do anything that might unduly excite one of their residents.

That left me with the long day ahead and nothing to fill it. Except for thoughts of Healey and Dobrygowski digging around, narrowing their search, closing their net. The idea was too much to bear. I yawned and thought I could really go back to sleep, I was that tired, like the food had weighted me down and I couldn't even find the energy to stand up. But I made it back up to my bedroom. I collapsed on the bed, and before I knew it I was dead to the world.

15.

The next few days passed in much the same way. I woke up some time before noon and Connie gave me a meal in the kitchen. I'd go back to my room, try to pick at a book from Great Aunt Alice's library, and then fall asleep after a few pages and be out until dinner. I only saw Great Aunt Alice at dinner. And then the conversation was only of books and it didn't really matter how much I contributed, Great Aunt Alice could talk enough for both of us, which was all she really wanted anyway. Otherwise, I managed to sleep as much as eighteen, twenty hours a day.

The funeral was scheduled for Thursday, one week exactly after Joe's death. I would have liked it to be sooner—I felt I would be safer with the body in the ground—but once it was declared a murder, the city wouldn't release the body until two days after the autopsy, which put it on a Sunday, which in the police bureaucracy really meant Monday. So the earliest the funeral could have been was Tuesday. But Mary was in charge, along with Frank Palmer, and she wanted to get it just right. She'd gotten very particular as a widow. Only of course she wasn't even a widow since they never were married. I just slept, letting it all happen without me, at a distance, and so I was told the funeral was on Thursday and the funeral was on Thursday.

I saw Mary only once in that time, on Sunday. She came to the house all fired up with the distraction of planning, and said that she was in the midst of all of these decisions—the flowers, the clergy, the eulogy, the obituary, everything—and she was afraid that she had overstepped her bounds. She was afraid I would be angry. I put my arm around her and told her it was all right, it was great, it was the way it should be, and the weight of the whole thing suddenly showed on her face. It went from pinched to slack, and her eyes got shiny, but she didn't let a tear drop. She was a good sport like that. She said again that she wanted to think of me as a dad, and I said I wouldn't like anything better, and she managed a smile at that, even if it was pained, and she left, back to her organization, keeping busy to keep her mind off of it.

When I was awake, however, I couldn't keep my mind off of it. It would creep up on me, Joe's fall, carrying his lifeless body up the stairs, the glow of the lighter... Even if it had been an accident, covering it up was surely a crime, and when your kid got hurt, even if you had nothing to do with it, you felt guilty and thought, if only I had...if only...and here I had everything to do with it. Mary wanted to see me as a father, but it was I who needed a parent. With that thought, I'd roll over and force myself right back to sleep.

There was a phone call with Palmer. I *had* come into money. Since Joe died without a will, the estate was distributed according to the order of succession, first to Joe's kids if there were any and there weren't, and then to Joe's parents, which was me. Surprisingly, I didn't feel one way or the other about the news, and we agreed it was best dealt with after the funeral. I knew I should at least tell Vee that much, but I didn't know what her situation was with Browne, and it still felt too risky to make contact. And every time I thought about calling Clotilde, I couldn't face the idea of having to put off Director Philips once more, or worse, on the weekend, one of the sub-directors.

On Tuesday, I was finally forced out of my lethargy. I was

dreaming about the funeral, and the bell tolled, but it wasn't one sonorous note but a stream of notes, up and down. They ran through their sequence again, and I became aware of the room, the bed, the leathery dry interior of my mouth, and I realized the ringing wasn't in my dream. It was the doorbell.

I lay there on my stomach in my suit pants and shirtsleeves, one arm hanging off the bed, feeling too tired to get up, but awake enough to know I wouldn't be going back to sleep any-time soon. Then there was the sound of Connie on the stairs, and a knock at my door.

"Mr. Shem. There's a man here to see you."

I didn't move. I was so numb to everything that I wasn't even worried it was the cops. They could come and take me for all I cared.

"Mr. Shem? Should I send him away?"

I called, "I'll be right there, Connie." There was a pause, and then I heard her walk away. I pulled up my arm, swung my feet around, and sat on the edge of the bed. Man, did my head feel like it weighed twenty-five pounds. I brought a hand to my fore-head to support it. If Vee could see me now... I deserved what-ever vitriol she could spew, and she was expert at vitriol.

I pulled myself together and got up. I felt a little lightheaded and dizzy at first, but that was to be expected. I rubbed my cheeks to get some blood into them, and they were like sandpaper. I couldn't remember the last time I'd shaved.

From the top of the stairs, I could see a young man in a blue suit with no tie and a gray hat. He was familiar, I knew I should know him, but I just couldn't place him. In the back of my mind a note of panic edged in with the sense that this man knew something about Joe's death. He was linked to it in some way.

He looked up when I was halfway down the stairs, broke into

a nervous grin, and hurried off his hat. "Mr. Rosenkrantz." His expression got a little funny as he took in my condition, but what was that to me?

"I'm sorry, I..." I said as I reached the bottom of the stairs.

His face fell a little, but he managed to keep his grin. "Taylor Montgomery, sir."

"Who?" I said out loud. I couldn't remember any Montgomery.

His face fell even further, and he looked down. "Oh, I'm sorry, maybe I shouldn't..." He darted a look at me to see how he was faring. "I knew I shouldn't have come."

Montgomery? It dawned on me. It was the kid from the newspaper who I'd shot the breeze with the day I... That was why I thought of him and Joe. It felt like a year ago. "Montgomery. Sure. Sure. No, the kid from newspaper. It just slipped my mind for a minute."

"Because I could come back. Or if you'd rather be alone..."

"No. It's all right. What can I do for you, Montgomery?"

"I got your address from the hotel. They said this was where your messages were to be forwarded. I hope it's all right. I mean, I know with your son and all... I just wanted to tell you how awfully sorry I am. I just feel terrible."

And he looked it too. It embarrassed me to see how deferential he seemed, how worshipful. I couldn't look him in the eye. "Thanks, kid." I put my hand on his shoulder, and he looked up at me with his chin still tucked in.

"It's all right I came?"

"It's swell you came. It's better than all right. I've been alone too much. Your mind dwells on things..."

He rocked on his heels, uncomfortable.

I put my whole arm around him then. "Come on, come in." I led us into the nearby sitting room. There was a sideboard with a small wet bar, and just the sight of the alcohol made me stand up straighter. I'd been very near a teetotaler since coming to Great Aunt Alice's, but now I had a guest, I could have a drink. I went across to the bar and flipped over two glasses.

He looked around for where to sit, and settled on a delicate colonial couch with two-tone yellow upholstery. He perched on the edge. "It's really okay I'm here...?" he said.

"Of course. Of course. What'll you have?"

"Oh, none for me. I'm fine. I'm just here to pay my respects."

"Don't make me drink alone." And I made us each a Gin Rickey. I crossed the room, handed him his drink, and sat in one of the armchairs, an uncomfortable Louis XIV.

He held the drink in both hands, and stared into it, not drinking. Then he looked up at me with equal parts reverence and embarrassed concern. It was how I'd had the strength to go talk to Joe, that look, and you know where that had led. Remembering that made me shift in my seat. He looked down again. "You probably think I'm crazy. Coming like I have a right to visit you. I'm probably ruining my chance to work with you. You probably won't be staying in Calvert much longer anyway."

"Probably not," I said, trying to remember what he meant, 'work with me.' And it hit me that we had been writing together that night, a play. Me, writing.

"Well even if we don't work more together, it's been a real honor." He met my eyes and his were just beaming, and it really made me feel like the rottenest person that ever lived, him looking at me like I was sacred, and me knowing that I was a philandering alcoholic hack screenwriter killer.

"Yeah, it's been an honor for me too," I said, and took another drink so I didn't have to decide what expression to give to my mouth.

He swallowed, looked for a place to put his glass down, and settled on the floor beside his foot. "I shouldn't even say anything," he said, "but even if we're not going to work together, I brought along something I worked up…if you don't mind, it'd mean a lot to me if you looked at it."

I didn't want to look at it. I was too tired. But there was something in his fawning that made me feel like somebody again. And with just that glimmer of self-worth, I started to think, I wasn't bad. I'd just ended up in a compromising situation. And not for any gain. That was the thing. It had been self-defense. This kid would believe that. He knew I was a good guy. So I leaned forward, and held my hand out for whatever it was he'd written, and said, "Sure, why not?"

His face lit up, and he pulled out his pad from his inner coat pocket, the same pad from the bar. He started to flip through it. "It's just an idea for a scene I think would come at the end of Act I." He handed it over, and at first I just stared at the script unseeing. "It hit me what you were saying about the Furies being mortal. And I thought if one of them killed the other, you see, if one Fury killed another Fury, that would be like a sister killing a sister, and then that's exactly one of the things the Furies punished people for, killing a family member, you know, in the old myths." My face must have changed colors, because he stopped and said, "Mr. Rosenkrantz, are you all right? I'm sorry if, well I knew I shouldn't say anything about tho play. My mom would kill mo if sho know I was here acting like this with you having just lost your son."

I shook my head and held out a hand when it looked like he might try to get up. "It's fine, it's all right. I want to read it, I do," and to prove I did, I started reading. I could feel him watching me and then looking away and watching me again, but I furrowed my brow and focused on what he'd written. And it was pretty good. It was really good, actually, and I felt some of the excitement I had felt with him in the bar the other day. I finished my drink and balanced the glass on the arm of my chair, and flipped through to the end of the scene. It was only four handwritten pages, but it was really good. "I like it," I said, handing the pad back to him.

His eye opened wide. "You do? I mean, you really do?"

"Yeah, it's a great idea. It's a great way to end the first act."

His smile was open and giddy.

"I'd cut that crying and laughing part at the end there."

He knit his brow and stuck out his lower lip in seriousness, nodding. "Sure, I could see that."

"A small action carries a lot of weight on a live stage. And you have this murder. That's going to be big enough. You just let the other two sisters stare at the body in shock. They lead the audience, you see. Everyone's in shock. Because you *are* in shock when it happens. You're looking down and thinking, this couldn't be, it doesn't—it just couldn't. You're in shock, you see." I realized what I was saying, and I got up to fix another drink.

"I see what you're saying," he said, writing something down. "Yeah, that's better than the murdering sister breaking down, if she just looks at her sister's body, and then the third one looks at her accusingly, their eyes meet, and the murderer runs off the stage, lights out." He was writing the whole while he was talking.

I drank half my drink on my way back to my seat. "And then when the innocent sister seeks vengeance on the murdering sister, then she's only left the choice to do the same thing, to kill her sister, and then she's no better off than the other one. Because really, we're all guilty in the end, right? It's not just one person who's guilty, but everyone, because they let it happen, they made it too."

He wasn't quite following me there, and I wasn't even following myself, I wasn't making any sense. "I like it," he said. "I hadn't thought of that."

"Here give me that," I said, reaching for the pad in order to hide my own confusion. He handed it back to me. "And a pen." He handed me that too. I looked at what he'd just written, and I started to jot some dialogue down. It just came to me:

"Don't you accuse me. How dare you accuse me. She would have killed me if she'd had the chance." "Do you think self-defense is an excuse? How many times have we ended a life even when self-defense has been invoked?" "I'll never let you get to me. I'll get to you first." "And that'll be self-defense too?" "It will." "Well you have to get to me first."

It felt good, the dialogue flowing like that. And you read it now, and I know what you're thinking, that I was trying to make excuses for myself. Only I didn't see that at the time. At the time it was just a play I was writing. And the important thing was that I *was* writing. And not the nonsense I'd written in the hotel the other day, but actual dialogue that fit into a play. Montgomery would take care of patching it all together, like the script doctors that come in and touch up a screenplay after you're finished with it.

I looked up for a moment, and saw that Montgomery was watching me with fierce intensity. It made me self-conscious, and I lost the flow of what I was writing. I handed back the pad and mixed myself another drink. He looked at what I had written and then immediately started writing something else down. I watched him work and it was exciting to see his enthusiasm and self-confidence. I wondered what had happened to my own self-confidence. If only I had a young man like that with me, I'd be unstoppable again.

And then I found myself wishing again that Montgomery had been my son. I would have been a different person with a boy like that looking up to me like I was king of the world. With a son like that you could really make something of yourself. You just about had to with a son like that, because he had you so great that you'd bend over backwards to prove he was right. But Joe had said that he thought the world of me as a kid, and what did I do? I made him think I was worse than I was and it seemed like I had proven him right in the end too.

But that didn't matter. What mattered was that I was up and awake and my mind was sharp.

He started talking. I offered him a drink, and he waved it off, and went on about another plot point in the play, and then we really were working again, just like the night in the bar. Everything else fell away. All of my guilt, my anxiety, my self-loathing, those things evaporated in the creative flow of hashing out murder and drama on the stage. It was so much easier on paper than in— But I couldn't think like that.

I kept drinking and finished the bottle. Montgomery nursed the first drink I had given him, learning from his mistake the last time. He took the role of secretary so I didn't have to worry about my handwriting. We hashed out most of the second act in what must have been something like four hours. I'm not sure how long it was. It wasn't dark yet outside, but it was getting there, that late evening summer twilight.

Montgomery filled up his pad at some point, but he had another one. He'd really come prepared; he was that eager and hopeful. To him, I really was somebody, even if everyone else in the literary establishment had forgotten me, and my call girl girlfriend didn't want to see me, and I owed money all over, and the police were probably going to arrest me any day. No, for him, I was a big-time writer. And we had that perfect give-and-take you need to get something good. I could feel it was good as it was happening. And maybe, I'm not ashamed to say it, maybe I began to believe it too. *The Furies* by Shem Rosenkrantz and Taylor Montgomery! The new smash hit! Yeah, we wrote.

And I didn't once think of Joe or anybody else.

16.

That was Tuesday, and the funeral was set for Thursday. Montgomery and I wrote all that Wednesday with only two notable interruptions that I guess I should mention. The first was a letter from Vee telling me to meet her at the hotel's luncheonette first thing Friday morning. She didn't know when she could get away so I was to just go and wait. Then we could figure out what we were going to do, and get the hell out of Calvert.

The second was two phone calls back to back, so if you count that as two things, then I'd have to say three things happened that Wednesday. The first phone call really threw me for a loop. Connie announced that someone was on the line for me, and I ran upstairs to take it in my room, expecting that it was Vee and I would need some privacy. But when I picked up, a familiar man's voice came through the line, "Shem Rosenkrantz, I can hardly believe it's you."

I sat heavily on the bed. "Hub." Hub Gilplaine was a night-club owner and pornographer in S.A. who I used to pen smut books for. We'd been friends, but I soured that the second I asked to borrow money. How had he found me?

"Shem, how long have we known each other?"

"A lot of years," I said.

"A lot of years. So you know what I hate more than anything, don't you?"

"For someone to waste your time."

"For someone to waste my time. That's right. So how come I

find out that you've skipped town and I've got to waste precious hours getting you tracked down?"

"Hub, I haven't skipped town. Quinn died, and then Joe—"

"How come?" He'd raised his voice. Then I knew it was personal. He never raised his voice.

I was silent.

"Huh?" He waited for me to answer. "How long have we been friends? You're afraid to call me?"

"I'm coming into some money—"

"Money! Money…"

I could hear him shaking his head through the wire. So he was going to take this offended compatriot act through to the very end.

"Shem, I had to put your name out in a lot of places to track you down, and we've already established that my time is too valuable for that. When somebody offered to buy up your debt, I didn't say no. You and I are square as far as money goes. It's not my problem anymore. I've washed my hands of it."

"But, you don't understand, I'm coming into a lot of money. That's why I'm here."

"Then you'll have no trouble paying your new creditors off."

I had no answer for that.

"That's all I wanted you to know," he said, "that you have someone else to pay back now, Shem. Someone less patient than I've been."

"Hub…"

"I'm sorry, Shem, I gave you all the time I could."

"Sure. Yeah." But he'd hung up.

I put the receiver down and just sat there, unable to get up. All of the energy that Montgomery had brought out in me in the previous thirty-six hours was gone, just pulled right out of me and across the country. Who was I kidding writing a play? I couldn't get away from my life. In America, you got one chance, and if you hit it big then you hit it big, but if you fell, there was no climbing back up. You might as well just die or go off somewhere where you weren't in the way. Yeah, I might have come into a lot of money, but I owed a lot of money too. And now some gangster had bought up my debt... Who knew how much he'd expect from me? There was no pretending. I was on my way out, not up.

But thoughts like that were doing me no good. I picked up the phone again, and got the Enoch White clinic on the line. I asked for Clotilde, and the nurse on the other end got icy and told me to hold on, and then the phone delivered me a voice that was as relieving as the last voice had been frightening.

"Shem, you haven't called."

"I know, baby. I've been real tied up out here. Joe died."

There was quiet, but not quite silence. She squeaked out, "No," and I sank again. She was supposed to comfort me, and now I'd have to comfort her.

"It's okay, honey, listen..."

"Shem, where are you?"

"I'm still in Calvert. The funeral's tomorrow. Then I'll come home."

"I miss you." She was crying, but quietly.

"I miss you too."

"I love you."

"I love you too. Listen, baby, it's going to be okay. I'm getting the money now. The whole thing, the estate. I'll be able to pay Philips. You'll be set up for a long time."

"Oh, Shem, I'm so happy," but she sounded just the same as she had a second before.

"It's all going to be okay now."

"But Joe died?"

"It's okay, honey."

"I miss you."

I sighed. This was actually worse than the conversation with Hub. He'd sent some gangster on my trail, but Clotilde…she tore it right out of me, you know? She emasculated me. All the no-good things I'd done to her. I just needed to lie back and go to sleep and never wake up.

"You'll pay Director Philips now?" Clotilde said. She'd stopped crying, but her voice still sounded small, like a shy little girl's.

"Yes."

"I'm so happy, Shem."

"Yeah." It went on like that a little longer, with the I-love-yous and I-miss-yous. I'd planned to tell Director Philips the good news about the money, but I didn't have it in me anymore, so when I was able to, I let Clotilde hang up. I don't know how long it took me to get up, but I eventually made it back downstairs to Montgomery, and at first I was morose, but after a drink and a half he was able to pull me back into it, and we wrote until late in the evening, and he stayed and we had dinner with Great Aunt Alice and Connie.

The next day was the funeral. It was unseasonably cool thanks to the rain of the previous night. We gathered at the same funeral home where Quinn's service had been held just under two weeks before. Mary and her parents, Great Aunt Alice, and I sat in the first pew, with Connie directly behind us, and Montgomery a row behind her. Palmer Sr. was also there, and some other acquaintances I didn't recognize, friends of Quinn's from her life without me. It seemed that Joseph had had almost no friends of his own or maybe they were just all far away, seeing as how he'd always boarded at school. I half expected Vee to show up too, and I couldn't decide if I was relieved or disappointed when she didn't. I'd see her the next day at the hotel anyway.

In front of our pew, there was a waist-high wooden barrier that separated us from the closed casket and the podium from which the minister spoke. He did a hell of a ceremony, quoting the Bible about how the Lord giveth and the Lord taketh away, to every season, you die in body but live on in spirit, etc., etc. He threw in a bit about Abraham's test with Isaac on the mountain, and tried to make it that God tested us every day, and some trials were harder than others, but we should always trust in God. I guess he brought that up for my benefit, seeing as I was a father robbed of his only child. It was a nice try, but it only made me sick to my stomach.

When he'd finished, a man from the funeral home announced the location of the cemetery and informed us that people outside would be handing out maps to anyone who needed them. The pallbearers, just members of the funeral home's staff, wheeled the casket up the aisle and we all stood to follow it out.

It was then that I saw Healey and Dobrygowski standing in the back of the room. I had really hoped to not have to see them again, and the sight of them there started me sweating. Fortunately, they filed out ahead of everyone else and were gone from the lobby by the time I reached it. But I couldn't shake the feeling that they had come because they knew something, that they had wanted me to see them so that I could stew a little, and would be more likely to make a mistake when they actually talked to me.

I was on edge the entire ride to the cemetery. I didn't even attempt to talk to Mary or her parents. I told myself that the cops were just paying their respects, that there was no other reason for them to be at the funeral. Even the police couldn't be so cold as to arrest a man at his own son's funeral. They probably had already gone back to work. Surely Joe's case wasn't the only case they were working. They felt obligated to make an appearance, but that was all it was, an appearance, and I didn't have to worry about them anymore.

I'd just about gotten myself believing it when we pulled into the cemetery through an enormous granite archway, the wings of a black iron gate folded back into the grounds. The narrow road was just large enough for a single vehicle. The driver of the hearse expertly drove through the winding hills until he came to the Hadley plot. The large family marker, engraved with the umbrella that had made their fortune, was visible from the car, as was a four-foot pile of dirt.

And on the other side of the road, pulled off on the grass, was a black Lincoln with Healey and Dobrygowski standing up against it.

I got out of the car on the opposite side, and reached back to take Mary's hand. My reflection in the car's window—pallid, pinched face, shoulders hunched nervously, rumpled suit—was frightening. I looked like I had a big 'guilty' sign around my neck, and my only luck was that it was my son's funeral, and I hoped the guise of mourning still masked my expression.

I focused studiously on Mary, and even when Dobrygowski gave me a wry smile and a nod, I acted as though I hadn't seen him. We walked between the graves, picking our way up an incline towards the Hadley marker. It was shocking to see how many of the gravestones, even in the old part of the cemetery, were marked with the war years, '43, '44, '45. And all of them with birth dates as much as twenty-five years after mine.

We got to the grave where several folding chairs had been

arranged facing the empty hole. Mary hung onto me for support, but I felt as though I could just as easily topple over on her. I hadn't had a drink that morning, and I was feeling shaky.

I poured her into a seat, but continued to stand myself, facing the grave. I could feel Healey and Dobrygowski behind me, watching from their respectful distance. I began to worry that they were allowing me to attend my son's funeral out of courtesy, and were planning to arrest me as soon as it was over. At the thought, my mouth went dry and my chest grew taut, and it was sheer exhaustion that prevented me from bolting. Exhaustion and the knowledge that making a half-hearted attempt to escape two younger men in a cordoned-off cemetery was crazy and would just make my case look worse.

Great Aunt Alice grabbed my sleeve, startling me. She had her cane in the hand that held my sleeve, and Connie had her other arm. "Shem, help me will you?" Her back was hunched, so that she couldn't look up at my face.

I took her arm, and with Connie's help, we guided her to the empty folding chair on the end, leaving two chairs between her and Mary. I insisted that Connie take one, and Mary pulled me down in the other.

The pallbearers, along with two gravediggers in dungarees, worked the coffin onto a set of canvas straps that hung over the grave on a large stainless steel frame. When it was in place the minister began. He had asked me before the ceremony if I'd wanted to say anything, but I'd declined. He invited Mary to say a few words.

She brought out a much-worried crinkled paper from her small handbag, and stood but did not turn, instead addressing the grave. Her voice was thin, and she had gotten through barely a sentence before she broke down in tears. She waved away any help, managed to regain herself, and continued, although I think she left a lot of it out, the writing on the paper was so small and she only spoke for another minute tops.

Hearing Mary bawl like that nearly made me lose it too. I felt like it was kind of my fault that she had to feel that bad, but I bit down and did what I could to not let it bother me. I wasn't going to give the cops the satisfaction of seeing me cry.

When she finished, the minister asked us to rise. Connie and I stood, but Great Aunt Alice stayed seated, her hands propped on the top of her cane. The cemetery workmen stepped forward and began to undo the locks on the canvas straps, lowering the coffin slowly into the ground as the minister talked about dust to dust. The workmen expertly pulled the canvas straps from the grave and moved off to be unobtrusive. Mary continued to cry, and it kept making me feel worse, but I made it. All of the other funereal trappings were just trappings, things I had long ago internalized and drained of feeling.

The minister finished, and went around the grave. The rest of the little crowd broke up, and started to make their way back to the street where the line of cars was still facing further into the interior of the cemetery. Having been closest to the grave during the ceremony, I was one of the last to leave. Palmer had waited for me.

"Shem, it's been a hell of a month. Just a goddamn hell of a month."

"Yes," I said, not knowing what else to say.

"We still need to meet. Could you come around to my office sometime in the next few days? I'd like to sit and talk with you a minute, let you know what's going on with the estate."

"What's going on with the estate?"

"This isn't the place to go into it. It's just what we talked about on the phone. But since Joe died intestate it's not going to be quite as straightforward as it could be. We don't have to meet for long. You think you can swing by?"

"When do you want me?"

"Anytime is fine. Just drop in."

"Okay."

"You'll do that?"

"Okay."

"Good. Good." He paused, and his voice grew much more somber. "Shem, I'm so sorry."

I said nothing.

"It's been a real hell of a month." He clapped me on the back, rubbed once or twice, and then guided me forward with a hand on the back of my neck, leading us out. Healey and Dobrygowski were still by their car watching me, and when Healey saw that I was looking, he gave a little wave.

Great Aunt Alice and Connie stood at the end of the path at the edge of the road. "Shem, are you coming back with me or you going back with the hearse?" Great Aunt Alice asked.

Neither option would move quickly enough to avoid the detectives. The entire entourage had to drive forward before getting to a turnaround where they could head back. I was as good as trapped.

While I stalled, Palmer walked past us towards his car. Mary's parents had her in the front seat of their car, and I saw her father hand her a flask, and it made me feel awfully thirsty.

"Well?" Great Aunt Alice said.

The detectives started towards me, staying on the grass, out of the way of the mourners, but walking along until they were even with me. They stepped between the cars.

"Mr. Rosenkrantz." It was Detective Healey. "A word."

"Oh, enough's enough," Great Aunt Alice said. "If you catch us, you catch us, otherwise you can make your own way."

Healey and Dobrygowski were beside me then. "We won't be long, ma'am," Healey said, but Great Aunt Alice didn't even look at him. He turned to me. "I'm sorry to be doing it like this, Mr. Rosenkrantz. This isn't really the place for it."

"No, it isn't," I said. My stomach was in my throat, but I tried to make my expression fierce.

"It won't take a minute. You haven't heard anything of Ms. Abrams?"

"Ms. Abrams?" I said, and my shoulders dropped and my knees went weak. They weren't going to arrest me. Not just then anyway.

Dobrygowski gave a little 'huh' at that to show he was amused.

"You were staying with a Victoria Abrams at the Somerset," Healey said.

"Right. Vee." I turned to Dobrygowski, making sure to look him in the eyes. I just needed to be indignant, the way that anyone would be if the cops showed up at their son's funeral. "Maybe you remember all your friends by last name five minutes after you bury your son."

He held up his hands palms out in apology, but he didn't look sorry. "I didn't mean anything."

"He didn't mean anything," Healey said, giving him a chastising look. He turned back to me. "Have you heard from her?"

Up and down the row of cars, engines came to life.

"I haven't heard from Vee," I said, trying to decide how to play this. It was probably best not to deny the relationship, but to deny everything else. "I'm worried. Why? Is she okay?"

"Sure, she's fine," Dobrygowski said. "Just peachy."

"We don't know," Healey said. "We're looking for her."

"What's your relationship with Victoria Abrams?" Dobrygowski said.

"She's my girl—She, we're…We live together." I decided to switch back to anger. "What's this all about? You come out to the cemetery, pester me at my son's funeral, in front of all of my family, my friends."

"You don't really have much family left," Dobrygowski said.

"Listen, you," I said, forcing myself to take a step towards him, all the while my heart beating so hard I could hear the blood in my ears. "I've had just about enough—"

Healey put his hand out as if to block me. "You'll have to forgive Dobrygowski." He looked at his partner. "That was uncalled for."

Dobrygowski gave another 'huh.'

"Did you know that she also goes by the names Nancy Martin and Michelle Grant?" Healey said.

I swung around to face him. "How would I know? I don't know. She did?" It wasn't that much of a surprise that Vee had other names, but I was flustered by the fact just the same.

"We got a pretty interesting rap sheet from Cleveland on her."

I narrowed my eyes. "I don't care."

"Oh, but you might care about this," Dobrygowski said. "Yeah, I'm pretty sure you'll care. When 'Vee' went by Nancy Adams there was a fire in her house. This was in the suburbs right outside of Cleveland." I waited for it. "There was this fire and her husband was killed."

17.

They watched for a reaction to that. "Her husband?" I said, confused.

"You didn't know she was married before?"

"What do you mean before? I didn't know she was married ever."

A horn honked, and I jumped bringing my hand to my chest. The police looked back at the car we were standing in front of just as the car to our other side pulled away. The caravan was moving again. We stepped off onto the grass.

"Look, I need to go," I said. "I can't handle this right now."

"Of course, of course," Healey said. "Just a few more questions. We can take you anywhere you need when we're done."

I didn't like that, but it was probably better to get it over with.

They took my silence for assent. "So Vee, Nancy, Ms. Abrams. You didn't know about her husband."

"I just told you I'd never heard of Nancy whatever-you-said or this other name. I don't understand what this has to do with me."

"Please, don't get upset, Mr. Rosenkrantz. I know you've got a lot on your mind. We're sorry to have to tell you more."

"I don't understand," I said again, but then I flashed on it. Vee had used the murder/arson combination before. How could she be so stupid! I proceeded cautiously. "So what are you saying? Vee killed her husband and set the house on fire?"

"There were those who thought that," Dobrygowski said.

I looked at him, and he gave me a steel look back. I had been wrong to dismiss him as an oaf. If there was any danger of being found out, it would come from him, not Healey. Healey came on with all of the talking, but he was a good guy at heart. He didn't want to do it. It was just his job. I knew how that was. But Dobrygowski...I knew his kind too, they got an idea and they never let go.

"There was some question with the insurance company," Healey went on. "And the police there—it was just a small town—they just weren't sure, but they weren't going to give anything to that insurance company, so they wouldn't get behind the murder theory, and the insurance company paid up and that was that."

"Why are you telling me this?"

"Just that it's a funny coincidence," Dobrygowski said.

"Funny!" I flared, and I didn't care if I was overreacting.

Healey put his hand out again to restrain me. "He didn't mean anything by it, Mr. Rosenkrantz."

"I didn't mean anything by it," Dobrygowski said.

I took deep breaths and tried to count to ten in my head. If I lost my temper, I was liable to do something stupid.

"You've just become very rich," Dobrygowski said. "That must be some consolation to you."

"What consolation?"

"We spoke to Mr. Palmer," Healey said. "He told us that your son doesn't have a will. That you stand to come into a lot of money. The family might contest it, of course, but that's something."

I had to be careful here. "I just lost my son, and you're talking about money," I said.

"I'm sorry. I know it's crude. It's an unpleasant job."

"So I've heard," I said.

"You didn't know about the money?"

"Palmer just told me now. But not before."

They switched back to Vee.

"So you lived with Victoria Abrams?" Dobrygowski said.

"Why?" I said, narrowing my eyes.

"We just want to establish what she might have to gain."

So they knew. "Yes, we live together. In San Angelo."

"So she could expect to see some money if it came your way."

"She could, but she wouldn't be getting any. She won't be getting any."

"No?" Dobrygowski said.

I crumpled my features into a question. I needed to still look confused. I needed to be stupid.

"Do you know where Victoria Abrams is?" Healey said.

"No, I don't." It was technically true. They weren't asking where she had moved when we checked out. Just where she was now. "Why?"

"Can you believe this guy," Dobrygowski said.

I made as though it had just dawned on me then. "You think she killed my son and set his room on fire?"

There was an uncomfortable silence. "So you have no idea where she is?" Healey said.

And Dobrygowski jumped in, "Did you know her boyfriend was Carlton Browne, a well-known gangster here in Calvert? Her *other* boyfriend, I mean."

"I…" The caravan of cars had turned and was almost upon us on its way back out of the cemetery. "I…I'm sorry, I've told you what I know. And quite frankly, right now, I don't want to know any more of what *you* know."

"Why'd you leave the Somerset?" Healey said.

I stepped towards the road. Great Aunt Alice's car was almost upon us. "Because Vee's boyfriend found out about me," I said, my eyes on the cars.

Healey took a step towards me to try to recapture my attention. "So you think she's with Browne?"

Great Aunt Alice's car was abreast of us now, and slowed. I walked to the rear door, relieved to have an excuse to be done with them.

"Don't you want to know what happened to your son?" Healey said behind me.

I jerked open the front passenger door. "I know he's dead," I said. "Isn't that enough?" I slammed the door behind me. I could feel both detectives watching me as we pulled away, but I kept my eyes forward.

Yeah, I was stone cold. On the outside. But in fact I was badly shaken. Only days before it had sounded as though things were exactly as Vee had said they would be. Now it sounded like the police knew just about everything.

I got angry. Vee had done this before! Why hadn't she told me? How would I have handled it if she had? Badly. Very badly. Like I said, I'm not one for physical altercations, believe me, I'm not. But she still should have told me. Of course the police would put two and two together with something like that in her past. I thought Vee was too smart to make such an obvious mistake. But she had. She'd used the same ploy twice, and now they were on to her for it.

And then it hit me. They were on to *her* for it. They thought *she*'d done it. For all of Dobrygowski's innuendo, they had only asked about her. Because if they'd asked at the hotel, they'd know that I'd come back that night before the fire could have started. Because I had. And if the deskman told them that, he'd probably also told them that Vee had gone out. She'd had a car brought up from the garage. The garage people would remember that, too, that time of night. If the police thought Vee had done it, well, then part of her plan had worked. The important part. The part about me.

But probably it was just a matter of time until they stumbled upon me. And when they did, I was going to be arrested. And thinking more on it, I was pretty certain they had the death penalty in Maryland. Sure they did. I was going to die here, and there went all of the Rosenkrantzes in one fell swoop. No, not all. Clotilde in her clinic out west was one more. What would become of her?

I had to warn Vee. The way they'd get me for sure was if they got her. She'd spill everything, especially if she thought it might save her.

At Great Aunt Alice's I went right up to my room. I called the Somerset. The front desk answered after only one ring. "Somerset Hotel. How may I assist you?"

"I'd like to reach a party in Suite 12-2," I said. For some reason I knew that I shouldn't ask for Vee by name.

"Of course, sir."

There was a dead click, and then the phone was ringing. "Hello?"

It was a man's voice. I couldn't tell if it was Browne's or someone else's. My tongue was frozen. If it was Browne, the last thing Vee needed was for him to know I was calling. I hung up the phone without saying anything.

I lay back on the bed and tried to think it through, only my mind was caught on a loop thinking the same thing over and over. Vee needed to be moving, she needed to get out of Calvert, and she needed to get as far away as she could, because with that other incident in her past where she'd used arson to cover up murder, there was no way that they wouldn't try to hang Joe's death on her now. How could she be so stupid to use the same scheme? She needed to get out of Calvert. I needed to get through to her, and she needed to get moving. How could she be so stupid?

When it got where I couldn't stand it anymore, I tried the hotel again. Twice. And each time the desk would put me through to Browne's suite and a man would answer the phone and I'd hang up and start my worrying all over. After the third call, I decided that a whole bunch of hang-ups would be just as bad for Vee as if I were to say who was calling so I resigned myself to waiting until I saw her at our rendezvous the next day. And my thoughts circled and circled all night.

18.

The next day was overcast. Thick ash clouds blocked the sun, but they didn't do one thing to help with the heat. Instead they just trapped the humidity, making the day heavy and draining. I walked from Great Aunt Alice's and arrived at the Somerset ahead of our meeting with a sheen of sweat covering my whole body, my shirt stuck to my back. I took out my handkerchief and wiped my brow and the back of my neck and put it away. My nerves were as frayed as they could be, thinking on it all night, and the only thing that kept me from ducking into the bar for a drink was my heartburn, so bad I thought I might throw up.

Since I was early, I went to the desk to check if I had any messages. I'd asked for them to be forwarded to Great Aunt Alice's—that's how the police had found me last week—but I thought it was odd that I hadn't gotten any messages from *anybody*. I didn't recognize the man at the desk. They had an awful lot of people working there.

"I just checked out about a week ago," I said. "I was wondering if I had any messages that might not have reached me. My name's Shem Rosenkrantz. I was in room 514."

"One moment, sir," the deskman said with no change of expression. Then he turned and went through a door behind the counter.

I looked around nervously. Did the police have the lobby under surveillance? We probably didn't rate that much attention.

They had more important things to do than wait around for some woman who *might* have been involved in a death years earlier that *might* have been a murder. It was just my guilty conscience. But I felt exposed and I worried that I was making a mistake even if I didn't know what it was. At least checking my messages gave me a legitimate reason to be at the hotel.

The deskman came back, and said simply, "No messages, sir."

"No telegrams even?"

"I'm sorry, sir," he said.

No phone calls. No telegrams. I wouldn't need the money now that I had come into the Hadley estate, but still, the idea that my people in New York had forgotten me... All the work we'd done together over the years, all the books we'd published —and I had made them some money, my books had sold pretty well for a few years in there—the idea that a desperate telegram no longer elicited even a response, even a no. I had expected a no, but nothing...

I nodded, and forced a grin, though it didn't feel like it fit my face just then. "Well, thanks," I said.

"Of, course, sir."

I turned back to the lobby, and as I did, Browne went by with two other men in suits. They were intent on the door and didn't see me, but my heart rate jumped so fast I felt lightheaded. Browne scared me back into childhood. I was a killer now too, I reminded myself; so what if it had been an accident, with the police and my "motive," it had almost gotten to the point where that didn't matter, the whole thing confused in my mind the way it was. But with all that, I certainly didn't feel like any killer watching the gangster and his bodyguards stroll out of the hotel.

I swallowed and forced myself to move. I didn't want to give the deskman an extra reason to remember me, and standing around like a halfwit was exactly the kind of thing that might get remembered if someone made a point of asking. I started for the luncheonette, but after only a handful of steps it struck me, if Browne had gone out, that meant Vee would be alone on the twelfth floor. We could meet in Browne's suite, and that would be much better than meeting downstairs where anyone could see us and remember the two of us together. I hurried to the elevator, praying that we wouldn't miss each other as I went up to twelve and she went down to the lobby. I pushed the call button, and waited, watching the dial run down the numbers until it reached one, and a bell rang, then rang two more times in quick succession, and then the elevator door slid open.

A slender young mother ushered two children—a boy with Air Force insignia pins on his shirt and a girl in a dress with a bow—out into the lobby. Why had Clotilde and I never had any kids? She would have been such a beautiful mother. And now my only son...

I got in the elevator, and tried once again to organize my thoughts, how the police were onto her and she needed to get out of town. I jiggled with nervous energy, and when the elevator door opened on twelve, I practically ran to Suite 12-2. I knocked at the door, looking along the hallway, hoping to get inside before anyone else went by. When I heard no movement inside, I pounded with a closed fist, painfully aware of the sound traveling.

At last the door jerked open, Vee already saying, "What's the idea—" She was dressed in what was a modest dress for Vee. The bruise on her face had faded to a piebald mess of greens, yellows, purples, and blues. She registered that it was me and said "Jesus H. Christmas, Shem, what the hell's the matter with you? I said downstairs."

"I saw Browne leave and thought it would be better if we met up here out of sight." I pushed her back into the room and closed the door behind me. "We've got trouble."

" 'We've' got trouble? Ha!" She turned her back on me and stalked across the room. "*I'm* the one living like a prisoner." And she disappeared into the master bedroom. From there, she called, "What's this trouble, you bastard?"

I took a step towards the bedroom, and stopped. The sight of the place hit me hard, almost as if I had only just seen Browne beating on Vee, and my mouth went dry.

"Hello? Idiot! Back here!"

I followed her voice back to the bedroom. She was sitting on the edge of the bed, reaching down to sling a pair of black and white heels over her stockinged feet.

"This is the last time I let you pimp me out to a gangster. You nearly got me killed the other night, you know that?"

"Will you lay off of me on that. I'm not a pimp."

She ignored that. "Did you talk to the lawyer yet? You find out when you'll be getting that money? Then I can get out of here."

How had this conversation gotten away from me? I was there for a reason. "You need to go now," I said, but it came out weak.

"And wait for you like a fool, just hoping you show up with the money? Right." She stood up and went over to the bureau, where she picked up a silver pendant earring and cocked her head to put it on.

"Vee, the police…"

She paused, her head still turned to the side. "What about

the police?" Her features grew pinched, and if I didn't know before, I knew right then that I could not let Vee hang around and get caught under any circumstances. Because even if right now the police genuinely thought that Vee had acted alone, once they had her in custody she'd be quick to set them straight about that. Hell, she'd probably have a way of putting me in the hot seat without her in it at all. She'd show that broken face of hers and say that I had done that to her if she didn't go and clean up Joe's body. That's exactly what she'd say, and then I'd be right back in it, on my way to death row. If she left, I could sit easy waiting for the money while they chased Vee around the country.

"Shem, you tell me what the hell about the police right this instant."

"You need to get out of here. You need to leave right away."

"Shem—"

"Were you married?"

Her eyes narrowed. "What?"

"The police came to Joe's funeral yesterday. They wanted to know where you were. They say you killed and burned your husband."

"My husband?" Her arms had turned to gooseflesh. With just the one earring hanging, her head looked lopsided.

"In Denver. No. Cleveland."

"What else did they say?"

"They know Joe's skull was fractured. They said they aren't sure it was murder, but…"

"But they brought up Cleveland. Paul. That was years ago." She started forward, but stopped, not sure where she was going.

"Did you kill your husband?" I said.

That woke her back up. She grabbed the other earring. "You don't know what he was like, so don't you even start. And what does it matter to you anyway?"

She wasn't saying no, and even though I knew the answer was yes, I began to feel uneasy with the idea of her running, where I wouldn't know where she was, and I'd worry each minute we were apart.

"Paul had no vision," Vee said. She went to the armoire and pulled out a handful of clothes on their hangers and threw them onto the bed. "He was keeping me trapped in that little town, and a girl can only take that for so long, you know? But he just wouldn't listen."

"What are you doing?"

"What am I doing? I'm leaving. I'm getting the hell out of this city. I'm not stupid. If they're talking about Paul, it's because they want to hang your kid on me too, and I'm not getting sent up for something I didn't have anything to do with."

Hearing her say it, that she was going to leave, that she was doing what I wanted her to do, suddenly filled me with an even greater sense of dread.

She dumped more clothing onto the bed and pulled out a suitcase. "You better get out of here. Carlton's supposed to be out all day, but you never know with him."

That threat didn't even stir me. My mind was trying to catch on something. Something I hadn't thought through in the whole night of thinking. "Where will you go?" I said.

"Who cares? Not here."

Yes, 'who cares?' That was Vee. I knew then what I had probably already known. Even if she ran, they would catch her.

She had her bag half packed, and was forcing stuff into it with no regard.

Yeah, they would catch her, because if she ran it would look guilty as anything, and they'd put everything into catching her. "You can't run," I said.

She looked at me and put her hands on her hips. "You're the one who said I should leave."

"I was wrong. I hadn't thought it through. They'll think for sure you did it then, if you run."

"So I'm supposed to wait right where they probably know where I am. That's your brilliant idea."

I was desperate suddenly for a way to keep her from walking out the door. "You can't leave me," I said.

"Oh, Mr. Sentimental. You got my face beat in and then got me tangled up in a murder. I should have left you the day I met you. You'd have thought I'd never been around the block before, starstruck for a has-been writer. All because one of your books made me cry as a girl."

"I got the money."

That stopped her. She did want that money. "What do you mean you got the money?"

"I got the money. I'm getting it. The whole two million, it's mine. Now that Joe's dead." I knew she wouldn't be able to resist the money, just like I knew they'd catch her when she ran, and she'd pull me into it.

"You're sure?"

I nodded.

She blinked rapidly, and shook her head. "How long till you get it?" She spoke deliberately, as though she was afraid I might skitter away if she talked too suddenly.

"I don't know. I'm meeting with the lawyer soon. Today maybe. These things take time. Maybe a week or two. Certainly by the end of the month."

"The end of the month!"

"It'll be sooner than that." I had no idea how long it would be, but as badly as I needed her to run before, I needed to keep her there with me now.

Her face was dead serious as she looked at me across the clothing-strewn bed. "I want us to get married," she said.

I almost laughed at that one. Married! I couldn't even believe she'd been married before I knew her. And she killed that guy. "I can't. I'm still married to Clotilde."

"You can get a divorce. She's in the loony bin."

I shook my head. "I'm not getting a divorce."

"Well, something. I need to know that I'll get my cut of what's coming."

"You'll get your cut," I said. I saw in her eyes that I had her hooked. I'd be able to keep her where I could watch her. Having killed Joe was already nearly killing me, my whole chest on fire from reflux, but I wasn't going to sit in any electric chair.

"Fifty-fifty."

"We'll see."

"Fifty-fifty," she said again. "It's my neck hanging out there."

I saw then what you probably saw at the start. They'd get her if she stayed or if she left.

"Sure. Of course," I said. "That's fair."

She searched my face, still wary. "You know what I'd do to you if you cross me."

"I'd never cross you."

She was reluctant, but she must have decided that was the best she was going to get right then. She started putting clothing back into the armoire. I watched her do it, and I was suddenly more exhausted than I'd ever been in my life. Exhausted because there was only one way I would know she wouldn't talk, and being in the room with her after thinking that, well, it just got real hard. Carrying my body around seemed like a horrible inconvenience. My head was falling off my neck and my eyelids were like quarters over my eyes. I wanted to lie down and never get up again. Because I had to kill her, and that was worse even than thinking about how I'd already killed Joe.

"I'm so tired," I said.

She went around the bed and sat down at the vanity. "So get out. Go home, sleep."

I could tell by the way she said it that she was still awfully unsettled by the fact that the police were asking about her and bringing up what she thought was ancient history. If her nerves could be rattled so easily... Killing her really was my only choice.

"It's going to be all right," I said.

"I know that," she said. "I'm probably safer with Carlton than anywhere else anyway. The cops wouldn't touch one of Carlton's girls." She folded a tissue, put it between her lips, and closed her mouth quickly and opened it, blotting her lipstick.

As she talked I felt heavier and heavier. Could Browne really protect her from a murder charge? And what about protecting her from him? He'd attacked her at the sight of me. I had a feeling he wouldn't take it too kindly if he knew where she had gone afterwards, what she had done with me. Men like Carlton Browne don't let any of the dirty work get anywhere near them, so they always have deniability, and this was right up next to him.

Vee finished her makeup, stood, and turned to me. "Well, how do I look?" The bruise was still visible, but it wasn't as pronounced. Even with the puffiness on that side of her face, she looked like a million bucks. She knew what she had, and she knew how to use it.

"Like a killer," I said.

She laughed, a big open-mouthed laugh, throwing her head back to really get it out there. "Come here. Let me give you a present." I didn't move, and she pouted a little, but then she came over to me. She gave me a kiss on the cheek. It made me think that there was no way I'd ever be able to go through with it.

Then, with her mouth right near my ear. "Who was that girl you were with the other day?"

I looked at her, incredulous, and I knew I'd be able to kill her after all. "You're all dolled up for some other man, and you're going to be jealous?"

Her face turned mean again. "That's work, and you know it. Carlton expects me to be on call."

"That was Joe's fiancée," I said.

Her expression softened. "Is that why her face was all runny? Oh little girl, you've got a lot to learn." And she laughed her ugly laugh again, and I could have killed her right then if I knew how to do it without putting me in it.

"I better go," I said.

"We ought to celebrate," she said.

"Celebrate?"

"The money," she said. "We can have a lunch in the dining room. I think that's safe enough, don't you?"

"I don't know."

"Yes, it is. Just give me a couple of hours to get myself together. I need to, I don't know, untwist my mind. Two million dollars! Sweet Mary! I always knew I deserved this." And she kissed me again and then that horrible laugh. It made my stomach turn over. "Ha! Two million dollars. My luck's really changing now."

"Yeah, sure," I said, thinking, if only she knew. "Noon, we'll say. Downstairs. I'm going now."

"Wait," she said, and she stepped forward, and wiped some lipstick from my cheek. It was such a gentle gesture, and it made me sick. Because sure I'd killed Joe, but that was an accident. And this... This wouldn't be.

She stepped back. "Okay," she said.

But nothing was okay. Nothing.

19.

The thing about killing is… You see, when you've decided to kill someone… What am I trying to say? I think I mentioned that Joe wasn't the first person I'd seen who'd met a violent end. I had a girlfriend, a girl I knew, back when I could get a little work in Hollywood, even if it was only because Clotilde pulled some strings. This girl, she was a waitress at a nightclub with aspirations to Hollywood stardom. What I'm saying is that she was one of thousands of girls out in S.A. who all are waiting for their moment to come, convinced they'll be discovered, that someone on the street will stop them, and say, 'You oughta be in pictures.' Yeah, this girl was just a dime a dozen, but I'd met her, and I started seeing her, and I even got her cast in one of Clotilde's pictures. I've always been a real upstanding guy, huh?

Clotilde was starting to have more and more trouble with her nerves, jumping at shadows, playing the wronged woman, convinced that a slew of people were out to get her, including me. It didn't matter that I actually *was* stepping out with this other girl, the point is, I'd never have done anything to hurt Clotilde. I mean it. She was always the joy of my life, the one thing that mattered, and if I was going out with this other girl, it was only because I couldn't help it, I just needed something Clotilde couldn't give me, suffering the way she was.

Now that I think of it, that was about the time I started borrowing money from Hub Gilplaine. He owned the nightclub

where I met this girl, and we were friends... Gee, it's funny
how the pattern of your life gets stitched from all these different threads, none of which seem important at the time, just
day-to-day living, and then someone starts worrying one of
those threads, just gives it a little pull, and your whole life starts
to unravel. But maybe it was before that even, back when Quinn
and I were still married...

Anyway, I went over to this waitress' house in San Angelo,
late one night, and I let myself in with my key, and I went into
her bedroom, and there she was, all cut up and blood everywhere. It was a thousand times worse than what happened to
Joe. I shriveled up then. Anyone would have, even the toughest
cold-blooded murderer on death row. And I was just an effete
writer who told himself he was hardboiled but really wasn't
anything but a husk of a man, if that.

So I've seen the worst, and the only thing that made Joe as
bad as all that was that I did it myself. Now I was planning to do
it for real, on purpose, and it just about was all I could do to
make myself think about it. Because if you thought too much
about it, how a person was a body, just a biological machine that
was, honestly, quite easy to break, but a person was also so
much more, the stuff that all of the world's religions and artists
and writers had spent all of human existence trying to understand... Well, you see where your mind starts to go. It had been
that way for a long time after my girlfriend got cut up with me
trying to understand what and why. And now it was like that in
thinking about Vee, and what I needed to do. I had to kill her. It
was the only way I'd be safe. But my mind kept slipping back
to that cut-up girl in S.A., and I couldn't think straight, even if
I knew I *had* to think it out or I'd end up in a jam over Vee's
death too.

Well, there's no surprise that I was doing all of this thinking in the hotel bar, but I was tossing back far fewer than you would have thought. I was hardly even buzzed. I played out different scenarios. Getting Vee out of the hotel into a bad part of the city and making it look like a mugging. Only that was just improbable enough that the police would probably know she'd been killed to shut her up. Throwing her down the stairs. But why hadn't she used the elevator? Any good cop would find that too suspicious. I didn't know anything about poisons, didn't know much more about weapons. And it needed to look like an accident.

It didn't help that with each plot, the blood from that long-ago night in S.A. kept trying to drown out all of my thoughts. The only reason I hadn't been a suspect then was because I had a good alibi. Even if I could orchestrate a good alibi for Vee's death, it still might seem convenient enough to reinvigorate the investigation into Joe's death, which left me at risk. The police had to be certain that Joe had been murdered by Vee. These ideas twisted and curled in my mind, spiraling out questions that hit brick walls, banging up against them again and again, as I tried in vain to find an answer, increasingly anxious that I didn't have one.

And that was a familiar feeling. The steady flow of ideas discarded one by one, with each failure constricting me further and further in inaction. That was writing. Killing someone was a whole lot like writing, a creative endeavor. I was trying to manipulate characters to do what I wanted them to do while trying to figure out how it would all play out afterwards to get the effect I wanted. I was anxious, but a part of me enjoyed what I was doing. And with that realization, a door opened up in my mind to show me new space—it didn't have to be an accident if it was suicide.

But Healey and Dobrygowski thought she'd done it for the money. Why would she then kill herself? Maybe if she knew they were on to her, especially if they brought up that old husband case. It had really given her pause when I told her about that. Yeah, she found out they were on to her, and she killed herself.

Well, by the time I had it worked out that far, it was almost noon and I had to meet Vee for lunch in the main dining room. I didn't like that we'd be so exposed, but I couldn't do anything that would arouse her suspicion, and skipping our celebratory lunch would have done just that. Before I left, I put my plan into action. If I was going to do it, I ought to do it. I asked the bartender for a phone. He brought it to me, and retreated discreetly.

I had the operator put me through to the *Sun*. "Taylor Montgomery please." The switchboard did whatever it does, and Montgomery answered in a voice that sounded much gruffer than in person. "Montgomery here."

"Taylor, son, it's Shem Rosenkrantz."

His voice softened into the fawning young man I knew. "Mr. Rosenkrantz! What can I do for you?"

"Would the paper be interested in running a follow-up on Joe's death? The police think it was a murder now."

"Oh no, that's horrible," he said, genuinely pained.

I made sure to increase the sorrow in my own voice, although it was probably unnecessary. "They think this woman I know, Victoria Abrams, did it. She apparently did the same thing in Cleveland a while back under a different name. Killed her husband and burned the house down."

"Abrams, you said?" He was writing it down.

"Victoria Abrams." If the police found out I'd made this call,

planting the story would look bad for me, so I made my intentions very clear. "If this woman did this thing, I want her nailed
for it, and I don't trust the police to carry it through. But if the
Sun runs a story about it, maybe something'll actually get done."

"Of course, of course," Montgomery said, his voice somewhat muffled, so I knew he was holding the receiver with his
shoulder, using both hands to write or check a file or something.

"Will they let you run it? It's not big news, I know."

"They'll run it. You're still a celebrity and the Hadleys are a
big deal in this town, even if they are on the way down. I
mean—"

"No offense taken."

"I'll make sure they run it."

"Good. And check on this thing in Cleveland."

"As soon as we hang up the phone," he said.

"That a boy." And we rang off. I knew he'd do all that he
could to get it on page one of the city section. And it would be
thorough and it would be damning and I would be an innocent
victim, and me a great man. And if Vee was guilty in the paper,
it hardly mattered if she was guilty or not, the police would
have to do something. At least, that's what Vee would think.
And that's why she was going to kill herself. A stretch, but a
plan. I felt the high of a good writing session, the same energy
and self-assurance, as I left the bar to cross the hotel lobby.

We arrived at the dining room at exactly the same time. She'd
changed again, now wearing a royal blue tea dress with an oversized white belt cinched around her waist, an outfit I'd never
seen before that was no doubt a gift from Browne. She tried to
look demure, biting her lip to keep from smiling and failing. All
her teeth came out in a huge sappy grin. She moved towards

me, but then checked herself. She might have thrown Browne
over in her head, but she couldn't be seen getting too familiar
with another man just yet. I felt the same way, my confidence
waning, worried that the police had their eyes on us right then.

"Mr. Rosenkrantz," Vee said.

"You look stunning, Vee," I said.

She actually hung her head at the compliment. "I'm glad you
think so," she said, and then stepped forward and took my arm.
"Well, I guess I can be escorted by a gentleman friend without
anyone thinking anything of it."

Despite her hanging on me like that, I was surprised to find
that I didn't actually feel anything about what I planned to do
to her later. It was as though that part of me was closed off,
protected from what I was doing right then. I led her into the
dining room.

They sat us at a four-person table in the center of the room.
The lighting from the chandeliers was just enough to see by,
augmented by a shaded candlestick in the center of the table,
which cast a flickering circle on the tablecloth. A good number
of tables were filled with hotel guests and maybe some locals
there for the cuisine. Tuxedoed waiters moved quickly between
the tables. Jacketless Negro food runners and busboys carried
platters at shoulder height.

I held the chair for her like we were two regular people, and
then sat across from her. She leaned forward, and the candle lit
her face from below as though she were telling a ghost story at
a campfire. "We're gonna eat at places like this all the time,"
she said, "and I won't have to sleep with any more gangsters to
do it. We're coming up in the world finally."

"I've been up in the world. This is still coming down for me."

She crunched her face into a pout. "Well, excuse me, Mr. Big-time New York Writer. Not all of us had movie star wives and vacationed on the Riviera."

I shouldn't have done that to her, taken the air out of her balloon. She had a right to be happy for a little while. But I felt like being mean for some reason. I said, "*Have* a movie star wife. I'm still married to her."

Her face turned into that familiar hard-boiled stare, and she said, "I'm your woman now, you got that? I don't want to hear about any wife or anybody. We're in this thing together. That money's mine just as much as it is yours."

"Oh, just the two of us? But I know you're always for hire. If we're each other's one and only, how are you going to ditch your boyfriend?"

"You pimp—" she started, but she saw where this was going, and she visibly stopped, closed her eyes and took a deep breath. "Let's just forget all of that," she said. "This is a chance for us to start again."

Seeing her try so hard like that really made me feel like scum, and I said, "Of course. You're right." I reached across the table and gave her hand a squeeze.

Her expression softened, and soon she was smiling. She laughed to herself, and I knew she was thinking about all that money that was hers.

I grabbed a passing waiter and ordered a Gin Rickey. Vee asked for a Manhattan. Then we both fell silent over our menus. And the whole thing felt perfectly natural. We were a wealthy couple enjoying a wealthy meal in a wealthy hotel. It's true that there was a time in my life when that was a regular occurrence, but just then, I couldn't help but feel as though we were playacting.

And that started me wondering if I was playacting at the other thing also, but…I couldn't think about that right then. I couldn't risk Vee thinking something was up.

And then suddenly, a loud voice cut through the room from the doorway, and I turned to see Carlton Browne striding for our table.

20.

He came at us, with the maître d' following him.

"Would you look at that," Browne said. "It's your cousin, Vee." He emphasized the word 'cousin' as though it were a shared password that should be taken to mean something else. He came right up to me and gripped me around the arm where Joe's ice pick had sliced me. The pain shot through my arm. I sucked in and held my breath as my stomach turned. "This really is a small hotel, huh? How you doing?" He ground his fingers into my bicep leaving no doubt that he knew exactly what he was doing.

He looked at the maître d', who was standing a few steps back, his hands out and his mouth open as though he were trying to catch something delicate. "I'll join this table. How about a bottle of red and a bottle of white? And a scotch for me. Anyone else?" He looked between Vee and me, then turned to the maître d'. "A scotch for both the men." He released my arm, and I let out my breath.

"We've already ordered drinks," Vee said.

"Good. So you'll have some more." He took the chair to my right with Vee on his right. "You don't mind. The lady and I like to sit together."

Vee kept her eyes on the tablecloth, her hands fidgeting with the napkin in her lap.

I did what I could to avoid looking at Browne, which wasn't much. He was younger than I had thought, no more than forty, probably younger. He was balding, his hairline eroded in two fierce arches from his forehead back to the top of his head. He was big in every way, tall, muscular, and fat, if you can imagine that.

Our drinks came, and I took half of mine in one gulp.

"It's funny us all being here like this," Browne said. He seemed to revel in our discomfort. "Huh, Vee?" He gave her a playful tap on the chin with a closed fist, but the intent was far from playful, carrying what it did behind it. "Sorry, what was your name?" he said, turning to me. "I was a little distracted the other night, I'm not sure I got it."

"Shem Rosenkrantz," I said.

He frowned. "That's a Jew name, isn't it? Vee, I didn't know you were a Jew."

"I'm not," Vee said, leading with her whole body. "You see—"

He raised a hand, silencing her without even looking at her. "Sure, sure. It's not important. We're all white. What's it matter? Still, I'd like to have known you were a Jew, Vee. You should have told me that."

Vee looked at her hands in her lap. A small ring of silence had fallen at the tables around us, like Browne sucked all of the energy out of his surroundings.

"So how are you related? I'm still not clear on that," Browne said.

"Carlton—" Vee started.

He sneered at her. "I wasn't asking you. Was I asking you?" She said nothing, her head down, chastised. "You'd think you could knock some sense into her, huh?" He grabbed her bicep as he had grabbed mine, and Vee's face turned sour, and she looked away from him. I had never seen her so cowed, and it frightened me even more than Browne's patter. When the maître d' set down our Scotches, and then turned to a busboy behind him holding the bottles of wine, I picked up my Gin Rickey and drank the rest of it down.

"Shem Rosenkrantz…" Browne said, ignoring the wait staff and still holding Vee by the arm. "Oh, wait, did I read something in the paper about your son getting killed?"

"My son died, yes," I said. "But he wasn't killed."

"Oh, sure. I read the paper," and he gave me an exaggerated frown. "But I get the real news, too. Outside the paper. He was killed and someone tried to burn his body."

I tried to tell if he was just talking or if he knew something. It made me nervous, and as I shifted in my seat, I tried to catch Vee's eye to see if she had told him, but she was sitting with her eyes down like a kid in trouble with her folks.

Browne leaned back, and grabbed a passing busboy by the sleeve. "I want to order," he said.

"I'll find your waiter, sir," the busboy said.

"I don't want you to find my waiter. I want you to tell him. Whatever's not on the menu, that's what we want. All around." He spun his finger to indicate the whole table.

"Yes, sir," the busboy said, nodding more than he needed to.

"Ha. 'Sir.' And they say kids aren't learning any manners these days. You're smart, kid, you'll go far if you keep that up." He released the boy, who hurried back in the direction of the kitchen.

Browne grabbed a bottle of wine, and poured Vee a glass before filling his own. "That's tough about your son," he said to me. He shook his head. "Nothing's more important than family. I've got three little angels myself, and they're my whole world. Ask Vee, she'll tell you. I talk about 'em all the time, don't I?" He waited. "Don't I?"

"He does," Vee said, as though she needed to plead his case to me.

"You see that. I talk about 'em all the time, because there's nothing more important than family. Isn't that right, Rosy?"

I exhaled through my nose.

"Yeah, you're in mourning. I see that. If anything happened to my kids, I'd kill the bastard who did it. I mean with my own hands, right here, I'd kill him."

The comment made me think about how all three of us at the table had killed someone at some point, and I was planning to do it again. This was what my life had become.

I drank, while Browne stared at me intently. I was supposed to speak. "I feel like my life is over," I said, and I really did. I'd probably have been happy if Browne'd stood up and shot me right there. Not that he'd ever do that, he was too cagey for that. That's why he could sit out in public like this, like a respected citizen, because he was a respected citizen. Nothing ever stuck to him.

"You always feel like that," Vee said, deciding that the best course of action was to ridicule me, which she had a lot of practice doing despite our newfound camaraderie.

"Hey," Browne snapped. "He's in mourning."

"But he does. He whines about everything—"

"If you don't shut it," Browne said, "I'm gonna shut it for you." He brandished his fist. Then turning to me: "You tell me about your son. I want to hear. It'll be good for you to talk. I've learned that the hard way. You can't keep it all pent up inside you. Go on, tell me."

I looked at Vee. She looked like she was going to throw up at any moment. She crossed her arms, and rubbed as though she were cold.

"What can I say? I never really knew Joe," I said.

Browne was nodding with deep understanding.

"He lived with his mother all his life. I wasn't even there when he was born. I think he was maybe two when I saw him the first time. It seems stupid now. Stupid that I didn't know him. But I guess I would say that my parents didn't know me, and I grew up right in the same house with them. They could never understand my love of books. But they read everything I wrote and were proud of me, even if they didn't understand them."

"You're a writer, huh? What do you write?"

"Novels. Movies."

"What movies?"

I shook my head and shrugged.

He didn't seem to care that I didn't have an answer. "My mother lives with us now," he said. "You got to keep the whole family together, tight." He reached over and patted Vee on the cheek. The gesture was to show ownership. "You don't even have a mother, do you, Vee? Nah, no mother'd let her baby be like you." He looked back at me. "You can't even imagine loving somebody until you have a kid. You can hardly love a woman," he said. "Maybe your brother. It's family, always family." He looked me straight in the eye. "We never know what we've got when we've got it, and we always kill what means the most to us, huh?"

I still couldn't tell if he knew, if Vee had told him. He seemed to be needling me purposely, going on about family, making the remarks about killing, like he really wanted to get to me, to see if I'd crack. Was it possible that he was afraid of being caught up in the murder if it went the wrong way? Nah, he couldn't worry about that in this town. Nothing would come near him. He wanted to tear me down because I had violated his space, and it was certain he knew about Vee's and my true relationship.

The food was brought over, a team of three men, two carrying plates, and the chef himself standing next to Mr. Browne with his hands clenched together. He went through a detailed description of what was being served, but I didn't hear any of it, and I don't think Browne or Vee did either. When the serving team had left, Browne dug right in. Apparently there was no talking while eating, and since Browne had fallen silent, neither of us was going to make any attempt at small talk.

I finished my scotch and had several glasses of wine too. As Browne was wiping up his plate with a piece of bread he said in a quiet, measured voice, "Rosy. You're sleeping with my mistress and you've been living the high life on my dime." Vee and I froze. "I could have you killed tonight if I wanted to, but you've already taken a pretty bad blow, and you're set to take another at any moment."

I knew then that he knew, and I knew my life was over.

"You know," he said, and took a gulp of wine, "you and I have a mutual friend."

My stomach boiled. I could feel it in the back of my throat.

"Great guy, out in S.A."

I knew what he was going to say before he said it, and now I knew who had bought up my debt.

"Hub Gilplaine," he said.

I felt my face grow slack.

He took another gulp of wine, nodding to indicate he was still going to say something. "Vee tells me that you just came into some money. She said something about two million dollars."

He paused for me to say something, but I couldn't even swallow, my mouth was so dry.

"Now, really, I don't care who Vee sleeps with, I'd be crazy if I did. If it was my wife, I'd kill you both, but Vee, she's not wife material. She just needs to know who's boss. And you know who, right, honey?"

Vee looked like she might cry. I'd never seen her like that. She was the strongest, loudest, most demanding woman I'd ever met, and I'd met a lot of loud women. But I knew now that she could be beaten, in both the literal and metaphorical sense, and that my concern over her setting me up for a fall should she take a tumble was absolutely correct. Yes, she had to die. That Browne had gotten it out of her was trouble enough. Now neither of us was going to see any of that money.

"I've got a wife too," I said.

"Good for you. Remind me to send her a present."

"She's sick. She needs to stay in the hospital. It's very expensive."

"I'm crying on the inside."

"Please." I thought about all his talk about family. "She's the only family I've got left," I tried.

"We'll take that into consideration," he said. "Now, you owe me five hundred thousand dollars."

"But I only owed fifteen grand to Hub," I said, and could hear I was whining.

"Let me explain to you how this works," Browne said. "When someone buys up your debt, it's like refinancing your house. The deal changes. And you owe me five hundred thousand dollars."

I didn't say anything.

He stood. "I'll give you a little time for the estate to come through, but if I don't get my money on that day, it goes up by five grand a day until I get it, because you're gonna have the dough." He stood, and put his hand on the back of Vee's neck. "That leaves you some for your wife's hospital bills, right?" Vee winced, and I knew he had tightened his fist. "You didn't think you were getting any of that money, did you, Vee?"

She looked across at me, and her eyes were shiny with tears. "No."

"Of course not," he said. She winced again. "There's something I've got to go see about. You'll be in the room when I get back." It was an order. "Here's the key." He dropped it beside her, and I remembered I still had the other key to the room. Either he didn't remember or he didn't care about getting it back. Instead, he looked at me, and said, "Stay. Enjoy some coffee. Dessert. It's all on me. I think it's going to be nice doing business with you, Rosy." He raised his voice. "Excellent as always," he said to no one in particular, and he wove his way through the tables and out the door.

The two of us sat in silence. It was as though I'd been hit by a truck. I was so despondent I wished I actually *had* been hit by a truck. I thought about going out into the street to see if it could be arranged. *Wham!* Goodbye troubles.

At last, Vee stood up, threw her napkin on the table, and walked out without a word.

I just kept sitting, looking at nothing, and wishing I were dead.

21.

I sat there a long time. It wasn't until the third time the waiter came around to offer me coffee that I could look him in the eye when I shook my head no.

But that wasn't good enough for him. He was a real sentimentalist. "Are you all right, sir?"

I couldn't do more than press my lips together and shrug over and over, exposing my palms again and again: I don't know, I don't know. I was on the verge of tears.

"Take your time." And he stepped away.

My mind circled. I needed to get out of Calvert. Healey and Dobrygowski wouldn't like it, it would look suspicious, but I wasn't going to risk any more time in the city than I needed to. Browne could get at me too easily if I stayed. Five hundred thousand dollars! What was I going to do? Palmer had said I was getting some money from the estate, but I certainly didn't know if it was going to be that much. Sure, it was *supposed* to be two million, but it wasn't in the bank yet. And the will might still be contested, and there would be legal fees… How could Hub do this to me? I was going to pay him back! We were supposed to be friends. And just like that, my fear turned to rage—I wanted to kill Hub. I wanted to kill Browne, and Vee, and everyone else. I wanted to kill them all.

But I couldn't think like that. It was thinking like that that would get me all fouled up. I'd had too much to drink with lunch. I needed to get straight.

I looked around. Most of the lunch crowd had left, and busboys were clearing tables into a bin on a rolling cart. My waiter hovered a few tables away, watching me. I gave a weak smile and nod, pulled myself together, and got up to leave.

In the lobby, I stood halfway between the elevator bank and the front entrance, unsure where to go and what to do. My anger had drained off, leaving me exhausted, and now there was only one thought running through my head: I needed to get out of town if I wanted to live.

But what about Vee? I couldn't trust Vee. And I couldn't bring her with me. That would look far too suspicious. I thought of my original plan, before this lunch fiasco, the decision I'd made with a clear head, not out of anger. For peace of mind, to at least neutralize the risk of the police, Vee had to die. If there had been any doubt before, I didn't have the luxury to entertain it now. Now it needed to happen and fast. Tonight. And I needed to figure the way to do it.

That's what I was thinking as I stood there, working out again why Vee needed to die, when all of a sudden I got the feeling that I was being watched. I hated that feeling. It reminded me of Clotilde's paranoia, and it always made me worry about my own mental health. But I just couldn't shake it. So I scanned the lobby, and zeroed in on a man sitting in one of the overstuffed easy chairs across from the front desk. He wore a tailored suit and had one foot resting on the opposite knee, with a paper spread out before him on his lap. I watched him, and I was certain that his eyes kept darting up from the paper, focusing on me. Did the police have me under surveillance? That would be bad. That would be very bad.

I turned suddenly and went out the revolving doors, and hurried across the street into the First Calvert City Bank. It was a large edifice, the ceiling rising three stories above with two exposed balconies hanging over the tellers. A line of people, men and women, stood watching the "Next Teller" sign light and ring and following its command like Pavlov's dogs. I turned my back on them, and stepped over to a chest-high counter that ran along the front windows, where I pretended to make out a withdrawal slip. I kept my eyes on the hotel's entrance, waiting for the man I had seen to come out after me, expecting him any moment.

I waited long enough to fill out the withdrawal slip ten times, but he never appeared, nor did anyone else who seemed on the lookout for where I had gone. This worried me almost as much as if he had followed me. Maybe I really was going crazy like Clotilde. People who decide to kill other people aren't sane, right? But thinking like that wasn't going to get done what needed to get done. So I pushed it away into the same corner of my head where I'd hidden Joe's death as best as possible, and made a pact with myself to wait another five minutes, measuring them on my watch.

After three minutes no one had appeared and I'd had enough. I left the bank and began to wander the streets with no clear plan, but heading uptown towards Great Aunt Alice's all the same. Halfway there it occurred to me, if the man at the Somerset wasn't a cop, maybe he was one of Browne's men. I tried to place him as one of the men I'd seen walking out with Browne that morning, but my mental image of them was almost nonexistent. Browne had been alone when he came into the dining room, and he'd been alone the night I'd...visited him. So it was just as likely that he didn't have men with him all of the time. And I didn't even know for sure that the man in the lobby had been looking at me.

My thoughts chased one another like that, and I traversed the
blocks without seeing the city around me. I was lost again in the
same way I got when writing. I could thank Taylor Montgomery
for that. He had reawakened my creative impulse after it had
remained unexercised so long, and now I was putting it to good
use. In a way, he was responsible for my new career as a criminal.
He was even setting Vee up for me with the article in tonight's
evening paper. That made him practically an accomplice. I
started to feel guilty about leaving him, what with how important my interest in his writing was to him. A blow to a writer's
optimism like that could set him back years. I promised myself
I'd write him a letter before I left. If I left...if I...no, when I
left. After I'd done this one last difficult thing.

I got to Great Aunt Alice's then. Connie let me in. Her expression at the sight of me was one of heavy concern. I must have
looked worse than I knew, and I wondered if it was my fear or
my new grim conviction that showed. It could have just been
the day's liquor.

"Will you be to dinner tonight, Mr. Shem?" she asked.

"I can't say that I know," I said.

"Mrs. Hadley is wanting to see you and she was hoping you
would be to dinner."

Great Aunt Alice. I couldn't handle Great Aunt Alice on top of
everything else just then. But I was staying in her house, eating
her food... I bit the bullet. "I could see her now," I said, taking
the attitude that the sooner it was started, the sooner it would
be over.

"Mrs. Hadley is indisposed for the rest of the afternoon. She
really hoped you'd be to dinner."

I tried to smile, but it wasn't in me. "I'll see what I can do," I
said, and went upstairs without waiting for another exchange.

The last thing I needed was to worry about what Great Aunt Alice and Connie thought of me.

In my room, I retrieved my duffel bag from beneath the bed, and started pulling my clothes out of the closet and stuffing them in without any semblance of order. It couldn't have been more than five minutes before I was packed and ready to go. I stood beside the bed, supporting some of my weight by leaning on the duffel bag with two of my fingers. I stood that way for three or four, oh, I don't know how many minutes, and asked myself again why I couldn't just pick up and leave right then. It was twenty to two.

I picked up the phone with the intention of calling the Enoch White clinic and getting Clotilde on the line. She'd remind me what I was doing this for. Just hearing her voice, the relief and good will she'd had when I told her we'd gotten the money, that would shore up my nerve. But instead of dialing California, I found myself calling Joe's girl Mary.

A maid answered the phone. How come you could never get anybody just straight? She put the phone down, and I could hear the echoing sounds of her walking away, and then a door closing. There were some loud clanks as the receiver was picked up, and Mary said, "All right, Louise," another clank as the maid set the receiver back into the cradle, and then, "Mr. Rosenkrantz, I'm so glad you called."

I let out my breath, and found that I didn't know what I had intended to say to her. "Mary, I'm so sorry," I said, and it came out as a sob. What was I doing? Was I going to break down and throw it all away? I shook my head, regaining control of my voice. "I'm sorry," I said again.

"No, I'm sorry, Mr. Rosenkrantz. I'm sorry I ran off yesterday after the service. I was so stunned I didn't know what to do."

She laughed, but it sounded hollow. "My father even made me drink out of his flask, I was so distraught."

"I saw that," I said, pinching the bridge of my nose with my free hand.

"You did," she said, guilty. "Oh, well, I guess it was all right under the circumstances. That's what my father said."

"Of course. Of course."

"So you weren't angry that I didn't say anything to you."

"I was in shock myself," I said. "If I could do anything about all of this…"

"I've been saying that to myself for a week now," she said in a brave voice.

"The estate—" I started, but she interrupted.

"I don't care about that. It's not about that. It never was."

And that made me feel better. Maybe that's why I had called, to hear her say that, to assuage at least some of my guilt. A fine murderer I was, let me tell you.

"I just wonder if I'll ever stop missing him." She paused. "Did you ever stop missing Quinn? After the divorce, I mean," she said, and hurried to add, "if that's not too bad of me to ask."

"It wasn't the same with Quinn. We hated each other as much as we loved each other."

"Like Joe and you."

That hit me in the gut.

"I'm sorry," she said, realizing what she'd said. "I didn't mean that."

"No, it's okay. It's true. Like me and Joe. Not like what you had at all."

"So you think it won't go away?" she said.

I wondered that myself. Would Joe's death ever go away for me, the clunk of his head, the weight of his body as I carried him up the steps? And soon I planned to add Vee to that. And Browne, flashed into my mind. If I wanted to be certain that enough of Quinn's money went to setting Clotilde up for a very long time, Browne would have to die too. After all, Vee must have told him about the murder when she'd told him about the money. If they both were to die, then no one else would know, and I could walk away from the whole thing free. But not other-wise.

"Mr. Rosenkrantz?" Mary said.

"It'll go away," I said, needing that to be true. "You'll meet someone else. You'll move on. And every now and then you'll wonder, what if?, maybe around the anniversary of his death, but as you get older, things seem less important." Was that true? I sure as hell didn't know.

"I don't think it'll ever get better," she said, resolute.

"I hope you're wrong," I said.

"But we can still write, can't we? You wouldn't be mad if I sent you letters. It would be kind of like—" She broke off.

"Kind of like writing to him."

"Yeah."

And if that didn't make me feel like a heel, then what would. It had been a mistake calling her. It was a mistake to expect anybody to be of help then. That's what this was all about, car-rying it on my own.

I realized she was waiting for me to answer. "Sure," I said. "You can write any time."

"Thank you," she said, and expelled a sigh.

"I better be going now," I said, needing this call to be over.

"I'm so glad you called. I'm glad that Joe and you had made it up before he died. At least there was that."

"I'll wait for your letters," I said. I put the receiver down but left my hand on it. I felt better about the money, but about a thousand times worse about everything else, and that was exactly what I didn't need.

My mind ran back to my flash of insight while I was talking to Mary, that Browne had to die as well. Whether he knew about the murder or not, he didn't need to have something on me to blackmail me. He'd kill me if I didn't pay him, and that was all the motivation he needed to rely on. Part of me knew somewhere the second he sat down at lunch with us this afternoon that it would come down to me killing him or him killing me. That's where all of the fear, the paranoia, was coming from, because for this to work, for me to set up Clotilde and myself, they both had to die...

I took my hand from the receiver. Nothing would be gained by calling Clotilde now. I had to do this alone. I sat down on the bed beside my duffel bag, and let it all sink in. I knew that killing two people, one of whom was bigger than me and much more accustomed to violence, was not going to be at all the same as a lucky push. But what choice did I have? And what did I have to lose? If I waited it out it would come to the same thing in the end, because I wasn't stupid enough to think Browne'd leave it at five hundred thousand dollars when he found out just how much I got. In the end, it would still be them or me.

And I couldn't feel bad for either of them. Browne was a criminal, after all. He knew the risk when he chose his way of life. He probably expected to get killed someday. And Vee? Vee was little better than a whore, and she knew it. If she was going to live by spongeing off of gangsters who beat her, she was playing Russian roulette already anyway.

And then it all fell into place. Browne could come home and beat Vee. Hell, he probably would. Maybe even strangle her.

But this time, during the struggle, Vee could manage to get her gun—the gun she kept in her bag, the one he made her carry—she'd get it and shoot him with it. She'd still die, but she'd get him first. Yeah, killing two people could actually make the whole thing much easier, because I could make it look like *they'd* killed each other. And the cops would have an open-and-shut case with one of the biggest criminals in Calvert dead, so no one would be eager to check too closely. They could even pin Joe's death on them if Montgomery's article stirred up any noise about that. It was like a present to the police. And I'd be home free. I just needed to let myself into the suite with my key before Browne got back, beat Vee to death, and then wait for Browne with Vee's gun.

I tried to think of holes in the plan, and it seemed sound any way I looked at it. I didn't think about the fact that I had never hit anyone in my life, let alone a woman. But would I have done anything differently if I had considered it? When you feel the noose tightening around your neck, you don't stop kicking because the movement's pulling the knot tighter. You kick right to the end. Yeah, I would have still done it, kicking all the way.

22.

I had to pass a few hours before I could go back to the hotel. I needed to kill them both within as short a time as possible or it wouldn't look right. You can tell how long a body's been dead, and even if the police wanted the same outcome I did, it might be hard to sell it to the press if there were glaring inconsistencies. At lunch, Browne had said he was going out to take care of business, so that meant he was probably coming back in the evening, which meant that *I* had to wait until early evening. At least that made the most sense, and I just had to stick to my plan and hope.

I tried to pass the time with a book, but instead of being able to concentrate on the pages in front of me, my mind picked over little things, like whether I should take my duffel bag with me in case I needed to run, and what I'd do if Browne had gotten there before me. I decided the duffel bag would be unwieldy, and that I'd just call to make sure Browne was still out. There were dozens of other ways I started to second-guess myself, but then I'd think of the money and Clotilde and I'd be able to focus on the book I was reading for another half a page.

It was just before six when I left Great Aunt Alice's house. I didn't let them know I was leaving. They would have to miss me at dinner. I walked the twenty minutes downtown to the Somerset. The humidity hadn't let up, so it was hot even though the sun had sunk below the tall buildings. The streets were still crowded with the tail end of rush hour, and the people jostling me on either side made me feel as though I were taking a natural evening walk, as though it had nothing to do with murder. I was sweating, but it might just as well have been because of the heat.

A block from the hotel, I went into a phone booth and called up to Suite 12-2. I wiped my forehead and the back of my neck with my handkerchief as I waited for the phone to be answered. At last Vee picked up.

"Hello."

"Hey," I said, talking into my hand to disguise my voice. "Mr. Browne there? It's important."

"Nah, there's no one here but me."

"Know when he'll be back? It's really important."

"Does he tell me anything? I'm just supposed to sit here, like always. Put the dame on ice."

"Okay," I said, and hung up.

I leaned against the wall of the phone booth. I could feel the blood throb in my neck, and I was sweating like crazy, my whole undershirt soaked, large dark patches under my arms, the back of the shirt sticking to me. And it wasn't just because it was hot.

I took a deep breath and pulled open the phone booth door, and with that I shut my mind right off. I was only concerned with the physical.

I went by way of the back alley, just like Vee had taught me, and I walked the twelve flights of stairs too, which was just about enough to kill me, but somehow I made it, and the next thing I was standing outside Suite 12-2, lightheaded and with sweat running down my face. I slid the key into the lock, turned it, and opened the door.

There was no sound coming from within. I stepped inside, and closed the door silently behind me, easing it into its frame with the door handle still turned, so that there was no click when the door closed all the way. I released the handle. There was no one in the living room or dining space. A bottle of champagne sat at the head of the dining room table closest to the door. I picked it up by instinct, thinking it would make a good weapon, and continued on, the weight of the bottle a comforting heft in my hand.

The brief hall to the bedrooms—there were two—was dark, and there didn't seem to be any light coming from either of the rooms. In the first, I could just make out two twin-sized beds fit tightly to either side of a nightstand, a setup that filled the whole room. That made the other bedroom Browne's, which was where Vee had to be.

I made a little sound, brushing against the wall, to give some indication that I was coming. That way she might come to greet me. It wouldn't do to have her in the bed, if that's where she was waiting.

I stepped into the room. A blade of light came from the bathroom through the slightly cracked-open door. The bedroom it illuminated was almost indentical to the one we had had downstairs—bed, nightstand, armoire, vanity—except this room was twice the size, which left space for some reclining chairs, a couch, and a coffee table. Vee was in the bathroom, the water in the sink running.

I hurried along to the other side of the bathroom door, where I pressed myself against the wall. I held the champagne bottle upside down by the neck, as though it were a club.

The bathroom door opened. Vee strode out for the bed where I could see she'd left her purse—almost too perfect.

I took one step towards her.

She heard me and turned, and I slammed the bottle into the

side of her face, right where the bruise from Browne's attack was fading. She staggered, and gave almost a skip hop, reaching out to steady herself on the bed, which she missed, but managed to continue standing. The sound the bottle had made was almost the same as the thud of Joe's head hitting the cabinet, but with a metallic ring to it as well. Before I could get my head around the idea that this was Vee, the woman I had slept with for more nights than not in the past year and a half—but I was a pimp; and she was a whore—I brought the bottle back up into her face, breaking her nose, and she tripped backwards now, falling against the bed, but sliding down to the floor.

The sound of bubbles escaped her with each breath, like sipping up the final bit of soda through a straw. "Whh... Shhh... Wh..." They were noises, but it was unclear if it was a voluntary attempt at speech. I was heaving, and I dropped the bottle to the floor. Then Vee started to move, to try to get up. She shot one foot out and dragged it along as though trying to catch at something. I knew I needed to finish her before she could get her senses in order, and it had to be with my hands.

There was blood on her face. I took a moment to roll up my sleeves. Then I gripped her around the neck. It was so small, so easy to get my hands around, so soft, pliable, and I made myself squeeze, leaning my whole weight into her, forcing her head back against the bed, which gave me a support to push her against. Her legs jerked again, and her hands reached up trying to get at me, but in that position, she couldn't even reach as far as my shoulders. The sound coming from her faded into a staccato cough. I felt something hard give way in her throat. She stopped moving, but I kept leaning on her throat, unable to raise myself. I was certain already that I'd made a mistake. That Joe had been bad enough. That I didn't need anything more than

Joe on me. And this was worse, much worse. There was all that time, and the sounds she was making, and her neck giving way. This was more than I could bear.

I was able to get myself to let go eventually, and I leaned against the bed, trying to bring my breathing back to a normal rate, ignoring as best I could the throbbing pain in my head. Still leaning over, I grabbed Vee's handbag. It was heavy, like it should be. That was good. I unzipped it and pulled out the gun. I'd never fired a live round, but I'd been taught to shoot blanks by an effects man out in Hollywood, so I knew the basics of how the thing worked. I dropped the bag, trying to approximate where Vee would have dropped it if she'd grabbed it while being strangled.

I stepped aside so the light from the bathroom could show me the scene. She was in almost the same position that Joe had been in. I smudged the champagne bottle as much as I could in case of fingerprints. There really wasn't much blood on my hands or wrists. The fact that I was considering that almost made me retch. I couldn't stand anymore, which was good, because I needed to shoot Browne as though I were in Vee's position. This was going to be much trickier than Vee had been, because he'd no doubt see me before I could shoot him. I was counting on him coming after me.

I sank to the floor beside Vee, rested my head against the bed, and waited. After five minutes, the air conditioning dried the sweat on my body, making me feel sticky and cold. I shivered, and found I couldn't stop. So I sat there, gun in hand, shivering.

23.

I waited for ten thousand hours, although really it was less than an hour. I stopped crying after about ten minutes, and even the muscle memory of the jolt the bottle gave when it connected with Vee's head began to fade, so that I couldn't tell if I was still feeling it or if I was just imagining I was feeling it. The gun heated up in my hand where it rested on my lap.

You may think I'm crazy when I tell you that I started to talk to Vee then, out loud. I know it seems crazy, but just wait until you're in my position and see how crazy it is. So I started talking on any old thing, about how Quinn and I had fallen in love, about how we had fallen in hate, and all of the violence of that non-violent confrontation. I talked about Clotilde. Talking about Clotilde, I almost cried again, but I didn't. I'd promised her so much and I had failed at everything every step of the way. I still loved her more than anything, which is maybe why I stayed away from her as much as possible. That's what I told Vee, at least, although I don't know if it was true. I reminded myself that all of Quinn's money was going to provide for Clotilde, that that was what really mattered. (You see, I wasn't crazy. I knew exactly what I was doing.)

Then somebody banged on the front door and my thoughts froze. They banged again, with more violence.

It had to be Browne. He'd given Vee his key and I had the other. If I had to let him in, it would ruin my plan. I could still frame him for Vee's murder; he'd be the number one suspect.

But he had the police in his pocket, and he probably knew how to dispose of a body without it ever getting to the police. If I wanted to protect Clotilde's money, it had to be both of them.

I stumbled to my feet, as he pounded again, shouting this time, "Vee, you better open up."

I approached the door, the gun lowered in my right hand.

"I'm going to beat your ass black and blue if you don't open this door this second!"

This was good, I thought. People would be able to say they'd heard him threatening her. I stepped up to the door and put my eye to the spy hole.

Browne was very close, his face distorted by the fisheye lens into a bulbous cheek with retreating features. Another man stood behind him, squat and overweight, bald except for a bushy hedge along the sides of his skull. Two people was no good. What was I going to do with two people?

They talked, and then Browne yelled one last time, "You better be ready for the beating of a lifetime, woman!" and the two of them stalked off.

I stood there, my eye still to the spy hole, calculating, trying to decide if I should go after them, or wait, or disappear altogether. My chest felt tight and I gripped the gun in my fist so tightly that my fingernails dug into my palm.

Before I'd reached any decision, the two men were back. Browne had a key in his hand, and was reaching for the doorknob.

I jumped back, and hurried into the bedroom, resuming my position crouched to the far side of Vee's body. All I could do was stick to the plan and improvise along the way.

The door banged open, rattling the mirrored closet doors, and Browne called from the living room. "Vee! You better have been taking a shower—" He cut off. "Where's the champagne?"

I could hear him moving around, but the sound was muffled. Perhaps he was in the kitchen.

"Vee! Get your ass out here. You better not have taken my champagne."

I waited. My heart was pounding again, the pulse rising from my stomach right through my neck, and with each beat the pain in my head swelled. I had the safety off, and the gun cocked.

"I'm going to kill you…" He trailed off as he flipped the light switch and came in. I'd been sitting in the path of the light from the bathroom, so fortunately the overhead light didn't blind me. "What the—?" Browne said, and took a fast step towards me, his hand going for the holster under his arm.

I knew I wouldn't have two chances, so I shot him, right in the gut, because that's where Vee would have shot him. The blood spread on his shirt immediately, and I shot him again in the same place, and then a third time.

He still staggered towards me but his hand never found his gun. I hurried to my feet, standing stock straight, still awaiting an attack, waiting for the other man to come in from the living room.

Browne tripped past me, and leaned over Vee. "What in the hell?" He looked down at himself. Some of his blood was spilling onto the carpet, some even onto Vee's legs. "Bastard." His voice was strained, not at all the strong man he had been at lunch, or even a minute ago. The room smelled. It could have been feces, or it could have been rotting meat, and of course there was the gunsmoke.

The other man still hadn't come in. There was no sound in the suite.

I watched Browne with no words. I needed to be certain he

was dead, and I needed to get out of there. Even if his body-guard hadn't responded, I didn't want to push my luck that the shots hadn't alerted somebody else.

He sank to a knee. There was still no response. I'd have to take my chance. I wiped the gun on Vee's blouse, stooped, and set it against her hand.

Browne watched me do it. He was completely white. I stood up, and as I did, he fell onto his side next to Vee. His eyes looked at the ceiling, but focused on nothing. The wounds in his stomach were still oozing, and there was a sucking sound there as the blood spread on the carpet, pooling under Vee's hand closest to him. His breathing was shallow, and I was satisfied.

I walked away without looking back, and into the living room, my hands empty, unprotected. There was no one there.

I crossed to the door, and stepped into the hall. I looked back in the direction of the elevators, and there, halfway down the hall, was the squat bald man. His face crumpled into a question and he paused mid-stride, before he started to run towards me.

I turned, and crashed through the fire door, as he yelled behind me, "Wait!"

I took the stairs so fast that I tripped halfway down to the next landing, skidding down several steps without falling. I hurried on, already at the eleventh floor landing before I heard the fire door open above me.

"Hoy! You!"

I kept going, my steps echoing in the enclosed space.

At the next landing I looked up, but there was no one above me. I pushed on, not even wondering where the bald man had gone.

I burst into the heat of the night, which felt, if anything, hotter than the stairwell. My chest burned, my throat was dry, and my knee kept shooting spikes of pain up and down my leg with every step. I needed to get away fast, which meant a cab, and the only guarantee for a cab was the cabstand at the front of the hotel. I didn't think about an alibi or witnesses or anything at all other than the need to get away, to run for my life.

I rounded the corner, and ran towards the doorman, waving at him as I approached, and then I recognized the car idling in front of the hotel as Browne's, the one Vee and I had used to go back to Joe's house and set it on fire.

"Good," I said, between breaths, going right for the driver's side door. "Mr. Browne said the car would be ready."

I got in before the doorman could respond, and as I turned the key, the bald man pushed his way out of the revolving door. He'd decided he couldn't handle the stairs and taken the elevator.

"Hey! Hey!"

The engine turned over, and I pulled away with a jerk before getting into gear, rounding the corner just as the light changed, taking George Street uptown.

Most of the downtown traffic was gone. I raced up to Washington Hill, but I knew I couldn't go to Great Aunt Alice's—they would know how to find me then—so I continued on past the monument, all the way up past the university, past even Underwood where Quinn and Joe had lived, and was almost at the city line when my mind slowed down enough to realize I couldn't leave the city just yet. I still hadn't met with Palmer, and I needed to be certain that the money was going in the right direction.

I'd have to wait until morning.

24.

I spent the night in the car, parked in the lot of a combination garage and gas station, where an unfamiliar vehicle wouldn't look out of place. I didn't sleep much. I knew that Browne's entire criminal organization would be after me, and that had a way of making it hard to sleep.

When the sun came up, I closed myself into the phone booth at the side of the station and got Palmer Sr.'s number out of the book. His voice was strong when he answered. I hadn't woken him.

"Mr. Palmer, it's Shem Rosenkrantz."

"Shem. Is everything all right?"

"Can you meet me at your office this morning?"

"It's Saturday, son."

"I need to get out of town."

"It can't wait until Monday?"

"No, sir." I didn't offer any more explanation and he didn't ask.

There was a pensive silence, and for a moment I thought he wasn't even there, that he'd hung up. "I'll be down there right away," he said at last.

"Thank you."

He hung up.

I got to the Key Building before he did. Downtown seemed surprisingly empty even for a Saturday, and I felt terribly exposed waiting in front of the locked building. A dejection, a sinking feeling that it wasn't going to work, none of it was going to work, settled over me. Browne's men would find me and kill me, and the money would get tied up in probate for years, and Clotilde would end up in a state hospital, and the whole thing made me tired, so tired...

I don't know what I would have done if Palmer hadn't appeared just then. "Good morning," he said, his key already out.

"Good morning," I said. He let us into the building, and we went up to his office without another word.

The elevator opened onto the dark offices of Palmer, Palmer, and Crick. Palmer stepped out ahead of me and flipped a switch, and the overhead fluorescent lights started to flicker to life, revealing the waiting room I had last been in what felt like a lifetime ago. He led me back past the dark conference room, into his office, where the outside light lit the space but he turned on the overhead lights anyway. The office was dominated by an enormous desk with neat stacks of papers along its edges, and more bookcases filled with uniform leather volumes, a continuation of the law library I'd seen in the conference room at the reading of Quinn's will.

He sat in the leather chair behind the desk, and pulled one of the piles of papers closer to him, extracting a folder without any trouble finding it. He gestured with it to one of the armchairs in front of the desk, and said, "Please, have a seat."

I sat and waited.

"As we talked about the other day, this doesn't really have anything to do with Quinn's will anymore," he started. "You're next in line as Joe's father, since Quinn's estate passed to him, and it would then pass to any of his children, and after that his parents, so there's no problem about that. Alice could try to make a fuss, but I don't think that's going to be a problem."

"How long will it take?"

"It will need to go through probate since you weren't the named holder on any of the accounts or the named beneficiary on Joe's or Quinn's life insurance policies. Probate could take four to six months and it'll cost you a chunk of the estate, but you'll still walk away with a little more than one and a half million."

And there it was. One and a half million dollars. That justified everything I had done. I'd be free. Except I was now a hunted man. I took a deep breath and let it out slowly. "I want to make out a will," I said.

"That's exactly why I wanted you to come in." He pulled out a drawer beside him, and brought out a typed document that looked several pages long. "Since you're in a hurry…"

"I'm sorry about that."

He waved this away. "I've got a template here. I only need to fill in the names, and I'll write in any other provisions, and have the whole thing typed up on Monday."

"Do we need a notary? I can't wait until Monday."

"Is everything all right?" he said, his eyebrows raised in fatherly concern.

I pressed my lips together and took another deep breath.

"It's this thing with this woman you knew and the gangster, isn't it? I saw it in the paper this morning. They said she was suspected of murdering Joe. Sometimes God metes out justice after all, although to be beaten to death like that…" He shook his head.

I nodded my head, unable to say anything. I didn't trust myself to speak.

"I'm sorry, son," he said. "Money's never a consolation in these matters, but think of that at least."

I nodded again.

"Well, don't worry about the notary. We aren't supposed to, but how many years have I known you? I know you're you, I know it's your signature. We can take care of notarizing it without you, given the circumstances. We like to accommodate our clients. Now..."

He started in on the details. All my assets—including the new money from Joe—would go to Clotilde in the event of my death. He'd add her name to all of the appropriate accounts. She was already the beneficiary on my life insurance. I had him add a clause to the effect that the money would be put in trust for her if she were determined to be incapable of managing it herself, and we filled in a template for the trust too. I made provisions for my loans to Auger and Pearson to be paid back, and then I signed and initialed a whole bunch of papers, and Palmer did the same, and he said he'd get his son to make it official first thing Monday morning. The whole process took a little less than an hour.

He stood with me when we'd finished, and shook my hand. "This business has been a damn mess," he said.

"Yes, well..."

"Yes, well..." he echoed with deeper resignation, staring off for a moment. Then he broke into a false grin, and extended his hand, and said, "May it all work out for the best."

I took his hand in mine, and gave a pained smile. "Mr. Palmer."

"Frank," he said, still holding my hand.

"Frank," I agreed. Then: "Listen. I'm embarrassed even to ask this, but is there any way you could advance me a little money to help me get back to S.A.? I haven't got it, and I really do need to get back, Clotilde needs me there."

He blinked, and there was a little flicker in his smile, but he released my hand, nodding, and said, "Of course, of course."

He looked down at his desk, and slid open the center desk drawer from which he took a business checkbook. "Is a check all right?"

I thought about the challenge of getting a check cashed out in the country, and that it would be even harder out of state. I couldn't risk being in town any longer. "If you could make it cash…"

He blinked again, and I could tell he was concerned. The whole exchange felt too familiar, too like Friday nights when I was a kid, begging the old man for fifty cents so I could take a girl for a soda and a picture show. And just like my father, Palmer at last reached into his pocket and brought out some money. Only this was a wad of bills in a money clip, instead of a handful of coins. He pulled off the clip and unfolded about half of the roll. He counted the bills twice and wrote a note in the file, under the word *Advance*. Then, with only a moment of hesitation, he handed it over to me. "Take care of yourself, Shem."

"Thank you. Frank. You've saved my life." I put the money in my pocket, feeling like a heel, but feeling even more strongly relief. "I'll pay you back—"

He waved that away. "We may not know exactly how much the estate will throw off, but we do know it will be more than a few hundred dollars. We'll net this against the ultimate payout, charging appropriate interest of course. It'll all come out even in the end."

I nodded, my lips pressed tightly together. He walked me out of the office, shaking my hand again at the elevators, and then waving goodbye as the elevator doors closed.

25.

I ran then. I didn't think I really had much chance of getting away from Browne's men. He had been connected enough to strike a deal with Hub Gilplaine on the other side of the country, so I wasn't so foolish as to think that there wouldn't be people all over the country looking for me. If it had gone off the way I had hoped, I would have been safe, but having been spotted... Yeah, I ran.

That first night, I checked into a little motel just off of Route 40. Like a million other motels across the country, it was called the E-Z Motel and it wrapped in a U around a central parking lot, which was mostly empty. The clerk was a boy who couldn't have been more than sixteen. He didn't even look at the false name I put in the register. I went to my room, which smelled of mildew, but was otherwise clean, and I lay on top of the bedspread in my clothes since I didn't have any other clothing with me. I stared at the ceiling, and I thought.

What did I think? I thought I wanted to die. I thought that was the only way I could escape from the utter exhaustion I was feeling. I thought about the girl who'd been my mistress who got killed, her body mutilated, and how I had been the one to find her, that smell, that sight. I thought about how Clotilde could have been killed like that, how close a thing it might have been. And I wondered why I had seen so many dead bodies brutally treated. Of course the last several were because I had killed them. I knew that. I hadn't forgotten that. But still, it seemed to me that I'd seen too many. A man could only take so much of that, and I'd had too much. It would be better if it were just over. But it wasn't, and I didn't have what it took to do anything about that, so I had to live with it.

I tried to tell myself things would be different if Clotilde were here. If I hadn't started going with a whore, none of this could have happened. It was Vee's fault really. She couldn't blame me for doing what I did. She'd have done the same to me if I'd given her the chance. Yeah, Clotilde would have saved me.

There were no long-distance calls allowed from the rooms and I didn't want to have a conversation with the kid at the desk standing right there. I thought I'd write a letter, several letters actually. I got up and looked in the nightstand for a pad, but it wasn't the kind of place that offered a complimentary pad and pen. These places never were. They didn't get many writers among the traveling salesmen and wayward tourists. Why would they waste money on pads and pens?

I pulled myself together and went back to face the kid at the desk. He handed over a pad and pen, and I asked for a few envelopes and stamps, and for that he had to get up. He rolled his eyes and huffed his annoyance, but he got me the envelopes and stamps all the same.

I took my supplies back to the room and wrote three short letters.

The first was to Clotilde, and it basically said, I love you. It said a little more than that, but that's what it basically said, so we'll leave it at that.

The second letter I wrote to Great Aunt Alice, and I told her

I was sorry I'd had to miss dinner when I knew she wanted to talk to me so badly, but that things had come up, and I'd had to leave town, and I couldn't thank her enough, and if she could send my duffel bag back to my home in S.A., I'd pay the postage, and I'd write again soon. I felt guilty writing it, but there was nothing more I could do about it.

The third letter was the hardest. It was to Taylor Montgomery. I wanted to tell him how much it had meant to me to work with him the few times we had worked together. How fulfilled that time had made me feel, because of the writing, but even more because of him, a young man's interest and respect, the only thing an old man like me could hope for. I almost wanted to say he'd been like a son to me, but I knew that was going too far, and anyway, how do you write any of that to a man you'd met only a week ago, not even? Well, I'm sure it came out all jumbled, and I filled three sheets of paper front and back, but I sealed it into the envelope before I could reread it and make any changes.

I passed a bad night that night, but I managed a little sleep.

And after that, a week went by in a series of motels and lonely highways and gas stations and all-night diners. Every time I encountered someone new, I had a moment of panic that this was the one who was looking for me, who was going to gun me down. That kind of stress makes your stomach burn straight up into your throat and I was nearly sick any number of times during the day.

But when it finally came, I knew immediately.

I was in a diner in Iowa. There was nothing but corn all around and enough sky for everyone on the planet. Judging by the number of pick-up trucks parked on the dirt shoulder outside the diner, it seemed to be the meeting place of everyone around. Inside all of the booths were taken and about half the counter space as well. The place was loud, and loud waitresses ran through the crowd with coffeepots they never put down, even when carrying someone's meal.

I sat at the counter with a coffee and some crumb cake in front of me, but I wasn't able to take much of either on account of my stomach. Maybe I knew the door opened behind me, but when I saw a man in a blue suit head straight for the bathroom, it struck me as funny, and before I knew it there was another man in a suit sitting beside me. I'd never seen him before, but I'd watched him in the movies a million times, right down to the diamond tiepin puckering the center of his tie.

To my surprise I wasn't frightened. In fact, it was just like when I killed Vee and Browne, my mind shut off and I was focused physical energy.

I didn't move or say anything, and I tried not to stare.

The first man came back, and the man beside me slid off of his stool and headed for the bathroom, while his friend took the stool he'd just vacated. He looked at me, but just the way that neighbors look at each other when they first sit down at a counter. He ordered a soda, and then he looked at me again, and this time I could feel it was a more considered look.

I took a sip of my coffee. It had gone cold. Then I slid off of my stool and started for the door. When I was halfway there, the man behind me called, "Hey, Shem."

I paused for just a second out of instinct, but I knew it was enough to give me away. I quickstepped out the door then, and ran to the car. I could see through the windows of the diner that the man was hurrying to the bathroom to get his companion, and this gave me enough time to get the car started, back up onto the road, and tear off before they had come out of the diner.

I had the road to myself for maybe five minutes, but their car appeared in the rearview mirror after that, and I knew there was no way I could outrun them. I was in a good car, and I had the pedal to the floor, but they'd still get me, because it didn't matter if they got me then or later, they knew where I was, and that was all they needed to know.

I watched the rearview more than I watched the road. They were sitting back there, barreling down at me.

I'd say I thought something then about Clotilde, about Joe, about everything I'd done, and about how bad my stomach hurt, and how tired I was of it all, and all that kind of junk you would think would be going through a man's head when he's about to do what I did, but I didn't think anything. I thought nothing. I simply saw the wide dirt patch beside the road, and I swung out into it. I swung out, and skidding sideways as I turned, the car slammed into a row of corn, the stalks hitting with enough force to break out the windows on that side of the car. I jerked on the wheel, grinding the gears, and I managed to fishtail back onto the road facing back in the direction from which I'd just come.

The other car was closer to me now, but still several hundred yards off.

I ground the gears some more, and put my foot to the floor again, and started in their direction on the wrong side of the road, headed straight for them.

I don't know if they thought I was just playing chicken or what, but they didn't show any sign of turning.

I leaned forward on the wheel as though that could make me go faster. I leaned forward and all of a sudden I broke into a grin. My trademark grin, as big as ever and one hundred percent genuine. Yeah, I grinned, and I looked for any sign that they were going to turn, because if they were, I was going to turn, too. I wasn't going to make any mistake about that. They'd caught me, but I was ready for them.

And I grinned all the way.